BAD PREACHER

JOHN FRADY

WestBow Press
A DIVISION OF THOMAS NELSON
& ZONDERVAN

Copyright © 2017 John Frady.

All rights reserved. No part of this book may be used or reproduced by any means, graphic, electronic, or mechanical, including photocopying, recording, taping or by any information storage retrieval system without the written permission of the author except in the case of brief quotations embodied in critical articles and reviews.

Scripture quotes are taken from the King James Version of the Bible.

This is a work of fiction. All of the characters, names, incidents, organizations, and dialogue in this novel are either the products of the author's imagination or are used fictitiously.

WestBow Press books may be ordered through booksellers or by contacting:

WestBow Press
A Division of Thomas Nelson & Zondervan
1663 Liberty Drive
Bloomington, IN 47403
www.westbowpress.com
1 (866) 928-1240

Because of the dynamic nature of the Internet, any web addresses or links contained in this book may have changed since publication and may no longer be valid. The views expressed in this work are solely those of the author and do not necessarily reflect the views of the publisher, and the publisher hereby disclaims any responsibility for them.

Any people depicted in stock imagery provided by Thinkstock are models, and such images are being used for illustrative purposes only. Certain stock imagery © Thinkstock.

ISBN: 978-1-5127-9581-3 (sc)
ISBN: 978-1-5127-9582-0 (hc)
ISBN: 978-1-5127-9583-7 (e)

Library of Congress Control Number: 2017911114

Printed by Bookmasters in the United States of America

WestBow Press rev. date: 08/01/2017

For the girl

For the good that I would I do not: but the evil, which I would not, that I do.

—Romans 7:19

CHAPTER 1

My name is Brad Johnson. I'm a bad preacher. I don't mean to be bad. I just am. Sometimes I simply choose to do dreadful things, things I hate. I don't know why, and I'm not sure I can change.

Let me explain. I've been the pastor of Lee Community Church in Aucoin, Louisiana, for six years now. Funny, it only seems like seven. The people in our congregation are the best folks in the world, but they "have no desire to see anything change, thank you very much." This is most evident in our worship services. Every Sunday, we sing a few songs, collect the offering, have the sermon, pray for the sick, and then finally go home.

Doesn't sound too bad, does it? When you do it every week for six years, it is beyond monotonous.

I suppose I shouldn't complain. I knew the drill long before I was the pastor. I grew up here at Lee Community Church. My parents brought me to church the second Sunday after I was born. I would have been in attendance my first Sunday, but Mama had just returned from the hospital and was just plain worn out. Until I graduated from high school, she apologized to me every year on Sunday school awards day. Her laziness, in her own eyes, had heaped shame on our family because I was never able to win the lifetime perfect attendance button, since she had caused me to skip church on the first Sunday of my life.

I used to tell her it was no big deal because the award went unclaimed every year—no one could possibly meet the criteria—but Mama didn't care one bit. It was her belief that Jimmy Rice, our Sunday school superintendent, announced the award every year to make her feel bad about skipping one Sunday years ago.

Our senior adult members often remind me about my first Sunday at Lee Community. Rumor has it that I cried so much that Mama had to leave the service. While Daddy stayed and listened to the sermon, she carried me to the Dorcas Sunday school classroom, where the seats were cushioned, so she could calm me down. The following Wednesday, in an emergency church business meeting, Mrs. W. P. Gurdon, the Sunday school teacher for the Dorcas class, made a motion that the church create and staff a church nursery so babies wouldn't disrupt the service and so mothers wouldn't wear out the Dorcas class seat cushions. Mama immediately seconded the motion. Since no man in his right mind would dare comment, the motion passed unanimously without further discussion.

I sometimes wonder if the establishment of the nursery has been my greatest achievement at Lee Community Church, even though it happened before I was two weeks old. It makes me wonder if I would do better in another church, any church, outside of Aucoin. However, whenever I've seriously considered moving on, I've thought of Jesus saying that "a prophet is honored everywhere except in his own hometown." His words are certainly true, but I've known these people so long that they're like family to me, even the ones I don't like.

Yet no one can get under your skin like family. No one.

I do occasionally try to move the Lee Community family forward, hoping the congregation will grow to new spiritual and ministerial heights, but I'm most often met with limited success. That's when my atrocious acts begin. I guess it's the discouragement that brings it out of me, but I'm not sure.

This past Sunday was one of those times. Apparently, I did the unthinkable in the eyes of the Lee Community congregation. Without authorized permission from the deacon body, I had the audacity to suggest that our ushers receive the weekly offering at the end of the service instead of before the sermon. Because our donations have been rather sparse for the past three months, I had prepared a sermon on stewardship and tithing. I thought the change in the order of service and the topic of the sermon might inspire our folks to be more generous in their giving. Sounds logical, right?

Well, obviously, it wasn't logical to everyone. From the reaction I received, you would have thought I had suggested we have our ladies dress in boas and sombreros and then limbo in front of the pulpit during the offertory hymn. Needless to say, the deacons threw an absolute fit.

In order to stop this blasphemous heresy delivered directly to my consciousness from the mind of Satan, the deacons gathered for an emergency meeting in the church office, which doubled as my office, during the Sunday school hour. Apparently, the placement of the offering was more important to everyone than our ongoing system of Christian education.

"Three of you are Sunday school teachers, aren't you?" I asked them. "Is someone else teaching your classes right now?"

"Not at the moment, Pastor Brad," answered Jimmy Rice. "Instead, we asked our classes to pray for the deacons while we met with you to attend to this spiritual emergency."

"Which spiritual emergency are you referring to?" I asked.

"So there's more than one?" asked Jimmy, shaking his head. "What is this church coming to?"

"I'm sorry," I replied. "I don't understand."

"Why would you ever do such a thing, Pastor?" asked Archie Arceneaux, our deacon chairman. "We've been collecting the offering in the middle of the service for at least sixty years, and I don't see why we should change anything now!"

"Let me try to explain," I said. "Congregational giving at Lee Community has been down considerably for the past several months. In response, I'm preaching on tithing today. I was hoping people might be more generous in their giving if they had the opportunity to give *after* the message instead of before. Can you see the logic in what I'm saying?"

Earl Bishop, the assistant deacon chairman, stepped forward and pointed his short, fat finger in my face. "That's the silliest thing I've ever heard. If you go changing when we collect the offering, you'll confuse everyone, half the people will get mad, and then nobody will give anything. Have you given any thought to that?"

After taking a deep breath, I said, "I can appreciate what you're saying, Earl. But don't you think the topic of the sermon could have an impact on the amount people give? Doesn't it make sense that we should ask people to give after they've been taught about giving?"

Earl Bishop threw his hands in the air and shouted, "Wake up and smell the coffee, man!"

I folded my arms and replied, "I'm guessing you disagree with me?"

Archie shook his head. "Pastor Brad, I know you have high hopes for the results of your sermon today, but you've been with us since you were born. You know all about our people here. They get all suspicious when there's the slightest hint of money problems in the church. Our offerings have been down recently and—"

"Considerably down!" interrupted Earl.

"Yes," said Archie, holding up a palm toward Earl. "They have been considerably down recently, and no one understands why."

"It's just like the book of Jonah," cried Earl. "We're all on a sinking ship, casting lots to find out who's at fault here."

"What are you talking about?" I asked.

"I'm talking about you, Jonah!" cried Earl. "People are worried about their giving. They feel like they're giving to a black hole, and they're plain fed up."

"That's why I wanted to move the offering, just for today," I said. "Let me do this to help everyone understand. The content of the sermon will—"

"Just hear me out," said Archie. "You know better than anyone that people around here don't handle change very well, and today's sermon probably isn't going to alter their minds. Everyone sees the stress we're having around here because of our account balances. This kind of thing might make some of them really mad. We simply can't risk it."

"I don't understand what's going on with our offerings," cried Jimmy Rice. "No one's left the church recently. For crying out loud, we even had two visitors last week. No one seems mad about anything. I just don't understand it."

Archie nodded and continued, "What Jimmy's saying is exactly what I'm trying to convey to you, Pastor. Our folks feel the same way. They don't understand why we suddenly have less money in our offerings."

I grimaced and replied, "I know that better than anyone, Archie. I suppose I was just hoping that the Holy Spirit might actually speak to some of our people today about their giving and inspire them to take action."

"Come on, man," groaned Deacon Earl. "These people have already heard everything you could possibly teach them about giving. Besides, you're not that good of a preacher. Do you honestly think anyone sitting in the pews is really listening?"

I swallowed hard and took in a deep breath, opting not to answer.

"Now, Earl," said Archie, putting one hand on his shoulder, "that wasn't a very Christian thing to say."

"Maybe not, but everyone here knows it's true," said Earl, shaking Archie's hand from his shoulder. "Don't you think he's a bad preacher?"

Archie's lips tightened, and he glanced at me sympathetically before answering, "Now that's beside the point, Earl. We're here because we've got to make a decision about the placement of the offering collection in today's service. It's a delicate matter because everyone knows that as a church, we're broke. Because of that fact, and after much prayer, I say we ask Ernie Plaisance and let him decide. He's the church treasurer, for crying out loud."

"We're going to pray?" asked Jimmy Rice.

"Ah, no, Jimmy," answered Archie.

"But you just said 'after much prayer,'" said Jimmy.

"Well," said Archie, "what I meant was that all of us have already been praying about the financial situation, so now it's time for us to hear from Ernie."

"Ah," said Jimmy. "You're right about that. I've certainly been praying a lot about this whole mess."

Ernie, who had been standing in the back of the room, said nothing but slowly made his way to my desk. He paused, smiled awkwardly, and then looked back at the rest of the deacons.

"Go ahead, Ernie!" snapped Earl. "Straighten him out!"

"Well," said Ernie, straightening his tie nervously, "I'm not sure my responsibilities include selecting the time in the service when the offering is collected. I am pretty much given the authority and responsibility after we actually have the money in hand."

"Oh, come on and make the decision!" cried Earl. "You're the church treasurer for crying out loud!"

Jimmy Rice patted Ernie's shoulder and said, "Give yourself a bit more credit, Ernie. You know the church's financial struggles more than anyone."

"That's right!" cried Earl. "You've been our treasurer for years now. We trust you with our money. It's your decision, and we all know it."

"I'm not so sure about that, fellas," replied Ernie. "The church treasurer is responsible for the money received during the service, not for scheduling when it's collected in the service, no matter what our financial statements reflect."

"Just tell us what you think, Ernie," said Archie.

I looked down at the red carpet in the office. It hadn't changed since I was a boy, except it was slightly more worn now, like most of the men in the room.

"I still don't think the decision should be mine alone," said Ernie.

"Sure it is!" cried Jimmy. "You can do it."

"Spit it out, man!" said Earl. "I'm just betting your opinion is the same as the rest of us. Tell us, and then we will all agree with you. You'll feel better, and we can all get back to our classes."

"Yes," said Archie. "Who knows what's going through their minds right now? Financial issues can be a huge load on the minds of any congregation, especially a small one like Lee Community."

Now, I wouldn't say that Ernie and I were friends, but we did meet almost every week to count the offerings. He understood my concerns about our low offerings better than anyone in the church. Over the years, we had developed a sincere respect for each other, and I was pretty sure he would agree to let me try collecting the offering in new ways. However, Ernie also had a powerful position in the church and would have to save face with these men, especially considering our financial situation. I didn't envy him the next few seconds and whatever his final decision would be.

"Well," said Ernie, "I, uh, of course agree that the offering should be in the middle of the service, no matter what the topic of the sermon is going to be. I can see some benefit in changing it around from time to time, especially if the sermon is on tithing, but for the time being, I think everyone in the church would have to receive advance notice if such a change were to take place, especially when considering our current financial circumstances. I'm sorry, Pastor Brad, but I have to agree with Archie and Earl on this one."

"So there it is!" snapped Earl. "It's settled. The offering will be taken as usual in the middle of the service, just as God intended."

"I guess I have no other choice," I replied.

"You got that right," said Earl. "Justice has prevailed!"

Archie patted me on the back and said, "It will be all right, Pastor Brad.

In the end, you'll see that this is all for the best. We can try something radical like this when things look better."

"Radical?" I asked.

"Well," he replied, "you know what I mean."

"I was hoping this would help things look better," I replied, "for all of us."

"Well, I'm sorry," he replied. "Thanks for understanding."

I didn't know what else to say, so I mumbled, "You're welcome."

The deacons left my office and headed back to their respective Sunday school classes to inform the members of Lee Community Church that their prayers had been answered, holy righteousness would prevail, and their pastor had no spine.

I glanced at my phone for the time. I had twelve minutes to adjust my sermon, leaving out the parts about the offering we were going to collect at the end of the service. I picked up a red pen and scratched through a few sentences in my notes. I could have continued, but after a few seconds, I could force myself no longer. I gripped the pen tightly and then threw it across the room. "Thanks for understanding, Pastor Brad," I said softly, repeating Archie's words, before slamming my Bible shut.

"What does it really matter when we take the offering anyway," I asked out loud, "since I'm such a bad preacher and nobody ever listens? Our church is about to run out of money, and I'll be released from my duties anyway." I sat alone with my Bible in my hands and stared at the white cinder-block wall in front of me. There was a small red mark where the point of the pen I had thrown had struck the wall. Something about the mark gave me a sense of satisfaction.

I know it seems silly, but I found myself thinking, *Yeah, you may have done that to me, but I threw a pen at the wall, and it left a mark, a big red one, so there!* Even though it could probably be wiped clean without any cleaning solution, I vowed to leave it there so that I could glance at it whenever one of the deacons was especially cruel to me. It would be my monument of rebellion, and I would celebrate it often.

I'm such a wimp.

I retrieved my pen and started a second time to open my notes and adjust my sermon further, but I couldn't bring myself to do it. "I'll just wing it," I said. Suddenly inspired by righteous indignation, I reached for my phone and composed a text message to Deacon Earl Bishop: "Thank you, Earl, for challenging me today regarding the offering. Obviously, 60 years of tradition could never be wrong, especially in a church that is shrinking every year because they are afraid of trying anything new. And thank you for informing me that my preaching, the main emphasis of my lifelong ministry, is so bad that no one actually listens. You've given me such hope! By the way, you're a jerk!"

Putting my feelings into text somehow made me feel better. I bit my bottom lip as my thumb hovered over the send button. I glanced up at the red mark on the wall. "Should I send it?" I asked the wall, waiting like a goober for a response.

No response came, but the red spot stood strong, which gave me a hint of satisfaction. "I see," I said before taking in a deep breath and exhaling slowly. Slowly, I deleted the message and composed another for my wife: "Hey, baby. I'm having a tough morning. Can you pray for me?"

I locked my phone and heard the buzzing of the Sunday school alarm, informing everyone that they had ten minutes before the service was to begin, not that it did much good. I glanced back up at the dot and muttered, "If everyone's giving faithfully, where is all the money? Something's not right here."

I took another deep breath, blew it out slowly, put on a fake smile, and walked out of the church office toward the church auditorium, which everyone at Lee Community called the sanctuary. As I entered, Ernie Plaisance smiled at me awkwardly. I returned the smile and took my seat in the first pew.

Mrs. Nettie Longwood, our pianist, walked past me and said, "Good morning, Pastor Brad. It's good to see you this morning."

"Good morning, Nettie. It's good to see you too."

Even though I didn't always care for her musical selections, Nettie was always friendly, and I appreciated that. She walked to the left side of the stage (affectionately called the piano side) and fiddled with her large-print piano-edition hymnal.

Trying to avoid conversation with anyone, I opened my Bible and pretended to look over my sermon notes. I should have set them to the side, stood proudly, and greeted the congregation as they entered, but I couldn't put myself through the humiliation. I couldn't muster the enthusiasm to face the men of the deacon board who had just put me in my place or all of the Sunday school members who had stopped their Bible study in order to *pray* about my heretical suggestion.

I could feel the stares of church members as they passed. I tried my best not to wonder about what they were thinking, but as usual my imagination got the better of me. In my mind over the next few minutes, every church member from the oldest deacon to the youngest infant insulted me. Even though this notion was a fabrication of my own brain, by the time Mrs. Nettie played the first note on the piano, I was ready to kill someone.

The service began and proceeded as normal. Jimmy Rice stood to welcome the congregation and gave a quick Sunday school report, which everyone could almost quote word for word. Freddy Lambano, our monotone volunteer music director, asked us all to stand and sing together. Fortunately, Mrs. Nettie played loud enough to drown out Freddy's singing.

Poor Freddy, I thought as I did my best to sing along. *He has no idea that he can't carry a tune in a bucket. Ironically, no one here cares as long as he doesn't try to change the order of worship.* When the singing was finally over, Archie Arceneaux walked to the platform and introduced the offering with a smile. A hush fell across the small crowd, which was thankful that the offering was taking place before the sermon.

As Archie spoke, Ernie Plaisance, Earl Bishop, Jimmy Rice, and Burt Luketich rose from their seats and made their way to the front, where they retrieved the offering plates from the communion table and then turned to face the congregation. Without introduction, Ernie said, "Let's pray."

As every head bowed, every eye closed, and Ernie began praying, I committed a cardinal sin, at least in Lee Community standards. I peeked at the five men at the front, all of them practically clinching their eyes in prayer. *I should be listening to the prayer and praying along in my heart*, I thought. Jimmy sniffed, and my thoughts returned to his words from the meeting. *As hard as it is for me to admit*, I thought, *Jimmy did have a good question. If everyone is still giving, why have the offerings been lower? I don't understand.*

Jimmy sniffed again and then sneezed terribly. Ernie paused his prayer for a moment but soon started again. *Surely we can figure out what's happening with the money*, I thought. *What would it take to figure it out?* I wanted to ponder this further, but Ernie said "Amen," and everyone prepared to give.

While the offering was being collected—or received as the good people of Lee Community preferred to say—I could feel the stares on the back of my head like daggers waiting to strike if I dared make the slightest move. Needless to say, I didn't. Instead, I sat quietly as Nettie Longwood continued to play the offertory hymn, "Spirit of the Living God, Fall Fresh on Me." I wondered what would happen if the Spirit of God really did fall fresh on everyone at Lee Community. If that were to ever happen, we surely wouldn't argue about the placement of the offering in the service, would we? We would be too busy praising God to worry about such trivial items. We wouldn't be experiencing the financial woes we were currently going through because everyone would be giving freely. Then maybe I wouldn't be going through frustrating budget struggles and the sheer agony of trying to change the order of the worship service.

Then again, if the Spirit really did fall fresh on our congregation, Archie, Earl, and Jimmy would probably call a special deacons' meeting to set specific guidelines on what the Holy Spirit was allowed to do in our services. I could hear them say, "You know, Preacher, everything must be done in order and without spontaneous chaos. Besides, the good people at Lee Community don't like being taken by surprise, thank you very much."

As Mrs. Nettie finished her song, I glanced at the sermon notes protruding from my Bible. I didn't dare look at anyone. I'd have to look at them soon enough during the sermon. Unfortunately, the music stopped, and I rose to preach with no confidence whatsoever. Apparently, we were evenly matched because it seemed the congregation had no confidence in me either. Everyone fidgeted, young people texted, older people pretended to listen, and Archie Arceneaux fell asleep. I searched for the reassurance I often found in my wife's face, but she had been called upon to serve in the nursery. I wished I could have volunteered instead of her.

My parents were also nowhere to be seen, oddly enough. Only Nettie Longwood paid attention throughout the entire sermon. She was always attentive, but I'm pretty sure she was simply listening for her cue to move to the piano for the decision song. I wished Freddy Lambano would be as attentive, but mostly he dozed through my sermons and stirred only when he heard the music playing.

I fumbled my way through thirty minutes of tithing scriptures and illustrations, wishing as much as everyone else, maybe more, that this horrific sermon would soon be over so we could all go home.

I did learn one thing for sure that day: Earl Bishop was right. I was a bad preacher.

CHAPTER 2

My first week of seminary, I was walking across campus when I came across a quote carved in marble over the entrance to the Biblical Studies building.

> *It is the business of a virtuous clergy to censure vice in every appearance of it.*
>
> —Patrick Henry

I immediately declared this as part of my calling. It enhanced my plans to be a fiery, charismatic, virtuous preacher, leading the charge in destroying sin whenever it reared its ugly head. I imagined my deacon board, like David's mighty men, serving as mighty warriors alongside me, willing to give their lives for the sake of holiness. I never realized that the one I would be condemning would be me, but I'm getting ahead of myself.

I am the senior pastor of Lee Community Church. The title "senior pastor" has always been humorous to me because we have no other staff members. I suppose Nettie Longwood and Freddy Lambano could be considered staff, but they hardly qualify as clergy. Freddy is a volunteer, thank God, and Nettie is minimal part-time. Although Nettie is paid for playing the piano and organ, she receives only $100 per month and is expected to use a portion of that money for purchasing music and for the annual tuning of the piano.

When I was hired as senior pastor, I was assigned three main tasks. The first was the weekly preaching in the regular worship services, funerals, weddings, and special events of Lee Community Church. At the time of my hiring, I thought this part would always be my favorite because I've always prided myself on my communication skills. However, consistent rude comments from Earl and Archie, not to mention Freddy falling asleep every week, have caused me to wonder whether I need to reevaluate my strengths.

My second responsibility is caring for and leading the people of God at Lee Community Church. This sounds simple enough, right? However, it does come with its own set of complications. Everyone at Lee Community agrees with the "caring for the people of God" portion. But as you can probably imagine, the exact meaning of *leading* the people of God is still an ongoing source of conversation and debate.

My third responsibility is overseeing the care of the house of the Lord. I used to think that meant I would be meeting with a team of leaders responsible for the care and expansion of the building and property. Most of the time, however, it means I am the custodian and caretaker who does whatever no one else wants to do. That often includes, but is not limited to, custodial work, plumbing repair, lawn care, and building security. That being the case, on most Sundays, I have the task of locking and securing the building after the worship service, especially if there's a big Saints football game on at noon.

On this day, out of sheer duty alone, I went through the process of fulfilling responsibility number three. I walked the hallways and turned off the lights in each of the classrooms. Making my way to the sanctuary, I put away the microphones and powered down the sound system. Then, before leaving, I checked to make sure the church office was locked. As usual, the door was wide open, and the lights were on.

I was reaching for my computer bag when I noticed that someone, probably Earl, had brought in the Saturday mail and placed it on my desk. I picked up a few letters and glanced through them quickly. I dropped the bills back on my desk and tossed the junk mail in the trash. I paused when I came to a letter addressed to me from Pastor Jeremy Sullivan from Grace Church, a large church in Baton Rouge. Not wanting any further stimulation, I dropped it on top of the bills on my desk.

I grabbed my things and pointed myself toward the door. It was my intention to leave the building and not give it or the congregation a second thought for the remainder of the day. However, in that moment, something unusual caught my eye, something green. On the floor next to our locked safe was a crisp $100 bill. I blinked to make sure I was seeing properly. I was.

"This must have fallen from the offering collection somehow," I said aloud to no one in particular. "But surely one of the ushers would have seen it fall." I picked up the crisp bill and held it tight in my hands.

Ben Franklin smiled back at me as if to say, "Thank you for picking me up off of that ugly carpet. It looks and smells as if it hasn't been cleaned in years."

"Well, hello there, Mr. Franklin," I said. "Where did you come from?" I glanced around the floor to see if Mr. Franklin had any friends who had gotten loose. I didn't notice any, but I did find three paper clips on the floor close to the where the bill had been. I picked them up and placed them in my front pocket.

Now, I knew from the start that the honest, upright thing to do would be to return the money to the offering collection. Simple enough, right? It's money I found in God's house, so it must be God's money. I should just open the safe and deposit the cash, right? Absolutely. Only I couldn't open the safe.

It may seem ridiculous, but I was purposefully denied access to the combination for the safe. That way, I could never be accused of stealing the church's money. That policy had been put in place after the deacons accused one of my predecessors, Rev. George P. Legendre, of misappropriating church funds in a business meeting. The meeting ended with the cursing out of and subsequent forced resignation of Pastor George, followed by the immediate initiation of this policy.

That meeting was the first time I'd seen a grown man cry. It was also the first time I'd heard cursing in church.

I was about ten years old when the business meeting happened. I remember sitting between my mother and my sister Elizabeth on the hard wooden pew, my rear end longing for a cushion from the Dorcas class. My mother leaned over and whispered loudly, "What are you smiling about, Bradley?"

At the time, I thought she wanted to share in my humorous moment, so I smiled and answered, "I didn't know you could use those words in church."

She pulled my ear to her mouth and whispered, "You better be careful what you say, young man. You could be the pastor here one day, so you better stop laughing and start paying attention!"

What? I thought. *She doesn't know what she's talking about. If this is the way people act in church and treat their pastor, I wouldn't ever want to be a preacher.*

"Mama's right," whispered Elizabeth.

"About what?" I asked.

"You will be the pastor here one day."

"What do you mean?" I asked.

"Everybody knows it," she replied.

"Well, I don't know it!" I snapped. "I'm not going to cry in church, not ever!"

Mama turned and stared us both down before saying, "You two had better be quiet, or I'll give you something to cry about!" Mama whispered so loudly that Myra Boudreaux, secretary for the Dorcas Sunday school class, turned around and gave Mama a nasty look. Mama smiled in return and gripped my hand tightly until all the blood rushed from it, warning me to be quiet or else.

Back in my current reality, I contemplated my situation. Since I wasn't able to place the money in the safe, I knew I needed to contact Ernie Plaisance, the finance committee chairman who had been forced by Earl Bishop and his deacon cronies to decree earlier that morning that the offering must be collected in the middle of the service. Even though I was hurt by Ernie's declaration, I understood from counting the offering with him weekly that he was a good man who loved his church and respected me. I pulled out my phone to call but opted not to when I saw the time. Ernie and his wife Connie almost always drove to McComb or Hammond for Sunday lunch. They were most likely already sitting down in a restaurant to eat, and I hated to disrupt their weekly date.

I made a mental note to contact Ernie later in the afternoon and give him the cash tomorrow when we met to count the offering. I opened my Bible and placed the $100 bill next to Proverbs 10:2, which proclaims, "Treasures of wickedness profit nothing, but righteousness delivers from death."

"Duly noted," I said to myself, figuring the Lord would help keep me accountable since the money belonged to Him and was now hidden in His Word.

As I closed the Bible, I noticed Ben Franklin's eyes staring at me. I imagined him winking at me with his left eye while loudly whispering, "Keep the money."

I suddenly felt self-conscious and jerked my head to look behind me, to ensure that I was indeed alone. I was. "I can't do that!" I said aloud. "I'm a holy man of God!"

What difference does that make? said a voice in my mind. *No one will ever know.*

"But I'll know," I said, "and the Lord will know."

Come on, Pastor Brad! the voice persisted. *Don't you deserve it? When was the last time you got a bonus?*

"Last Christmas," I answered. "The Dorcas class gave Allison and me a fruit basket."

Answer the question. When was the last time you were given a bonus? And I'm talking about a real bonus of serious cash money, not some basket of fruit.

"I've never received one from this church."

That's what I figured. Keep the money. You deserve it.

I still didn't feel right about it, so I prayed to the air around me. "What should I do, Lord? This whole situation just doesn't sit well with me. It's almost like someone left that bill there on purpose to test my integrity. But why would they do that?"

I waited for a moment for a divine answer. It never came.

Well, I thought, *I'll put the money in my Bible for now. I can text Ernie Plaisance and ask him to call me later. I'll tell him about how I found the money and how I'll give it to him tomorrow when he comes to count our Sunday offering.*

I grabbed my Bible, stuffed it into my computer bag, and finished locking up the office. I had taken only the first step toward the parking lot when I froze, turned around, and unlocked the office door once again. "No harm checking," I said to myself. "Who knows what I could find?" I knelt down on the floor where I had found the money. I put my face as close to the carpet as possible and scanned the carpet. I scanned the floor around the safe and found nothing but an old paperclip, bent in the middle.

I then searched the area around my desk, looking for anything that looked unusual. I found two more paper clips, one under my chair and another leaning against the leg of my desk. I then rose to my knees and surveyed the rest of the carpet in all corners of the office. I found nothing but last week's worship guide and three more used paper clips. "Where did all these paper clips come from?" I asked myself as I tossed them onto my desk. "I can't remember the last time I used a paperclip."

I stood up and quickly surveyed the floor of the office again. Finding nothing, I shrugged and picked up my computer bag. I placed the strap over my shoulder so I could lock the office once again and then quickly walked to my car, locked the bag in the trunk, and finally sat in the driver's seat.

I locked my doors and pulled out my phone. I found Ernie's name in my contacts and texted the following message: "Hi, Ernie. Can we talk after lunch when you get a minute? Something strange happened after church, and I need your help. Thanks."

Finally, it felt like things were settled. The money was in my Bible, and my Bible was in my computer bag, locked in the trunk. I had sent a text message to Ernie, and I was on my way home. Everything was going to be just fine. I breathed a sigh of relief and headed home for a relaxing afternoon of nothingness.

CHAPTER 3

As a child, I attended Aucoin Elementary School. My fifth grade teacher was Mrs. Doris Melancon. I don't remember much about what I learned that year, but I do remember her fingers. She had long bony fingers and would point her right index finger in the face of any student who complained or misbehaved.

Once, after I complained about the amount of homework we were being assigned, Mrs. Melancon pointed her finger in my face and said, "Well, young Bradley, as you will come to learn, there is no rest for the weary and the wicked."

I didn't know what to say, so I just replied, "Yes, ma'am."

Now I understand. Mrs. Melancon has long since retired and moved to Florida, but her saying has stayed with me. I thought of it today when I knew I was already way past weary. However, unbeknownst to me, I was about to become more wicked. In my defense, I only wanted an afternoon nap after a leisurely meal at home with my wife and son. However, as I was nearing our street, something happened that altered the course of my day and, as providence would have it, my life.

My wife called. "Hi, honey," she said. "I got your text. I'm so sorry things were going so badly for you. Are you okay?"

"I might as well be," I responded. "I don't have many other options. How was your morning?"

"It was okay," she said. "But there's something wrong with the restroom plumbing in the nursery. It smelled bad no matter how much I cleaned it."

"I'm sorry, baby. I'll ask Burt to look at it."

"Since it was only Gabe this morning, I took him to the church office for a few minutes to escape the smell. However, he was getting into your office supplies and crawling over everything, so we left once the deacons arrived with the offering."

"I'm sorry you had to go back to the smelly room."

"I am too," she replied.

"Is that why you called?"

"No, I wanted you to know that we're completely out of milk. Would you mind picking up a gallon on your way home?"

"Can't it wait, Allison?" I asked. "I'm almost home, and I really don't feel like—"

"No," she interrupted, "I'm sorry, but it can't wait. Your parents are coming over, and your mother always complains if we don't have enough milk."

"Oh man," I said, tightening my grip on the steering wheel. "I forgot all about them coming today. Is it too late to cancel?"

"Yes, it is!" she exclaimed. "We set this date with them a month ago, and I'm sure they're going to pull into the driveway at any moment. Your mom already thinks we're terrible parents."

"Mama doesn't think we're terrible parents," I replied with a grin. "She just thinks you're a terrible mother."

"Very funny," said Allison. "Well, this terrible mother wants her husband to go wherever he needs to go to get us a gallon of milk."

"You know what?" I said. "I've had an extremely hard morning, and now I'm almost home. The One Stop is the only place open today, and it's way on the other side of town. Mama will just have to get over it. People just don't drink milk like they used to."

"I don't care what people do," said Allison. "I don't want to deal with her about it when she arrives, and I don't want to argue with you about it now. Please stop and get us some milk, okay?"

"I really don't want to, Allison," I replied. "And like I said, I'm almost home."

"Fine," she snapped back. "Then you can be the one to tell her that *she'll just have to get over it* while she's inspecting our refrigerator."

Realizing there was no way to win this argument, I replied, "Okay, you win. I'll try to get us two gallons if we can just stop talking about it."

"Thanks, honey," said Allison. "And pick up some ice cream for dessert."

"I will if I can swing it. Remember, I don't get paid until next week."

"Well, if it's too much, don't worry about the ice cream. But don't forget the milk, okay?"

"Yes, ma'am."

Ten minutes later, I placed two gallons of milk on the counter at the One Stop Shop, our small-town version of a grocery, gas station, deli, bakery, diesel truck wash, wedding supply, and cattle feed store all rolled into one.

"Hello, Preacher Brad!" said the stringy blond clerk clad in a worn red T-shirt, blue overalls tight-rolled above her ankles, and black Chuck Taylor high-top sneakers.

"Well, hello there, Sally Mae Watson," I said with a smile. "How's everything at the One Stop Shop?"

Sally Mae stared across the counter and straight into my eyes without blinking. "Everything's just fine and dandy here, Pastor," she replied. "I sure am glad you dropped by to see me this afternoon. Do all of your parishioners receive this type of personal treatment?"

I looked away from her eyes, not able to tolerate her lack of blinking. "Sorry, I'm not sure what you mean."

"Are you sure?" she asked with an evil smile.

"I, uh, well …" I stammered.

Sally Mae dropped her stare and smacked the counter. "I'm just teasing you, Brad!"

"Oh," I said, laughing nervously. "I see."

"You've got to lighten up a little and relax. You remember how to relax, don't you? You know, like when we were in high school."

Sally Mae and I had been classmates. She was more reserved in those days and wasn't quite as hygienic then as she was now. Teenagers, especially young teenagers, can often be the meanest people on the planet. The youth of our high school were merciless, especially with their comments to Sally Mae. Because of this, I had always tried to be nice to her. Once, when a few kids were making fun of her at the skating rink, I asked her to do a couple's skate with me. It was only one song, but even now, years later, she always acted like we'd had some type of romantic relationship.

"Well," I said, suddenly feeling extremely awkward, "we, uh, all missed seeing you in church this morning."

"And I sure did miss being there too," said Sally Mae. "I absolutely love hearing you speak. I could listen to your voice—I mean, your sermons—all day long."

"Yeah, I'll bet," I replied sarcastically without thinking.

Sally Mae's jaw dropped to the floor. "I beg your pardon?" she asked, crossing her arms and raising one eyebrow.

Suddenly, I realized what I had said and how it had sounded. "I'm sorry," I said, awkwardly smiling. "I didn't finish my sentence. What I meant to say was, I'll bet … you have to get here really early on Sunday mornings to open up the store."

Apparently, Sally Mae bought my excuse. She dropped her arms, shook her head slightly, smiled, and winked. "Yeah, well, that's the truth. I have to get here before the crack of dawn so I can open up this place at six on both Saturday and Sunday mornings. I don't get off until two in the afternoon."

"Well, it certainly seems like a lot of responsibility," I replied.

"Oh, it is, Brad," she answered, her eyes staring into mine. "And then I go home all by my lonesome to a big empty house. Can you believe that?"

"Well, uh … oh yeah, I almost forgot to tell you. My wife—you know Allison, right? Well, she wanted me to tell you she sure does miss seeing you as well."

"Oh, really?" she replied, dropping her gaze and her enthusiasm. "Well, that's right nice of that sweet wife of yours, Preacher."

"Yeah, she's a good one," I said. "A really good one."

I looked away for a moment and hoped Sally Mae would catch the hint. If she did catch it, she didn't hold on to it for very long.

"You met her when you were off at college, right?"

"That's right," I replied, nodding my head. "Sure did."

She once again stared right at me without blinking and said, "I always knew I should have gone to college."

After a slight pause, I said, "Well, I guess I'll get this milk."

"Sure thing," Sally Mae replied while ringing up my order. "So what's going on at your house today? I'll bet your mama must be fixing to visit with y'all for lunch."

"Yes, she is. How did you know?"

"Y'all always buy lots of milk when she's coming over. Everyone in the parish does, for that matter."

I finally chuckled slightly and said, "Well, what can I say? She's a woman who really likes her milk."

"I'm just teasing you, Brad," said Sally Mae with a giggle. "She was in here a few minutes ago, telling me how she was headed over to your place for Sunday dinner."

"You really had me going there, Sally Mae."

"You always were gullible, Brad, even when we were dating in high school."

"I'm sorry, what?" I asked. "I don't remember us dating …"

"I sure do like your mama. I wish I had a mother-in-law like her, but I guess I missed my chance since I didn't go off to that college you went to."

Sally Mae was going overboard, and I had to change the subject. Not knowing what else to say, I blurted out, "You know, my mother … we were just talking about her … she sure does know a lot about milk."

"She sure does," said Sally Mae.

"Now," I said, "if she ever comes in here, you can't tell her we were making fun at her expense."

"Don't you worry, honey," said Sally Mae, reaching out and grabbing my arm. "I wouldn't tell a soul, and I'd certainly never tell your mama."

"Thank you," I said, wondering why she hadn't released my arm.

"You're welcome, Brad," she replied, staring once again into my eyes. "It'll be our little secret."

I gulped, not sure of what to do. I looked down at her grip on my arm. "Well," I said, "I guess I should be going. My family's waiting, you know."

"You know," she said, "your daddy and I get along really well too."

"I can believe that," I replied, opening my eyes wider toward her grip on my arm. "My dad can be a very likable person, as long as you're not too pushy."

Suddenly, as if she finally sensed the awkwardness, Sally Mae released my arm and jerked her hand away. "Well, that will be $7.87, Pastor Brad."

I pulled my debit card from my wallet and held it out to her.

"Oh, I'm sorry," she replied. "I should have told you. Our card machine is down today. We can only take cash right now."

I looked inside my empty wallet. "Well," I said, "my mother will just have to be disappointed."

"You know, Pastor Brad," said Sally Mae, as her foot twitched nervously, "I can spot you the money, and you can drop it off by my place later this evening, if you like."

"It's okay, Sally Mae. I'll figure something out."

I glanced down at the milk and was contemplating my next move when I heard the voice in my head. I still have no idea whether it was Satan, my own imagination, or indigestion.

Use the hundred-dollar bill you found.

I froze. "I can't use that money!" I said. "I'm a holy man of God!"

"What are you talking about?" asked Sally Mae. "I know you can't use your card. I'm the one who just told you our card machine is down."

Why not? said the voice. *You can replace it later. No one will ever know.*

"But I'll know!" I cried. "And God will know too!"

Sally Mae's right eyebrow shot up. "What will God know? Is He telling you when our machine will be repaired? Are you having a revelation? Do you see me in it? How do I look?"

"Huh?" I blurted. Suddenly, I realized I had been having this strange, seemingly one-sided conversation with the voice in my head out loud, all the while staring at the containers of milk, right in front of a mystified Sally Mae.

Sally Mae cocked her head and whispered, "God just spoke to you about our debit card machine, didn't He?"

I shook my head to pull myself together.

Sally Mae took a strand of her hair in one hand and twisted it. "Tell me about my appearance in your revelation. Was I dressed in a white ball gown? Were we dancing?"

"Excuse me, Sally Mae," I said, turning toward the door.

"Where are you going?" she cried. "Are you okay?"

I looked up, startled. "Oh, uh, yes, I'm fine, thank you. Sorry if I zoned out for a moment there. It's been a long day for me already."

"I imagine so," she replied. "I heard about the deacons voting down your decision to change the placement of the offering."

"You did?" I asked.

"Oh yes," she said. "You hear a lot of gossip when you're the only convenience store in town."

"I see."

"For the record," she whispered with a wink, "I agree with you completely."

"Okay," I said. "I guess that's good."

"Oh, it is," she said, "and I don't think you have anything to do with the lower offerings."

"What?" I asked.

Before she could answer, the door to the One Stop Shop flew open, and one of my old friends ran inside.

"Billy Ray Broussard!" snapped Sally Mae. "You scared me half to death!"

Billy Ray had gone to school with Sally Mae and me. He also used to come with me to Lee Community when we were kids. He stopped coming after my dad caught him kissing my sister Elizabeth in the Dorcas classroom after church. Daddy just pointed at the door, and Billy Ray instinctively knew what to do. He ran out and never came back.

"I need gas right away!" cried Billy Ray. "Melissa is having a baby right now!"

"Right now?" I asked.

"Right now!" he repeated.

"Oh my!" yelled Sally Mae. "Well, the pump is outside!"

"I can't get it to work," he snapped back. "The pump won't take my card!"

"Billy Ray!" yelled Melissa from the passenger seat of his truck. "Hurry up, please!"

"Oh, that's right," said Sally Mae. "Our card machine is broken. Do you have cash?"

"No, I don't," he said hopelessly. "Please, I'll pay it later! We don't have much time."

"I'm sorry," said Sally Mae. "Store policy. I can't give away gas for any purpose."

Billy Ray looked at me and said, "Brad! Do you have any cash? Please help me!"

"You know what?" I said. "I just remembered that I do have some cash in the car. Sally Mae, put twenty dollars on his pump, and I'll pay for it."

"Bless you, Brad!" cried Billy Ray.

"I'm praying for you and Melissa," I said hastily.

"Right now?" he asked with a blank look on his face.

"Go, Billy Ray!" I cried. "Pump your gas and get your wife to the hospital."

Without another word, Billy Ray rushed through the door, slamming it open hard and once again startling Sally Mae. Through the open door, I could hear the happy couple.

"Where have you been?" yelled Melissa. "I'm having a baby, and you just leave me here?"

"I'm sorry!" yelled Billy Ray.

"I'll be right back with the money, Sally Mae," I said as I exited the store.

"No problem, Pastor Brad," said Sally Mae with a smile. "You hurry back now!"

I ran to my car, opened the trunk, yanked the Bible from my computer bag, and pulled the $100 bill from within.

Billy Ray was nervously willing the gas to pump faster, gripping the pump handle as tightly as possible.

"Which hospital are you headed to, Billy Ray?" I asked.

Without looking at me, he yelled, "We're going to McComb!"

"Billy Ray!" yelled Melissa from inside the car. "Stop talking and take me to the hospital!"

"I'm coming!" he yelled.

"I'll leave you to it," I said, not expecting a response, and walked back inside. Sally Mae was leaning on the cash register with one fist beneath her chin.

"Can you break a hundred-dollar bill?" I asked.

"We wouldn't for everyone, but I think we can trust a strong man like you, Pastor Brad."

I smiled but thought, *Where are you going with this, Sally Mae?* "Thank you," I answered.

"Let's see," said Sally Mae. "That will be $7.87, plus twenty for the gas."

"You know what?" I asked.

Sally Mae leaned across the counter and batted her eyes. "What is it, Brad?"

"I want more."

"Really?" she asked, batting her eyes once again. "I want more too. Is it just a coincidence, or is it fate?"

"What I meant was, is it too late for me to add to my order? Allison—you know, my wife—wanted me to pick up some dessert if I was able."

"Oh," said Sally Mae, deflating like a pricked balloon. "That's fine. What would you like?"

I glanced around the store. "I'll take these two gallons of milk, two gallons of ice cream, and two of your homemade apple pies."

"Good choice," said Sally Mae, shooting me a quick wink. "The pies are sinfully delicious today."

"I bet they are, Sally Mae," I replied. "I bet they are."

CHAPTER 4

Love is the best emotion in my opinion. If it had an evil nemesis, I'd say that would have to be shame. No matter how good we are feeling about ourselves, shame can jump in, kick us in the butt, and shout, "What makes you think you can be happy? Look at who you are and what you've done. You'll never be good enough." Unfortunately, we often don't see shame coming our way until it's right upon us.

My drive home from the One Stop Shop was serene at first. I was happy that I had been able to help Billy Ray and Melissa get away from the gas pump and head toward the hospital. I was also pleased with the treasures I had for my family: ice cream, pie, and milk. But then shame stole my happiness, pummeled me in the gut, and reminded me that I had spent God's money to satisfy my own selfish desires. Earl Bishop had been right, but he hadn't taken it far enough: I was a bad preacher, but I was also a bad Christian.

"Get a grip on yourself, Brad," I said as I pulled into our driveway. "You might have saved their baby's life by spending that money. You're supposed to be going about doing good, right? Oh, but doing good by buying pie and ice cream was really only being good to yourself. Don't worry, you can figure it out this afternoon."

I placed the car in park and took a few deep breaths before I stepped onto the pavement. Remembering my promise to Allison, I opened up my contacts and tapped on Burt Luketich's name. I held the phone to my ear and waited to leave a message. Being one of the only plumbers in town, Burt had learned not to answer his phone on Sundays.

But surprisingly, Burt answered. "Hello, Pastor Brad," he said.

"Burt, sorry. I didn't expect you to answer today."

"Well, I saw it was you and thought it might be important."

"Thank you. It is, Burt. It's about the church."

"I'm not changing my mind about the placement of the offering, Pastor."

Good grief! I thought. "Oh, this is not about that. I need your expertise as a plumber in the church nursery."

"What's the problem?"

"I'm not sure, but I've been hearing reports that there's a terrible smell that won't go away no matter how hard they clean."

"Okay, I'll check it out tomorrow. You going to be around?"

"Yes," I replied, "unless there's some type of emergency."

"Well, if there is, I'll just let myself in with my own key."

"Thanks, Burt," I replied. "I'll see you tomorrow."

"Sounds good, Pastor Brad," said Burt before he ended the call.

"Why was I so nervous talking to Burt?" I mumbled to myself as I collected my purchases from the back seat. "And why did I use that money? I'll have to replace it somehow."

Once inside, I quickly surveyed the situation. Sunday lunch was always interesting when my parents came to visit. Daddy, not surprisingly, was already asleep in front of the TV when I walked through the front door. Gabe, my three-year-old son, was asleep in his arms. My mom stood in the doorway to the kitchen with her arms crossed and her nose twitched to one side of her face.

"Hi, Mama," I said, lightly kicking the door closed. "Is everything okay?"

"What?" she asked before softening somewhat. "Oh, yes. I'm sorry. I was just lost in thought, son. It's good to see you."

"It's good to see you too, Mama. It looks like Daddy and Gabe are enjoying the game."

"Well, you know your father, Bradley. He falls asleep faster than anything."

"If anyone deserves it, it's Daddy. He's worked hard his whole life."

"And I didn't?" she asked, playfully shaking a finger at me as she walked toward my dad. "Bob!" she cried. "Wake up. Bradley's home."

Neither my dad nor my son stirred.

"Ah, let them sleep, Mama," I said. "They'll wake up when it's time to eat."

"That's Bob Johnson for you," she replied. "You could shoot bullets around him, even set off bombs, and nothing will wake him up until you shut off that TV. Then he'll pop up and say, 'Hey! I was watching that!'"

"But what about you, Mama? How are you doing? I noticed you weren't in church this morning."

"I'm sorry we missed the service, Bradley," she answered, reaching to take a gallon of milk from me. "Here, let me help you with that."

Mama is the queen of changing the subject during uncomfortable discussions. When I was seven, I asked her where babies came from, and she suddenly jerked and cried out, "There's a fly in this house! Go fetch me the flyswatter."

Her avoidance wasn't going to get the better of me today. "But you never miss church," I said, "never, that is, unless—"

"I heard the deacons gave you a run for your money."

"That's one way to put it," I said, "but that's not what we're talking about right now."

"Well, that's what I heard, Bradley."

"What's going on, Mama? Why didn't you come to church? Are you sick?"

"I'm fine, son."

"And Daddy? Is he okay?"

"We're both fine. Everybody's fine. Now give me that pie. I bet—"

"Forget the pie for a moment, Mama."

"Well," she said, "aren't you the bossy one?"

"This has something to do with Elizabeth, doesn't it?"

After a brief pause, Mama sighed and said, "Well, if you must know, then yes. Yes, it does."

"It figures."

The corners of her mouth turned down. "And just what, pray tell, is that supposed to mean?"

"Nothing at all, Mom. It's just that whenever she comes around, you and Dad start acting all unpredictable."

"Is that a fact?" asked Mama.

"Yes, it is, and you're trying to change the subject."

"I'm certainly glad that milk was on your shopping list. Gabe needs lots of milk, and so do you and Allison! Calcium and vitamin D are essential, Bradley!"

"Well, it certainly does a body good," I interjected, "unlike my sister."

"You leave your sister out of this. She never did anything to harm you."

"I know, Mama, but the way she's living just might end up harming you, and that concerns me."

"Are you being smart with me?" she asked, pointing her right index finger in my face.

"No one's ever accused me of being smart, Mom," I replied, "especially not today."

"You're smart enough, son. And you can hear all about our time with Elizabeth when she gets here for lunch. Now let me help you with this milk and pie."

"What did you say?" I asked. "Elizabeth is coming here?"

"Yes," she answered. "That's what I said all right."

"But she's not invited."

"Of course she's invited, son. She's your sister."

"I don't believe this," I said. "I have one of the worst days of my life, and now I have to put up with Elizabeth."

"What's so wrong with Elizabeth?" she asked.

"Nothing at all," I said. "She's just fine. I must be the one who's crazy. I mean, what was I thinking, studying hard in school, going to college, staying away from wild parties, keeping myself pure, not mooching off of my parents?"

"That's enough, Bradley! Quite enough!"

Suddenly, I was ticked (that's southern for really mad). The emotions of the entire day poured into my head while images of Archie, Ernie, and Earl flashed before my eyes. I imagined them all huddled together, listening to Elizabeth tell stories about me, shaking their heads and pointing.

"Bradley," said Mama, jerking me out of my thoughts, "if I could have just one wish, one tiny fulfilled desire, it would be that you and your sister would finally get along."

"Did you see a falling star?" I asked.

"No," she replied. "Why?"

"Then it's probably not going to happen today."

Mama sighed and dropped her eyes. Remorse suddenly attacked me. Why in the world had I spoken to my mother in such a fashion?

"I'm sorry, Mama," I said. "That was uncalled for."

"I can't believe you said those words with the same mouth that you eat with."

"Like I said, Mama, I'm sorry." I looked at my father and my son still fast asleep in the recliner and wished I could join them.

"Brad?" Allison called from the kitchen. The sound of her voice felt to me like a death-row presidential pardon. "Are you home?"

"Yes," I said. "I'm here with the milk. I managed to get the ice cream and a surprise dessert as well."

"Oh, that's wonderful!" said Allison from the kitchen. However, her cheerfulness changed as soon as she walked into the foyer, where Mama stood staring up at the ceiling and I stood looking down at the floor. "Is everything okay?" she asked.

"Yes, Allison," said Mama. "My son is just telling me how much he hates his sister."

"I'm sorry, what?" asked Allison.

"I don't hate Elizabeth, Mama," I said. "In fact, I love her. I just can't stand being around her. She was okay when we were kids, I guess. But then she grew up and started treating us all like dirt."

"Well," said Allison, "it looks like it's time for the preacher to start forgiving because she's coming to eat with us."

"Allison's right, dear," said Mom.

"I guess this is not the best time to tell you that I also can't stand milk, is it?" I said.

Mama looked straight into my eyes and said passionately, "But milk is nature's health remedy! You need to think about your wife and son."

"I know, Mom," I replied. "Can we just not talk about it for at least one day?"

"What took you so long, honey?" asked Allison. "We expected you earlier."

I smiled awkwardly. Allison knew where I had been.

"Oh," I said, seeing her wink at me behind Mama's back. "I went to get milk at the One Stop Shop and …"

"Was Sally Mae still there?" asked Mama. "I stopped and spoke to her on our way here. She's always been such a nice, sweet girl."

"She's a terrible flirt!" said Allison. "One day I thought she was going to grab Brad and kiss him right in front of me."

"Oh," I said, "she's not so bad. You just have to get used to her."

Allison looked at me quizzically. "Are you saying you're used to her, Brad?"

"Uh, no," I replied. "Not in the slightest. Oh, never mind! Did I tell you Melissa Broussard's on her way to the hospital to have her baby?"

"Oh, that's nice," said Mama. "How do you know?"

"I saw them at the One Stop Shop."

"They stopped at the One Stop Shop on their way to the delivery room?" asked Allison.

"Everybody needs gas, baby, even in an emergency."

"Is that what took you so long?" asked Allison.

Suddenly, like a gift from heaven, my phone started buzzing. As if on cue, Mama, Allison, and I all stared at my pocket, where my phone was stored. Dad and Gabe, of course, continued to sleep.

"Why don't you just call them back later, honey?" said Allison. "I know you're the pastor, but it's your off time, and your parents are here for lunch."

"I agree," said Mama. "We're about to sit down to dinner, and your sister will be here any minute."

Inwardly rejoicing for the diversion, I said, "Excuse me," with insincere enthusiasm. "But I really shouldn't neglect a call from anyone. It may very well be someone in need of sincere pastoral attention."

Allison rolled her eyes and repeated my words. "Sincere pastoral attention?"

"Go ahead," said Mom. "Make sure to keep it quiet about how you hate your sister and how you're neglecting the temple of the Lord by ruining your own body, not to mention the bodies of your wife and son, by not drinking enough milk."

I stepped outside the front door and answered without checking the caller ID. "Hello?" I said.

"Pastor Brad?" said the caller.

"Yes?"

"It's Ernie Plaisance."

Oh no! I thought, panicking to myself. *Ernie's coming by, and I've spent some of the money! Have I told him about what happened yet? I can't remember!*

"Pastor?" Ernie's voice jerked me out of my thoughts. "Pastor Brad? Are you there?"

Remorse over what I had done swallowed me up once again. I had taken money given to the work of the Lord and had used it to purchase ice cream, milk, and pie to impress my mother and my wife. How could I explain it to him?

"Yes, Ernie. I'm here."

"Good. I thought I had lost you. I saw I had a text message from you."

"Yes, I sent one earlier."

"Well, I'm sure it's about something important."

"Yes, it is," I replied.

"Yeah, well, I hope it can wait. You see, my wife and I were just in a car accident in McComb."

"Oh no! Are you both okay?"

"I'm fine, but Connie's hurt. I don't know how bad it is yet. It looks like she may have a concussion or even something worse. We're at the hospital now. I'm really worried about her, Pastor Brad."

"I'm on my way, Ernie, and I'm praying for you both."

"Thank you, Pastor Brad. I appreciate it."

"You're welcome. I'll call you when I arrive."

I know that as a pastor, or even as a Christian, I should have felt sympathy for both Ernie and Connie in that moment. Then, as a son, I should have felt remorse for having to miss a family meal and get-together. Finally, as a husband, I should have felt guilty about leaving Allison alone to deal with my parents and Elizabeth.

But I didn't experience any of those feelings. Instead, all I felt was relief. I could delay speaking with Ernie about the money I had found and spent. I had an excuse to drive to McComb, where I could find an ATM and withdraw funds to replace the portion of the money I had already used. I wouldn't have to spend the afternoon listening to Mama complain about our lack of milk consumption or enduring my sister's never-ending shenanigans.

"Thank You, Lord!" I cried aloud, startling the neighbor kid who was riding his bike down the sidewalk, causing him to jerk his head my way and almost run into our mailbox. "Sorry!" I called out to him.

He shook his head lightly, waved, and rode quickly away.

Suddenly, the door opened, and Allison walked out. "Is everything okay?" I shouted with joy, "Connie has a concussion!"

"What?" she asked. "Connie Plaisance? Ernie's wife?"

"Yep!" I said. "They were in a car accident this afternoon!"

"Oh no! That's terrible! Where?"

"In McComb, on their way to lunch."

"How awful," said Allison.

"Oh, uh, yes, it is," I replied. Realizing that I had been smiling this whole time, I hugged Allison and toned down my enthusiasm. "I really should go to the hospital to check on them."

"Of course," she answered. "You should go. I hope they're okay."

"I'm sorry to leave you here with my parents and Elizabeth, though. Do you think you'll be okay here without me?"

"What's a couple of more hours?" she said. "Go. Take a sandwich and a glass of milk and go."

CHAPTER 5

Theft and deception are good partners. In Genesis, there's a story about a man named Jacob who tricked his twin brother Esau out of his inheritance. Then, to make matters worse, he deceived his elderly father into believing that he was his older brother so he could receive the family blessing as well.

When I was a child in Sunday school, I watched my teacher tell this story using felt characters on a flannel graph board and vowed I would never act so selfishly. However, as I drove into McComb, I wondered if I was like Jacob. No matter how I twisted the truth, it didn't change the fact that I was guilty of spending money that wasn't mine. Granted, I had spent the first part of it helping out a friend in need, but that certainly didn't give me a license to throw away my values for the hope of a pleasant afternoon eating ice cream and a supposedly sinfully delicious pie, which I had missed completely.

"I can't believe that a hundred-dollar bill was lost from the offering," I said to myself. "Are Earl, Ernie, Jimmy, and Burt running through the church office with the collection like the Marx Brothers, throwing caution and sensibility to the wind? Surely not. These guys take the offering as seriously as I do. So losing the hundred dollars was simply an accident."

I shook my head and laughed it off. "Certainly, it was just an accident. I should just forget for today and turn the money back in tomorrow. Maybe Allison will save me some pie and ice cream."

When I finally arrived at the Southwest Mississippi Medical Center, I let out a deep breath. I wiped the crumbs from my lap, glanced at my phone, and read a text from Ernie: "I'm in the surgery waiting room on the second floor."

"Surgery?" I cried aloud. Embarrassment swept over me. Suddenly, I couldn't believe I had been so pleased at Connie's misfortune and just now had been selfishly dreaming of pie I had acquired through ill-gotten gain. "Man," I said.

I found a spot designated for clergy, parked my car, dropped my head into my right hand, and prayed. "God, are You sure You have me serving in the right place? I'm just not very good at pastorly stuff. Apparently, I also have issues with poor leadership, theft, and honesty, not to mention disrespect of my elders. God, I'm so sorry about everything that has happened. Please help Connie be okay and help me care more about others than I do about myself. Amen."

I sat still for a moment, waiting for something to happen. Honestly, I was hoping that the Almighty would zap me with a feeling of overwhelming forgiveness partnered with outstanding confidence.

It didn't happen. In fact, instead of the euphoria I was hoping for, I felt devoid of feelings altogether. So I did what I always do when I feel inadequate, even after praying: I kept going. I quickly typed a response to Ernie's text: "I'm in the parking lot. Be right up."

A few minutes later, I found Ernie sitting in the surgery waiting room, wringing his hands and staring into nothingness. I paused when I saw my friend, wondering for a moment if I should disturb him. He must have sensed my presence because he leaned back in his chair and nodded without speaking. I'd never seen him like this before, and I suddenly didn't know what to say.

"Hi," I said awkwardly.

Ernie motioned for me to sit across from him.

"How's Connie?" I asked as I took my seat.

In a brief moment of silence, Ernie's eyes met mine in search of comfort. I tried to keep mine open but suddenly felt like I was playing the staring game and had to blink. When I did, Ernie closed his own eyes for a moment and let out a long breath.

After a few moments of silence, I repeated, "How's Connie?"

"Well," he said, opening his eyes but looking away from me, "I don't really know. At first, the doctors thought she was okay and might just have to stay for observation overnight. But then, just a few minutes ago, a different doctor came and told me she might need to have further extensive surgery."

"I'm so sorry, Ernie."

"Thanks," he replied, continuing to wring his hands.

With the exception of my own father, Ernie was the most solid Christian man I had ever met. He loved the Lord, loved his wife and family, served the church, and respected me. He was always courteous and considerate of others, even when going through a crisis.

"What kind of surgery?" I asked.

Ernie looked up, tightened his lips for a moment, and said, "He said she might have some sort of brain injury."

"He doesn't know for sure?"

"He said he couldn't be certain."

"So this could mean brain surgery then?"

"Yeah, possibly. He said he couldn't be sure without the opinion of a specialist."

"The uncertainty sounds strange to me."

"I suppose," he sighed, "but I guess I'd rather have a doctor who knows his limitations than one who's trying to fake it at Connie's expense."

"That makes sense," I replied. "So what happens now?"

"Another doctor, some kind of brain specialist, is taking a look at her as we speak to determine the extent of her injury, to see if she needs surgery."

"So there's a good chance she might be okay?"

"Maybe," said Ernie. "That's all I'm hearing now: *maybe*."

"I'm sorry, Ernie," I said.

"It's not your fault," he replied.

"I know, but I'm sorry just the same."

Ernie looked toward the entrance impatiently and began to rock back and forth. "Where is that doctor?" he asked nervously. "Why aren't they telling me anything?"

"I'm sure they're doing all they can. Your job is to pray and be strong for Connie."

"I guess you're right," said Ernie as he leaned forward, placing his elbows on his knees and burying his face in his hands. "It's hard to pray right now, Pastor."

"I'm sure it must be," I answered.

In that moment, I knew I should grab Ernie's hand, kneel down right there in the waiting room, and pray the house down. But I didn't, even though

I knew it was the right thing to do. Something was holding me back. I don't know if it was fear or unbelief or stupidity. Just as I was about to move my knees to the floor, Ernie spoke.

"You know," he said, "none of this would have happened if we would've just gone where she wanted to go, but I was stubborn. I insisted on coming to McComb, going out to eat, then taking care of a few business things from here."

"It's not your fault," I said. "You were trying to be nice to your wife by not making her cook."

"I only wish that were the case," he replied. "To be honest, I was only thinking of myself. It was my greediness that caused this accident."

"I don't understand," I said.

"Connie wanted to go to New Orleans," said Ernie. "She wanted to try to find ... well, our son. But I told her I didn't want to fool with that today. I told her McComb is a lot closer than New Orleans, and I didn't want to spend my whole day driving. It's all my fault."

"That's nonsense!" I said sharply. "What happened here was an accident, and it could have happened on your way home or in New Orleans just as easily as it happened here in McComb."

"I suppose you're right," he said before sniffing hard.

"Are you okay?" I asked, looking around for some tissue. A box of Kleenex was on the end table to my right. I offered one to Ernie.

He took it, wiped his nose, and tossed the tissue into the trash. "I think so," he replied. "I'm just worried about Connie now."

"You're a good husband, Ernie."

"Not really," said Ernie. As he turned to me, he said, "You know, it should be me in there, Pastor. I'm strong, but Connie's not. She's the best wife in the world, but she's really fragile. Why did the car have to hit us on her side?"

"Is that what happened?" I asked.

"Yeah. We were on our way to Maggie's Restaurant here in McComb. I stopped at a light. It turned green, we pulled forward, and we were hit by an old Ford truck. I guess the driver either didn't see us or didn't stop for the red light for some reason."

"What did he say?"

"He didn't say anything. Nothing at all."

"What do you mean?" I asked. "He didn't talk to you?"

"No, he didn't."

"Was he injured?"

"Not at all," said Ernie. "In fact, he just drove off after plowing into our passenger-side door."

"He left the scene of the accident?"

"Yes. He'd probably been drinking, didn't have insurance, or both. You know those old trucks were made out of real metal. He slammed into us, then just backed up and drove away without a word."

"That's terrible!" I exclaimed. "I'm so sorry this happened."

"I am too," said Ernie.

"I'm sure the police will find the guy who ran into you."

"I hope so, but for now I just hope my Connie's okay."

"Yeah," I said. I put my hand on his shoulder, not knowing what else to say. His face went back into his hands, and I could tell he was crying. *Oh, God*, I prayed silently, *what do I say to a grown man, a strong man like Ernie, almost old enough to be my father, when he's crying?*

Even after my prayer, I still couldn't think of anything to say, so I kept my hand on Ernie's shoulder and continued to pray silently. *Lord, please help Connie be okay. Help Ernie be strong for her. Comfort them both. Help their family, and please, help me know what to say to them.*

After a few minutes of silence, Ernie wiped his eyes and sat up straight. I offered him another tissue, which he took without a word. After a moment, Ernie regained his composure and said, "Thank you for coming today, Pastor Brad. I didn't know who to call, and it helps knowing you are here to help me through this."

"You are most certainly welcome," I answered. "I may not always know what to say, but you can call me anytime."

"You don't have to say anything. You being here means so much. Thank you."

"Have you called your son?" I asked.

"I tried, Pastor, but it's no use. Paul wouldn't be much help to me in this situation anyway. Besides, I couldn't reach him."

"I'm sorry about that. Is there anything I can do? Do you want me to keep trying to reach him?"

"No," he replied. "Sooner or later he'll get my message. I'm just thankful that you're here."

Feeling like we had just had this conversation, I said, "It's the least I could do."

Ernie pulled another tissue from the box and wiped his eyes once again. "I'm sorry, Pastor Brad."

"You don't have to be sorry either, Ernie. Like I said, the accident wasn't your fault. Connie would never blame you for—"

"No, not about the accident," he inserted. "I'm sorry about what I said at the deacons' meeting this morning at church."

"What do you mean?" I asked.

"I'm sorry I went along with the others who were insisting that the offering must be taken in the middle of the service. What you were saying made perfect sense, but I let Archie and Earl get the best of me. Then, after I heard your sermon, I realized how beneficial it would have been to have taken the offering at the end of the service."

"Really?" I asked.

"Yes," he replied. "I believe it would have inspired people to give more. Our offering would have—"

"No, uh, not that," I interrupted. "I'm sorry, but what I mean to ask is, uh, you listened to the sermon?"

Ernie smiled through his pain. "Of course I did. I pay attention to all of your sermons. Don't listen to Earl and Jimmy and those other guys, Pastor Brad. You are a good preacher."

"Thanks, Ernie," I said, swallowing hard and putting my hand on his shoulder. "Do you want some coffee or something? I could get it for you while you wait."

Ernie looked around and shook his head. "Not right now, thank you."

"Okay," I said.

I sat with Ernie in silence for a few seconds, reflecting on what he had said. Never before had anyone besides my wife told me that I was a good preacher, not even my parents. Daddy would sometimes mention a point I had made in a sermon, but he had never gone so far as to say I had done a good job preaching. Mama, however, often had that glassy-eyed look people get when they're daydreaming. I often wondered if she was pondering the whereabouts of Elizabeth.

I think every pastor wonders from time to time if people are really listening. That's probably why Ernie's words meant so much to me. Even though I was sitting in a hospital with a grieving man, I wanted to bask in the moment.

"Mr. Plaisance?" said a doctor who was suddenly right upon us, clipboard in hand.

"Yes?" said Ernie, rising to his feet. "I'm Ernie Plaisance."

The doctor extended his hand and said, "I'm Dr. Carraway. I've just come from examining your wife."

Ernie shook the doctor's hand but said nothing.

"Is she going to be okay?" I asked, positioning myself beside Ernie.

"I'm sorry," said Dr. Carraway. "Are you a family member?"

"He's my pastor," said Ernie. "He can hear anything you've got to say."

"Excuse me," I said, extending my hand to Dr. Carraway. "I'm Brad … uh, Pastor Brad Johnson. Are you the brain specialist?"

Dr. Carraway shook my hand and said, "Yes, Pastor, and any prayers you've offered up must have worked today. Mrs. Plaisance is going to be fine. Your doctor was right to be cautious. Brain injuries can be very unpredictable, so we'd like to keep her overnight, but she can probably go home in the morning."

"Are you serious?" asked Ernie. "You mean she doesn't need brain surgery?"

"That's right," said the doctor. "She's going to be okay."

Ernie exhaled deeply and then grinned from ear to ear. "When can I see her?"

"No time like the present," said Dr. Carraway. "Follow me."

The doctor led us to Connie's room, where a nurse asked Ernie to sign a few papers, which he did while keeping one eye on his wife. He did so with good reason: Connie was the most peaceful-looking almost-brain-surgery patient I'd ever seen.

Ernie moved a chair beside the bed and reached for Connie's hand. "She looks good, doesn't she?" he asked.

"She looks great, Ernie," I said. "You're a very lucky man."

"No," he said. "I'm blessed, Pastor. Tremendously blessed."

I stayed with Ernie and Connie for another half hour. We didn't talk much, but when Ernie did speak, he never took his eyes off of Connie.

"Are you okay?" I asked him.

"Yes, thank you," he said. "I want the first thing she sees when she wakes up to be me looking back at her."

"You sure do love her a lot, don't you?" I asked.

"Yes. More than anything in the world."

"You said you were blessed, Ernie, but Connie is also blessed to have you for a husband. You're a very good husband."

He smiled. "Not really, Pastor. Not at all, actually. She puts up with a lot from me. She always has. Sitting here, looking at her, willing her eyes to open, helps me realize that I would be nothing without her. Every good thing in me is because of her … well, and because of the Lord, of course."

"That's awesome, Ernie. Do you want me to wait here with you until she wakes?"

"No," he replied. "Why don't you go on home and hug your own wife? I don't know whether you realize it or not, but you're blessed as well."

"You're absolutely right," I said with a smile. "I sure am. Please let me know how things go."

"Sure thing, Pastor. Again, I can't thank you enough."

"No problem, Ernie," I said as I stood to go.

I was almost through the door when Ernie called to me. "Pastor Brad!"

I stopped and looked back at him. He was still staring at his wife. "Yes?" I asked.

"I meant what I said before. You are a good preacher. Don't let anyone ever tell you different."

"Thanks, Ernie. Take care of that wife of yours."

"I will," he said.

"Good," I replied.

With my first sense of accomplishment for the day, I smiled and walked down the hall toward the elevators. I had come to offer encouragement to Ernie, but he had encouraged me. It was exactly what I had needed, and for that I was very thankful.

CHAPTER 6

In rushing home to see Allison and Gabe, I completely forgot about checking in on Billy Ray and Melissa at the hospital. Replenishing the church's money also slipped my mind. By the time I realized, I had already phoned Allison to let her know I was almost home. I didn't want to waste what was left of my afternoon.

"I can't believe I live so far from an ATM," I said to myself. "Why couldn't I have found a hundred-dollar check? I'll just have to wait until tomorrow to replace the money."

Almost as if on cue, as I entered Aucoin, my phone started buzzing, alerting me to a text message. I know you're not supposed to text and drive, but I was curious. I glanced down quickly to check the sender's name: Elizabeth. "What does she want?" I said aloud.

I imagined her saying, "Hi, Brad. How's about joining me tonight for a tall one and a good joint? You know it's legal in Colorado."

"Then why don't you just move to Colorado?" I asked the air in the passenger seat.

I realized I was having a conversation with imaginary Elizabeth and shook my head slightly before turning onto a side road leading toward my home. After a moment, curiosity got the better of me, so I slowed to a crawl and clicked on Elizabeth's name to read the text message.

"Hey, bro. Sorry I missed you at lunch. Let's talk soon."

I drew in a breath and let it out slowly. "I can't deal with you right now, Elizabeth," I said to my phone. "You can wait until tomorrow. I'm going home to see my wife."

I pulled into our driveway about four thirty, expecting Allison to be exhausted from hosting my parents and Elizabeth. Instead, I was surprised to see her sitting in a rocking chair on our front porch, reading a book and waiting for me to arrive. When she saw me, she smiled, dropped her book, and rose to her feet. I love it when she smiles. When Billy Joel sings "She's got a smile that heals me," it feels like he's talking about my wife. He had better keep his distance if he ever comes to Aucoin. I don't care if he is the piano man.

"Welcome home, Pastor Brad," said Allison as she wrapped her arms around me.

"Why, thank you, ma'am," I said, pulling her close to me. "Where's my wife?"

She laughed. "Why, she's standing here in front of you, happy that her husband is finally home."

"Well, it's good to see you too," I said, giving her a quick kiss. "Where's our son?"

"Oh, he's run off somewhere down the street. He was carrying a box of matches and a pair of scissors. You know how toddlers are. I'm sure he'll make it back eventually."

"Oh really? Just like that?"

"Yeah, he really wanted to, so I let him. You know, you're not supposed to squash your children's desires."

"That's good parenting," I said. "I mean, it's good as long as you gave him a glass of milk for the road."

"Well, he's actually gone with your parents for the rest of the day, so I'm sure he's getting plenty of milk."

"Did Elizabeth go with them?"

"Uh, no," replied Allison. "She never showed up."

"Surprise, surprise," I said. "She sent me a text message just now, saying she was sorry she missed me at lunch. I assumed she meant because I wasn't here."

"Did you see the baby?" asked Allison.

"What baby?"

"Billy Ray and Melissa's baby. Didn't you say they were headed to McComb to have their baby?"

"Oh yeah," I said. "I honestly never thought about it. I was pretty focused on Ernie and Connie."

"And you're also a man."

"Yes, and that."

Allison smiled, took a step closer to me, and said, "Well, Mr. Man. Why don't we forget about your sister, your parents, and the church for a while?"

"Ah, so it's just you and me?"

"Yes, sir, Pastor Brad," she replied, kissing me on my cheek. "We're all alone."

"Really?" I asked, hugging her tight.

"Absolutely positive."

"And my parents have Gabe for the rest of the day?"

"That's right," she said, smiling gently.

"Awesome," I replied, releasing my grip on her. "Let's go doze in front of the TV."

She let go of me, crossed her arms, and said, "I can't believe this. We have the entire house to ourselves, and you want to watch TV and take a nap?"

"Oh!" I said, seeing the look in her eye and realizing what I had done. "Uh, no, you were … um, what I meant to say was …"

"And here I was waiting for you on the porch!"

"Wait!" I cried. "Let's start over. I'm just getting home, you're really cute and smiling when you see me, I'm ruggedly handsome getting out of the car, and you walk up to me and say …"

"You know," she said, turning toward the house, "taking a nap does sound really good now."

"But you know," I said, "the nap really could wait."

"I get the love seat," she replied. "And you could use a nap anyway. You've had a pretty hectic day."

Sunday afternoons at home typically are amazing. I lie on our sofa, allowing myself to forget about the struggles of the past week and lose myself in nonsense on TV. However, this day seemed to be fighting against me. Nothing seemed interesting, and I felt restless.

First, my mind kept wandering back to the offering confrontation with the deacons that morning. It was ridiculous that I even had to endure that interaction. The pastor of a church should have full authority to change the order of service anytime he deems it necessary, even every week if he is so inclined, especially considering our bad financial state. To make things worse, Earl had called me a bad preacher, and none of the deacons had disagreed with him, at least not in front of the others. Ernie had expressed his disagreement later at the hospital, but I wondered if he did so only because I was there with him in his time of need. Would he have said the same words to me if his accident had never happened?

Second, I was guilty of stealing from the church. I had found offering money in the church office and had spent a portion of it instead of reporting it to the chairman of the finance committee. To my credit, I had crawled around on the office floor looking for any clues as to what might have happened. However, I now wondered if I had done so only because I hoped to find more lost money. If Earl ever found out about this, he would surely have me arrested for fraud, theft, or embezzlement or at least misappropriation of funds.

Third, I couldn't get over my argument with my mother about Elizabeth. I didn't know why I let my sister get under my skin so easily. Sure, Elizabeth had a past. Who didn't? She had hurt the rest of the family and wanted us to jump every time she called us with a relapse issue. It made me feel strange because I was supposed to be all about ministering to people in need, and now I was rejecting my own sister. I knew I should feel differently about her, but she had just put us all through too much.

And finally, the results of the car accident with Ernie and Connie had shaken me. On one hand, I was amazed by the love I saw in Ernie's eyes for Connie. He wouldn't even look away from her to talk to me because he wanted the first thing she saw when she woke up to be him gazing back at her. That kind of love was inspiring and convicting at the same time. The love they had for each other was the same type of love I wanted for Allison and me. It was the depth of love I wished for Gabe to feel toward his wife whenever he grew up. It was the kind of love every husband should have for his wife.

Then, in the midst of everything, Ernie had stepped out of his situation for a moment while his wife was suffering to tell me that he listened to all of my sermons. He had even called me a "good preacher." He had given me hope, and he didn't even know it. I just hoped he really meant what he said.

I glanced over at Allison, who had forsaken the idea of finding something decent to watch and was now curled up on our love seat reading. Suddenly, I felt incredibly small and completely unworthy of being her husband. She deserved so much more than living in our small home, worrying about the cost of ice cream, being married to a man who was constantly pulled in a thousand different directions. She deserved to be whisked away to some exotic place, far away from the craziness of Aucoin and Lee Community Church.

Allison had stuck with me through all of my seminary training, taking on whatever work she could find to help support us since I had only a part-time job because of my full-time study load. Then she had never complained as we traveled the southeast portion of the United States, enduring the agony of multiple pastoral candidacy opportunities as I searched for the Lord's will regarding where I should serve. Finally, she had agreed to join me in our ministry journey with Lee Community, sitting faithfully through all of the church business meetings, even when people said mean things about my preaching, our marriage, and me.

I watched her reading, unable to look away. I noticed how she smiled naturally, even when she was totally focused. I loved that.

"Why are you looking at me?" she asked.

"I like the way you look."

"What?"

"You're cute. I like to look at you."

"Well, cut it out. You're making me nervous."

"Can I ask you a question?"

"Sure."

"Do you ever get tired of me being a pastor?"

"Yes, I do."

"Wow!" I laughed. "You certainly did answer quickly."

She smiled. "It's easy when you know the answer."

"So I take it you've spent considerable time thinking about this?"

"Of course," she smiled. "I've thought about it quite a bit, actually."

"So are you sorry you married me?"

"Not at all."

"But if you were married to someone else, he could better provide for you financially, take you on expensive vacations, and even make sure you have plenty of milk in the house."

She smiled. "That is true, and all of that does sound tempting, but then again, he also wouldn't be you, so I'd eventually have to kill him."

"Really?" I asked. "You'd do that for me?"

"Certainly," she replied with a smile. "It's a good thing I married you and spared myself from serving a life sentence in prison."

"I was just looking out for you," I said.

"How very thoughtful," she said. "You're so good to me."

My face turned serious for a moment. "But really now," I said, "wouldn't you rather be married to someone who could give you lots of money and security and lots of fancy vacations?"

"I don't need security and fancy vacations and lots of money," she replied. "I'd rather be married to you."

"Thank you, I guess."

She smiled without saying a word.

"You know what?" I asked.

"What?" she asked back.

"I'm really glad we're married."

"Me too."

Suddenly, I felt restless, and before I realized it, I was on my feet.

"What are you doing?" she asked.

"Do you want to go do something?"

"Like what?" she asked.

"I'm not really sure. Why don't we do something exciting?"

"Something exciting?" she asked. "That sounds fun, but what?"

"I'm not sure."

"What do you want to do? Take a walk?"

"No, I mean actually do something. You know, something like … uh, well … why don't we at least go to dinner and a movie or something like that?"

"What about Gabe?" she asked.

"We can pick him up from my parents on our way home."

"Can we afford it?"

"Who cares?" I replied. "Let's throw caution to the wind!"

Her shock turned to suspicion, and she crossed her arms. "Just what are you up to, Pastor Brad?"

"No," I replied.

"What do you mean, 'no'?" she asked. "We're not going anywhere?"

"Don't call me Pastor tonight. I'm not Pastor anybody right now. Tonight, I'm just Brad Johnson, a regular guy who loves his wife and wants to take her on a date."

"I'll be ready in ten minutes," said Allison, dropping her book to the floor and heading toward the bedroom.

"I'll be waiting," I replied.

As she disappeared into the hallway, I sat down so I could put on my shoes. I picked up my keys and my wallet from the floor where they lay and placed them on the sofa. With the feel of my leather wallet still on my hands, something within me, perhaps my conscience or at least common sense, asked a very simple, honest question: *how are you going to pay for it?*

Almost by instinct, I opened my wallet and pulled out the remaining cash. I had given Billy Ray twenty dollars for gas and spent twenty-one dollars on milk, ice cream, and pie, which left me with fifty-nine dollars. "Well," I whispered to myself as I looked at the cash, "I guess spending a little more couldn't hurt. I'm replacing it all tomorrow anyway."

A thought entered my mind: *it's still stealing though, isn't it?* I knew in my heart that I should agree and not spend any more of the money, but I also felt like I'd burst if I didn't give my wife a night on the town.

Suddenly, a competing voice said, *Go ahead. You'll give Ernie a hundred-dollar bill tomorrow. What difference will a few more dollars make?*

"I'm still not sure this is the right thing to do," I said aloud. "Maybe we should just stay home."

"Did you say something, honey?" asked Allison from the next room. "You want to stay home?"

"No, just talking to myself," I replied. "I want to take you out and show you a good time!"

"Good!" she cried. "I'll be just a little bit longer."

You don't want to disappoint Allison, do you?

I stuck the remaining fifty-nine dollars back in my wallet, rubbed my temples, and then reached for my keys.

An hour later, I pulled our car into the Sonic Drive-In in Kentwood,

Louisiana. I parked in the first available spot, turned off the ignition, and hung my head. "I'm sorry," I said.

"Sorry about what?" asked Allison.

"I'm sorry that all of the movies sounded stupid and that every place we wanted to eat was closed, and I'm sorry we ended up at the Sonic. Nothing has turned out how I thought it would."

She smiled and patted my hand. "Well, you always did know how to show a girl a good time."

"I'm just warming up," I said, leaning in for a kiss.

She kissed me quickly and then backed away. "None of that, Mr. Man! I'm hungry."

Not wasting any time, I pressed the red order button, waited for the clerk to respond, and said, "We'd like the brown bag special with two cheeseburgers, fries, and Cokes, please."

"That will be $10.95," said the voice over the speaker. "Your order will be out shortly."

"Wow!" said Allison. "Aren't you the big spender tonight?"

"I'm sorry," I said. "I didn't even ask you what you wanted. I just ordered the same thing we used to get when we were in college."

"The brown bag special was all we could afford in those days, wasn't it?" she asked.

"Yeah, it was," I said, looking down. "Some things never change."

"I really miss college sometimes," she said. "Those were fun times, weren't they?"

"Yeah, they were. Did you want something more than what I ordered?"

"No, it's fine," she replied. "We're kind of tight money-wise right now anyway, aren't we?"

"Why do you say that?" I replied as I pulled thirteen dollars from my wallet for the bill and the tip. I made a mental note that I had only forty-six dollars left.

"Earlier today you said you might not be able to buy ice cream because we won't get paid until next week."

"Yeah?"

"But then," she continued, "I was sort of confused when you came home with not only milk but ice cream and pie, which I didn't even ask for."

"Well," I said, "it turns out I had more cash on me than I thought."

"Oh, okay," she said. "That's strange because you usually know the amount of money we have to the penny."

"Yeah, that is weird," I said, smiling nervously. "I'm sorry about that, and I'm sorry about everything else too."

"You don't have to be sorry. I already told you it's okay that we're eating here."

"No, it's not just about that, sweetheart. I'm sorry I don't make more money than I do. I'm sorry we can't live in a bigger place and eat at fancy restaurants. I'm sorry I haven't given you a better and more fulfilling life."

Allison smiled. "You've given me a great life. I love you, and I want to be with you a lot more than I want fancy dinners, big houses, and lots of money."

I returned her smile. "Thanks, honey. I love you too."

Silence suddenly filled the car, and I wondered if she really meant what she had just said or if she was just making the best of the sorry deal she had been handed.

"Even so," I said, trying to lighten the mood, "if money were no object and you could go anywhere on vacation and do anything you wanted to do, where would you go, and what would you do?"

"Do you get to come with me?" she asked.

"I would hope so."

"Well," she said, "I guess the first thing I'd want to do with you is drive to New Orleans, eat in some swanky restaurant, then stay in a fancy hotel on Canal Street."

"Really?" I asked. "Is that all?"

"I get to choose more?"

"Certainly!" I replied. "Price is no object for my wife while we're planning a pretend vacation."

"Then I'd want to go on a cruise that leaves from the French Quarter, travels down the Mississippi River, and spans the Caribbean, visiting beautiful islands."

"That sounds nice," I said. "Which islands?"

"It really doesn't matter to me," she replied, "as long as they have pretty water and white sand and I'm with you."

I smiled and then pondered her answer as I turned and pretended to read the backlit menu.

Later that evening, Allison lay beside me, sound asleep. I stared restlessly at the ceiling, my mind racing through affordable vacation possibilities for the two of us on a pastor's salary. *Could we possibly afford to take a cruise this year, even a short one?*

Allison and I had dreamed of taking a cruise for years. We had spent two nights at Pensacola Beach for our honeymoon. Even though we had enjoyed the white sandy beaches and the emerald water, we had spoken then about how it would be nice to take a cruise someday. But then seminary classes, tuition, church, bills, and life happened, and our thoughts of taking a cruise disappeared in the midst of the urgent. Musings about a fabulous cruise vacation would come up whenever we really talked about our lives, but we never took them seriously enough to take any real financial steps toward making such a cruise a reality. It was destined to remain a dream, or so it seemed.

But this time, something was different. The idea was eating me alive. I had to find out if there was any way we could make it work. I slipped out of bed and tiptoed down the hall past Gabe's room, made my way into the living room, and turned on my laptop. Soon, I was scrolling through numerous cruise line websites, noticing one recurring theme. Cruises, though a tremendous value for what travelers received, still seemed really expensive for someone without any money. Even if I could manage to reserve the cheapest of interior rooms, we would still be hurting for port excursion funds and extra spending money. Before I knew it, I was checking our various bank and credit card accounts, searching frantically for at least one possible way I could make this happen for us. After a half hour of financial scheming and wondering how much we could save if we didn't eat for a couple of months, I finally had to admit that even the cheapest cruise didn't look feasible for us, at least not this year. Next year wasn't looking all that great either.

Then I picked up my wallet and looked inside. I recounted the forty-six dollars I had left from the hundred I had found. *What am I doing?* I thought. *I can't even afford to pay back the money I've spent since yesterday. Allison will just have to be happy with a staycation this year. It will be fun. We can sleep late,* watch television with Gabe, play cards, go to the movies (maybe), or spend extra time with our families this year. It'll just have to be okay. But I didn't mean it. Not one bit.

Feeling more depressed than ever, I closed my laptop, slightly harder than usual, and slipped it back into the computer bag. "I don't understand my life," I whispered.

As I glanced around the room, every flaw jumped out at me, and I suddenly felt poor and stupid. Our furniture was old, our walls needed painting, and there were cracks in our tiles. Beside the sofa sat a toy box Gabe had inherited from me. We loved Gabe so much, but when Allison told me she was pregnant, I had no idea how much raising a child would cost. Next year, we were planning on sending him to preschool, which was another priority expense I had no idea how we were going to cover. How could we possibly make it if we had a second child? Silently, I prayed, *What's wrong with me, God?*

The sound of a car driving down the street jolted me. I stood and looked through the window at the new Lexus SUV passing my house. *What must it be like to own and drive a new car like that? That's really what you wanted for me, right, Lord? Surely it wasn't your plan for me to be an ineffective, boring, broke preacher who constantly struggles with doubt and debt.*

The Lexus continued down the road even though I was secretly willing it to pull into my driveway. I imagined a tuxedo-dressed driver stepping out, handing me the keys, and saying, "Hello, Pastor Brad. The Lord is so pleased with your leadership and preaching that He wanted you to have this new vehicle."

I was jolted from my thoughts by a dog barking down the street. I looked for the Lexus, but it was nowhere to be seen. I sighed deeply and resumed my prayer. *I know my thoughts should be more on You and less on me, but I can't stop these thoughts. Is my ultimate purpose in life so small that I constantly have to worry about money? Is my integrity so loose that my morals can be so easily swayed by a hundred-dollar bill? Why did I spend this money when I know it's wrong? Why do You even put up with me?*

I waited silently for an answer, feeling like an elementary school student who had just confessed to his own actions while subsequently questioning the motives of his vice principal. I hoped for some type of answer, anything, even disappointment in my lack of faith or in my recent thoughts and behavior. I waited for either an encouraging embrace or a trip to the spiritual woodshed. Nothing.

After a few minutes, I started feeling stupid, so I turned out the lights and quietly made my way back toward the master bedroom. I glanced in at Gabe, who slept peacefully, having no idea of the inward struggle taking place in the mind of his old man. I envied him. Well, I did until I remembered that I was the one who would be paying for his college education. Then I pitied him. "Poor kid," I said. "I hope you study hard and get lots of scholarships."

As I climbed back into bed, Allison rolled onto her side but didn't wake. Slowly, I pulled the extra covers over myself and lay flat on my back beside her. As I lay there, I spoke silently to God once again. *Lord, this whole preacher life at Lee Community is driving me crazy. The deacons are stressing me out, especially Earl and Jimmy. The pay is ridiculous. And people are constantly reminding me of my faults. Tithing must be at an all-time low. With everything going on, should I just find something else to do? I mean, why should I continue doing what I hate, or at least strongly dislike?*

There, in the darkness, I waited once again for God to speak to me. "I'm not going to sleep until I hear from You," I mouthed silently.

Even though I had made that ridiculous statement, somehow in the midst of my waiting and self-pity, I drifted off to sleep.

CHAPTER 7

The ocean wind blew in my face as I reclined in my chair with my bare feet on the railing of our private balcony. I watched Roatan Island growing smaller as our cruise ship sailed away from it and toward our next tropical destination. I sipped from the soda in my glass and picked up a mystery paperback from my favorite author.

"Brad?" called my wife from within the cabin. "Where are you?"

"I'm on the balcony," I replied, glancing at the tropical waters below. "Come see me."

Allison peeked out from our stateroom wearing a white bathrobe.

"Well, hello there, Mrs. Johnson," I smiled. "I really like your outfit."

Allison returned my smile and took a seat in the chair beside me. Then she leaned over and kissed me gently on the cheek. "This is a wonderful vacation, honey," she whispered in my ear. "Thank you so much for making it happen. I'll remember it forever. I love you so much."

"You're welcome, baby," I replied. "Now I'm just curious about one little thing."

Allison's eyes caught the reflection of the Caribbean water. "And just what might that be?"

"Well," I whispered, "would you like to show me just how grateful you are?"

Allison smiled once again, leaned in close, and kissed me again, on my lips this time.

"I'll take that as a yes," I said.

Allison nodded as she reached for my hand. I took it in my own, stood up, and pulled her close to me. She kissed my cheek again and then placed her mouth beside my ear. Softly, she whispered, "Brad, are you awake?"

"What do you mean?" I asked. "Of course I'm awake."

"It's way past time to get up, Brad!" shouted Allison, poking me in the chest. "I'm sorry to tell you, but we've overslept."

Suddenly, my dream cruise melted away. I opened my eyes and glanced around at our bedroom. I closed my eyes again, only tighter this time. "Can't we both just go back to my dream?" I asked. "You'd really like it there, especially for the next half hour or so."

"Sure," said Allison. "But you're going to be really late if you don't get up."

"You're joking," I said, realizing what she was saying for possibly the first time.

"Look how bright it is outside," she replied. "It's really late."

"Why didn't you wake me?" I asked.

"Please pardon me, your majesty," she said. "I realize that I've been negligent in fulfilling my servant duties of waking you. Please forgive me and withhold the flogging this time. Would you like me to change your diaper now? Or perhaps you would prefer for me to draw your bubble bath."

"The dream is definitely over," I said. "The nightmare has begun."

"I'm glad I can be of assistance, Your Highness."

"Okay, I get it," I said. "I'm sorry." I reached for my nightstand and grabbed my phone. It was almost 8:00 a.m. "I can't believe this!" I cried as I jumped out of bed. "I really have to get going."

"What time do you usually meet Ernie to count the offering?"

"Eight thirty, sharp," I said as I hurriedly pulled on a sweatshirt over my T-shirt. "If I hurry, I can still make it."

She cringed. "Do you think he'll still be coming this morning? I mean, the man's wife is probably still in the hospital, and she wasn't even awake when you left yesterday."

"I'm pretty sure we're still on," I said. "Ernie's a rock. He never misses anything like this. Besides, the hospital might have even let Connie go home yesterday. If so, he's probably so grateful for my visit yesterday that he's already there in the parking lot, just waiting for his negligent pastor to show up. Even if he isn't, he would never be late for our weekly offering counting without letting me know."

"You better head that way then," she replied. "But you should let him know what's happened. It's not that big of a deal."

I paused for a moment, thinking of how I had yet to replace the money. I stood in a frozen state, pondering my situation while staring blankly at my wife. *If only that were true*, I thought.

"What is it?" she asked. "What are you doing? I thought you were in a hurry."

I shook myself out of my thoughts. "I am. Sorry. Yes, I'd better hurry."

Without showering, I reached in the closet for whatever pants my hands could reach while also scanning the room for my car keys. I pulled on an old pair of jeans and laced up my running shoes. I practically ran through the hallway, stopping quickly to pat my son on the head and to kiss my wife and then hurrying through the front door to the car.

I was starting to unlock my car when I realized something wasn't right. I held the keys to my face. "Man!" I yelled out, before noticing the neighbor kid pushing his bike down the sidewalk.

At the sound of my shout, he glanced over at me and made eye contact for a brief second.

"Excuse me," I said. "I brought out the wrong keys."

He shrugged his shoulders and looked ahead as he continued down the sidewalk.

Realizing I had just apologized to an elementary-school child, I sighed and then ran back for my keys.

Twenty minutes later, I pulled into the church parking lot. Thankfully, Ernie's car was nowhere to be seen. "Thank You, Lord!" I mouthed as I reached for my phone to send Ernie a text: "Hi, Ernie. How is Connie this morning? Allison and I are still praying for you both."

I was just about to walk through the front doors of the church building when Ernie texted back: "Hi, Pastor. Thanks for praying. We're still at the hospital, but Connie did wake up yesterday. She's back asleep now, but we should be able to come home today. Can we hold off on counting the offering until tomorrow?"

His text was like a breath of fresh air. Realizing that I had another day to replace the hundred dollars, I let out a sigh of relief. I looked up and mouthed another silent "thank you, Lord!" before texting back. "No problem, Ernie. Allison and I will keep praying for you and Connie. Please keep us informed as to how she's doing. I'll try to stop by later today."

I unlocked the church door, stepped inside, and then quickly relocked the door. *Awesome*, I thought. *I have time to travel to an ATM before seeing Ernie.* I practically ran to the office. After placing my computer bag on the desk, I sat down to gather my thoughts. I ran my fingers through my hair and closed my eyes tightly. *I have to get to an ATM so I can withdraw the hundred dollars I need. If only I hadn't found that money. Where did it come from in the first place?*

I let out a deep breath and lowered my hands to my desktop. They landed on top of the paper clips I had found yesterday. "And where did these paper clips come from?" I whispered to myself, as if someone was really listening. I scooped them up and instinctively tossed them into the trash. "Wait a minute," I said out loud. "I might need those if I discover that something fishy is going on around here."

I dug through the papers in the trash can until I found the paper clips. I pulled my hands out and turned so quickly toward my desk that I inadvertently knocked over the trash can, dumping the contents onto the floor. "Goodness," I exclaimed. I set the paper clips on my desk and knelt down to clean up the mess I had made. That's when I saw it. Three silver paper clips had been taped together to the bottom of the overturned trash can.

"Huh," I said as I examined it closely. The trash can had a metal lip on the outside bottom that touched the floor. If someone clipped something underneath the trashcan, it could be hidden from the world, at least temporarily. "Could someone be stealing money from the church, clipping it to the bottom of the trash can, and leaving it here right under my nose? Surely not." I shook the nonsense from my mind and continued to pick up the trash from the floor.

"Hello, Pastor Brad," said a voice from nowhere. "Digging through the trash today?"

I almost jumped out of my skin. After regaining my composure, I looked up to see who was speaking. From the dark hallway appeared the assistant chairman of our deacon board. "Earl!" I said. "Sorry for being jumpy. You really took me by surprise."

"Obviously," he replied, pointing at my clothes. "I see you're dressed pretty casual today."

I looked down at my clothing, suddenly embarrassed. In this light, I could see some very noticeable coffee stains on my sweatshirt. "Yes," I finally answered. "I woke up late and dressed quickly so I wouldn't miss Ernie when he came to count, but it looks like he's not going to make it today."

"Is that a fact?" asked Earl. "Why not?"

"Well, Ernie and Connie were in a car accident yesterday. Connie suffered a head injury, but it looks as if she's going to be okay. She's still in the hospital in McComb."

"Now that's truly a shame," said Earl with no concern in his voice whatsoever. He turned his head to the side and said, "Something stinks around here."

"What do you mean?" I asked nervously.

"Something in this hallway. It stinks."

"Oh, that must be the nursery restroom. Burt's coming in today to take care of it."

"Well, that's good," said Earl. "At least something around here is going to be in good hands."

"I guess so," I replied, deciding to ignore his rude comment.

"But answer me this," said Earl. "If Connie Plaisance is in the hospital, then why aren't you there with her? Aren't preachers supposed to be about visiting the sick and offering divine comfort to their families?"

I wanted to slap him. The most infuriating thing about Earl was that there was always a slight bit of truth in just about everything he said. He reminded me of Satan, twisting the truth to fit his own purposes. I wanted to ask, "Do you want me to hate you, Earl? If so, you're doing a good job!" But I didn't. Instead, I took a deep breath and held my anger in check. "I went to see Connie yesterday, and I figured she would have been released by now. Ernie just texted me to let me know about her condition and asked me about moving our counting session until tomorrow."

"That's probably a good idea," said Earl. "The money's not going anywhere, is it?"

"Not that I know of," I said.

"At times like this," said Earl, "I thank God that we spent the money to have a strong, reliable safe."

"That's a good point," I said.

"Yes, sir," he said, raising one eyebrow. "No one's getting at the Lord's money collected at Lee Community, Pastor Brad. It's locked up, good and tight."

"You're right about that," I said, looking away.

"I'm right about a lot of things, Preacher. Even respectable attire for ministers."

"What are you trying to say, Earl?"

Earl smirked and crossed his arms. "Well, it seems to me that if I was the preacher around here, I would keep myself looking presentable—at least dressed nicely and clean shaven—at all times in case someone became sick or in need of pastoral care."

This jerk was really starting to annoy me. I should have said nothing, but I just couldn't hold it in any longer. "Well, Earl," I replied sharply, "you've got a good point there, but sometimes, it's better to make sure ministry happens in a timely fashion, which can happen no matter if the pastor is nicely dressed or not."

He pursed his lips. "And I see you're out to prove that point today?"

"No," I replied. "I'm just trying to serve the Lord in the best way I know how, relying on the Bible, the Holy Spirit, and the education and training the Lord has graciously afforded me in the context where I find myself. It's not always easy to do that, Earl, when certain people continue to fight me, continually questioning every move I make."

I realized right away that I had answered a little too harshly, but I didn't care. Earl deserved whatever he got. Grouchy old goat.

"Well, Pastor Brad, I'd say that smart mouth of yours is probably something you picked up in that fancy seminary you attended, isn't it? Because it's certainly not coming from the Holy Spirit or from the Holy Bible!"

Suddenly, I saw myself as a child in my Bible drill competition, called upon to quote Proverbs 15:1 in the King James Version. I had stepped forward and said, "A soft answer turneth away wrath, but grievous words stir up anger." I knew I should heed the scripture I had learned as a child. I knew I should be more careful with my words, but something inside me was about to burst. "No, Earl!" I snapped. "Not at all. I picked those words up here at Lee Community Church in our last deacons' meeting."

"Is that a fact there, Mr. Preacher Man? I guess I can call you that."

"Yes," I replied. "In fact, I learned that lesson very well."

"It appears you have. It also looks like you've got a few more lessons to learn."

I wanted to tell him off right there, but instead, I took a deep breath and replied, "Lessons are things we all have to learn from time to time, Earl. Is there something I can help you with today?"

He chuckled to himself, sensing that he had gotten the better of me.

I stood perfectly still, determined to wait him out.

After an awkward moment of silence, Earl finally replied. "No, not at all, Pastor Brad. I just thought I'd stop by to help Earl count the money. Since our offerings have been down lately, people are beginning to wonder if something fishy is going on."

"Well, that's very nice of you," I said, "but like I said, Ernie's not going to be able to do that until tomorrow."

"I guess so," said Earl. "I'll just have to come back then. You know, someone has to keep an eye on things around here, especially with Ernie's wife in the hospital."

"I suppose that's true," I replied politely. "I'm sure Ernie will greatly appreciate any help he receives."

Earl started toward the door, before turning back and saying, "Shouldn't you be headed to the hospital?"

"I already told you that I was there yesterday."

"What have we come to?" snarled Earl. "Here is our church with our treasurer's wife injured and in the hospital, probably suffering and calling out to God for Christian sympathy and comfort, and our unshaven, sloppy, argumentative preacher won't even lower himself to visit her in her hour of need."

"You know what, Earl?" I replied. "You are exactly right. I should be visiting Connie and Ernie right now. Both of them are always so faithful, selfless, friendly, Christlike, compassionate, and caring. It's the least I could do for them. Please excuse me."

Without another word, I nodded goodbye to Earl and walked right out the door.

CHAPTER 8

Aucoin is no different from thousands of other small towns across America. We have small businesses, fireworks stands in July, and pride in our local high school football team. We also have our share of jerks, with Earl Bishop leading the pack. I'm not sure what the problem is, but that man either truly loves to torment me or really wants me fired. I knew that arguing with him might one day result in the ending of my ministry at Lee Community Church, but it felt really good to finally have the last word in an altercation with him.

Earl had always been cantankerous. Daddy was a deacon when I was growing up, and I didn't remember him returning from a single deacons' meeting or business meeting without saying, "I can't believe the nerve of that man!"

Mama would always respond to his complaining by asking, "Who are you talking about?"

"Earl Bishop, of course!" Daddy would always say. "Who else could I mean?"

I wasn't surprised when Daddy stopped being a deacon the year I left for seminary. I once asked him if he had resigned because of Earl and his antics.

"Not really," he said. "I just figured when you went to seminary that it wouldn't be long before you would become the pastor at Lee Community. I figured it would be too awkward for you if I was serving in that capacity when you moved into that position."

"Why did you think I was going to move back here and become the pastor?"

"Oh, Brad," he chuckled. "You were born for that position. Everybody knows that."

"Elizabeth said that to me when we were kids," I replied.

"Yeah," he said, "she was another reason I resigned as a deacon. She was struggling, and your mother and I wanted to help her."

"It figures," I said. "It really does."

"Yep," he replied.

As I headed toward McComb, I-55 seemed almost deserted, an unusual occurrence for a Monday morning. I slowed to five miles under the speed limit, enjoying the solitude and the replays of my verbal victory. It wasn't long, however, before the billboards of the city advertising new home sites, local restaurants, chain hotels, and lottery tickets came into view. "That's what I need, Lord!" I said aloud. "I need to win the lottery! Then if I'm fired, I won't ever have to worry about receiving a salary again. Problem solved."

Without warning, I heard the same voice I had heard the day before. *Why don't you buy a ticket, Pastor Brad?*

"What?" I cried.

You can't win if you don't play. Stop somewhere and buy a ticket.

"This is stupid!" I said. "I'm not going to do that. Lottery tickets lead to gambling, and that's not something I want to get involved in."

I'm not telling you to go and bet the farm at a Las Vegas casino, Brad. Stop at a convenience store on your way to the hospital. No one knows you in McComb, you're not dressed like a pastor today, and who knows—you just might win. If you do, you can take Allison on that cruise you've been dreaming about. Wouldn't she like that?

"Yes," I admitted, "she would like that, but she wouldn't like me playing the lottery."

Come on, Brad. What harm could possibly come from it?

"This is ridiculous!" I said aloud. "I am not buying a lottery ticket. People in my church don't even buy charity raffle tickets for the local children's home."

Oh, come on. Haven't you always wondered what it would be like to play?

"Yes, but no, I'm not doing it. I need to be thinking about replacing the money I spent yesterday, not wasting more of it on gambling. If the deacons of Lee Community found out I'd even given this a second thought, I'd be fired and run out of town. Besides, I've got too much ministry to focus on to worry about buying a lottery ticket."

Energized by righteous indignation, I drove straight to the hospital, determined to make a difference in the lives of two church members entrusted to my spiritual care. I drove through the parking lot and received a disapproving look from an older lady when I parked in the "Reserved for Clergy" parking space and stepped out in casual clothes, but I didn't care. I walked tall as I entered the main entrance doors.

Evangelistic fervor surged through my veins, and I felt more determined than ever to fulfill my pastoral duty by ministering to a church deacon and his wife. However, as I stepped off of the elevator, a twinge of fear hit me. *What if she's worse?* I thought. I instantly quickened my pace. *What if she never woke up? Or what if she never wakes up?* I swallowed hard and continued moving toward Connie's room. *What if she's dead?*

"Now that's ridiculous!" I said aloud as I stopped outside Connie's room.

"What's ridiculous?" asked a voice from inside.

I stepped through the door and found a young nurse's assistant stripping the bed of its sheets. "Excuse me," I said. "I'm looking for Connie, uh, Mrs. Connie Plaisance, who is, or uh, was, in this room."

"I'm sorry," said the girl. "I'm afraid she's gone."

"What?" I asked. "She's gone? What happened?"

"I'm not sure," she replied. "I guess it was just her time to go home."

"This is dreadful," I said. "I can't believe it."

"I wouldn't worry about it too much," said the nurse. "It's not like you're never going to see her again."

"Well," I said, "I suppose that's true. We will all be united in heaven."

The nurse's assistant looked at me strangely for a moment but didn't say anything.

I felt tears welling up in my eyes. Poor Ernie. How would he possibly survive the guilt? "How did her husband take it?" I asked. "He was so worried about her."

"Oh, he was so happy. You should have seen him, grinning from ear to ear."

"He was pleased that his wife was dead?"

"Dead?" she asked. "What are you talking about? She was discharged from the hospital. She went home."

Relief washed over me. "Oh, you mean she went home as in where she and her husband live together?"

"Yes, isn't that what I just said?"

I could have kicked myself for not coming to the hospital sooner, partly because it turned out that Earl had been right. I should have been visiting Connie instead of arguing with him. I hated it when Earl was right. Absolutely hated it.

I made my way back to the elevator and pulled out my phone to text Ernie. "Sorry I missed you at the hospital. The nurse told me Connie was released. I'll catch up with you later today."

As I stepped from the elevator, I was determined to get back to Aucoin as soon as possible. However, I heard a voice calling, "Brad! Hey, Brad!"

I turned toward the voice and discovered that it was coming from Billy Ray Broussard. I had completely forgotten about him and his wife Melissa having a baby. "Billy Ray!" I cried. "How are you? How's Melissa?"

"She's awesome," he replied, reaching to shake my hand. "Both mother and baby are doing great."

"Congratulations to both of you!" I said. "Did you have a boy or a girl?"

"I have a son," said Billy Ray. "William Raymond Broussard Jr."

"And he's got his daddy's name!" I said.

"Hey, Brad," he said. "Thanks again for paying for our gas when we were on our way here. I don't know what I would have done."

"No problem," I said. "What good is money if you can't use for it helping a friend in need?"

"Well, you certainly helped me," said Billy Ray. "Now, I'm going to pay you back for—"

"You'll do no such thing," I said. "You can pay me back by taking good care of Melissa and Junior."

A few minutes later, as I walked toward the parking lot, my thoughts faded from Billy Ray and Melissa to my own schedule. I tried to calculate how much time I had wasted this morning. "Why don't I do a better job with my calendar?" I asked myself. "If I did, maybe I could stop wasting time doing so many things I really don't want to do."

I had almost come to an answer when I found a parking ticket on my car, sticking out from beneath my windshield wiper. "What?" I cried out as I snatched it from under the wiper. I quickly scanned the ticket. Under "Description of Violation," the barely legible handwriting declared, "Car was illegally parked in a space reserved for ministers. $20 fine."

"I don't believe this!" I said, stomping back toward the hospital. "Do I look so bad that people can't believe I'm a pastor?"

I found the security office and finally convinced the officer on duty that I was indeed the pastor of Lee Community Church in Aucoin, Louisiana, by showing her my driver's license and a pay stub from my wallet.

"I guess we'll let you off this time," she said condescendingly, "but next time you come to this hospital and park in a ministers-only parking space, it would be advisable for you to look more like a pastor."

"Does it really matter how I'm dressed?" I asked. "What if it's an emergency and I'm pulled away from bed in the middle of the night?"

"Is that what happened today?" she asked.

"Well, no."

"Are you really a pastor?"

"Yes, absolutely."

"Then look like one next time you come."

I sighed. "I'll do my best," I said as I turned to go.

"See that you do," she said. "And have a nice day, Pastor."

"Thank you."

"You're welcome," she replied, obviously needing to have the last word.

I walked away with my head down, feeling defeated and stupid. "This has been a terrible day," I muttered. "What else could possibly go wrong?" I was about to find out. "Oh man!" I exclaimed as I approached my car once again. Another parking citation was sticking out from underneath my wiper blade. I pulled it out and read the offense. "Car was illegally parked in minister's parking. Second offense. $25 fine."

I crumpled the ticket into a ball and thrust it into my pocket. "I don't believe this," I said. "Not only am I a bad preacher, but I'm so far from having the appearance of a pastor that hospital security guards are giving me double parking tickets!" I jumped into the car and quickly moved it to a regular parking space a few rows over. I turned off my ignition and practically ran back to the security office.

"It's me again," I said as I walked through the door.

The officer looked up at me as if she had never seen me before. "I'm sorry," she replied. "Who are you?"

"I'm the pastor who was just in here five minutes ago."

"Oh, sorry," she replied with a smirk. "I didn't recognize you as a pastor because of the way you are dressed."

I paused for a moment, taking in a deep breath. "Point taken," I said. "Anyway, I'm back."

"And?"

"And when I made it back to my car, a second ticket had been placed on my windshield."

"You mean you didn't move after the first time?"

"No!" I exclaimed, slightly louder than before. "I came straight to you with the ticket!"

"Ah," she replied. "There's your problem."

"What? Not moving my car?"

"No," she replied, "yelling at me just now."

"I wasn't yelling!" I exclaimed loudly before calming myself. "I'm just exasperated by all of this."

"Doesn't matter," she said. "Your attire and demeanor are not pastorly, Mr. Johnson, making it hard for me to believe you truly are a pastor. You're going to have to pay the fine."

"You're not serious, are you?"

"Do I sound like I'm joking?" she asked.

"No."

"Am I onstage in a comedy club with a microphone?"

"No," I said with a smile.

"So what does that tell you?"

"That you're not joking."

"Which means I must be …"

"Serious?"

"Always. Now show me the ticket."

I reached into my pocket and pulled out the ticket, still crumpled into a ball.

"What's that?" she asked.

"My ticket," I replied. "I was angry."

"Very mature of you, Pastor, Minister, whatever you are," she replied, taking it from me and unfolding it carefully.

I looked down, completely ashamed of myself.

"That will be forty-five dollars," said the officer.

"What?" I asked. "I thought the ticket said twenty-five dollars."

"It did," she replied, "but your attitude added made the first fine payable as well."

"I don't believe this," I said.

"Cash is best," she replied.

Without another word, I reached for my wallet and pulled out the cash. After paying her, I realized I had only one dollar in cash left. "It figures," I said.

"Thank you so much, Reverend," she said as she took the money. "You have a nice day now."

"Thank you," I replied weakly as I left the office.

"You're so very welcome," she replied.

CHAPTER 9

As I pulled out of the hospital parking lot, I noticed my low-fuel light flashing. "Great," I said. "This might as well happen."

I turned right and headed to the nearest gas station, about a mile away. I parked by pump 4, pulled out my wallet, and reached for my church credit card. Fortunately, the church paid for my gas for ministry-related purposes. "At least I don't have to use stolen money to fill my tank," I said as I inserted the card into the payment slot.

A woman at the pump next to me heard what I said, glared in my direction, and then escaped into her car and hastily locked her door.

I shook my head, selected my fuel grade, and pumped my gas. As it flowed into my tank, a commercial played on the advertisement screen above the pump:

> POWERBALL! The biggest lottery sensation the world has ever known. Imagine yourself having millions of dollars to spend however you choose. Somebody's gotta win—it might as well be you!

As I watched past winners jumping up and down, my mind began to wander. *What would it be like to win the lottery? I could take Allison on cruises whenever I wanted, and I wouldn't feel like such a prisoner of the deacon board. I could lead the church and wouldn't care what they thought because it wouldn't matter if I lost my job. Like the commercial said, somebody's gotta win. Why shouldn't it be me?*

When my tank was full, I returned the nozzle and waited for my receipt to print. The pump display instructed me to "please see attendant for receipt." "Fabulous," I said to myself as I walked into the store. "One more thing to make this a red-letter day."

I took my place in line, which was quite long and very still. I would have left without the receipt, but it was a church credit card purchase, so I was responsible for turning it in. I blew out a breath of air and cocked my head to see what was taking so long. A young girl was arguing with the cashier because he wouldn't sell her cigarettes.

"What's the big deal?" she cried. "I buy cigarettes here all of the time!"

"Not from me, you don't," said the cashier.

"So?" she replied.

The cashier threw his arms out and looked as if he was about to explode. "So it's against the law! You have to show me your ID if you want to purchase cigarettes. It's plain and simple. Now come on. You're holding up the line."

"Who's to know?" she yelled.

"I'm to know," yelled the clerk, pointing to himself. "I could get into a lot of trouble if my boss found out."

"I won't tell a soul," she said.

"You won't have to," he replied, "because I'm not selling you cigarettes!"

"What difference does it make?" she asked.

"It makes a lot of difference to me," he cried, pointing to himself once again. "You might be mad at me, but at least I know I can sleep at night because I did the right thing."

He has a point there, I thought. *I'm going to use this story in a sermon sometime.*

As the argument continued, the other customers rolled their eyes and checked their phones. I reached for mine but realized I had left it in the car. I glanced at the soft drinks and suddenly became thirsty. I reached in the side cooler and grabbed a small bottle of Coca-Cola. I looked at it, shook my head, replaced it, and then pulled out the larger-size bottle. *Well*, I thought, *if I'm getting a Coke, I might as well have a candy bar too.* I had just grabbed a Snickers bar when the line began to move.

Apparently, the underage girl had finally given up on her cigarette purchase. "I'm leaving and never coming back!" she yelled as she stormed toward the door.

"Fine by me!" yelled the store clerk as the girl exited the building.

Poor girl, I thought. *She wants those cigarettes so bad and just can't have them.*

How is she all that different from you? asked a voice in my head. *You want what's in your hand, but how are you going to pay for them?*

"But what she was doing was illegal," I said aloud.

And you would be using the church's money to pay for your items. Sounds like stealing to me, Brad. Besides, you only have one dollar left.

"You're right," I said. "I'll just put them back then."

The man in front of me looked back as if I were talking to him.

"Oh, excuse me," I said with a smile. "Just thinking out loud."

"Can you think a little quieter please?" he asked as he shook his head.

"Certainly," I whispered to him, trying to be funny. "On second thought, I don't want to buy these after all. Sorry if I disturbed you."

The man stared at me for a couple of seconds without smiling. I smiled back at him as I leaned over to replace my items. He looked like he wanted to kill me.

Fortunately, the lady behind me said, "The line's moving, guys."

"Thank you," I said to her, giving myself a reason to look away from the man in front of me.

"Whatever," she said. "Just pay attention. I'm in a hurry."

"Sorry," I replied.

The man in front of me finally had his items on the counter and was pulling cash from his wallet. Seeing his money reminded me that I had only one dollar. I thought, *What am I going to do now?*

"I don't know," I said to myself, in a normal voice. "I'll also have to find an ATM, and that could take a while."

The customer at the counter turned around once again, pointed, and said, "There's an ATM across the street at the bank, fella."

"Thanks," I said, slightly embarrassed.

"Whatever," said the man, and he took his items and left.

You will have to go into the bank, I silently told myself. *You know the ATM probably won't give you a hundred-dollar bill.* "Oh man," I said out loud.

"You're next," said the clerk. "Sorry about the wait."

I hurried to the counter like a goober and said, "I need a receipt from pump 4, please."

"Anything else?" asked the clerk.

How about a lottery ticket? I thought. *Who knows? I just might win.* "Yeah," I answered. "Give me one lottery ticket."

"What kind?" asked the clerk.

"I'm sorry, what?"

"What kind of lottery ticket do you want?"

"I'm not sure," I answered, much to the chagrin of the lady behind me, who sighed loudly.

"Come on, man," said the clerk. "You're wasting everyone's time."

"I apologize," I said. "I didn't even know there were different kinds of lottery tickets."

"Can you believe this guy?" the lady behind me asked the others in line.

"Look, buddy," said the clerk, "you're holding up the line. Do you want a pick-three, a Powerball, an instant scratch-off, or something else?"

"Is the Powerball easy to play?" I asked.

"It's the lottery," he sneered. "It ain't like you're playing chess."

"Okay, thanks. Uh, which one costs a dollar?"

"Almost all of them, man!" said the clerk. "Except the Powerball, which is now two dollars. Where have you been living?"

I thought, *At Lee Community Church in Aucoin,* but blurted out, "I guess I'll try the instant scratch-off."

"Good choice," said the attendant as he handed me the ticket. "That will be one dollar for your ticket. Here's your gas receipt."

I paid him in cash with the one dollar bill I had remaining in my wallet, took my gas receipt, and quickly placed the ticket in my front jeans pocket. I turned around to face the line of people, holding my receipt chest-high and smiling big like an idiot.

"Do you mind?" asked an annoyed woman. "We're trying to get out of here today."

"Excuse me," I replied as I stepped out of her way and almost ran to my car.

The few steps between the store and the pump felt like the length of a football field. I climbed in my car and locked the doors. The scratch-off ticket in my pocket felt like a load of bricks. In my mind, everyone in the world, especially those at the gas station, now knew I was on my way to a terrible gambling addiction. I felt ashamed and wanted to bury my head. I envisioned Kenny Rogers sitting in the passenger seat strumming a guitar and singing, "You've got to know when to hold 'em, know when to fold 'em ..."

"What have I done?" I cried out loud. "I've bought a wicked lottery ticket with the Lord's money. I am now officially living a wayward life of sin." Slowly, I reached into my pocket and pulled out the scratch-off ticket. I held it before me on my open palm as if it were a balloon of heroin. *I wonder if the clerk would give me a refund*, I thought. *I still have my receipt.*

I pulled out my phone, pressed the control button, and asked, "Do people ever return unused lottery tickets?" My screen suddenly showed an ad for Gamblers Anonymous. "I can't take it back," I said, suddenly realizing that returning the ticket would mean I'd have to interact with more people. I wasn't doing so well in that department.

I'll just play the stupid scratch-off thing, lose, learn my lesson, and then never do it again, I decided. *How do I even play this?* I held the card and noticed the instructions written on one side. There was a scratch-off area at the top of the card, which was supposed to reveal the number I was to look for in the five other scratch-off areas.

"This is sort of like the McDonald's Monopoly game," I said to myself. I pulled out my keys and scratched off the key number. It was a two. I scratched off the first scratch-off play section, revealing a twelve. I looked around once again to make sure no one was watching and then scratched off the second play area, revealing a seven. "I never should have done this, Lord," I prayed. "Give me the strength to never do this again."

If my own prayer had impacted me, I would have crumpled up the ticket and stopped playing right then and there. Instead, I scratched off the third play area, revealing the number ten. "But it would sure be nice to win some money, Lord. You understand, right?" The fourth scratch-off play area revealed a three.

"What am I doing?" I asked myself before scratching off the last number. "I don't even bet on the Super Bowl with my own family." I looked down at my card as a scratch with my key revealed the final number, a two.

I stared at the card in disbelief. "Holy cow!" I looked away, shook my head, and looked again. The results hadn't changed. "I can't believe it," I said. "I won."

Suddenly, there was a rap on my window. I turned slowly, just knowing I was going to see Earl Bishop's face smiling back at me. I braced myself for his hurtful remarks and mentally began writing my resignation letter and rehearsing my final sermon. But instead I turned my head to see the gas station attendant standing outside my car. Impatiently, he motioned for me to roll down my window, which I did quickly.

"Yes?" I asked timidly. "Is there a problem?"

"You're going to have to move your car, buddy!" he cried. "We've only got four pumps working today, and you're cutting into our business."

"Oh. I'm sorry about that. I'll move it right now."

"Good," said the clerk, turning to go.

"Hey!" I yelled through the open window.

"What?" he asked, irritated that he should have to waste any more time on me.

"I just won something with this scratch-off ticket. What do I do now?"

He shrugged his shoulders and said, "Celebrate." He turned to leave.

"Wait a minute!" I yelled.

"Come on, man. What is it?" he asked, looking back. "I've got customers waiting."

"How do I claim what I've won?"

He rolled his eyes. "For a scratch-off, I can give you the money. How much did you win?"

"I don't know," I said. "This is my first time playing."

"I can tell you how much you've won."

"So what do I do?"

He folded his arms, blew out a big breath, and said, "Park your car around back, then come inside."

Ten minutes later, I exited the store and walked toward my car with my head down. I paused at the sound of tires spinning and imagined Earl peeling off to report my sinful activities to the deacon board and my lack of milk consumption to my mother. "It's okay, Brad," I whispered to myself. "Just calm down. No one knows what you've done—well, except for the clerk and the people inside the store."

Once inside my car, I pressed the car lock button twice. I glanced around the parking lot, extremely grateful that I did not see anyone I knew. I fell back into my seat and felt my pulse. My heart was beating extra fast. I took in a long breath through my nose and released it through my mouth.

Slowly, I pulled my wallet from my pocket and peered inside. The green bills within seemed to glitter in the sunlight, like buried treasure exposed to the light of day, except this was green currency. Twenty-four hours earlier, I had been completely out of cash. Now my wallet held one thousand dollars. It was awesome and frightening at the same time.

"This is unreal!" I cried. "I can't believe I won so much money! I never win anything. It's probably because I never play. I don't even participate in raffles, much less play the lottery. Wait until I tell …" I stopped short. "What have I done?" I said. "I can't tell anyone about this, not even Allison."

I rubbed my thumb over the edge of the currency, watching the bills change from ones to fives to twenties to hundreds. "What am I going to do with all this money?" I asked. "It's tainted! It's ill-gotten gain! How can I possibly keep it? It's practically stolen from the church, the house of the Lord. I don't know what to do."

Suddenly, my phone buzzed with a new text message notification. I opened my messages, pressed Ernie's name, and read. "Thanks again, Pastor Brad, for visiting us yesterday. We're home and Connie's doing much better. My sister's coming over. Can we meet at two to count the offering?"

"This must be the Lord," I mumbled, "giving me a way to return the money I found. That's the first thing I need to do to make things right." I texted back, "I'm glad Connie is doing better. We've been praying for you both. Yes, I can meet you at two. I'll be there all afternoon. I've been waiting to talk to you."

As I pulled out of the parking lot, I called Allison.

"Hi," she said. "Did you make it in time to count with Ernie?"

"Not exactly," I said. "I'm in McComb at a gas station."

"What?" she asked. "You're in McComb? I thought you were headed to church."

I quickly explained how the morning had gone: about Ernie not making it to the office, about Earl showing up and mouthing off, about missing Ernie and Connie at the hospital, about seeing Billy Ray, about my parking tickets, and finally about Ernie's text message. I opted not to tell her about my scratch-off lottery and my winnings.

"Oh my!" Allison replied. "You've certainly had a full morning. Why don't you come home for lunch? You can shower and change before you head back to the office to meet Ernie."

"That sounds great," I said. "See you soon, sweetheart."

"Oh," she said, "and when you get home, you can tell me all about how you laundered money from the church, how you used it to gamble in another state, and how you're now hiding everything from me."

"What?" I cried. "How did you know?"

"How did I know what?" she asked.

Was I hearing things? I wasn't sure. "Didn't you just ask me about something?" I asked.

"No," she answered. "I only asked you about Ernie and Connie."

"Okay, honey," I said. "I'm sorry."

"Are you okay?" she asked. "You sound funny."

"I'm okay," I answered.

"Are you sure?"

"Yes, honey. I'll see you soon."

"Bye," she replied.

I hung up my phone and blew out a breath of air. "That was close," I said aloud as I gripped the steering wheel a little tighter. "I have to tell her everything. I just wish somebody could tell me how."

As if on cue, my phone rang. I glanced at the caller ID: Elizabeth. "No, I don't think so," I said as I pressed "decline" on my phone. I didn't feel like I had the fortitude to deal with her on top of everything else. "Sorry, Elizabeth," I said. "Not today."

CHAPTER 10

B ack home in the shower, I watched soapsuds run off my feet and wash down the drain as a million thoughts flooded my brain.

I wish my troubles would disappear down the drain like these suds. If that were the case, I could make a horrible decision and then simply turn on the water, rinse off the suds, and watch them vanish. However, this trouble I'm in is a lot thicker and denser than the suds on my body. I'd also need stronger water pressure and a much larger drain. But afterward, everything would still be gone. That would be nice. What am I going to do with all that money?

A voice in my head replied, *Use it for a down payment on the cruise your wife wants to take.*

"I could," I said quietly, "but I don't think I'd be able to enjoy it."

You wouldn't be able to enjoy a cruise?

"I don't think so. I wouldn't be able to stop thinking about how I'd paid for it."

So you found some cash, and you bought a scratch-off ticket—what's the big deal? Return the original hundred dollars you found, and the rest is profit.

"Well," I replied, "that's the least I can do. I can return the money today. I'll explain to Ernie how I found the money on Sunday and then add it to the offering. He won't think anything of it."

Sounds like a solid plan. Then you can soothe your conscience and use the rest of the money you earned to put a down payment on that cruise.

"Maybe, but is winning money from a scratch-off ticket really earning money?"

Sure it is. You didn't have it before, and now you do because of something you did, so you earned it.

"I guess. But I'll have to report that money as income. My accountant will know that I played the lottery."

So what?

"So my accountant is cousin to one of our deacons. In fact, he knows everyone in Aucoin. Everyone."

Stop worrying about it so much. So you'll tell him about winning a scratch-off. You'll both probably have a big laugh over it.

"I guess if this is my money, that means I'll also need to tithe from my winnings."

Good grief, man. Live a little.

"Shut up."

When I arrived at the church, Ernie was leaning on the hood of his car in the parking lot, waiting for me.

"Good afternoon, Pastor Brad!" he called.

"Hi, Ernie," I replied. "How's Connie?"

"She appears to be getting better," he answered as he shoved his hand out to me. "Thanks again for coming by. It meant a lot to both of us."

I took his hand in mine to shake, but he pulled me closer to him and wrapped his arms around me. I must admit, it took me by surprise. Hugging was not something that the men of Lee Community did on a regular basis, except with their wives and children.

"Oh, uh, you're welcome, Ernie," I said as he released me.

"So you went to the hospital this morning?" asked Ernie, taking the conversation away from the awkward moment.

"Yes," I replied. "I must have just missed you. Sorry about that."

"No problem," he replied. "I appreciate you trying. You need to know that Earl Bishop called me."

"Oh really?" I asked.

"He wanted to make sure I didn't feel neglected by my pastor during this time of crisis."

"And do you?"

"Not at all," said Ernie with a smile. "Just the opposite actually."

"That's good to hear," I said. "Sorry if I've kept you waiting."

"No problem at all. I'm just anxious to get started. You know I like to stay on top of things."

"I certainly know that," I replied.

"Oh yeah," said Ernie, "I forgot to tell you. Your sister Elizabeth stopped by just before you pulled up."

Not sure what to say, I joked, "Now I keep telling her the worship service is on Sunday morning, but she just can't seem to remember."

"That's funny," said Ernie in a way that people respond when something really isn't funny. "She just said she was looking for you and would catch up with you later."

I hope not, I thought, but aloud I answered, "Okay, great."

"Is she doing okay?" asked Ernie.

"Ah, yeah," I said. "I guess so. It's so hard to tell with Elizabeth. Her life is so very different from mine."

"You know, that's not always a bad thing," said Ernie.

"Yeah," I said, "I know. She's a little unpredictable is all I'm trying to say."

"Does she still make her living as an artist?"

"Among other things," I replied. "She sells paintings and T-shirts to vendors from Jackson, Mississippi, to the New Orleans French Quarter. She keeps pretty busy."

"That's nice," said Ernie. "I guess."

We walked through the building to the office. I glanced at my desk and suddenly felt ashamed over the messiness of the papers on top. I quickly straightened them and set them on one corner. Three or four paper clips lay across the desk as well, so I gathered them and put them into my desk drawer. Ernie, of course, paid my desk no mind as he knelt to open the safe.

I'd been waiting for the perfect moment to tell him about the money. While he was hunched over to enter the safe combination didn't necessarily seem like perfect timing, but it at least provided us with a moment when it was just the two of us. "Ernie, I've got something I really need to tell you."

"Oh yes," he replied, leaning up for a moment. "You were trying to talk to me about something yesterday when I called you about the accident."

"Well," I replied, "you had good reason to be distracted."

"I guess so," he said. "What is it?"

Okay, I thought. *Here goes nothing.* "Well, it's like this. On Sundays, after everyone leaves, I usually walk through the building … you know, making sure everything's okay and that all of the lights are shut off and—"

"I'm glad you're telling me this, Pastor," he interrupted.

"I'm sorry, what?" I asked.

"You shouldn't have to do all of that by yourself. The rest of us should really be helping you with those responsibilities. I'll bring that up at the next deacons' meeting."

"Oh," I said, wondering how much arguing I'd have to listen to about that. "Thanks, Ernie, but that's not really what I wanted to talk with you about. You see, this Sunday afternoon—I guess that was yesterday, right?"

"Yes, it was," said Ernie as he once again reached for the combination lock. "I know a lot has happened since then."

I scolded myself internally, *Get a grip on yourself, Brad!* "Well, anyway," I said, "I came to the office after everyone had left, and I found—"

"My, would you look at this!" Ernie suddenly cried.

"What is it?"

"Right here between the safe and the wall. There's some cash!"

"What?" I asked, kneeling down to look. "There's money there too? How much?"

"Well, let me pull it out, and we'll count it."

One by one, Ernie pulled out a small stack of twenty-dollar bills. He ran the bills through his fingers, counting them quickly. "Looks like two hundred dollars," he said, looking up at me slowly. "How do you suppose it got there, Pastor?"

"I have no idea," I replied, suddenly self-conscious.

Ernie held the money tightly in one hand and scratched his head with the other. "It's weird. There's really no way it could have fallen between the safe and the wall, is there?"

"I don't think so," I answered, running my fingers through my hair. "But that makes what I wanted to tell you even more important."

"Oh yes," said Ernie. "You were about to tell me something. What is it?"

"Well," I began, "yesterday, when I was packing up to leave for the day, I came here into the office, and right here on the floor by the safe, there was—"

"What are you saying about the safe?" asked Earl Bishop as he suddenly stepped through the office door into the room.

"Earl!" exclaimed Ernie. "We didn't even hear you come in."

"So I gathered from your conversation," smirked Earl. "What's all this about the safe?"

"Man," said Ernie, "this is so strange. I just found two hundred dollars in twenties shoved in between the safe and the wall."

Earl looked at me suspiciously. "Really? Where?"

"Right here," said Ernie as he pointed to the place.

Earl glanced at me and tightened his lips before bending down to examine the area. "It couldn't have just fallen there," he said.

"My thoughts exactly," said Ernie.

"Yes!" I interjected nervously. "We were just discussing that."

Earl frowned. "The answer is obvious. Someone must have placed it there."

"What makes you think that?" I asked.

"It's the only explanation," said Ernie, feeling along the top of the safe. "This wooden ledge that comes out over the edge of the safe would have kept the money from falling into that slot from above. There's no way it could have just landed in that position if the money fell, especially not that many bills. Someone must have planted the bills there so they could return later to claim them. But why would anyone do that?"

"Someone's been stealing money from the church!" cried Earl. "No wonder our offerings have been down and no one could understand why."

"But who would do such a thing?" asked Ernie. "Why would anyone steal from a church?"

"Yeah," said Earl, staring up at me. "Why indeed, and who could it have been?"

"Why are you looking at me?" I asked.

"A guilty dog always barks," said Earl, crossing his arms.

"What is that supposed to mean?" I asked.

Earl pursed his lips together. "It means that whoever did the crime usually speaks up."

"I understand the expression, Earl," I said. "What I meant was, why would you think I had something to do with hiding this two hundred dollars?"

"How did you know it was two hundred dollars?" said Earl, looking at Ernie but pointing right at me. "You must have been the one who planted the money!"

"For heaven's sake, Earl," said Ernie. "I had just counted it and shared the amount with Pastor Brad before you walked into the office."

"Well, you're a crafty one, ain't you?" snapped Earl, staring into my face without blinking. "Maybe Ernie did tell you how much was there, but you are in this office an awful lot."

"I work here, Earl," I said, pointing to my desk. "And if I was stealing money from the church, would I have just been trying to tell Ernie about some money I found on Sunday?"

"What money?" asked Ernie. "Where did you find it?"

"That's what I've been trying to tell you," I replied. "Yesterday afternoon, I found a hundred-dollar bill on the floor next to the safe."

"What were you doing in here on Sunday afternoon?" asked Earl.

"I'm in here every Sunday afternoon, at least for a little while."

"I don't believe that," he replied.

I sighed heavily. "Part of my responsibilities is the care of God's house, remember? So I usually make my rounds after the service, turning off the lights. Then I come back here to pick up my things. This Sunday, right here on the floor by the safe was a hundred-dollar bill."

Earl pointed his finger in my face. "Then why didn't you tell anyone?"

My eyes grew large. "I texted Ernie as soon as I found it."

"That's true," said Ernie, "but then before we could talk, Connie and I were in the accident."

"I knew we'd be meeting to count the money today or tomorrow, so I decided to just hold it until I could give it to Ernie in person."

"You decided, huh?" questioned Earl.

"Yes," I replied.

Earl snarled. "Well, then why didn't you give it to Ernie at the hospital?"

"Come on, Earl," I said. "That's hardly the time or the place to bring something like that up."

"Then why didn't you put it in the safe?" asked Earl.

"I don't know the combination," I replied, throwing my arms out. "I've never known the combination."

Earl stared me right in the eye and said, "Can you tell me why you, as our so-called preacher, wouldn't have the combination to our church safe?"

"Certainly, Earl. As you should be aware, when I was called as pastor of this church, I told the finance committee I didn't want to know the combination, so I would never be tempted and could never be accused."

Earl turned to Ernie. "Sounds to me like our preacher has been tempted to steal church money before."

Ernie shook his head. "Now, Earl, that's not what Pastor Brad meant."

"But how can we know for sure?" asked Earl.

"Come on, Earl," said Ernie.

"Don't 'come on' me, Ernie. He's stolen church money before!" cried Earl.

"When?" I cried. "When have I ever stolen church funds?"

"Back when you were the treasurer of our Christian Boys' Club!"

"I was eight years old, Earl!"

"It still happened," he smirked. "Some people never change."

"What's he talking about?" asked Ernie.

I rolled my eyes. "When I was a kid, my dad led the Christian Boys' Club here for a short time. I was the treasurer. One day, as a child, I took fifty cents from the collection box and used it to buy a soda."

"What happened?" asked Ernie.

"Well," I said, "I started feeling bad about it, so I told my parents what had happened one Sunday morning at church. My dad took me out back and gave me a spanking, then forced me to confess to the entire church during the worship service."

"And he's still stealing money today," said Earl.

"I am not!" I cried. "I was just about to give it to Ernie. I would have put it in the safe, but as we've already established, I don't know the combination."

Earl shook his head and closed his eyes. "Well, I see you've got an answer for everything, don't you, Mr. Seminary? If what you're saying is true, then don't you think now is a good time to hand over the money you claim you found on the office floor?"

"You know what?" I asked, reaching for my wallet. "I do believe it is, Earl. What a fine idea. I was planning to give it to Ernie as soon as the safe was open anyway."

"That's a likely story," said Earl.

"Now, Earl," said Ernie, "you're not being very nice right now. Pastor Brad was trying to tell me about the money he found right before you came in. He's been trying to tell me about it since yesterday. Up until now, things just haven't worked out for him to do so."

Earl took in a breath as if he was about to say something but then tightened his lips and kept quiet.

"Thank you, Ernie," I said as I opened my wallet, fished out one of the $100 bills I'd won from the scratch-off game, and handed it to him.

"Here you go," I said. "One hundred dollars found, one hundred dollars returned, safe and sound."

"Well, would you look at that!" exclaimed Earl, jerking my wallet from my hands. "It looks to me like either you have been stealing offering funds, or we've been paying you too much money."

"Can you please leave my personal property alone?" I exclaimed, snatching my wallet back from him.

"Good Lord! There must have been more than a thousand dollars in there!" cried Earl. "Did you see all that money, Ernie?"

Ernie raised both eyebrows and looked at me sympathetically. "Well, yes, I did, Earl."

Earl shoved his finger in my face. "How long have you been stealing church money?"

"I haven't been stealing anything!" I cried.

"How can you stand there and lie to our faces?" cried Earl. "I am the assistant deacon chairman, and Ernie is the church treasurer and finance committee chairman. We represent the church body of Lee Community Church, and you will respect that."

"I'm very aware of your positions," I replied. "And you should be aware of mine. I am the senior pastor of Lee Community Church, and I did not steal money from the church."

Earl put his hands on his hips and shook his head. "Well, all that money in your wallet makes me think you've been stealing money from somewhere, and the most obvious place is our church offering. You're a sneaky one, ain't ya?"

I was irritated to the core. "I found one hundred dollars on the floor of this office yesterday, and I just gave it back to Ernie. What's the big deal?"

Ignoring me completely, Earl said, "I'll bet that's why you wanted to preach on tithing yesterday! It seemed really odd to everyone that you were so dead set on taking the offering at the end of the service, even though we told you we'd never done it that way before. You were scheming to guilt the good members of our congregation out of their money because you're greedy and you're a thief!"

"I would never do those things to this church family. I am neither of those things!"

"Yes, you are!" snarled Earl. "Otherwise, how could you ever have so much cash in your wallet when it's still another week before you get paid?"

I looked at him and then at Ernie and shook my head. "I don't have to put up with this. I didn't do anything wrong."

"I believe you, Pastor Brad," said Ernie, patting me on the back. "I really do."

"Thank you, Ernie. It's nice to know I have at least one advocate around here. You're a great example of a true deacon."

Earl shot a piercing look at Ernie, who squelched a laugh and then glanced at me.

"You're welcome," said Ernie. "But as much as I hate to admit it, I would venture to say that Earl is asking a valid question. That is an awful lot of cash for anyone to carry around, especially when you're a part of counting the weekly church offering."

I took in a deep breath and looked at Ernie. He was right, but I didn't want to admit it. After a few seconds, I breathed out and nodded. "I suppose you're right," I said. "It is a valid question."

"So what's the valid answer then?" blurted out Earl.

Can I tell them I played the lottery? I wondered. *I don't have to tell them I did it with the church's money.*

"We don't want any more secrets," Earl said with a slight snarl. "We want the truth."

I was tempted to yell, "You can't handle the truth!" in Jack Nicholson style, but I restrained myself. Instead, I replied, "And the truth is exactly what you'll get."

Even as I spoke the words, I knew I couldn't tell them the entire truth. Even if I didn't mention that I'd used the church's money to buy the ticket, Earl would have me run out of town on a rail if he learned that I'd played the lottery. It wouldn't matter if Billy Graham and Mother Theresa had combined their money and asked me to buy them lottery tickets; for most of our church members at Lee Community, including Earl, playing the state lottery, or any lottery for that matter, was the same as gambling in a Las Vegas casino. To this congregation, who believed that premarital sex was wrong because it might lead to dancing, gambling was worse than all of the seven deadly sins rolled into one.

"Well, spit it out, man!" snapped Earl.

"Well," I said, folding my wallet and placing it back in my pocket, "since you have to know, I'm using this cash, which I earned outside of the church, for a down payment for a vacation. I'd like to take Allison on a cruise for our next anniversary."

"Do you always use your wallet as your savings account?" asked Earl.

"To be honest," I said, "I was going to deposit it into my checking account later today so I could make the down payment after I get paid this coming weekend."

"That's good enough for me," said Ernie.

"Thank you, Ernie," I said. "What about you, Earl?"

"Well," said Earl, "I think you just made up that story and that you're lying to us right now."

"Well, I've said all I have to say," I remarked. "You can believe whatever you want. I'm not a thief, and I haven't been stealing from the church. The one-hundred-dollar bill I found yesterday is the only money I've ever found on the church premises, and I've just returned it."

"It's okay, Pastor," said Ernie, giving a stern look to Earl. "What you've said makes sense to me, and I'm the church treasurer."

"Yeah, well," said Earl, "I'm the assistant chairman of the deacons, and it doesn't make sense to me at all. Not one bit."

I have to get out of here, I thought. *Come on, Brad. Think of something.* I looked around the office and caught a glimpse of the red mark on the wall. It wasn't offering me much help at the moment.

"What are you doing?" asked Earl.

"Are you okay, Pastor Brad?" asked Ernie.

I turned to Ernie and realized that I had my out. "Ernie," I said matter-of-factly, "is anyone looking after Connie right now?"

Ernie shot me a quick look of compassion. "Yes, my sister is there with her now. Why?"

"I was thinking that Allison might want to drop in on her. If you can spare me here, and since I missed the two of you this morning at the hospital, and since Earl is here to help, maybe I could pick Allison up, and we could go together to pay Connie a visit."

Ernie smiled. "That sounds like a great idea, Pastor. Earl and I can take care of the offering. In fact, it's probably best considering the circumstances."

"I agree," I said.

"At least you're properly dressed this time," said Earl.

"Come on, Earl," said Ernie. "I appreciate what Pastor Brad is trying to do."

Earl shook his head. "You wouldn't have if he had gone to see Connie wearing what he was in this morning."

"Thank you, Ernie," I said, trying to keep from getting angry. "Should we call ahead?"

"No need to," said Ernie. "I'll check in with her and let her know that you're coming. Do you remember my sister?"

"Shirley, right?"

"That's her. She's my youngest sister."

"She's a real nice lady, if I remember correctly," I said.

"Oh, she's a gem," said Ernie. "Just don't mention politics to her. She has strong political opinions, and she doesn't know when to drop it."

"Thanks for the warning," I said as I headed toward the door.

"Pastor Brad?" said Earl.

I turned to him. "Yes?"

"This is not over," he said, "not by a long shot."

I swallowed hard as I looked at him. "See you gentlemen later," I said before stepping into the hall and closing the door behind me.

I heard the door lock click behind me before I'd taken two steps down the hall. I should have just kept walking, but something made me stop and listen. I'd like to say it was righteous indignation, but honestly, it was probably fear.

"Can you believe him?" said Earl. "Now where could a pastor get that kind of money? He's no good for us, I tell you, and it's not hard to see that he's been up to something, probably stealing money from the church."

"I like him, and I believe him," said Ernie. "I don't see why he would steal money from the church. Besides, he's been really supportive to Connie and me."

"It's a cover-up!" said Earl. "Archie and the rest of the deacons are going to hear about this. I'm going to make sure about that."

"Why don't you just drop it, Earl? What's done is done."

"Not going to happen," said Earl. "No way, no how."

My head fell to my chest. Suddenly, I felt guilty and defeated. I was being reported to the deacon board. I had returned the money I found and had told the church treasurer all about it, but I had used it selfishly and had lied about the results. Snapping back at Earl hadn't improved my situation either.

Earl was a loud-mouthed idiot, but I was beginning to believe that he was right about me. Maybe I was no good for this church. Maybe I was no good period.

CHAPTER 11

Groucho Marx once said, "The secret of life is honesty and fair dealing. If you can fake that, you've got it made." I'd worked hard to live a life of genuine integrity, but here lately, I wondered if I'd been leaning toward Groucho's version. Could it be that I simply faked my integrity?

One thing was certain: I hadn't been completely honest with Allison. As I pulled into our driveway, I wondered how much longer she would accept my counterfeit explanations of recent events. I'd never been able to keep anything from her. All she ever had to say was "What's going on, Brad?" and I'd open up to her like a fire hose on full blast. That usually meant the pressure was off of me, but it left her all wet, which meant I had to deal with the issue all over again, only from her perspective.

I need to tell her, I thought as soon as I saw her exiting our front door. *I just can't do it yet, not until I figure out what's happening with the church money. And I definitely want to know where all those paper clips came from. Has someone been using the clips to hide money during the offering collection and then returning to retrieve the money later? I have to find out, somehow.*

I parked the car outside our home and smiled gently at Allison as she stepped from the house onto the front porch. "I'm a very lucky man," I said to myself as she smiled and stepped into the car.

"Hi, honey," I said. "Thanks for going with me. I thought it would help to have a lady present."

"No problem, Pastor Brad," she replied. "I always enjoy spending time with you."

"Where's Gabe?" I asked.

"He's inside with Ashleigh."

"Your sister Ashleigh?"

"The one and only," she replied.

"What's she doing here?"

"She called and asked if she could stay with us for a few days."

"And you told her she could?"

"Yes, I did. What else could I have done?"

"Why isn't she staying in her dorm room? This isn't a good time for her to visit."

"What do you mean?" she asked.

"It just isn't," I replied.

"She's on spring break from school," she replied, "and it seems to me that this is a perfect time for her to visit. Otherwise, Gabe would be with us right now and would soon be crawling all over everything in the Plaisance home while we're visiting Connie."

"I can't argue with you there," I said.

We sat in silence for a moment. I could feel the tension building between us, and I knew it was my fault. Ashleigh was actually very nice and had proven to be a big help with Gabe over the last year.

"I'm sorry," I said. "I don't know why I'm so irritable today. Of course your sister can stay with us."

Allison smiled and put her hand on my cheek. "Are you okay?" she asked. "You've seemed so stressed lately."

"I think I'm okay. I know I'm stressed, but I'll get over it. Are you okay?"

"Yep," she said. "Let's go."

A loud silence filled the car as I drove. I knew Allison could tell something was bothering me. She knew my feelings too well for me to pass off her questions for long. Inside, I wanted to tell Allison everything. I had to do something, anything, to share this burden with her, but I wasn't sure how to start, and I was afraid she would be so incredibly disappointed in me.

"Are you sure you're okay, Pastor Brad?" she asked.

Oh man, I thought. *There it is.* "Sure, I'm fine," I lied. "Why do you ask?"

"I'm not sure," she said. "But it seems like something is really bothering you."

"Ha!" I laughed. "I'm the pastor of Lee Community Church. Something's always bothering me."

"I guess that's true," she said. "But I've been married to you for a long time, and it seems like something is different this time. Am I right?"

I blinked hard and blew out a long breath. "I'm okay," I said. "I'm just a little stressed, I guess."

"Are you sure?"

"Yeah, I think so."

"Good," she replied. "You know you can tell me anything, right?"

"Yeah," I replied, "I know."

"Good," she said. "Can I ask you a question then?"

"Sure."

"Why aren't you at the church office counting money with Ernie right now?"

"What do you mean?"

"From the time we woke up late today, everything's been about meeting Ernie to count money. You went to the office this morning without showering because you thought you might miss Ernie, then you drove to the McComb hospital to see Ernie and Connie, and then you went to the church office to count the offering with Ernie. But now you've left Ernie there at the church office, and we're going together to visit Ernie's wife Connie. Something strange is going on, Brad, and it's got something to do with Ernie. What is it?"

"Uh, well," I stammered, "Ernie and I were all set to count the offerings until Earl showed up at the church office."

"Earl Bishop?"

"Yes, the assistant chairman of the deacons himself."

"You really let him get to you sometimes, don't you?"

"I guess I do, sometimes."

"I think you let him get to you all the time."

"Maybe," I replied.

"What is it about him that bugs you so much?"

I sighed. "It's the way he treats me. He's a bully, and he's always looking for something to get mad about. He's always stirring things up, getting people upset over nothing."

"Why do you put up with it?"

"What other choice do I have? He's the assistant chairman of the deacons."

"Why should that give him a license to insult you?"

"I don't know exactly. He's got some type of evil power over me, I suppose."

"Evil power?"

"Yes, and today I didn't really feel like hanging around with him. It really only takes two people to count the offering anyway, and since I missed seeing Connie this morning, I told Ernie you and I would check on her."

"Okay," she said. "Has Earl always been like this?"

"Well," I answered, "I don't remember much about him before I became the pastor here."

"Really?" she said. "Not even when you were growing up?"

"I saw him in the church building, but we never really interacted. He was involved with the Christian Boys' Club for a short time, but it didn't last very long."

"How long has he been the assistant chairman of the deacons?"

"For as long as I can remember. Long before Archie was voted in as chairman."

"I'm surprised he's never tried to become chairman."

"Oh, he has tried," I said, "but he has never been able to get the votes."

"I guess that's a good thing."

"I think so," I replied. "If he was chairman, I don't think I could be pastor. He thinks being elected deacon chairman is like being crowned the royal monarch of Lee Community."

"Really?" she asked.

"Yes," I replied. "He wants all of the attention and wants to make every decision for everyone about everything. He reminds me of …"

"Who?" asked Allison. "Who does he remind you of?"

"Weird," I said. "I was going to say he reminded me of Elizabeth."

"Funny you should mention her," said Allison. "She called earlier looking for you."

I sighed heavily. "This is not a good time for her to go off."

"Is there ever a good time?" asked Allison.

"No, there's not."

"You should probably check up on her this time, Brad. She is your sister calling out to you in need."

"I will," I said. "I just don't want to."

Apparently sensing that I didn't want to discuss Elizabeth, Allison said, "Well, I sure do hope Connie is going to heal quickly from this."

"I do too, honey."

"But you really do need to stand up to Earl."

"I know it, Allison, but …"

"But what?"

"I don't know. You're right. I need to stand up to him. I'm just not sure how to do it."

"Well, you need to find out. Otherwise, he's going to keep bothering you for the rest of your life, and I for one don't like the way it affects you and impacts our marriage."

"Okay, I'll try to figure something out."

"Good. I love you, but I do worry about you sometimes."

"I love you too."

We drove for the next couple of miles in silence. I glanced over at Allison. She always seemed content with the world and with me. But if she knew what I had done, she would be furious, partly for what I had done with the money, but mostly for not telling her about the struggles I had been going through internally.

You see, for as long as we'd been married, we had shared almost everything with each other. It was us, Brad and Allison, the two of us, against the world to the bitter end. However, with all my secrets, a small rift had been created in our marriage. I wasn't sure how to repair the damage.

I wasn't proud of what I had done. In fact, I hated it. But I knew I couldn't share any of the details with her in that moment. I had to make everything right first, and then I would tell her everything, from beginning to end. She would be angry, but she would soon forgive me, and things would finally feel right between us again.

Maybe.

CHAPTER 12

Ernie Plaisance had become a Christian at Lee Community Church when he was a teenager. Even though it was his parents' idea, he embraced his newfound spiritual life with vigor, studying his Bible and praying daily. He was so devoted to Jesus that many believed he would become a pastor or even a missionary, but Ernie chose to serve the Lord quietly, as a deacon, as a Bible study teacher, and eventually as church treasurer.

Ernie had always been nice to me, even when I was a child. He was actually my Sunday school teacher when I was in the fifth and sixth grades. There were only three kids in the class, but Ernie did his best to help us grow in Christ. He and Connie took us on field trips to mission centers around the state and always bought us pizza and ice cream on the way home.

Ernie had worked at Aucoin Auto Parts store since he was in high school. He had put himself through college at night at Southeastern Louisiana University, working hard to receive his business degree by age twenty-four. He became assistant manager at the store when he was twenty-six and manager at thirty. Ten years later, he purchased the business for cash. There had always been talk that Ernie planned on opening a second location in Kentwood or Amite, but that was just talk. Ernie enjoyed his quiet life and wanted to keep it that way.

Ernie and Connie met in Ernie's first night-school class. She was from Independence, not far from Aucoin. They went on a date to the movies in Hammond two Saturdays later. Six months later, they were engaged to be married. Now they lived in the same house they had purchased as newlyweds and seemed very happy. Every year, Ernie hired neighborhood boys to help paint his home. Connie grew roses in their front yard. Their son Paul was an only child and a very talented musician, playing several stringed instruments. Ernie and Connie wished he would lend his talents to Lee Community Church, but Paul showed no interest in our style of music or in the church as a whole, for that matter. Paul once told me, "Sacred music is not my thing. It's extremely limiting, and you know I must be totally free in my music."

Okay, whatever. The last I heard, Paul had moved to New Orleans and was making a modest living playing music in various clubs and jazz venues. I once asked Ernie about how Paul was doing. He answered, "Well, Pastor, you know, he's a pretty free spirit, not really committing himself to anything longer than a one-time performance. If I understand correctly, he's really developing his talents and is keeping pretty busy with gigs and rehearsals."

"Do you ever get to hear him play?" I asked.

"No, we don't hear much from him. He probably thinks we'd disapprove of the clubs where he's playing."

"Ah," I said, "I understand."

As I pulled into the Plaisance driveway, Allison asked, "Do you think Paul knows about his mother's condition?"

"I think a better question might be, 'do you think he really cares?'" I said without thinking.

"Why wouldn't he? Connie's his mother."

"You're right, sweetheart," I replied. "I'd say it's pretty doubtful. He's pretty self-focused."

"That's a shame," she said.

"Yeah, it is."

I placed the car in park, and we crossed the neatly manicured lawn on stepping stones to the front door, which opened before we could knock. Ernie's sister Shirley appeared in the doorway. She smiled in a fake, polite sort of way. "Do come in, Pastor Johnson," said Shirley, motioning us into the living room. "Won't you have a seat? Can I offer you some coffee or a cold drink?"

"No, thank you, Shirley," I answered, not ready to sit just yet. If we weren't going to get to see Connie, I didn't want to get stuck in a political debate with her.

"Are you sure?" she replied. "I think we even have some sodas in the refrigerator."

"Yes, we're sure, thank you," I said. "Do you remember my wife Allison?"

"Yes, yes, I do," said Shirley, nodding to Allison. "How are you today, dear?"

Allison smiled. "Oh, I'm fine, thank you."

"That's wonderful," said Shirley.

Allison continued, "But what we really want to know is how Connie is doing."

"Oh, she's going to be just fine," said Shirley. "She's sleeping right now."

"Oh really?" replied Allison. "We were hoping to visit with her for a few minutes."

"I'm sorry," said Shirley. "She's been taking short catnaps periodically, but if you would like to sit and visit for a while, I'm sure she'll be awake before long."

"Okay," I said, finally giving in. "We'll do that. I certainly don't want to miss her again."

"Thank you so much," said Allison.

"Thank you so much," I repeated like a goober. *My gracious!* I thought. *It's exhausting being so polite, and I'm a pastor.*

Allison and I sat on the sofa across from a large easy chair, where Shirley sat properly on the front edge with perfect posture. Allison straightened up and nudged me until I obliged.

"It's certainly nice of you to stay here with Connie," said Allison. "I'm sure she and Ernie really appreciate your help."

"Thank you," said Shirley. "I do consider it my duty as Ernie's sister. Although it is a slight inconvenience, I do believe that it is necessary nonetheless."

"Okay," I said awkwardly.

"Shirley," said Allison, "I understand you're a very involved woman."

"Yes," replied Shirley. "I do keep myself busy with political rallies and candidate fundraiser events, but this is certainly a necessary diversion. Besides, family emergencies are often seen as good press for candidates."

"I suppose so," said Allison. "Are you running for office?"

"Not at the moment, dear," said Shirley, "but you never know when the right position is going to come along. This will serve as good practice for me."

"Perhaps you're right," said Allison. "Of course, it's always good to care for sick family members. I'm sure Ernie and Connie appreciate it so very much."

Didn't she already say that? I thought.

"Yes," said Shirley. "Now I'm just waiting my turn to serve my fellow Louisianans like I'm serving my sister-in-law today."

"That's just wonderful," said Allison. "Don't you think, Brad?"

"Oh ... yes," I answered, desperately willing Connie to wake up. "Absolutely."

An awkward moment of silence passed. Allison and I glanced at each other. Shirley continued to stare at us with blank eyes and a fake smile.

"You know," I said, hoping to change the subject, "maybe I will take some of that coffee after all."

"Certainly," said Shirley, rising to her feet. "I'll go and fetch us some. Will you be having some as well, Mrs. Johnson?"

"Oh ... ah, yes, please," answered Allison. "Thank you very much."

"You are quite welcome," said Shirley, disappearing into the kitchen.

After Shirley had left, Allison leaned to me and said, "She's quite formal and self-absorbed, isn't she?"

"Yes," I answered. "Ernie did try to warn me about her, but he didn't say too much because Earl was there."

"What did he say?" asked Allison.

"He only said we shouldn't engage her in a conversation about politics."

"I can see why," said Allison. "I guess it's too late now."

"He said that once she begins rambling about politics, she never stops. He didn't mention her intentions of running for office."

Suddenly, the kitchen door opened, and Shirley returned with two coffee mugs.

"Thank you," Allison and I said in unison.

"You're welcome," she replied.

"I do enjoy a good cup of coffee," I said, trying to continue the conversation.

"Oh, I do as well," replied Allison, still sitting very straight.

"Well," said Shirley, "if that is the case, then I have a question for you."

"Okay," I said. "What is it?"

"I've heard it said that you can learn a lot about a man by the coffee he drinks."

"That's so true," said Allison, nodding her head.

"Since that's the case," asked Shirley, "do you agree with the Democrats or the Republicans on the best establishments to purchase coffee?"

"I'm sorry," I replied, "but I guess I'm not up-to-date on the coffee purchasing practices of those political parties. I usually just buy Community Coffee."

"Well," said Shirley, "that is a good, standard Louisiana brand."

"Isn't that so true?" said Allison, causing me to glance at her. She was really burying herself in this politeness charade.

Shirley smiled politely before continuing. "Well, according to a recent survey, most Democrats prefer to purchase their coffee from Starbucks, while Republicans purchase theirs from Dunkin' Donuts. I'm curious, Pastor Brad—into which category do you fall?"

Allison shot me a warning glance, and I smiled back.

"Well," I said, "I'm not sure I fall into either category."

"And why is that?" she asked, leaning forward.

"Two reasons, really," I answered. "You see, first of all, living in Aucoin, Louisiana, doesn't often afford us the opportunity to purchase coffee at either of those places, unless we're willing to drive a good distance."

"Good answer, Brad!" said Allison, sounding like a family contestant from *Family Feud*.

"And second," I continued, "when you're in the ministry, the coffee you most often seek out is that which is free."

"Ah," said Shirley. "I see where you are coming from. Location and budget are two powerful items to consider when making decisions. You must be an independent!"

"Well," I said, "not exactly …"

"But from what I'm hearing," said Shirley, "you have your own set of problems when it comes to budgets."

"What do you mean?" asked Allison.

"From what I'm hearing," said Shirley, "the church is on the brink of financial ruin. People in the church say they're giving regularly, but the bottom line is about to fall out."

"We've had a financial setback," I said, "but—"

"Oh!" Shirley interrupted. "You made a bold move yesterday, trying to change the location of the offering and all, but it didn't work, did it?"

"Well," I said, "it certainly didn't go as I'd planned."

"Yes," said Shirley, suddenly cold. "It makes it look as if you've been stealing money from the church. That's surely going to put a damper on the giving of the Lee Community Church congregation, wouldn't you say?"

"Yes," I said, "it certainly could."

Trying to come to my rescue, Allison interjected, "I don't think—"

"Well, if your husband hasn't been stealing church funds, someone certainly has on his watch, which is also not good."

"Yes," I said. "Whatever is happening is not good."

Suddenly, like a gift from heaven, we heard a bell ringing from down the hall.

"Oh," said Shirley, popping up from her chair. "That would be Connie, requesting my prompt assistance. Please excuse me." With that, she disappeared down the hallway.

"Interesting lady," said Allison.

"Yes," I said, "and very knowledgeable about the coffee consumption practices of political parties."

Allison rolled her eyes, relaxed her posture, and shook her head. I loved that my wife was with me. I looked at her smile, her hair, and the way her arms crossed in front of her, with the fingers of each hand caressing her elbows. I wanted so badly to tell her about what I had done, but I knew this wasn't the time or the place. Instead, I held my breath for a moment.

After a moment, Shirley returned and said, "Connie would like to see you now. This way please."

We followed Shirley down the hallway and into the master bedroom. Connie was sitting up in bed with a slight grin on her face. Allison went right to her and gave her a big hug. I smiled and shook her hand gently but then kept my distance. With all of my ministry experience, I still felt awkward when visiting the sick. Fortunately for me, Connie began the conversation today.

"I'm so glad you could come, Pastor Brad," said Connie. "Ernie told me about how you came and sat with him at the hospital."

"I'm just glad you're okay," I replied. "That's the important thing."

"Yes, well, thank you for caring so much about us. It meant so much to both of us."

I blushed and said, "You're welcome. I'm just sorry you had to go through all of this."

"Oh," said Connie, "don't you worry about me. I'm fine. I do think Ernie is overly concerned, but I'm feeling better all of the time."

"That's good," said Allison. "I know Shirley is here, doing a fine job of taking good care of you, but is there anything we can do to help?"

"Not that I can think of," said Connie as she reached for an empty glass on her bedside table. "You've done so much already, and like you said, Shirley is here and seems to know what I want even before I ask."

Probably even more than you want, I thought.

Shirley seemed to stand even taller by the door frame of the room. She beamed with pride at Connie's kind words. "Now that's enough about me," said Shirley. "They came to see you, Connie."

"As you can see, Pastor Brad," said Connie, "I have everything I need, but I do thank you for the offer."

"Well, okay then," I said. "Can we pray for you?" I asked Connie.

"Certainly!" said Connie, sitting up straighter in bed. "Thank you for suggesting it."

"It's the least we can do," said Allison.

"And the most," said Connie as she placed the empty glass back on the bedside table.

"You're absolutely right," I replied, moving closer to the bed. "Why don't we all hold hands, and I'll pray."

Allison and I walked to opposite sides of the bed and reached out for each of Connie's hands. She instantly grabbed our hands tightly and smiled.

"Would you like to join us in praying, Shirley?" asked Allison, reaching out to her with her other hand. "You don't have to worry—Brad will make sure that it's a bipartisan prayer."

"I suppose it will be okay this one time!" said Shirley, rushing to hold Allison's hand. "Thank you for asking."

"Let's pray," I said. "Lord, please continue to heal our friend Connie. She loves You and has been a faithful Christian for many years. Please comfort her during this time. Restore her fully so she can continue serving You. Provide for her every need. Thank You for Ernie's love and for Shirley's care. In Your name we pray. Amen."

"Amen," repeated Connie, gripping our hands even tighter. "Thank you so much."

When we finally released hands, Shirley wiped her eyes and disappeared through the bedroom door.

"Is she okay?" asked Allison.

"Oh yes," said Connie. "She likes to pretend like she's an atheist and only interested in politics, but she always cries during prayer. We recognized that a long time ago, so we pray a lot when she's here."

I couldn't help but smile.

"Now," said Allison, "you should probably get some rest."

"You're right," said Connie. "Thank you so much for stopping by."

"Are you sure there's nothing else we can do for you before we go?" I asked.

"Well," said Connie, "there is one thing, but it seems too much to ask."

"What is it?" I said. "We'll do anything you want."

"Could you deliver a package to Paul?"

"Paul, your son?" I asked.

"Yes," answered Connie. "It's very important."

"Well, uh …" I stammered.

"We'd be happy to," said Allison. "Where is it?"

Before Connie could answer, Shirley yelled loudly from down the hall, "Can I get you anything, Connie? I noticed your water glass was empty."

"Yes," answered Connie. "Could you make me a glass of lemonade? The water was good, but every so often, I like a little bit of flavor."

"Consider it done!" cried Shirley.

Connie glanced toward the door. "Can you see Shirley?" she asked.

I looked in the hallway and then turned back. "No. She must have gone into the kitchen to make the lemonade. Do you want me to get her for you?"

"No," she replied. "In fact, would you close the bedroom door?"

"Sure," I said, doing as she asked.

"Is everything okay?" asked Allison.

"Yes, thank you," answered Connie. "Shirley doesn't approve of what I'm about to ask, especially while I'm recovering, so I don't want her to see.

Now would you be a dear and reach under the bed? You're looking for a large manila envelope."

"Okay, sure," said Allison as she knelt down, reached under the bed, and pulled out a large, padded manila envelope. "Is this it?" she asked.

"Yes," said Connie. "This needs to go to my son Paul in New Orleans, today if possible."

"Today?" I asked. "Can't we just mail it to him?"

"No, sorry," said Connie. "These are very time-sensitive, and I couldn't entrust them to the post office."

"What's inside?" asked Allison.

"Oh, it's mostly legal papers. You see, he's got himself in trouble again. Ernie and I are hoping the contents of this package will help him out."

"I didn't think you heard much from Paul," I said.

"Well, it depends on what's going on with him."

"Yes," said Allison, "he is very talented and must be very busy."

"That's true," said Connie, "but he also has a talent for getting himself into trouble. When that happens, we hear from him a lot."

"Okay," I said. "So Ernie knows about your request?"

"Don't you worry about Ernie," she said. "He knows all about Paul's troubles. He prays for him every night."

"But would he want Paul to have what's in the package?" I asked.

"Absolutely," said Connie. "He was going to take them himself tonight but thought it best not to because of my condition."

Allison held the envelope tight in her hands. "We'd be happy to deliver this for you. Where does Paul live?"

Connie looked down and suddenly became very serious. "I believe he's between addresses at the moment. His cell number is written on the envelope. He usually texts back. You know, he's so busy with his music and all."

"I'm sure that's the case," said Allison.

"So," I remarked, "I suppose that's another reason you can't mail these documents to him."

"That's right," she replied. "I should have said that before, but it's all so embarrassing."

"Don't you worry about a thing," said Allison, putting her hand on Connie's shoulder. "We'll deliver it to him this afternoon."

"Oh, thank you!" said Connie, placing her hand on top of Allison's. "This means so much to us!"

"You're welcome," I said. "I guess we should be going if we're going to drive to New Orleans. It might take us a while to find Paul once we get there."

"You're probably right," said Allison, releasing Connie's hand.

Connie motioned for us to wait. "When you find Paul, there is one more thing I'd like you to say, Pastor Brad."

"What's that?" I asked.

For the first time, Connie looked sad. She looked me straight in the eye and said, "Please tell Paul that we love him and to please be careful with the contents of this envelope. These legal papers will not be easy to replace if he loses them."

"Certainly," I said.

"Now," said Connie, "you be safe driving now."

"We will," said Allison as we walked toward the door.

"Oh, one more thing," said Connie.

"Yes?" I asked as we stopped in our tracks.

"Make sure to thank your sister Elizabeth for stopping by the hospital this morning. She sure was encouraging to me."

"What?" I asked. "Elizabeth stopped by to see you?"

"You didn't know?" asked Connie.

"No, I didn't," I replied.

"Yes," said Connie. "We had a really good conversation."

"Hmm," I thought aloud. "What do you know about that?"

CHAPTER 13

Allison and I sat in our car in the Plaisance driveway. I put the key in the ignition, started the engine, and shifted into reverse, but before I backed into the street, I gripped the steering wheel, sighed heavily, and closed my eyes tightly.

"Are you okay?" asked Allison as she buckled her seat belt.

"I just can't believe this," I said.

"What do you mean?" asked Allison.

"This whole thing!" I cried. "I can't go to New Orleans today. I've got too much to do."

"We have to! We told Connie we'd help her in any way we could."

"I know that, Allison," I said. "But I'm a pastor. I am not a courier service. Why can't Ernie take the package to Paul?"

Allison shook her head. "Because he and his wife have been in a traumatic accident, and now she is in bed with a very strange lady watching over her."

"That strange lady is Ernie's sister, and she seems to be doing just fine."

"Were you and I just in the same house? Shirley may have seemed to be doing just fine to you, but I missed out on that completely when she started talking about the political affiliation of coffee buyers. Besides, like I said, we asked Connie if there was anything we could do."

"Well, we didn't exactly mean *anything*, did we?"

"What did *we* mean then, Pastor Brad?"

I pursed my lips together, completely irritated. "I meant something like going to the grocery store for them or getting a prayer chain going or something like that. I certainly didn't mean for us to drive all the way to New Orleans. That'll take over an hour each way."

"Well, that's what we're doing. I don't understand you. Yesterday when Connie was hurt, you couldn't wait to leave the house. You drove this morning to McComb to see Ernie and then practically insisted that I come here with you today."

"Exactly," I snapped. "Haven't I done enough?"

Allison glanced at me suspiciously and tapped her forehead. "I think I know what's going on here. This has nothing to do with Connie. You're mad because your sister got to visit with her in the hospital, and you didn't."

"No, I'm not!" I exclaimed.

"Yes, you are," she said. "You're a pastor, Brad. Start acting like one."

"What's that supposed to mean?" I asked.

"Come on! You're throwing a fit because your wild sister accomplished some ministry that you, the high and mighty pastor, were not able to complete."

"I don't act high and mighty!" I retorted.

"You're right," said Allison. "But right now you are, and it's very unsettling. It's time for you to stop being mad about it and start driving toward New Orleans."

"What are you saying?" I asked. "You mean we should go there right now?"

"There's no time like the present," she responded. "Let's do it."

"You're going with me?" I asked. "But what about our son?"

"My sister's staying with us, remember? Gabe loves her, she loves him, and she knows his routine. I'll call her and explain what's happened. I'm sure she'd be happy to take care of him for a few more hours. Besides, you seem to need me right now."

"Oh man," I said, "this is terrible."

"Now what are you mad about? Being with me or my sister helping us?"

"That probably means she's staying the night with us, doesn't it?"

"Of course, Brad! I already told you that she's staying with us for a few days. She's helping us right now, so you should be pleased to have her with us."

I took another deep breath. "You're right," I said. "I'm grateful that Ashleigh is with us."

"Just try to calm down," she replied. "It's all going to be okay."

"I'm trying," I said. "I'm just not sure we should be doing this."

"Why not?"

"I'm just not sure that Ernie would agree to all of this. He doesn't seem the type to want to put me out in any way."

For a moment, we were both quiet, not really knowing what else to say, so I backed into the street and started driving.

Allison patted my leg and asked, "So we're going?"

"I guess so," I replied. "I should call Ernie on the way, just to make sure."

"That's probably a good idea," she replied.

"I'm going to let myself calm down a bit first."

"That's probably best. You always seem to let yourself get so worked up over everything."

"Are you telling me this doesn't upset you at all?"

"What's there to be upset about? Aren't surprises like this normal in ministry?"

"Yes. Very normal as of late."

"And isn't ministry all about working with people?"

"I suppose."

"And weren't we just trying to find a good place to eat dinner last night and couldn't?"

"What do you mean?" I joked, trying to turn the situation. "I took you to a pretty swanky place!"

"You took me to Sonic," she replied. "I want to go someplace nice where there are tablecloths and where you don't order by numbers."

"You think there's a place like that in New Orleans?"

"There must be thousands there," she said matter-of-factly. "And I think it's high time you took me to one."

"Okay then," I said. "Let's go to New Orleans."

As Allison and I drove down I-55 between Lake Pontchartrain and Lake Maurepas, I reflected over everything that had happened in the last day and suddenly felt nauseous—the disagreement with the deacons, preaching to an increasingly unresponsive congregation about tithing, finding the one-hundred-dollar bill, breaking it to pay for Billy Ray's gas, spending more of it to impress my mother, comforting Ernie after the car accident, waiting for Connie to wake up in the hospital, spending the rest of God's money, arguing with Earl time and again, winning with the scratch-off lottery ticket, Ernie finding even more money in the church office, and Earl yanking my wallet from my hands and finding one thousand dollars inside and then accusing me of theft and/or embezzlement. I thought about us visiting Connie at home and now delivering a package to her son in New Orleans with no real explanation. All of these things together made me feel out of control. My stomach gurgled, and I sighed heavily.

Allison, as usual, could tell I was deeply troubled and, as usual, tried to talk me into feeling better. "What's going on with you?" she asked. "You've been fidgeting nervously in your seat since we left."

"I'm not sure what you're talking about," I said, lying through my teeth.

"You know exactly what I'm talking about," she replied. "Tell me what's going on, babe."

I glanced at her. I didn't know how much longer I could keep from telling her everything, but then again, I knew she would be so disappointed in me. "Do you really want to know?"

"Of course I do," she said, putting her hand on the back of my neck. "I'm your wife. I'm here for you. Whatever is bothering you is something you don't have to go through by yourself."

I looked in her eyes for a brief second, took in a deep breath, and let it out slowly. "You're not going to like it," I said.

"Try me," she replied.

"Okay," I said. "The other day when I told you—"

In one of the top interruptions of all time, my phone started to ring.

"Don't answer it," said Allison, her eyes watching my hands reach out for my phone. "Whoever it is, you can call them back later. Tell me what's going on."

I glanced at the screen. It was Archie Arceneaux, the chairman of the deacons, probably calling to tell me that the deacons were calling for my execution. Fear shot through my spine. "It's Archie," I said. "I should probably take it."

"Okay," she said, turning to stare at the lake, "if that's what you have to do."

"I'm sorry," I said. "But I really should take this."

"Like I said," she replied, still not looking at me, "go ahead and take it if it's so important that you have to stop talking to me."

"It is important. I'm sorry." Hesitantly, I accepted the call and held the phone to my ear. "Hello," I said.

"Pastor Brad, this is Archie Arceneaux."

"Oh, I thought that was your number, Archie. How are you today?"

"Well, Pastor, I'm not quite sure how to answer that question at the moment."

"Okay," I replied, knowing exactly where he was heading next. "What's wrong?"

"Well," he answered slowly, "I just had a conversation with Earl Bishop. He told me all about Ernie finding cash in the church office, about your confession regarding the hundred-dollar bill, and about how he and Ernie discovered around a thousand dollars in cash in your wallet."

"Well, I wouldn't necessarily call me telling Ernie about the money I *found and returned* a confession."

Allison, hearing only my half of the conversation, raised one eyebrow and cocked her head to listen.

"What would you call it then?" demanded Archie.

"Well," I said, stuttering slightly, "I would call it reporting exactly what happened."

"But you admit to keeping the hundred-dollar bill instead of putting it in the safe?"

"I couldn't put the money into the safe," I replied. "I don't have the combination. So I was keeping it safe until I could meet with Ernie."

"So are you saying you were purposefully hiding the money?" he asked.

"That's not how I would explain it," I answered.

"Then exactly how would you explain what you were doing with the money?"

I swallowed hard. "I suppose I was keeping it safe until counting time. I just didn't want to leave a hundred dollars out in the open on the floor for anyone to find."

"This is not looking good for you at all, Pastor," said Archie. "Not good at all. You should have just left the money there until Ernie arrived."

"Well, what would you have done if you were in the same situation, Archie?"

"It's not a question about what I would do, Brad. I'm not the pastor."

"I tried to contact Ernie. He and his wife were in a car accident!" I said.

"Yes, that's right, Pastor. But you didn't know that when you found the money. Like I said, you should have just left it there."

"You think I should have left a one-hundred-dollar bill on the floor of the office where anyone could have found it?"

"Yes, I do."

"Well, I'm sorry, but that just sounds ridiculous to me," I said. "Anyone could have come in there and taken it at any time."

"Anyone with a key, you mean."

"Yes," I said. "Anyone with a key could have entered the office and taken the money at any time."

"Who all has keys to the office?" he asked.

"As far as I know, only Ernie, Earl, you, and I have keys."

"So are you saying you think one of us would have stolen the money if we would have come across it?"

"No!" I exclaimed. "I'm not saying that at all."

"Well, what are you saying then?"

"What I'm saying, Archie, is that it's not a good idea to leave hundred-dollar bills lying on the floor of the church office, no matter if the door is locked or not."

"I suppose a much safer option is to keep the money in your wallet," said Archie.

"I tried to contact Ernie," I said. "I wanted to let him know what I had found."

"Why didn't you explain it to him when you saw him that afternoon?"

"Because he'd just been in a car accident," I cried. "The man didn't need to hear about church finances at the time! His wife was in the hospital, and he was desperately praying that she wasn't critically injured and that she was somehow going to be okay! Me finding money was the last thing he needed or wanted to hear about."

"Are you sure that's the way it happened?"

"Yes, Archie, I am. When Earl finally called me back, he said that he hoped whatever I had to say to him could wait because he and his wife had been in an accident. There was too much on his mind to process anything else at the moment."

"Well, he's all ears now," said Archie, "as is the rest of the deacon board."

"Good grief," I said.

"This doesn't look good for you, Pastor Brad."

"You already said that."

"That's because I really mean it. Our people have been continuing to give their tithes and offerings, yet our financial records show a deficit. Either all of our people are lying about their giving, or something fishy is going on. With all that's transpired today, Pastor, it just does not look good for you."

I swallowed and glanced at Allison, who was intently listening to my half of the conversation. "So what happens now?" I asked.

"Well, we're having a special deacons' meeting tomorrow evening to discuss the issue so we can make a recommendation to the church body at an emergency business meeting this Wednesday evening."

"You can't be serious," I said.

"I'm afraid I am," said Archie. "This is a very serious matter, especially with your track record."

"What do you mean?" I asked. "What track record?"

"Well, everyone knows this is not the first time you've stolen money from the church."

"What are you talking about?"

"You once took money from the Christian Boys' Club treasury."

"For heaven's sake, Archie. I was an eight-year-old child. That doesn't have anything to do with this."

"Some of our deacons would argue with you on that, Pastor. It's hard to change someone's nature, even if they do go to seminary."

"My gracious!" I said. "I don't believe this! I found some cash on the floor of my office and later gave the exact amount to Ernie when he came to count the offering. What's the issue? No one would have even known about it if I hadn't said anything."

"So were you considering keeping the money and not telling anyone about it?"

"Absolutely not! I was trying to focus on all of my ministry responsibilities like a good pastor is supposed to do."

"Obviously, you weren't trying hard enough, Pastor."

"Do you really believe that?"

"I'm not sure," he answered. "I suppose that's up to the deacon board and the entire congregation at Wednesday's business meeting."

"I suppose you're right about that," I said, somewhat calmer. "Well, I'll see you tomorrow night."

"I'm sorry things are going this way," said Archie.

"Me too," I replied.

"I guess I'll see you tomorrow night."

"I guess so," I replied, ending the call and placing my phone on the seat beside me. I glanced over at Allison. She was staring at me with her mouth open.

"What is going on?" she demanded. "Are you in some kind of trouble? Why were you talking about leaving hundred-dollar bills all over the floor?"

I sighed. This was it. Allison was about to learn everything. In a way, I was relieved. I hated feeling like I was keeping something from her. However, she was still going to be mad.

"Okay," I said. "I'll tell you everything that's happened, but I want you to know that I think everything is okay now."

"I believe you, but if everything's okay, then why did Archie Arceneaux just call an emergency deacons' meeting before a church business meeting?"

I sighed heavily. "Because Earl's got him all worked up about something that's really nothing. After everyone was gone Sunday, I found a one-hundred-dollar bill on the floor next to the safe. I texted Ernie and was going to tell him about it when he called me on Sunday afternoon, but …"

"But you couldn't because Ernie and Connie were in a car accident," said Allison.

"Exactly! I didn't want to leave a hundred dollars lying on the office floor, so I kept it until I could turn it into Ernie for the offering."

"And why didn't you just put it in the safe?"

"I don't have the combination."

"You don't have the combination to the safe that's in your own office?"

"That's right," I said. "You know better than anyone that I don't have a real office. Everyone just thinks of it as the church office where I have a desk. When I was hired on as pastor, it was decided that I shouldn't have the combination so I would never be tempted and could therefore never be accused of stealing church funds."

"But it sounds to me like that's exactly what's happening now. Is it?"

"Sort of. I found a hundred-dollar bill and turned it in at my first opportunity. Everything looks worse because Ernie found more money between the safe and the wall. So now Earl thinks I've been stealing church money."

"That's kind of strange. How did it get there?"

"I have no idea. It does look like someone might have been hiding it there so they could return for it later."

"Oh no!"

"And what's worse is that Earl has it in his mind that I'm the one hiding the money on Sundays and then returning for it at a later time."

"But why would he think that?" asked Allison. "You don't collect the church offering, and you don't put it in the safe. You do count it with Ernie most weeks, but he's always there with you."

"Yes, he is," I replied. "Ernie seems to believe me. At least he said he does."

"Who puts the money in the safe after it's collected on Sundays?"

Before I could answer, my phone rang once again. Allison rolled her eyes while I glanced at the screen.

"It's Ernie," I said. "Maybe he can tell us what's going on." I accepted the call and answered in a less than enthusiastic voice. "Hi, Ernie."

"Don't worry, Pastor Brad. I know everything seems like it's falling apart right now, but trust me, things aren't nearly as bad as they seem."

"Really?" I asked. "Because right now it seems to me that things are really, really bad. From what I hear from Archie, it sounds like Earl and a few of the deacons are out to get me fired over this."

Allison grimaced but reached for my shoulder and rubbed it slightly.

"Well, that is true," said Ernie. "Well, at least it's true on Earl's part, and maybe Archie's as well, but I don't think that's going to happen."

"How can you be so sure?"

"Earl does seem like he's out to get you, but I think he's just wound up a little too tight."

"So what do I do?" I asked. "Our offerings have been short, I preached hard on tithing Sunday to hopefully increase our finances, and then you and Earl caught me with a wad of cash in my wallet."

Allison pulled her hand from my shoulder and covered her own mouth with it. I suddenly remembered that I hadn't told her about the lottery money yet.

"Since you mentioned it, where did you get all of that cash?" asked Ernie. "Did you find it in the office as well?"

"Absolutely not," I replied. "The fact that it was in my wallet when I pulled the one-hundred-dollar bill from there was purely coincidental."

"How much was there?" asked Ernie.

"What's that got to do with anything?" I asked. "It's my money that I earned outside of the church."

Allison instantly turned her head to look at me. Her eyes were scrunched up, and her mouth was tightly closed.

"I think it could matter a lot," said Ernie. "Tell me, Pastor. You can trust me."

I let out a deep breath before I answered. "It was right at one thousand dollars—well, before I returned the one hundred dollars to you."

Allison's jaw dropped, and her eyes grew wide.

"And you promise it wasn't church money?"

"Yes!" I cried. "The only church money was the hundred-dollar bill I found on the floor of the office, the money I texted you about and later returned before everything blew up and threw us into chaos! That's the truth! I promise!"

"And you didn't have anything to do with or have any knowledge of the money I found between the safe and the wall?"

"Absolutely not!" I replied. "The first time I saw it was when you found it."

"Do you have any notion of who else might have hidden the money between the safe and the wall?"

"I have no idea, Ernie. No idea at all. I'm baffled by the whole thing."

Ernie said nothing in reply, but I heard him sigh deeply. After a moment, I couldn't hold it in any longer, so I asked, "What are you thinking, Ernie? You're not saying anything."

After another long pause, Ernie said, "It's okay, Pastor Brad. I believe you."

I sighed heavily. "Thanks, Ernie. That's good to know."

"Where are you now?" he asked.

"Allison and I are on our way to New Orleans, delivering a manila envelope from Connie to your son Paul."

"Oh, okay," he replied. "I certainly appreciate that, but under the circumstances, are you sure you still want to deliver it? I mean, things are pretty rocky around here right now."

I glanced at Allison. She was shaking her head gently, looking out the window. Her eyes were narrow, and her lips were pursed.

"Yes," I replied. "I think a few hours away from Aucoin might do us some good. If nothing else, it will help me calm down."

"Did Connie give you Paul's number?"

"Yes, she did, but I haven't tried to call him yet."

"I'll call him and tell him to meet you at Café du Monde in Jackson Square. He often hangs out there between gigs and rehearsals. Do you know where that is?"

"Sure do," I answered, glancing at Allison. "Café du Monde is always a great place for a cheap date."

Allison didn't even flinch at my comment.

"Call me back if he doesn't show," said Ernie.

"Okay, I will," I replied. "Do you think that's a possibility?"

"I don't think so," he replied. "He's really needing the papers in the package. But you never know. Paul's got a mind of his own."

"Yeah," I replied. "He's very talented, though."

"We can certainly be thankful for that," said Ernie.

I finished the call and placed the phone in my lap. Allison had picked her jaw up off of the floor, but she was in no way ready to talk. That was perfectly fine with me because I wasn't quite ready to talk either. So we drove on in silence, until my phone rang once again. I reached for it, but Allison snatched it before I could.

Allison read the caller ID and then answered. "Hi, Elizabeth," she said.

Not her, please.

"Brad?" she said. "Why, yes, he's right here, ready to talk with you." Allison handed me the phone without looking at me.

"Hello," I said, secretly willing the phone to go dead.

"Hey, Brad," said Elizabeth. "I really need to talk with you in person."

"Sorry," I said. "I'm on my way to New Orleans."

"Really?" she asked, but she didn't wait for a reply. "What time will you be back?"

"I'm not sure," I said. "Probably late. What's up? The usual?"

"What is that supposed to mean?" she asked.

"I don't know," I said. "I shouldn't have said it. I'm sorry."

After a brief moment of silence, Elizabeth said, "It's okay. Both of us seem to hurt each other a lot on accident. I know I've done my share of it in the past."

"Are you okay?" I asked.

"Maybe," she replied. "Can we talk late tonight?"

"I'm not sure when I'm coming back," I said.

"How about tomorrow morning?" she asked. "I could take you to breakfast."

"That sounds good," I said. "Will you come by the house?"

"Yeah."

"Okay, see you then."

"Bye."

Before I could respond, she hung up. I turned to tell Allison the full story, but she had turned away from me. Josh Billings once said, "Silence is one of the hardest arguments to refute." He was so right.

CHAPTER 14

Sometimes silence speaks louder than words. Somehow, the emptiness of it has the ability to convey anger, comfort, disappointment, and love simultaneously. Interrupting this deep level of communication with words is often far worse than not speaking at all.

Allison and I drove on in silence, me overwhelmed by shame and her calming her anger. Obviously, she knew there were things I hadn't told her. Much worse, she knew there were things I hadn't planned on telling her, ever. Worst of all, we both knew I was eventually going to tell her everything, or things were going to get really bad between us.

I wondered if the silence was intended to calm her nerves, to allow our minds to rest, or to stay my execution. However, I wasn't about to ask. So we drove on in muted anticipation.

I-55 finally merged into I-10, and we drove along Lake Pontchartrain into the New Orleans metro area. Before long, we were in bumper-to-bumper traffic and could see the Superdome ahead of us. As we were approaching our exit, Allison finally spoke.

"Do you ever miss living here?" she asked.

"Oh," I said. "Ah, well, I don't really know. Sometimes, I suppose. I guess I don't think about it very much. Why?"

"Just wondering, I guess."

"Do you ever miss living here?" I asked.

"Every so often," she said. "When we lived here before, we were newlyweds without church or parental responsibilities, and you were still in seminary. When I remember it now, it feels like we were a million miles away from Aucoin and the church members at Lee Community Church."

I smiled and said, "We did have a good life here, didn't we?"

"Yeah," she answered, "we did."

"You know," I said, "back then, I never would have imagined that we would ever move back to Aucoin."

"Did you ever think you would be the pastor of Lee Community Church?"

"I never did, but Elizabeth used to tell me I would be."

"Our new lives felt like such a big adventure to me," she said. "A fun, romantic adventure with just the two of us, not out to conquer the world, but out to explore it from every angle, inside and out, from top to bottom."

"I guess it was like that, wasn't it? I don't think of that part very often."

She finally turned my way and smiled slightly, a huge improvement over her previous expression. "What parts do you think of then?" she asked.

I smiled and answered, "I guess I think about all of the traffic, the rudeness of some of the people, the hard living conditions, and how fast everyone talks."

"They do talk fast here, don't they?" said Allison.

"Yeah, they do, especially when compared with Aucoin. It could just be that people in Aucoin speak slow."

"That is true," she replied.

"However," I said, "I also remember how fun it was going to the French Quarter, eating at Café Maspero, watching the ferry boats go across the river, sampling the free hot sauce in the French Market, and standing outside of jazz clubs listening to music because we couldn't afford to pay the cover charge."

"I really liked going to Maspero's," she said. "Looking back on it now, it seems like we went there quite a bit."

"I never heard you complain about it before."

"I'm not complaining. I'm just curious. Why did you always take us there?"

I laughed. "I liked the atmosphere, I guess."

"Plus," she said, "I remember the food being really good."

"It was good, wasn't it?" I asked.

"Yeah," she replied, suddenly looking down.

"Would you like to eat there tonight? Maybe we can go when we finish with Paul. We'll just be down the street."

"Maybe," she answered, looking away. "I guess it will be close for us."

"Yeah, it will be. Then, if you want, we could also go hear some jazz somewhere tonight. Maybe Snug Harbor or some other place. What do you think?"

Suddenly serious, Allison answered, "I don't care. Something in me just wants to find Paul, give him this package, and get this all over with."

"Can we at least eat some beignets?"

"Sure," she replied, "if we've got the money for it."

"I've got plenty."

Allison breathed out hard.

"What is it?" I asked.

"You just said that you've got plenty of money. Well, that's really convenient, Brad. Where did it come from?"

"What do you mean?"

"Where did the money, which apparently you've got plenty of, come from? Yesterday, you didn't know if we could afford to buy a gallon of milk. You said you weren't getting paid for another week, so we had to watch our spending."

"Allison, I—"

"But now, suddenly, out of the blue, you have plenty of cash for dinner and jazz clubs and beignets. What happened? Were you lying to me before, or are you lying to me now?"

"I wasn't lying either time," I answered. "Things have just become sort of strange."

"When are you going to tell me?"

"Why don't we deliver the package, and then I can tell you everything over dinner."

"You're sure we can afford it? Legally, I mean?"

I laughed at her comment, but her facial expression didn't change. "Absolutely," I replied.

"Then let's deliver this to Paul and find a place to eat. Then you are going to turn off your phone and give me every last detail over dinner."

We parked in a lot I remembered from years before in the Faubourg Marigny near the French Market. Six years earlier, the lot had a manned attendant. Now it had a pay station and cameras on poles.

"I'll be right back," I said, opening my door and practically running to pay for the parking. As I went through the steps of paying, I took time to breathe. Allison was scaring me. She seemed harder and colder than I could ever remember her being. I was glad to have a short moment away from her to think. However, I went through the whole process of paying, and no solution came to mind.

I returned to the car. "We'll have to walk just a bit," I said as I opened the car door for Allison. "But this lot is so much cheaper than the ones closest to Jackson Square."

"Why should it matter?" said Allison, looking away from me stubbornly. "You've got plenty of money."

Even though her comment stung, I tried my best to ignore it. I grabbed Connie's package from the back seat, and we headed toward Café du Monde.

Allison walked beside me but didn't grab hold when I reached for her hand. *She must be really mad*, I thought. *It's rare that she doesn't want to hold my hand.* "Why don't we just walk through the market?" I said, trying to make conversation. "Even though there's lots of people, it's still the quickest route."

"That's fine," she said.

Because of the crowds, I immediately regretted my decision. Allison and I weaved our way through the souvenir vendors and fruit stands of the open-air market, exited onto the sidewalk, and continued down Decatur Street. It wasn't long before we saw the familiar green and white awnings, a trademark of Café du Monde, the Original French Market Coffee Stand.

"This brings back memories, doesn't it?" I asked.

"Do you see him anywhere?" asked Allison, ignoring my question.

"No, it's been so long since I've seen him that I don't really remember much about what he looks like."

"Why don't you try calling him?" she suggested.

"Let's sit at a table first so I can tell him exactly where we are."

"Whatever," she replied.

We entered the open-air café and were about to take our seats when I heard a voice from behind me. "Pastor Brad?"

Allison and I turned around to see a rough-skinned, bearded man wearing dirty jeans and a green T-shirt with the words "Kiss Me, I'm Irish!" emblazoned over a four-leaf shamrock. A guitar case was strapped to his back.

"Paul?" I asked. "Is that you?"

"Yeah," he said, suddenly looking ashamed. "I know I must look terrible to you."

"No," I said. "You look fine. You just, uh, took me by surprise, that's all."

"Sorry about that," he replied, not looking me in the eye.

"No problem at all," said Allison. "So how's everything with your music going? Are you playing anywhere tonight?"

Paul looked down and answered, "Oh … yes, it's, uh, going well … my music, that is."

"Are you playing anywhere tonight?" Allison repeated. "We'd love to hear you play."

"Well, uh, yeah," he answered. "I've got a gig later on tonight, but it's not somewhere you would really want to visit. It's a pretty rough place."

"Oh, okay," said Allison.

"We were just hoping to hear you play," I said, even though Allison and I hadn't discussed it.

Paul looked away. "It's just that it's not the best of places for a preacher and his wife to be hanging out, especially not at night."

"It's fine," I said. "We understand. Would you like to sit with us for a while? We can order some beignets and coffee."

He looked nervously to the right and then to the left before vigorously shaking his head. "Ah, no," he replied. "I don't think so. I've got a few people waiting for me. Dad said you had a package for me with some important papers."

"Yes," I replied. I handed him the package I had been carrying.

"Thank you so much," he replied as tears welled up in his eyes.

Allison reached out and touched his arm. "Are you sure you don't want to go with us to get something to eat?" she asked, glancing at me afterward.

"Yeah, Paul, why don't you join us?" I inquired. "We don't often get back to the city and even less to the French Quarter."

"Uh, I don't know," he said.

"Come on," I urged him. "It's our treat."

He smiled, looked at us briefly, and then stared down at his package. "I really appreciate it," he said. "But I've got an important rehearsal to attend in just a few minutes. I needed these, uh, papers to conduct my business. So thank you once again."

"Okay," I said. "If you're absolutely sure. Do you want us to wait for you? We could even give you a ride back to Aucoin so you could see your parents if you wanted."

"Yes," said Allison. "Then you could check on your mother."

Paul looked up quickly. "What's wrong with my mother?" he asked.

"Didn't your dad tell you?" I asked.

"No, nobody told me anything," he said. "What happened?"

Allison reached out and touched his shoulder. "Your parents were in a car accident yesterday in McComb."

"Oh, man. I didn't know," said Paul, staring down once again. "Are they okay?"

"Your dad is fine," said Allison. "But your mother was a bit shaken. She's home from the hospital now, but—"

"She was in the hospital?" he asked as a tear rolled down his cheek. "Why didn't anyone tell me?"

I nodded. "We didn't mean for you to find out like this. We had no idea you didn't know."

"Is Mom okay?" he asked.

"She's going to be fine," answered Allison.

"Are you sure?" he asked.

"Yes," I said. "Your aunt Shirley is taking care of her."

Paul wiped his eyes and then shook his head. "Well," he said with a tearful smile, "having Aunt Shirley as a caretaker is probably more frightening than being in an accident."

I couldn't help but smile. "Well," I replied, "I probably shouldn't say this, but you're just about right. She spent quite a bit of time talking to me about the coffee-drinking habits of Democrats and Republicans."

"That's my aunt Shirley," said Paul. Suddenly, he became serious again, looking over his shoulder nervously.

"Okay, Paul," I said as I reached for his hand.

Reluctantly, he took my hand and shook it limply. "Thank you," he said and then turned and walked away quickly, clutching the package as if it were an infant.

"He's kind of out there, isn't he?" I asked.

"It certainly seems that way," said Allison.

"Do you think he'll be okay?"

"Maybe the paperwork Connie was sending will help him."

"What do you think was in the package?"

"Probably his birth certificate, passport, and things like that, don't you think?"

"I guess so," I said. "I hope so."

Allison and I followed him out from under the canopy of the café and watched him until he disappeared into the crowd. I was about to speak when my phone rang. I glanced at the caller ID and raised my eyebrows. "It's my mom," I said. "I better take it. Who knows what she's heard."

Allison nodded in agreement, her anger somewhat subsided.

"Hi, Mama," I answered.

"What in heaven's name is going on, Bradley?"

"What are you talking about?" I said as I motioned for Allison to cross the street with me, heading toward the Jackson Square garden.

"I was just out shopping and heard all about it! You're in a heap of trouble, Pastor Brad!"

"Now, Mama, this is not as bad as it seems. I didn't do anything wrong."

"That's not what it sounds like to me. How can I possibly show my face in public again, knowing that my son's made a mockery of how I raised him?"

I led Allison to a bench where the two of us could sit while I spoke to my mother. "I'm sorry, Mama, but I don't see how this reflects on you at all."

"What do you mean, Bradley?" she snapped. "I go to the One Stop Shop and hear that my son has been avoiding his own sister in her time of need. Why won't you just sit down and talk with her, Bradley? She needs you. She trusts you."

"What are you talking about?" I asked.

"Sally Mae told me all about how Elizabeth has been chasing you all over creation and how you won't give her the time of day."

"You're calling me about Elizabeth?" I asked.

Allison rolled her eyes and shook her head.

"Of course," she answered. "What else would I be calling you about?"

I couldn't help but chuckle at the situation.

"I don't see anything funny about it," she said. "You've embarrassed me, and you're hurting your sister."

I swallowed hard and replied, "Well, that certainly hasn't been my intention, Mama."

"What's going on?" my mother demanded.

"You know what, Mom?" I said. "You're absolutely right."

"I am?" she asked. "You have been avoiding your sister? You've abandoned her in her time of need?"

"Yes," I answered, "but I wouldn't say that I've abandoned her in her time of need."

"Then what are you doing, Bradley?"

"I've been giving her some growing-up time and me some breathing room. But that's all over now. I'm meeting with her tomorrow morning for breakfast."

"You are?"

"Yes, and when I get back to Aucoin, I'm also going to stop by the One Stop and have a conversation with Sally Mae about this whole situation."

"Well, that's a start, but—"

"But I need for you to understand that we have to be tough with Elizabeth. She's got some issues that she has to accept and deal with."

"That's good, son, but—"

"And that means that we can't run and fix every problem she creates for herself. She needs professional help, Mama."

Allison's eyebrows raised as she listened to the conversation.

"Do you think so?" my mother asked.

"Yes, ma'am," I said. "I'm convinced of it."

After an awkward moment of silence, Mama said, "You do realize that you are the closest thing to professional help that she has right now, right?"

I paused and took in what my mother was saying. "You know what?" I said. "You may be right there. One thing I'm not is a substance abuse counselor, but I suppose I can meet with her again."

"Thank you, son," said Mama. "You don't want to get so busy serving the Lord that you neglect your own family."

"I understand," I said. "Will you please forgive me?"

"Well, of course, I forgive you, Bradley."

"And I want to take this opportunity to thank you, Mom."

"To thank me?" she asked. "For what?"

"For caring so much about me and my family. I mean, that's why you stay on top of us about milk, right?"

"Uh, yes," she chuckled. "That's right."

"I sure do love you, Mom."

A slightly awkward pause followed. "What?" she said.

"I said I love you, Mom."

Another awkward pause. "Well, that's real nice. I love you too, son."

CHAPTER 15

Daddy used to say that Aucoin was a place where people talked way too much, especially when they had nothing to say. This was certainly the case with my mama. I didn't mind, though. It was nice to have a civil conversation with her that didn't revolve around the subject of my sister or my family's milk consumption. When I was finally able to say goodbye, I stood up from the park bench, reached for Allison's hand, and said, "That went well. I only wish I could calm the deacons with the same amount of ease."

"Did you really mean all of what you said to her?"

"Yes, I did," I replied. "I seem to argue so much with her nowadays. She seemed to enjoy remembering how much I care about her. And it really made me feel good to tell her. Besides, what harm is it going to do me to drink a glass of milk every day?"

Allison tightened her lips and shook her head.

"What is it?" I asked.

"Well, I was just wondering about possibilities."

"What do you mean?" I asked.

"Well, you've given your attention to Ernie and Connie, to Earl and Archie, to Paul, and to your mother."

"Yeah?"

"Could it be possible that it is now my turn for your full attention?"

"Absolutely," I said, holding out my hand for her to take. "Let's go eat, and I'll tell you everything you want to know."

"No," she snapped, pushing my hand away.

"What do you mean, 'no'?" I said. "I thought you wanted me to tell you about everything that's happened."

"I do," said Allison, "but only if you promise to pay attention to me and me alone during our conversation. No texts, no phone calls, no social media—"

"Social media?" I asked. "You know I'm not really into that."

"I don't care," she replied. "Knowing what I know about you, I wouldn't be surprised if you tried to build an Instapic or Facelift page while we are talking over dinner."

"Don't you mean Instagram and Facebook?"

"I mean it, Brad," she said. "No anything with anyone else in any way during our conversation."

"Okay," I replied.

"Promise me," she said. "Promise me right now."

"I promise," I said, reaching for her hand. "Now will you come with me?"

"Okay," she replied as she reluctantly took my hand and stood up. "As long as you shut your phone off first."

"Yes, ma'am!" I said as I reached for my phone.

"And I don't mean turning down the volume," she said. "I mean shutting it off completely!"

"Gotcha," I said as I completely powered down my phone and showed it to her.

"Great!" she said. "Now put it away and let's go eat. I'm starving."

We walked a short distance and waited our turn to be seated at Café Maspero, our favorite dive from when we were younger.

"So," she said.

"So what?" I asked.

"The place looks like it's run-down a bit, doesn't it?"

"Did you want to go someplace else?" I asked.

"No," she said. "I want us to eat here for old times' sake."

"Okay," I said. "Sounds good to me."

"So," she said again.

"Yes?" I asked.

"So," she repeated, "did you do it?"

"Did I do what?" I asked.

"Did you steal the hundred dollars I keep hearing about?"

"You mean the hundred-dollar bill I found on the floor of the office?"

"Yeah," she said, "that hundred dollars. Did you steal it?"

"Do you think I stole it?"

"No, I don't think so, but I do want to hear you say it."

"No," I said. "I didn't steal that money."

"How did you get it then?"

"Like I said, I found it on the floor of the church office."

"And you couldn't tell Ernie because of the car accident? He was too out of sorts or something like that?"

"Right, but I told him everything when I saw him today."

"And you gave it back to him today?"

"Yes, today when we met to count the offerings, I told him the story and gave him the money."

"Was it the same hundred-dollar bill?"

"What do you mean?"

"I mean, did you give him the exact one-hundred-dollar bill you found?"

"Does it matter?" I asked.

"It could," she replied.

I sighed. "I'm not sure I understand the importance of the question."

"So you didn't give him the same bill you found?"

"No," I said, "I didn't."

"Oh," she said without emotion. She sniffed slightly. "That's very surprising."

"Yeah," I replied. "I guess it is."

I expected her to erupt, but Allison just stared out across Decatur Street, as if waiting for more than our table to be called.

"Okay," I said, "I can't take this anymore. I have to tell you everything that happened right now. Only then will you understand all—"

"Not yet," she interrupted.

"What?" I asked.

"I don't want you to tell me yet."

"Why not?"

"Because I'm not giving you the satisfaction," she said. "You've made me wait to hear this story, and you're not going to take away the atmosphere in which I want to hear it."

"Okay," I said. "So what happens now?"

"We wait for a table."

We stood waiting silently for the next few minutes. After a short time, which to me seemed like half an hour, a waiter finally waved us over and showed us to our seats at a table near an open window overlooking Decatur Street.

"Thank you," said Allison. "This is very nice."

"You're welcome," said the waiter, who handed us menus. "Someone will be with you shortly to take your order."

"Now let me tell you," I said, but Allison held up one finger, indicating that we still had to wait. Even in this stressful time, I admired her spunk.

Finally, another waiter brought us small glasses of water and took our order. When he left, Allison spread a white napkin across her lap, looked me square in the eye, and said, "Okay, now tell me everything."

"Okay," I said, "here's what happened …"

CHAPTER 16

It's amazing how spicy food can open your sinuses and your memory banks. While Allison listened across the restaurant table from me over fried shrimp po'boys and red beans and rice, I shared with her every last detail about what had happened, how I had responded, and—most importantly—what I had thought over the last couple of days. Surprisingly, she remained silent for the entire story, seemingly content to listen and nibble on her food.

Finally, when my confession was complete, I lowered my head and waited for the boom. When none came, I opened one eye to make sure she hadn't either run screaming or collapsed in disbelief. "Allison?"

She made no sound but simply stared ahead at me, the slightest look of displeasure on her face.

When I could take the silence no longer, I asked, "Aren't you going to say anything?"

She leaned forward on her elbows and asked, "What do you want me to say?"

"I want you to say whatever you want to say. How are you feeling right now?"

"What do you mean?" she asked.

"Well, I mean, are you mad at me? Are you disappointed? Are you happy?"

"I'm not any of those things," she replied.

"Then what are you?" I asked.

"I guess I'm just curious."

"Curious? What do you mean?"

"I'm curious about what we could do with the money you won if we really tried."

"I'm sorry, what?" I asked.

Allison suddenly grinned an evil grin. As I've told you, I usually always liked it when she smiled, but not this time. I'd never seen her smile like this before. I didn't like it.

"Give me your wallet," she said.

"What?" I replied. "You want my wallet?"

"Yes," she snarled. "Give it to me, now!"

"Okay," I answered, quickly handing her my wallet. "Here you go."

Allison held the wallet like it was a baby and then quickly dumped all of the cash onto the table between us.

I stared down at the money now spread across our table. "What are you doing?" I cried. "You can't do that here!"

"Why not?"

"Because we're in the French Quarter, that's why, right here by an open window with all of society walking by."

"So what?"

"So somebody could see it here, wait outside for us, knock us in the head, and steal it from us!"

Completely ignoring my response, Allison gathered the cash and ran it through her fingers like a deck of cards.

"Please put that away," I whispered.

"What's the big deal?" she asked. "You've got plenty, remember?"

"I won't for long if you keep doing what you're doing!"

I reached for the cash, but Allison pushed me away and shook an index finger at me. I could feel the stares from tourists at nearby tables. I slumped from the embarrassment.

"Please, Allison," I said. "You're starting to draw attention."

"Oh, all right," she replied, folding the money and reinserting it into my wallet. She winked at me before tossing the wallet across the table. It bounced across the table and onto the floor.

"What's wrong with you?" I asked as I reached behind my chair for my wallet.

"Why, nothing at all, Mr. Minister."

"What? I think something's wrong with you, Allison. You're acting very strange."

"No stranger than you, Pastor Brad."

"I know the last couple of days have been unusual for me, but I think—"

"You know what I think, Pastor Brad?" interrupted Allison.

"No," I replied as I stuffed the wallet back into my pocket. "What do you think?"

"I think we should take the rest of that cash from the lottery winnings, hit the casino, and turn it into some serious money!"

I looked into her eyes and saw no hint of pretense about her. "You're serious about this, aren't you?" I asked.

"Absolutely," she replied. "There's a large casino—Harrah's, I think, is the name—less than half a mile from right here. We should take our winnings, go gambling there, and try to quadruple them."

"What are you talking about?" I cried. "Neither of us would know how to gamble even if we tried."

"I'm sure we could figure it out."

"I don't believe what I'm hearing. You've never expressed interest in gambling before. Don't you think it's wrong?"

"You're right there," she replied, leaning down to rest her chin on one elbow. "I do think it's wrong, very wrong indeed. But you've shown me how easy it is to win when you forget about what's right and what's wrong and start living on the edge. Come on, let's throw caution to the wind, baby."

"What?" I asked, bringing my hand to my forehead. "Who is this person I'm sitting with? I'm not quite sure I recognize her."

"It's your wife, Pastor Brad. It's the woman you married, Allison Johnson, ready to finally let loose and live a little in the Big Easy."

"What?"

"Come on, preacher boy, let's do this thing and then party all night!"

"All night?" I cried. "What about our son?"

"What does it matter?" she snapped. "You didn't think about him when you took that money in the first place. Why should I be concerned with him now?"

My eyes grew large, and my jaw dropped.

"What's wrong, Pastor Brad? Cat got your tongue?"

"Am I dreaming?" I asked her. "This can't be reality."

"You know what else?" she asked, standing tall from her seat, reaching across the table, and grabbing my shoulders.

"What?" I asked nervously.

She pulled me to my feet, put her face next to my cheek, sensuously blew in my ear, and then yelled directly into it: "We've overslept again!"

Frantically, I shook my head. "What's going on?" I asked.

She shook me harder, and Café Maspero faded into Tuesday morning in our bedroom. "Wake up, Brad!" she exclaimed. "We've overslept again. You've only got a few minutes to bathe and shave. Your sister's going to be here at any moment."

My head fell back against the pillow. "Oh man," I exclaimed. "Why were you kissing me on my ear?"

Allison shook her head and pointed. "I think you're talking about your son," she replied.

I looked to my left and saw Gabe smiling back at me. "Good morning," I said.

"Daddy!" he said before striking me on the forehead with his hand.

"Ouch!" I said. "No, Gabe! That hurts!"

Allison quickly lifted Gabe out of the bed and placed him on the floor. He immediately ran into the living room.

"Did you see what your son just did?" I asked.

"So now he's my son?"

"Yes. Did you see him swat me on the forehead?"

"I didn't see it, and I really don't care," she replied. "Whatever it was, I'm sure you deserved it. Now get up!"

I rolled over and pulled the covers tighter to my body. "I don't want to get up. I just want to sleep. Elizabeth will just have to say no to whatever she's doing."

Suddenly, Allison snatched the covers from the bed and hurled them across the room. "Well, that's just too bad, Pastor Brad," she said. "Preachers who buy lottery tickets with stolen church funds don't get the luxury of sleeping in on deacons' meeting days, especially when they have a breakfast appointment with their sister. Get up. You're going to suffer through this like everyone else."

It was then that I remembered the reality of the previous night. Allison and I had had a very uneventful dinner during which I told her every detail of what had happened over the past couple of days. She was not sympathetic, not one bit. Instead, she was angry.

For the first time in our lives, we paid for our dinner and then left a nice restaurant without finishing our meals and without requesting a doggie bag. Then we walked back through the lively French Quarter and back to our car in silence, without holding hands. We didn't stop to listen to jazz music, even at the free places. We didn't stop for beignets, even though we were right by the original Café du Monde. We simply walked in silence to the car.

Needless to say, it was a long, quiet drive home.

CHAPTER 17

I sat on our front porch and listened to the rain pouring off of the roof. Inside, Allison had decided to go back to bed for a while. Gabe and Ashleigh were putting a puzzle together. And Elizabeth, well, she was nowhere to be seen. I wasn't surprised.

I dialed her number for the third time and listened to the rings until her voice mail picked up. "Where are you?" I asked the air around me.

Suddenly, my phone rang. I answered without glancing at the caller ID. "Elizabeth?" I cried into the receiver.

"No, it's your mother."

"Oh," I replied. "Have you heard from Elizabeth?"

"I'm sorry, I haven't."

"Why does she do this, Mama?" I asked. "Why does she hurt herself and us? What could she possibly gain from all of her addictions?"

"Oh, don't be too hard on your sister, Bradley."

"I don't understand how you can say that. Look at everything she's put us all through."

"Well, son, we all do things we don't want to do. We all make decisions on the spot that are contrary to our values and convictions."

"Well, I guess you're right there, Mama."

"I know I am, Bradley. You may be the preacher, but I'm still your mama."

I couldn't help but smile. "You're right there, Mama."

"You've got your own little set of troubles, don't you?"

"Yeah," I replied. "I sure do."

"Did you steal money from the church offering?" she asked.

"No, Mama, I didn't do that, but I have made some mistakes."

"Were they things that don't fit with your character?"

"Yes, ma'am," I said, expecting her to lower the boom on me. "They sure were."

"You see," she said. "Mistakes impact us all. Take care of your own problems, but watch out for your sister as you can. She needs you more than you know. I'll be praying for you both."

"Thanks, Mama," I said. "I appreciate that."

"Why don't you try her at least once more before you give up on her and move on with the rest of your day?"

"But I'm already getting a later start than I wanted …"

"Come on, Bradley. Do it for me. Do it for your sister. With all that's going on, what difference is it going to make if you're a few minutes late?"

"Okay," I replied. "I'll try once more."

"Good boy," she replied.

When my conversation with Mama ended, I dialed my sister's number for the fourth time. To my surprise, after two rings, it was answered.

"Hello?" said a man's voice.

"Hi," I said. "I'm trying to reach Elizabeth."

"Ah," said the man. "I'm sorry, but she is indisposed at the moment."

"This is her brother. She and I were supposed to have a breakfast meeting."

"Are you the preacher?"

"Yes," I replied. "May I please speak with my sister?"

"I'm sorry," he said. "She can't talk right now."

"Any idea when she might be available?"

"No, not really. In her condition, it could be hours."

"I'm sorry, who are you?" I asked.

"Bill," he replied. "My name's Bill."

"Is Elizabeth okay?"

"She will be, in a few hours," he said. "Maybe tomorrow."

"I'd like to come get her," I said. "My mama's worried."

"Well, that's not going to be possible," he answered. "I've gotta go."

With that, he hung up. I tried calling again, twice, but Bill, whoever he was, must have placed the phone on silent or was ignoring my calls.

I leaned back in my chair and listened to the rain draining from the roof. "Take care of my sister, Lord," I prayed aloud, "for everyone's sake."

CHAPTER 18

Since my breakfast plans had changed, I arrived at the church office a few minutes early. In the middle of my desk was an invoice from Luketich Plumbing. A sticky note was attached to it with a message: "Thanks for the work, Pastor. It was an easy fix, and the smell is now gone. Let me know if it comes back."

"Well, Burt," I said aloud, "the smell may be gone from the nursery, but something sure stinks up here. And I'm going to find out what."

I set my computer bag down on top of my desk and made my way to the sanctuary. I often used early morning hours to practice my sermons, but that wasn't my intent this morning. I walked to the front center of the room and then turned and faced the communion table in front of the pulpit. Stacked on it were the four offering trays our deacons had used to receive this past week's collection. Carefully, I examined each tray, in and out.

"God," I said, "I'm not sure what I'm looking for, but help me know what it is once I find it." Carrying one of the plates, I went through the motions of the offering collection, walking down each of the aisles. Nothing looked out of place, so I walked the only hallway between the sanctuary and the church office. Nothing looked out of sorts there either.

I placed the offering plates on my desk, next to my computer bag, and did another quick examination of my office. I turned the trash can over again, just to check. Nothing. I knelt on my hands and knees and crawled to each corner, intent on searching every inch of the carpet. Nothing. I even checked my bookcase, wondering if someone could be using my own books against me, or at least against the church, while stealing money from the offering. Once again, I found nothing. After a few minutes, I just felt stupid. I leaned on my desk, picked up the offering plates, and was starting to return them to the sanctuary when I asked myself, "Is there anywhere I haven't checked?"

I looked around the room. "Well," I said to myself, "I haven't checked all of my books, but certainly people would assume that I would be searching through those for sermon preparation. I don't know where else to look—that is, unless …"

I looked down at the desk upon which I was leaning. I returned the offering plates to my desk and quickly dropped to the floor. I rolled over on my back and slid under the desk. Right there, under the middle drawer, was a piece of tape holding three paper clips. "Oh man," I said. "Someone could easily sit at my own desk, reach underneath, and hide money there using the paper clips."

I started to remove the paper clips but then decided to leave them, in case I needed to prove my case. I quickly examined the rest of the underside of the desk, finding nothing else unusual. I pulled myself out and quickly stood, maybe too quickly. I balanced myself on my desk, feeling dizzy for a moment.

"Funny," I said to myself. "This is when Earl usually shows up. I have evidence under my desk and offering plates on my desk, and I'm obviously dizzy." I listened for his footsteps but heard nothing.

I returned the offering plates to their rightful place on the communion table and was starting back when I heard my phone ringing. After checking the caller ID, I answered. "Hello, Ernie. How is Connie today?"

"She's fine, Pastor. How are you doing?"

"I'm okay," I said. "About to do some sermon preparation."

"I understand that Earl is really spreading the word about tonight's deacons' meeting."

"Well, I guess that happens."

"I'm sorry to say that my sister Shirley has attached herself to it like it's a political campaign."

"What did I ever do to Shirley?"

"I don't know, Pastor. She never seems to need much incentive, though."

"Well, I won't let it bother me today," I lied.

"I hope you know that her actions don't reflect my opinions of you," said Ernie.

"Oh, I know that," I replied.

"Good," he said.

"Hey, Ernie," I said. "Can I ask you a question about the offering?"

"Sure."

"When the deacons bring the collection into the office and go through it before dropping it into the safe, does anyone sit at my desk?"

"No one sits at your desk."

"Really?" I asked. "Where do they sit?"

"No one sits. We just bring it in, separate it into checks and cash, and drop it into the safe."

"Okay, thanks," I said.

"Why do you ask?" he said.

"I'm just wondering," I said. "This whole thing has caused me to think about the process we go through with our funds."

"Oh, okay."

"Well, I'll see you tonight, Ernie."

"See you tonight, Pastor Brad."

I ended the call and decided to work on next weekend's sermon.

A few minutes later, I closed my computer and blew out a long breath of air. "Well," I said, "that was a complete waste of time."

From my desk chair in the church office, I stared at the red spot on the wall. I remembered the joy I'd felt over throwing the pen so hard at the wall a couple of days earlier. I recalled the satisfaction I had received from personally damaging the property in a way that would always symbolize a victory to me. It had been my plan to leave the spot and to always glance at it whenever I needed a feeling of personal victory over the madness of Lee Community Church.

However, viewing it no longer made me feel victorious. Instead, it made me feel small, weak, and stupid. *What's wrong with me?* I wondered. *No matter how hard I try, I just can't stay focused. Besides, I might be fired tonight or tomorrow night. Why should I waste my time on sermon prep if there's not going to be a sermon?*

I was thankful for one thing. The exasperating texts and calls from deacon officers and concerned church members had stopped. Instead of the incessant madness, I was now left in silence to confront my own guilt, partnered with the dreadful anticipation of the upcoming deacons' meeting. It was not going to be pretty.

I blew out a long breath and closed my eyes for a moment. "Help me, Lord," I whispered. I wanted to shout it out, but I refrained in case the assistant chairman of the deacons was lurking somewhere behind a door or even under my desk. "I'm so paranoid and confused, God. I do know one thing for sure. I am sorry for what I've done. I don't even understand why I did it in the first place. Please help me."

I opened my eyes and waited for an answer from the Lord. "Please, Lord," I said. "Just tell me what to do, and I'll do it." I wasn't sure if I was expecting a burning bush, an angelic appearance, or writing on the wall, but what I received was nothing. "Maybe you can just whisper it to me, Lord. You spoke to Moses face-to-face. Elijah heard a still, small voice. Can't I at least get a whisper?"

No response.

When no verbal answer came, I blew out another long breath of air and glanced down at my desk. There, on top of the incoming mail, was the unopened letter addressed to me from Grace Church in Baton Rouge, which I had forgotten about after setting it aside on Sunday.

"Oh my, a letter from the illustrious Grace Church. I wonder what event, concert, or life-changing conference they're hosting that they want me to share with the Lee Community Church people so they can prove how much better they are than us," I said as I opened the envelope and pulled out the form letter. I quickly read the message, addressed to me.

Dear Pastor Brad:

I'm writing you this letter because I'm concerned about you. In fact, I'm concerned about all Christian pastors across southern Louisiana. We all work extra long hours caring for lots of people. Most of us serve on committees that are important but far from our own strengths and passions. We are often forced to fight off criticism from parishioners and deacon board members on a daily basis, simply for trying to follow the Lord.

I don't know about you, but I don't see anything changing soon. I am hoping to meet with a few pastors to discuss how we can deal with the ongoing pressures of life and ministry.

Would you be willing to join me and a few other pastors at 11:30 a.m. on Tuesday, October 15, for a time of prayer, fellowship, and brainstorming? Lunch will be provided, and we'll be finished by 2:00 p.m.

I hope to see you there.

Jeremy Sullivan

I had heard of Grace Church and of its energetic, successful pastor. Even though we had never met, I felt a tinge of jealousy whenever I heard his name. He and I were roughly the same age but led vastly different ministries. Jeremy Sullivan was so far removed from the realities of my life in Aucoin that I never would have even considered attending such an event—that is, until today.

I checked the date once again. "Tuesday, October 15!" I cried. "That's today!" I glanced at the clock. "It's only 9:56," I said. "I can still make it." I grabbed my keys and headed out the door. I pressed Allison's name on my phone list and hoped she wasn't still upset with me.

"Hello," said Allison, somewhat coldly. Yep, she was still angry.

"Hi," I said. "I'm headed to Baton Rouge for a few hours."

"For what?"

"I was invited to a pastors' prayer lunch at Grace Church."

"Grace Church?" she replied. "And you're really going? You don't ever go to things like that."

"Yeah, I know. But I'm not getting anything done in the office, and maybe I can get some advice."

"Do you think there will be other pastors there who have played the lottery with church money?"

I paused for a moment and let her words sink in. "I doubt it, but other pastors have made bad decisions or have also been falsely accused."

"Which one are you, Brad?"

"What?" I asked.

"Into which category do you fall? The pastors who have made bad decisions or the pastors who have been falsely accused?"

"Well," I said, "I think I currently fall into both."

Silence followed.

"So I'm headed there," I continued. "Nothing may come of it, but I'll never know unless I try."

"Okay," she replied.

"I know I've made some mistakes, Allison, but not everything that's happened is my fault."

"I know it, Brad."

"I'm glad, honey. So I'm going to this thing, okay?"

"Okay, I hope it helps you," she said.

"Thank you."

"I'll pray that it does."

"You will?"

"Yes. I'm sorry I haven't been very supportive."

"Thank you for telling me. I was beginning to think I had lost you."

"You can't lose me, Brad. I love you."

"I love you too."

"That doesn't mean I'm not disappointed, though."

"I know, Allison. I'm disappointed too."

"Do you think we're going to make it through all of this?"

"I hope so," I replied. "I really do."

Upon arriving, I didn't remember much of the drive to Baton Rouge. I thought my mind would be racing, but apparently it was just numb. It was like one moment I was stepping into my car outside Lee Community Church in Aucoin, and the next I was pulling into the parking lot of Grace Church in Baton Rouge.

Almost instantly, I regretted the decision to come. I felt completely out of my league. Grace Church had neatly manicured lawns with a large fountain surrounding its welcome sign. Inside was a café and bookstore adjacent to an extremely modern 2,500-seat worship center.

"I have no idea what I'm doing here," I said to myself as I mindlessly followed the line of well-dressed pastorly-looking men walking toward the Grace Church prayer chapel. I looked down at my pants and suddenly noticed a few wrinkles. "Fabulous," I said, wiping my hands over my pants, hoping beyond hope that my touch would magically cause the wrinkles to disappear. It didn't.

"Well, I know why you're here," said a voice behind me.

I turned and saw a casually dressed man who appeared close to my own age. "Yeah, I bet!" I exclaimed to my own surprise.

The man laughed slightly and lowered his head.

"I can't believe I actually said that out loud," I said. "I'm usually much more polite."

"Don't worry about it," he said. "A lot of pastors like us have walked through here today wondering the same thing, wondering what we're doing we're here."

"It's a good question, isn't it?" I asked.

"It's the perfect question for us to be asking," he replied.

"What do you mean?" I asked.

"Well," he said, "no matter what size church we serve, most of us constantly struggle with nagging issues that those outside of our calling never seem able to fully comprehend."

"That's true," I said, thinking he was finished.

He wasn't. "We spend our lives giving and giving to so many different people, and we're often forced to choose between pleasing our spouse and family and pleasing the chairman of the deacons."

"I know what that's like," I replied.

"At the same time," he continued, "people don't understand that pastors struggle with the same issues and temptations that people everywhere face. We struggle with family and financial issues, boredom, health and fitness, jealousy, selfish desires, and lust. We need help. We need other pastors we can confide in."

"Amen!" I cried.

"So you agree with me?"

"Absolutely! I've always wanted that kind of help," I said, "only ... well, never mind. Let's just try to enjoy this event."

"No, please tell me," he insisted. "I bet I've felt the same way at one point or the other."

"Well," I started, "for one thing, I sometimes feel like I can't really trust other pastors."

"Really?" he asked. "And why is that?"

"Well," I replied, "it seems like most pastors are gun-shy. I know I am. We've all seen pastors turn on each other or on other hurting pastors if it benefits them in some way. I want to open up to a few other pastors, but I'm desperately afraid to share my own shortcomings with them because I'm afraid they might swoop down and join the swarming vulturous deacons and committee members who are coming in for the attack."

"Wow," he said, looking down.

Ignoring him, I continued, "And heaven forbid I should make the slightest mistake! I speak one wrong word to anyone, one sermon goes slightly long, one day I'm not dressed appropriately, one small financial problem, one tiny judgment error, and boom, I'm history. It's not fair, and I hate it."

"Man," he said, "you really understand the purpose of this meeting."

"I'm sorry," I said. "I guess I shouldn't have said all of that."

"No," he replied, "you're right to have these feelings. It's a serious indictment against our vocation, against our calling, and you're absolutely right. God help us."

We followed the crowd into the prayer chapel, which looked more like a reception hall. A smiling young lady stood at the door and smiled as we approached. "Hello, Pastors," she said. "Would you please take a moment to sign in? We have some substantial giveaways following today's meeting."

"Well," said my new friend, writing his name and contact info in the registry, "I could use all of the giveaways anyone has to offer."

"I might as well do the same," I said, following suit. I usually didn't like to give out my information, but I figured since this group already had my address, it couldn't hurt.

"Did you receive a letter?" he asked.

"Yes," I answered. "I wonder what the program here is going to be like."

"I'm not sure there is a program," he answered. "Why do you ask?"

"Just wondering," I said. "Most often, I hate these pastors' events."

"Really? Why is that?"

"Oh, you know, pastors going around introducing themselves, preaching to each other, sizing each other up depending on the size of their congregations, telling the same stories to twenty-five different people, trying to be impressive."

"And you don't like that?"

I turned to my unnamed friend. He was smiling in a funny way.

"I'm just kidding," he said. "I get it. I really do."

I assumed, since I had verbally flooded the man with my issues, that he would be seeking out other pastors with whom he could network. I extended my hand and said, "It was good talking to you. I didn't tell you, but my name's Brad. Brad Johnson."

"Pastor Brad," he replied, accepting my hand and shaking it vigorously. "Can we talk more about this sometime? Not very many people are so upfront with me, and I find your openness and candor very refreshing."

"Sure," I replied, "I would welcome it."

"I didn't ask you before, and I promise I'm not trying to do anything but get to know you, but where do you serve?"

Suddenly, while sitting in the lap of what seemed like luxury to me, I was embarrassed by the size and status of my church. "Oh, I pastor a small church in Aucoin called Lee Community."

"Lee Community Church in Aucoin," he repeated. "I know right where it is."

"You do?" I asked, not really believing him.

"Yeah," he said. "My dad is actually from Kentwood, and my relatives have some property outside of Aucoin. We used to go fishing there when I was growing up."

"Small world," I said.

"Yeah, it is," he replied, handing me his business card. "I'm sorry I didn't introduce myself before. I'm Jeremy."

"Nice to meet you, Jeremy."

"I need to take care of something now," he replied, "but will you call me later this afternoon? My number's on the card."

"Certainly," I replied. "I would be happy to."

"Thanks," he said before again shaking my hand enthusiastically.

"No problem."

"Now, please excuse me," he said as he quickly walked away.

I placed his card in my pocket and glanced around for someone else with whom to converse, but I stopped suddenly. Everywhere I looked, I saw men and women who looked more exhausted than I felt.

My phone buzzed in my pocket. I pulled it out and glanced at the screen. It was a text from Elizabeth: "I'm sorry, Brad."

"I am too, sister," I said. "I am too."

"Welcome, Pastors!" someone exclaimed from the front of the prayer chapel.

I glanced up and saw that it was Jeremy, the man to whom I had just been speaking. I quickly pulled his card from my pocket and held it out to read it.

Jeremy Sullivan
Lead Pastor
Grace Church

"I hope everyone found the place okay," he joked, receiving lots of fake preacher laughs from the crowd.

Suddenly, I felt embarrassed. I had allowed myself to be extremely vulnerable with a perfect stranger who I thought was in a position similar to mine. Instead, it felt like I had just lectured the professor.

"Oh man," I said to myself as Jeremy caught my eye from the front of the room. *What am I going to do?* I thought. *He knows I'm a nobody from a small church, a church he knows, and he's probably busy thinking bad thoughts about me right now.*

"Let me encourage all of you to come find a seat near the front," said Jeremy.

As everyone followed his instructions, I knew I needed to follow suit, but something started nagging me. My stomach tightened, and I suddenly needed a drink of water. Nearby, I saw a table filled with refreshments and bottles of water, presumably meant for us. I reached for a bottle of water and managed to knock over five others. I knelt quickly to retrieve them and bumped my head on the table. "Figures," I said under my breath, before looking around to see if anyone had heard. No one seemed alarmed, so I picked up the bottles and placed them back on the table.

Forgetting about my thirst, I stood and watched the other pastors file forward. For just a moment, Jeremy caught my eye and smiled. I smiled back and started to file in behind the other pastors, but I suddenly started to panic again. I felt small, insignificant, inexperienced, and unworthy. As much as I wanted to stay and become friends with Jeremy and others, I just couldn't do it. I turned on my heels, hit the door, and never looked back.

CHAPTER 19

"I just can't seem to concentrate," I said to myself. I had spent a few hours on sermon preparation, church budgets, and children's ministry plans, but the time was practically wasted. I would have been more productive at home taking a nap.

About to go stir-crazy, I pulled out my laptop and did a Google search for Lee Community Church, Aucoin, Louisiana. I scanned through the modest number of results. Most were for funeral arrangements. Only one or two mentioned me as the officiant.

When the time for the deacons' meeting finally arrived, I sat silently in my office, staring once again at the red dot on the wall. I remembered my previous satisfaction about it and wished I could feel that way again, if only for a moment. Instead, all I felt was shame. I had damaged, ever so slightly, the church building. Now, with my actions, I felt like I had damaged the church itself too, not the building but the people.

I looked down at my desk and noticed the letter from Pastor Jeremy from Grace Church. *He must have thought I was really stupid*, I thought as I picked up the paper. *No, pitiful is a better word.* I let the letter fall from my hands to the desk below me.

"Help me, Lord," I prayed. I dropped my head to my chest, hoping He would send a floating happiness bubble over me that would pop and disintegrate into my skin and help me feel better. It didn't happen. In fact, the opposite occurred. I felt worse somehow. All I could picture was Earl hiding behind my door with a phone to his ear, reporting my every move to Archie.

Suddenly, there was a knock on the door. "Come in," I said.

The door opened slowly, and Archie Arceneaux's head appeared through the opening. "It's time, Pastor Brad," he said. "The deacons will see you now in the Dorcas Sunday school classroom."

The deacons will see me now? What is this? I wanted to say. *A business-office personnel review? A visit to a junior high assistant principal's office where I have to wait my turn to see a bunch of aging, overweight jerks led by a clueless loser and his dork cronies? Well, you go back in and tell those fat, brainless, egotistical, power-hungry warmongers that I'm not ready to see them yet!*

What I actually said was, "Thanks, Archie. I'm ready."

Archie backed up, and I followed him through the office door toward the Dorcas classroom. The deacons, and everyone else for that matter, always held their meetings in that classroom. I used to think they did so because it was a bigger room until one day my dad let it slip that the deacons had officially moved their meetings there once the ladies had spent the money from their class treasury to purchase cushions for the seats of the hard wooden chairs. This meeting change had occurred much to the chagrin of the members of the class.

"Why would the ladies care about who used the room when they weren't using it?" I once asked my mother.

"Well," she replied, "I'm sure the members of the Dorcas Sunday school class didn't take too kindly to the deacons placing their oversized derrieres on their precious cushions. Now hush up and drink your milk."

Apparently, none of these senior adult women thought it proper to be so forward as to speak to this 100 percent male deacon board about anything pertaining to their backsides, so the subject was never breached by the members of the class or by the deacon board, at least not in public.

When I was a boy, I laughed almost every time I saw or heard the name of the Dorcas Sunday school class. I knew Dorcas was a lady in the New Testament who had gone around doing good works, but it didn't make a difference to me. Anything that sounded like "dork" was all that an adolescent boy in my day required for a good laugh, especially when it referred to a group of older women who proudly bore the title.

"Archie?" I asked as we walked down the dimly lit hallway.

"Yeah?"

"If I somehow manage to make it through all of this, I think I am going to suggest that we consider changing the name of the Dorcas class. What do you think?"

"Man, you are a glutton for punishment, aren't you?" he replied.

"Well, kids have been making fun of the name for years. I know I did."

"What's wrong with the name?"

"It sounds like we're calling the ladies a bunch of dorks."

Archie grinned but didn't say anything.

"Wouldn't it be better if we called it the Tabitha class? It's another name for Dorcas."

"What do you mean?"

"Tabitha was the name of the woman before it was translated into Greek. Doesn't Tabitha sound more appropriate than Dorcas?"

"I don't think that change is going to happen," said Archie as we stopped outside the closed door of the Dorcas classroom. "The members of that class are already angry that the deacons sit on their cushions. Can you imagine what would happen if you tried to change the class name they've been using for decades? You'd be strung up."

"You're probably right."

"Besides," said Archie as he put his hand on the doorknob, "you have much bigger things to worry about right now than the name of a Sunday school class."

I nodded my head, and he opened the door, revealing a packed house of silent, oversized men. "After you," said Archie as he motioned for me to enter.

I stepped in and said, "Good evening, gentlemen."

I received a few nods and half smiles, but no verbal responses.

"Go ahead and take a seat, Pastor Brad," said Archie.

"Sure thing, Archie." I looked around and took one of the two remaining chairs in the far corner of the room next to Ernie Plaisance. Somehow, the last two days had helped me think of Ernie more as a friend and confidant than as the church treasurer. He smiled and nodded as I took my seat.

My concentration suddenly shifted as the cushion on my chair flattened out as quickly as I sat upon it, releasing a brief whishing sound. I couldn't help but think, *What's the big deal about these cushions? They aren't even comfortable.*

Archie closed the door like there were other people in the building who would want to listen in on the deacons chewing me out. "Okay," said Archie, "let's get started. I'd like to ask Earl to lead us in an opening prayer."

"I would be most honored to oblige," said Earl. "Let's pray."

I bowed my head along with the deacons and wished I could be anywhere but here. Could I possibly dream up the cruise balcony again? That would be nice as long as none of these men were there with me. Of course, even a good root canal would be more enjoyable than this meeting was about to be.

Suddenly, Earl took in a loud, deep breath and began the most dramatic prayer I had ever heard. "Most divine, heavenly Father of all there is and ever will be, we thank Thee for the opportunity to gather together tonight, in this place of ongoing religious education and sanctimonious worship, to do Thy most excellent bidding. This holy ordained deacon body will not seek rest, dear Lord, until we have sought out and discovered the truth regarding this most sinful and heinous theft from the riches of Thy storehouse. Give us discernment and guidance as we seek out and convict the culprit who wouldst have the audacity to commit thievery of the widow's mite for his own personal, evil, sinful, and possibly even lustful and perverted gain. Give us extreme clarity of our own cognitive abilities as we attempt to expel this evil wickedness from the embrace of Lee Community Church. We, as Your favored deacon body, elected by our members and ordained by You, remain forever Thy eternally faithful servants. In Thy name we pray, dear Lord of Hosts. Amen."

Man, Earl, I thought. *This is really laying it on pretty thick, even for you.*

"Amen," echoed the deacons in unison.

"Gentlemen," said Archie, "we the members of this deacon board for Lee Community Church find ourselves in a difficult situation tonight. We are not here requesting a popularity vote for Pastor Brad."

Well, that's a relief, I thought.

"Instead," continued Archie, "we are here to uncover the truth in relation to the recent happenings surrounding the financial status of our church. Everyone understand?"

Even though I was certain many did not understand, they all nodded their heads in the affirmative.

"Very good," said Archie. "I'd like for us to first hear from Pastor Brad as he shares his version of these questionable discoveries. Pastor Brad?"

"I'm sorry, what is it you want from me?" I asked.

"It's okay, Pastor," said Archie. "Just stand up and tell us what happened."

"Okay," I said, rising to my feet, suddenly nervous to see every man in the room listening intently to every word I was sharing. Behind me, I could hear a slight hissing sound as my seat cushion refilled with air. I closed my eyes tightly for a second and began.

"I understand that some in this room may not believe the words I am about to say, but I feel I must share with you that everything I'm about to say is completely true. If you would, please let me share the entire story without interrupting. I'll be happy to answer any questions you may have after I've spoken. Is this acceptable to all of you?" I glanced around the room and noticed a few, not all, of the men nodding in agreement.

Archie halfway stood and replied, "That sounds good to me, Pastor Brad."

"Thank you," I said. "I never would have thought so many issues and so much discussion would come from this, but apparently I was wrong."

"You got that right," mumbled Earl under his breath.

I glanced at Earl but decided not to dignify his interruption with a response. Briefly, I told the deacons about how I had found the $100 bill on the floor of the office, how I had texted Ernie, and how I had decided to keep the cash with me instead of leaving it somewhere in the office.

"So," interrupted Jimmy Rice, "how did Ernie find out that you had stolen the money?"

"Well," I replied, "I wasn't quite finished yet, but I don't believe it's correct to say that I stole the money. I found it and tried to report it missing. I couldn't put it in the safe because I didn't have the combination."

"Why not?" asked Jimmy.

"Our church has a policy against me having the combination," I answered.

"If I may interject," said Earl, looking to Archie.

"Okay, Earl," said Archie, "but make it quick. Pastor Brad wasn't yet finished."

"Certainly," said Earl, beaming with pride. "Regarding the issue of our pastor not having the combination to the church safe, I took the liberty of discovering why that decision was made." Earl took a long dramatic pause and looked around the room.

"Why don't you enlighten us, Earl?" asked Archie.

"Absolutely," said Earl. "Apparently, the finance and personnel committee thought that it was the best decision for everyone involved to withhold the combination from Pastor Brad, especially considering his previous indiscretions when given access to cash money here at Lee Community Church."

"Actually," I said, "I agree that it is best for me to not have the combination to the safe."

"Why is that?" asked Jimmy.

"Because he's a thief!" shouted Earl. "He has a guilty conscience."

"Earl, that's a little harsh," said Archie. "Please continue, Pastor Brad."

I took a deep breath and said, "When I started serving here, I agreed with the policy of the personnel committee that I not know the combination to the safe, so that I could never be accused of theft."

"And," said Earl, "because of your previous financial indiscretions!"

"Okay, Earl," I said, "if we're going to play it that way, and if you're not going to let me finish, I'd like to know to which indiscretions you are referring."

"Oh," said Jimmy, "so there's more than one!"

"Of course not!" I said. "There's not even one! I don't even know what Earl's talking about!"

"Now, Pastor Brad," said Archie, "there's no need for you to get defensive here. We're just sharing information at this point."

"Thank you, Archie," said Earl. "To answer the question at hand, Pastor Brad admitted to stealing church funds when he was a member of the Christian Boys' Club."

"Is this true?" asked Jimmy.

"Yes, Jimmy," I answered, staring coldly at Earl.

"And there you have it!" cried Earl. "A full confession!"

"It most certainly wasn't anything of the sort," I said. "I was eight years old at the time."

"Oh, I remember that now," said Jimmy. "Your dad made you apologize to the entire church on Sunday morning."

"Yes," I replied, looking down at my shoes. "It was a wonderful learning experience for me."

"Obviously, you didn't learn enough," said Earl.

Jimmy continued, "And after your confession, didn't he take you out back and whip you good with his belt?"

"Yes, Jimmy, he did," I sighed, "except that took place before I confessed to the congregation. Thank you for sharing."

"If I remember correctly, all of the deacons came out to watch—you know, to make sure justice was served."

"Come on, Jimmy!" I said. "Isn't that enough?"

"Just trying to get all of the important facts out to the deacons," said Jimmy with a smirk. "You know they need to be able make an informed decision."

"How many licks did he give him?" asked Earl.

"Goodness gracious!" cried Ernie. "I think we've heard enough about the spanking Pastor Brad received when he was a child. That doesn't have anything to do with this conversation."

"Too bad we can't do that now," remarked Jimmy, leading to chuckles from most of the deacon board. "Because swift punishment would certainly be deserved in this case."

"Can we please get back to the business at hand?" asked Archie. "If we don't, we could be here all night."

"Archie's right," said Ernie. "Let Pastor Brad finish his story."

After a brief moment, the snickering finally ceased. Archie nodded at me and said, "Go ahead, Pastor. Finish your story."

"Well," I said, "there's not much else to tell. I couldn't get into the safe, and I didn't want to disturb Ernie in his time of trouble, so I kept the hundred dollars until I met with Ernie to count the offering money on Monday afternoon. I told him the story and returned the hundred-dollar bill to him at that time." I glanced at Archie.

"Is that all you have to say?" he asked.

"I suppose it is," I replied.

"Well," he said, visually surveying the deacon board, "any questions?"

"This seems pretty cut-and-dried to me," said Ernie. "Pastor Brad found one hundred dollars on Sunday and turned it in on Monday. He tried to communicate it to me, but I, of course, was unable to receive his communication because of Connie's condition following our accident."

"So," said Archie, "Pastor Brad did try to contact you on Sunday?"

"Yes," said Ernie. "He texted me while he was still at church."

"Did you text or call him back?" asked Archie.

"I didn't call him back until about an hour or so after I received the text."

"Did he tell you about the money then?" blurted out Earl.

Ernie tightened his lips and then answered, "Well, no, he didn't."

I suddenly sneezed and looked down at the floor as I wiped my nose with a Kleenex I had taken from the Dorcas class stash.

"Well, there you have it!" cried Earl. "The preacher should have told you right then and there about the money."

I glanced up at Earl and found his finger pointed at me.

"Why didn't you tell him about the money?" asked Earl. "Is it because you had decided to keep it?"

"Absolutely not," I answered.

"Then why?" cried out Earl, slapping his own leg with his right hand. "Why didn't you tell him?"

"Good grief, Earl!" snapped Ernie. "Pastor Brad was ministering to me. Connie was very possibly about to have brain surgery, and I thought I was about to lose her. I told Pastor Brad to just wait on telling me whatever he needed to tell me because I was afraid my wife was about to die! He agreed, left his Sunday dinner with his family, and rushed to my side in McComb."

"He was probably glad to leave his family dinner," said Deacon Wilson Day. "I heard he was fighting with his mama about his sister Elizabeth again."

"I heard that too," said Jimmy Rice. "It's not fitting for us to have a pastor who sasses his mother."

"See?" said Earl. "He doesn't even abide by the Ten Commandments."

"Earl," I said, "can you please—"

"Honor thy father and thy mother that thy days may be long upon the land."

"His days aren't going to be long around this church, at least," said Jimmy.

I dropped my head into my hands.

"Gentlemen," said Ernie, "we're not here to discuss Pastor Brad's family relationships."

"Thank you," I said.

"Maybe we should," said Jimmy. "They're all kind of unusual if you ask me."

I looked up at Jimmy. "I'm not sure what you mean."

"Well," said Jimmy, "we all know you're sweet on Sally Mae Watson."

"That's not true!" I said.

"Well, she's certainly sweet on you!" said Jimmy.

Archie held his hands out, calling for silence. "I think Ernie's right, fellas. If we want to talk about Pastor Brad and his mama fighting over his sister, over milk, or anything else, we need to call another meeting."

"Thanks, Archie," said Ernie. "May I continue?"

"Please do," said Archie.

Ernie stood up and held his hands out in front of him. "Men, during my crisis, Pastor Brad came to my side and waited with me at the hospital. I wasn't going to bring this up, but I have to say that not one person on this deacon board did the same. In fact, no one even called me to ask about Connie or our accident."

The room grew quiet as conviction settled in.

Ernie continued, "But Pastor Brad dropped everything and drove straight to the hospital. He did this right after I cast the deciding vote about the placement of the offering in the worship service. This deacon body had not treated him fairly, and I had not treated him fairly, but he didn't let it hold him back. He was totally unselfish about everything, and I for one am very grateful to him. As far as I'm concerned, he did the right thing by not leaving cash on the floor of the church office, and he turned in the exact amount the next day when he met with me to count the offering. I don't think anything worth all of this fussing has happened. Can't we just drop it and try for once to move forward as a church?"

"I think Ernie's right," said Archie. "I don't think there's any need for us to continue this discussion."

"Thank you, Archie," I replied.

Archie smiled briefly before saying, "Before we adjourn, are there any other questions?"

"Just one," said Earl.

"What is it, Earl?" asked Archie.

"I just want to know if Pastor Brad returned the exact one-hundred-dollar bill he found on the floor of the office."

All eyes turned to me.

"Now that's a good question," said Jimmy.

"What difference does that make?" said Ernie. "He found one hundred dollars and returned one hundred dollars to me."

Earl smiled without showing his teeth. "I know it may seem like a trivial matter to some of you, but I for one think we need to know if our pastor is trustworthy enough to hold on to a bill of that size without spending some of it."

"Okay," said Archie. "How many on our deacon board would like to know the answer to that question?"

Every deacon in the room raised his hand with the exception of Ernie. Earl Bishop raised both of his hands.

"Well, Pastor Brad, what do you have to say?"

"No," I said.

"What do you mean, 'no'?" asked Archie.

I took a deep breath and answered, "I mean *no*, the hundred-dollar bill I returned was not the original hundred dollars I found on the church office floor."

"And there you have it!" cried Earl. "He's been stealing money from the church!"

"I have not!" I cried. "And what difference does it make if it was the same hundred-dollar bill? I found one hundred dollars, and I returned one hundred dollars. End of story."

"If only that were the case," snapped Earl. "You've been hiding money in the church office from the offering and sneaking back in later to get it."

"What are you talking about?" asked Jimmy.

Earl pointed at me and said, "Our beloved pastor confessed to Ernie about finding the money only after Ernie found more cash hidden between the safe and the wall."

"Now, Earl," said Ernie, "that's not exactly how it happened."

"Are you certain?" asked Earl.

"Yes," said Ernie, "I am."

"But you didn't learn about the hundred dollars until after you found the other money, right?"

Ernie rolled his eyes and shook his head.

"Ernie," said Archie, "we all know you appreciate Pastor Brad's ministry, but you need to answer the question."

Ernie looked at Earl and said, "Yes, you should know, Earl. You were there."

Earl grinned wide and replied, "Yes, I was there, wasn't I? Which means that I also saw what appeared to be cash in excess of a thousand dollars in Pastor Brad's wallet. Do you all think it's a coincidence that he shows up with a lot of extra cash in his wallet the minute hidden money is found in the very office where he has a desk?"

The room grew silent. The deacons glanced at each other, waiting for the inevitable to come.

"Archie?" asked Jimmy. "Can I please make a motion?"

Archie turned and looked at me but answered, "Yes, Jimmy. What is it?"

"I make a motion that the deacons call a special church-wide business meeting tomorrow evening in order to present our findings about Pastor Brad's recent actions and ask for a vote."

"What type of vote?" asked Archie.

Jimmy looked at Earl, who nodded his head slightly. "Why," said Jimmy, "a vote of confidence."

"Do I hear a second to the motion?" asked Archie.

"Second," said Earl.

"All in favor?"

Every right hand lifted except for Ernie's.

"Motion carried," said Archie. "I guess we're meeting back here tomorrow evening. Everyone, please help us spread the word."

"No problem," said Earl. Spreading the word was something Earl was really good at.

CHAPTER 20

Ironically enough, because of my pastoral responsibility, I had to wait for everyone to leave the building before I could lock up. However, I just couldn't stand the thought of discussing fishing, sports, or the weather with this group of men who seemed so intent on firing me. I quietly made my way to the church office and sat behind my desk.

I stared up once again at the red dot. "Well, little dot," I said, "it looks like you might outlive me here at Lee Community."

Suddenly, I heard the faint buzzing sound of my phone. I had placed it on silent mode because of the deacons' meeting. I looked at my screen. "A 225 number?" I said aloud. "I wonder who this could be." Not having anything else to do, I answered. "Hello," I said. "This is Brad."

"Hello, man of God," said the voice on the other end.

"Excuse me?" I asked.

"This is Jeremy from Grace Church. I met you earlier today outside the chapel."

"Oh yeah," I said. "I remember. Is everything okay?"

"Yeah, it's great," he said. "I had hoped to talk to you more after our main session, but I couldn't find you."

"Sorry about that. I'm having a really difficult week, and I had to leave early."

"You left really early, didn't you?"

"Well, yeah, like I said, I'm having a difficult week."

"I understand," said Jeremy.

"Thank you for calling, though," I said. "I'd probably better—"

"Hold on for a moment if you would, man of God," he said.

"Why do you keep calling me that?"

"Because that's what you are," he said. "You are God's man at Lee Community in Aucoin."

"Probably not for long," I responded.

"What's going on?" he asked.

"Oh, you wouldn't believe me if I told you."

"You might be surprised," he replied. "I've heard and seen quite a few things in ministry."

That's when I hesitated. I didn't want to tell him. I didn't want to confess that I'd done wrong when I'd had the opportunity to do right. I didn't know what to do.

"Why don't you tell me?" he said. "It might help you feel better."

I closed my eyes and rubbed them slightly. "Why not?" I said, checking to make sure no one was listening from behind the door. "Why not?"

In one fell swoop, I gave him the five-minute rundown of everything that had happened, including my findings in my office.

"Wow," he said when I had finally finished. "That's quite a story."

"You're probably sorry you called me, aren't you?"

"Not at all," he said. "I'm glad I did."

"So what do you think I should do?" I asked.

"Well," he said, "I think you need to pray and ask friends like me to pray for you."

"Is that what we are?" I asked. "Friends?"

"Hey, man," he replied, "if pastors can't stand with each other and be friends, then the world is doomed."

"I guess so," I said, taking it all in for a moment. "Thank you."

"You're welcome," he said. "By the way, I'm really calling to let you know that you won one of the door prizes today. I'd like to bring it to you sometime."

"You know what?" I replied. "You keep it. Your encouragement to me means more than any gift I could receive."

"Are you sure?" he said. "You don't even know what it is."

"Absolutely," I replied. "I hope to talk to you again soon."

"I guarantee it," he said. "I really do."

"See you later, Pastor Jeremy."

"You too, Pastor Brad."

I ended the call just in time to hear footsteps heading toward the church office. Within seconds, Archie and Earl stepped into the office. Archie appeared gentle and unassuming. Earl, as usual, had a pious air about him.

"Pastor Brad?" said Archie.

"Yes, Archie."

"In light of the circumstances, the deacon body thinks it's best if you aren't here in the office by yourself until after this is all settled."

"We're going to search this office high and low and see if we can find any more stolen money!" said Earl. "That is, unless you just want to confess and show us where you've hidden it."

I sighed heavily and replied, "Well, I'd be happy to stay out of the office until after the business meeting. You can feel free to search all you like. I'd be as surprised as you if you find anything. I don't know anything about any stolen money."

"What will you do tomorrow?" asked Archie.

"I don't know," I said. "I suppose I'll spend some time praying. I might go out and do some visiting as well."

"What do you mean, you'll do some visiting?" cried Earl. "Are you trying to dig up supporters? 'Cause you won't find any if you do."

"Well, Earl," I said, "thank you for that vote of confidence, but that's not what I meant at all."

Earl scrunched his mouth together but didn't say anything else.

"What are you doing now?" asked Archie. "After a meeting like that, I figured you'd be heading home."

"I'm waiting for everyone to leave," I said with a smile.

"Why?" asked Earl. "Are you planning to dig up the rest of the stolen money?"

"No," I said. "It's part of my job to lock up."

"Well," said Archie, "under the circumstances, I think it's best if you go on home. Earl and I will lock up."

"Okay," I said as I stood and gathered my things. "I understand."

Archie and Earl stood awkwardly and watched my every move.

"Got everything?" asked Earl.

"Yes," I replied as I lifted my computer strap to my shoulder. "I believe I do."

"What are you going to tell the people tomorrow night?" asked Archie.

"I don't know, Archie," I answered as I walked toward the door. "I really don't know."

CHAPTER 21

I drove toward home in a completely confused and utterly defeated state. Aucoin seemed so peaceful in the evening hours when all you could see were the houses, trees, and landscaping. It practically reeked of wholesomeness. However, if you threw in a bunch of overweight, uptight deacons with sore rear ends who were angry from sitting on flat cushions, you got a completely different scenario. Then toss in the topic of church financial issues, and you had an absolute nightmare.

Humorist Dave Barry once wrote, "If you had to identify, in one word, the reason why the human race has not achieved, and never will achieve, its full potential, that word would be 'meetings.'" If I were a gambling man, beyond the lottery ticket I'd purchased, I'd bet that Dave Barry had never attended a church deacons' meeting at Lee Community. If he had, he would have intensified his statement dramatically—that is, if he didn't run away screaming first.

In my moment of desperation, I prayed, "God, I need Your help. I'm about to lose my ministry at Lee Community and my whole life here in Aucoin. They were so angry tonight, Lord, and they don't even know about the lottery ticket. Please let me know what I should do. I don't usually ask for things like this, but please, please send me some kind of sign."

As if on cue, my low-fuel light began flashing on my dashboard.

"Well, God," I said, "that's not exactly the type of sign I was looking for. I was hoping for something a bit more positive, but I suppose it's better than nothing."

Ahead, I noticed the One Stop Shop was still open, so I slowed the car, signaled my turn, and finally parked by pump 1. I pulled out my church credit card, inserted it into the gas pump, and waited for the prompts. I punched in my zip code and waited for approval. Instead of instructions about choosing my pump, the words "Purchase Denied" popped up on my screen.

"What's up with this?" I asked the air around me. I held the card tightly and walked into the store, surprised to see Sally Mae behind the register.

"Well," she said, "look at what the cat dragged in!"

"Hi, Sally Mae," I replied, trying to sound friendly. "How are you tonight?"

"Well, I'm right as rain, Pastor Brad," she replied. "But I was watching you closely, and you seem to be having some trouble out there at the pump."

"You can see the pumps from in here?" I asked.

"Oh yes," she answered with a deeper voice. "I've got hidden cameras outside, so I can see everything that happens out there."

"Uh, okay," I said awkwardly. "So you saw me having a difficult time with the pump."

"Yes, Brad," she said softly, looking me up and down. "I did notice. In fact, I noticed a lot more than that."

"Excuse me?" I asked.

"Like I said, with my hidden cameras, I can see everything that happens out there."

"Okay, well …"

"Everything," she repeated with a wink.

"Okay, uh, did your card machine ever get fixed? Because my card wouldn't work at the pump."

"Let me see your card," said Sally Mae, holding out her hand.

I handed her the card, which she took slowly, touching my hand a little too much in the process.

"Well, Bradley," she said while reaching beneath the counter, "our card machine is working just fine and dandy, but right now this card is no good at this store, or any other store for that matter."

"What do you mean?" I asked.

"I don't know how to tell you this, Pastor, so I'll just show you."

"What are you talking about, Sally Mae?"

At that moment, she pulled a pair of scissors from beneath the counter and cut my church credit card in two.

"What are you doing?" I cried.

"Sorry, Brad," she said. "But I got a call from Earl Bishop instructing me to do that if you stopped by. It seems your church credit card has been suspended."

"What?"

"He said you could no longer be trusted with anything connected to the finances of Lee Community Church."

"But why would you do what he said?"

"Well, Brad, you're cute and all, but he is the assistant chairman of the deacons."

"Oh man," I sighed, dropping my head into my right hand.

"You never should have stolen that money, Brad."

"What? How did you—"

"Oh," she said with a smile, "it's all over town about how you stole a hundred dollars from the church collection plate this past weekend and how you've probably been stealing money for the last six months."

I looked up at Sally Mae, who was suddenly no longer behind the counter but was standing in front of the Little Debbie display, about six feet away from me.

"I didn't steal anything," I said. "I found that money on the floor and was holding on to it until I saw Ernie the next day."

She took a step closer, winked once again, and said, "I believe you, Brad."

"Thank you, Sally Mae," I said. "However, I'm afraid no one else will."

"And don't you worry," she said, stepping closer to me once again.

"What are you talking about?" I asked, taking a half step back. "Don't worry about what?"

"You know what I'm saying." She smiled as she walked to the end of the candy aisle. "Don't you worry about us."

"What do you mean, 'us'?" I asked. "There's no us."

Sally Mae faced me once again. Her smile had turned to an evil grin, and her eyes looked like those of a cat about to pounce. "We don't have to hide anymore," she whispered.

"Hide what from who?" I asked. "We don't have anything to hide."

I didn't remember Sally Mae running track in high school, but she ran to me faster than any runner I'd ever seen. Before I could withdraw, she threw her arms around me and started kissing my cheek and forehead. I tried to pull away, but she pushed me against the counter.

"Oh, Brad," she slobbered. "I've been wanting to do this for so long."

"What are you doing, Sally Mae?" I cried.

"Come on," she howled. "I know you feel it deep inside just like I do. Pretty soon, you won't be a pastor anymore, and we can tell the world about our love!"

"Let me go!" I cried while pulling her face away from mine. "We don't have any love!"

"Oh, but we will, lover boy! We will! And you can take that to the bank. Now kiss me like you've never kissed anyone before!"

Her lips began stretching toward mine, so I turned my face away.

"No!" I said, finally able to push her away. "I'm a happily married man."

"You might be married," she said, "but I can tell you ain't happy. I can see it in your eyes when you look at me."

"I don't know what you're talking about," I said, "but I am very faithful to my wife."

"But you don't really want to be, do you?"

"Yes, I do, Sally Mae."

"Say it again."

"I am very faithful to—"

"Not that part," she said.

"I don't know what you're talking about."

"Say my name again, Brad."

"Look, Sally Mae, I—"

"Ooooo! Say it again. It sends chills up and down my spine."

"Stop coming on to me!" I said. "It's not going to work."

"Oh, I think it will, Brad, and I never lie in the presence of a holy man."

I slipped away from her and ran to the other side of the counter. However, she was close behind me and now had me trapped.

"I'm a married man," I cried, "and a pastor at that. You can't do this!"

"Oh yes, I can," she said, taking a giant step toward me.

"I'm very much in love with my wife!"

She took another giant step. "What's love got to do with it?" she said before jumping on me. Instantly, she started kissing my face once again.

I grabbed her shoulders, trying to push her away, and yelled out, "Stop it, please!"

"Oh, Brad!" she cried. "I love it when a handsome man is forceful with me."

I was about to shove her away again when she jumped in the air and wrapped her legs around my waist.

"Ahh!" I screamed, falling back into the counter.

"Leave Allison and come live with me!" she demanded. "I'll make you happy!"

"No!" I screamed. "I'm putting you down now."

Sally Mae tried to kiss me on my lips, but I pushed her away, causing us both to almost fall. I did some fancy footwork, barely keeping us both from toppling over.

"You need to get down now," I said. "I don't want to have to drop you."

"I don't want to get down!" she yelled.

Thinking I had no choice, I tried to drop her by throwing both arms out straight. Instead of falling, Sally Mae held on with her legs and took the opportunity to plant a huge smooch right on my mouth.

I tried to push her away, but her grip on me was tight. To make matters worse, the front door to the One Stop opened, and in stepped Earl and Archie.

Sally Mae removed her mouth from mine, but it was too late. Archie and Earl had already taken in the entire scene.

"Well, well, well," said Earl. "This gives the One Stop Shop a whole new meaning."

"Oh man," I sighed, lowering Sally Mae off of me and onto the floor.

Sally Mae fixed her hair, turned immediately to the men, and said, "Now how can I help you, gentlemen? We've got chocolate pie tonight. It's sinfully delicious."

"I bet it is, Sally Mae," said Archie. "I bet it is."

The long awkward pause that followed was horrific. When I could take it no longer, I took a deep breath, blew it out, and said, "I'm sure Allison is expecting me at home. Won't you all please excuse me?"

I was halfway through the door when I heard Earl say, "You didn't seem too worried about your dear wife's expectations when we walked in here."

I turned around slowly and stared at Earl.

He grinned an evil grin. "You got something to say, Preacher?" he asked.

"Now, fellas," said Sally Mae. "What you saw wasn't at all what it looked like. I forced myself on Pastor Brad, and that's all there is to it. He's a cutie, and I couldn't help myself. Now let's all forget it and have some chocolate pie, on the house."

"No, thank you, Sally Mae," said Earl. "But our friend the preacher here might want an extra slice."

Archie and Sally Mae looked up at me still standing there, staring angrily at Earl.

"What do you say, Pastor Brad?" asked Earl. "You want some pie?"

I sniffed and looked down at the floor. I'd had no idea how quickly all of this would escalate into such chaos.

"What's wrong, Preacher?" asked Earl. "Cat got your tongue?"

I regained my composure and stared back at him. "I don't want any pie," I said.

"Really?" asked Earl. "No pie? Well, I guess you've had your fill already."

Without another word, I turned and walked through the door to my car. I quickened my step when I felt a drop of rain on my face. I was reaching to wipe it away when the door to the One Stop Shop opened and Sally Mae stepped out.

"Brad!" she cried.

I opened my car door and looked her way but said nothing.

"I'm sorry!" she said. "It was my fault, what happened inside."

"Yes," I said matter-of-factly. "It most certainly was."

"Will you forgive me?"

"Sally Mae, you need to know that I am very much in love with my wife. I don't want to sneak around and mess around with you or anyone else."

"I understand, Pastor Brad. It won't happen again."

Suddenly, I was Pastor Brad again to her. I liked that. "Good."

"Will you forgive me?" she repeated.

I smiled. "I'm a man of God, Sally Mae. Forgiveness is what I do."

"Good," she replied.

"And Sally Mae?"

"Yeah?"

"Allison is the one you should be worried about."

"Oh my!" she said. "I didn't think about that."

"I figured as much. See you later."

"What about your gas?" she asked.

"I'll just have to wait until tomorrow," I said. I glanced at the low-fuel light, glaring at me, mocking me. "It's just going to have to wait," I said. "There's no way I'm going back in there with those two tonight." I stepped into my car and drove away, leaving Sally Mae standing in the misty rain.

Three miles down the road, my car sputtered. "Uh-oh," I said. "That doesn't sound good." It sputtered a second time, and I glanced once again at my fuel gauge: below empty. "I don't believe it," I said. "I'm going to have to go back to the One Stop."

I pulled the car to the shoulder, made sure no one was coming, and then attempted a U-turn on the highway. My car was still sputtering, but it made the turn okay—that is, until I went slightly off the shoulder as my turn was almost complete. The ground was level, so I didn't think there would be a problem. Once my car was safely back on the road, I began to slowly sputter back toward the One Stop, until my car started wobbling. "Now what, Lord?" I cried. "Haven't I gone through enough today?"

I managed to pull my sputtering, wobbling car to the shoulder before the engine completely stopped. I placed my head on the steering wheel and closed my eyes. "Well, this might as well happen."

CHAPTER 22

I once heard it said that expecting the worst is the highest point of anxiety. As I fell limply back into my seat and closed my eyes, I exemplified that quote to the fullest degree.

"I don't believe this!" I blurted out. "This evening is going from bad to worse."

I pumped the gas pedal and turned my key once again, hoping and praying for the car to start. It didn't. I tried a third time, closing my eyes, hoping to increase my faith and in turn cause the fuel in my tank to multiply. Nothing.

I reached for my phone and clicked on Allison's name. It rang twice before she answered.

"Brad?" she asked. "Are you okay?"

"No, I'm not," I replied. "Not at all, honey."

"I was afraid it went badly. I expected you home by now."

"I expected the same."

"How was the meeting?"

"It wasn't good," I said, grimacing.

"I'm sorry," she said.

"Thanks. It's worse now."

"What do you mean?"

"I ran out of gas, and I think I may have a flat tire. I'm on the side of the road, and I need some help."

"What?" she asked. "Where are you?"

"I'm about two miles your side of the One Stop. I was wondering if you could find the gas can and bring it to me. If your sister's still there, she can watch Gabe."

"I can do that. Are you going to be okay?"

"Oh, babe, this has been the worst night of my life. That's all I can say right now."

"Why didn't you just stop and get some gas on your way home?" she asked. "You must have gone right by the One Stop."

"Well, it's a long story," I replied, "but I did stop by there. But I had to leave quickly without pumping any gas."

"Why would you leave without getting gas?"

"I need to tell you when I get home, Allison."

No response.

"Allison?" I asked.

No response.

"Allison, are you there?"

I glanced at my phone's black screen. Dead. "Great," I said aloud.

I quickly stepped out of the car, closed my door, and ran into the light foggy mist to check all of my tires. Sure enough, the front passenger tire was flat. Looking closely, I could see the nail protruding from the rubber.

"Fantastic," I said, turning back to pop the trunk so I could change the tire. Right before I opened the driver's door, I heard the automatic door lock. "Oh no," I said. "My keys are still in the ignition. Please, oh please, no!"

I tried the driver's door. It was locked. I checked all of the doors. They were all locked. "No, no, no!" I yelled. "I am so stupid!"

I looked up at the sky and imagined the angelic hosts of heaven pointing down at me and laughing. I looked down and imagined the same from Satan and all of his demonic followers. In defeat, I slumped down to the ground and leaned against my car. I breathed in slowly through my nose and breathed out even slower from my mouth. "How could this evening get any worse?"

Suddenly, thunder crashed, lightning flashed, and the foggy mist turned into a downpour. "Well," I said, "ask a stupid question …"

When I was growing up and had gone through a bad day, my mother used to bring me cookies and milk and read to me from a book called *Alexander and the Terrible, Horrible, No Good, Very Bad Day*. At the time, it always brought me comfort. Now I realized that Alexander didn't know squat about bad days.

Not knowing what else to do, I turned toward home and started walking. "You know, God," I started to pray, "this just isn't right. I know I shouldn't have spent money from that hundred dollars I found. It honestly goes against everything I know is right. I can't say that I didn't mean it because I did. There were all sorts of opportunities for me to do the right thing, but I chose what was easiest because I was frustrated, and I wanted to save face with my mother. It didn't matter, though, because we ended up arguing anyway."

As I continued to walk, I could feel my socks getting more saturated with every step. "Lord," I continued, "you know I didn't have anything to do with how that money came to be on the floor in the first place or how the other money hidden in the office came to be where it was. Could you just reveal that mystery to me? It would make my life so much simpler if you would."

As if on cue, a thunderclap roared. I felt it in my chest, like a subwoofer at a rap concert.

"I know, I know," I said. "I shouldn't have spent any of it in the first place, but Billy Ray and Melissa needed to get to the hospital to have their baby. Then it was just so much easier to spend more because I had already spent some."

Lightning flashed, and I could sense God's disapproval at my bargaining techniques. I knew I needed to kick it up a notch, or I might not survive this prayer. "Lord, I know I did buy that scratch-off lottery ticket with change leftover from the church's money, and I did win, but I think that's really a different issue altogether, don't You?"

Thunder boomed, shaking the car before me and causing me to jump. "Okay, God, please don't let me die out here. I honestly don't even know what was happening with that whole Sally Mae thing. If I caused that or somehow led her on, Lord, I'm sorry. I love my wife."

About that time, I heard a vehicle coming from behind. I turned quickly and raised my hand, hoping for a ride. That's when I realized it was an eighteen-wheeler headed straight for me at full speed. I quickly ran to the shoulder and stepped into the grass at the top of the ditch. The huge truck flashed by me, throwing wind and rain my way, causing me to turn away quickly. When I did, I stepped into a small hole, lost my balance and my footing, and fell hard on my side. From there, I rolled sideways to the bottom of the ditch, into a stream of muddy water.

"Oh God," I muttered as I pushed my face up from the filth. I flipped over and sat down in the middle of the stream. "I'm about to lose my ministry, the church where You placed me. Allison probably won't leave me if she hears about Sally Mae, but she's going to be really mad. And now I'm drenched in mud."

After a moment of wallowing in self-pity, I stood and managed to crawl up the ditch to the shoulder of the highway. Not seeing any traffic, I turned toward home and started walking again. "I've messed everything up, God. I haven't responded well to Earl through this whole thing. He really is a mean, conniving, stupid jerk. Why do you put with him?"

Thunder clapped once again.

"I know I should love him, Lord, but he really makes it hard. He was right about one thing, though. I'm a bad preacher, or at least a really bad pastor."

I felt miserable when I looked down at myself. My clothes were sopping with a mucky mess, but I had no choice. I kept walking forward in the rain, which to my relief finally appeared to be letting up a bit. When I had walked at least a mile, I saw headlights, the first I had seen since the eighteen-wheeler. As it drew close, I could tell it was Allison's car. "Thank You, Lord," I prayed. "Thank You for such a caring wife."

The car pulled over to the shoulder, and through a foggy windshield I could see her arm waving me in. I ran to the passenger door, opened it, and stepped in as swiftly as possible. "Oh," I cried, "thank you for coming. I love you so much!"

"I love you too, Brad," said a voice that was not my wife's. "Wow! You're really wet and muddy."

To my surprise, my sister-in-law Ashleigh was sitting in the driver's seat, smiling at me. "So where are we going?" she asked.

"What's going on?" I asked. "Where's Allison?"

"So this is the thanks I get for picking you up off the side of the road in the middle of a rainstorm?"

I swallowed hard and said, "I'm sorry, Ashleigh. Thank you for your help."

"You're welcome," she replied. "I'm always happy to help."

"Where's Allison?" I repeated.

"She's at home with Gabe and Elizabeth."

"Elizabeth is there?"

"Yeah," she replied. "She's been there all night."

"Well, that's just great," I said.

"I can drop you back off at your car and go back and get Allison if you want."

"No, that's okay," I said.

"So where are we going?" she asked.

"Did you bring the spare key to my car?"

"I don't know," said Ashleigh. "Is it on Allison's keys?"

"Yes, it is," I said.

"Then I've got it," she replied.

"Gas can?"

"In the trunk."

"Well," I said, "I guess we're going to the One Stop."

"Okay," she replied as she pulled back onto the road slowly.

"Thanks again for coming," I said.

"No problem," she replied. "How have you been?"

"Just a little stressed, as you can probably tell."

"Obviously," she replied.

"When we get to the One Stop, can you go inside and pay while I pump the gas? I'll give you the money."

"Sure," she answered. "What's up?"

"Nothing really," I replied.

"Then what's the big deal?"

"Well," I stammered, "I just recently discovered that the lady who works there has a crush on me—a really big crush."

"And you'd like to make sure that she doesn't see you?"

"Something like that."

"Don't worry," she said. "I'll cover for you."

"Thank you."

"You're welcome. You know, it must be hard for you to fill up if she works there and this is the only place in town. How long have you been having to sneak around like this?"

"Well," I said, "it's a rather recent development."
"Does my sister know?"
"Ah, not as of yet."
"I see," she replied. "Are you going to tell her?"
"Yeah. It just happened a few minutes ago."
"Can I ask one question?"
"Sure."
"This One Stop girl, what is her name?"
"Sally Mae."
"Okay, this Sally Mae, is she covered with mud too?"

CHAPTER 23

When Ashleigh and I arrived at the One Stop Shop, there were no signs of Archie or Earl, at least none from the pump. I thought it best to remain unseen, so while Ashleigh ran inside to pay for the fuel and to check out the girl who was hitting on her sister's husband, I leaned back in the passenger seat of the car, hoping beyond hope that no one would see me.

Our plan seemed to be working well until Ashleigh walked back out to the car with Sally Mae behind her. Both of them were smiling.

I stepped quickly from the car. I wasn't smiling. "What are you doing, Ashleigh? You weren't supposed to tell anyone I was here."

"What are you doing?" she repeated. "I didn't say anything. We were just talking."

"Hi, Brad," said Sally Mae. "Boy, you're really messy."

"Yeah," I answered. "My car ran out of gas a couple of miles down the road. I slipped and fell into the ditch."

"If you would've pumped some gas before, none of this would've happened."

"You're right, Sally Mae," I said. "I just didn't want to run into Archie or Earl again. I've had enough of dealing with them for one night."

"They're still here if you want to see them."

"What? What do you mean?"

"They've been inside asking me questions since you left. I think they wanted to see if you would come back."

"And so you have," said Earl, stepping out from the One Stop with Archie right behind him.

"Pastor Brad," said Archie, "it looks like you need a shower."

"My car ran out of gas," I said. "I slipped in the mud."

"Looks like you've slipped in a lot more than that," said Earl. "You've really got a lot of nerve coming back here after your kissing incident with Sally Mae."

"Okay, guys," said Ashleigh. "That's enough picking on Brad for tonight. He's had a rough day."

"She's right," said Archie, patting Earl on the shoulder. "Let's go."

"Okay," said Earl, glancing first at me, then at Sally Mae, then at Ashleigh. "Too much going on here for me anyway."

"Come on, Earl," said Archie once again before the two of them stepped into Archie's Ford F-150 and drove out of sight.

"What do you suppose he meant by that?" asked Ashleigh.

"Never mind," I said. "Let's just get some gas and get out of here." I grabbed the gas can and started to fill it with gas.

"It's set for five dollars' worth," said Sally Mae.

"Thank you," I said without looking up.

Sally Mae took a step closer to me. "Brad?" she said.

The last thing I wanted to do was talk to anyone, especially Sally Mae, but it appeared that was the first thing she wanted to do.

"Yeah."

"I'm sorry," she said. "You know, about what I did when you walked into the store. You've only ever been a perfect gentleman to me, and I took advantage of you."

I stopped the gas flow at five dollars, returned the gas nozzle to the pump, and screwed the cap back on the can. Then I looked up at Sally Mae. "Why did you do it?" I asked.

"I don't know," she said. "I know it's wrong, but it's like I can't stop myself. You were so nice to me in high school, and now that we're older and I'm alone, I let myself dream up a fantasy about the two of us. I know it's not true. Everyone does."

"We all struggle with things, Sally Mae," I said, "but we have to take those thoughts captive."

"I can't," she replied. "It's like I have this voice prompting me to do things that I really don't want to do. I guess that's pretty hard for a pastor to understand."

"You'd be surprised, Sally Mae," I said. "You'd be surprised."

Ten minutes later, Ashleigh parked Allison's car by my own on the side of the road. "Ah," she said, "it looks so sad out here on the side of the road with a flat tire."

"Yeah" was all I could muster as I stepped out of the car with the gas can.

"So you really kissed that girl?"

"No," I said, "but she did kiss me."

Fortunately, Ashleigh's phone rang and spared me from conversation. I've heard it said that most men speak only about ten thousand words a day. If that's true, I was certainly over my limit.

I removed the gas cap, inserted the gas can nozzle, and listened as the gas poured slowly into my tank. In that moment, I finally allowed myself to breathe. I took air in through my nose and let it out through my mouth. My shoulders loosened, and I gave myself unspoken permission to close my eyes. The sounds of frogs and bugs joined together in a brief symphony with the trickling gasoline. Then suddenly, a steady rhythm joined the song, and it was beautiful—that is, until I realized that it was the sound of footsteps. As if part of a musical rest, the footsteps and the pouring of the gas stopped at the same time. *Maybe I'm just hearing things*, I thought.

"Hey, bro!" I heard from behind. "Looks like you're going to need some help here."

It couldn't be, I thought as I opened my eyes and pulled the nozzle from my gas tank. "Hello, Elizabeth," I said without turning to face her. "Fancy meeting you here."

"Well, you know I like to hang out in the gutters and ditches of this world," she replied.

"And once again," I said, "your timing is impeccable."

Elizabeth looked down for a moment but glanced back up with a slight grin. "I guess I deserved that," she said.

"Yeah," I said, "you did."

Elizabeth glanced down briefly for another moment, but this time when she raised her head, she wasn't smiling. She looked hollow.

"I'm sorry, sis," I said. "I went too far."

"It's okay," she replied.

I glanced back at my car's flat tire and opted to change the subject. "This is going to be an interesting tire change," I said. "The angle of the car is going to make it hard to—"

"I need your help, Brad," interrupted Elizabeth.

I stared back at her for a moment. Neither of us spoke. The only sound was that of the bugs and the frogs. In that moment, I thought of her not as she stood before me, but as her seven-year-old self, sitting next to me in the worship service, coloring with a crayon in one of the hymnals. Her coloring book lay on the floor next to my mother's purse and an open box of crayons.

"Elizabeth!" my mother whispered in that loud whisper that's actually louder than speaking normally. "Stop what you are doing this instant."

"But why?" asked Elizabeth. "It looks so much better this way."

That's my sister for you. One thing was for sure about her: she certainly kept family life interesting. Nothing could ever be black-and-white in her mind, whether in a book or in her life.

Suddenly, Ashleigh, who apparently had finished her call, interrupted my thoughts. "I didn't think I'd ever get them off the phone. How's the car repair going?"

"Well," I said, "I've only poured the gas into the tank. I was about to start on the tire, but …"

"But what?" asked Ashleigh.

"But I came along," said Elizabeth.

A strange, awkward moment followed in which no one spoke.

"Ashleigh," I said, "thank you so much for your help. Please don't be offended, but I need to talk to my sister right now."

"Right now?" she asked. "Right here on the side of the road, while your tire is still flat?"

I looked back at Elizabeth, whose mouth had dropped open. "Yeah," I said. "I think so."

"Wouldn't you rather fix the car and do this at home?"

"Absolutely," I replied, "but I'm not going to."

"Why?" she asked.

I smiled and said, "Because Elizabeth is my sister, and right now she needs my help. That's more important to me than the tire."

Elizabeth smiled and then sniffed slightly.

"Okay," said Ashleigh. "I'll leave you to it."

CHAPTER 24

You would think I would welcome the silence between Elizabeth and me. But I didn't. It was painful. We both knew it, but for some reason, in that moment, we chose the awkwardness—at least until I just couldn't take it anymore.

"So are you going to tell me about it?" I asked.

Elizabeth looked down and said, "I think so."

In that moment, I wanted to be more compassionate toward her. I really did. But I just couldn't keep myself from becoming angry. "You think so?" I asked. "What is that supposed to mean?"

"It means 'I think so,' Brad. You know me. I have to talk through things on my own terms. I've always been that way."

"Okay, so what's going on? You've texted and called and followed me all around over the past couple of days. What were you planning to say if you found me?"

"I was going to tell you that I need help, Brad, okay? I messed up, again, for the umpteenth time. Is that what you wanted to hear?"

Far down the road, I could see the lights of a semitruck heading our way. "Come on," I said. "Let's step out of the road before we get run over."

As Elizabeth followed me toward my car, she said, "That would be a fitting end for both of us today, wouldn't it?"

"I wish I could argue that with you, but I would lose big time," I replied. "So you've heard about my troubles?"

"Who hasn't heard?" she replied. "It's all over town that you've been stealing money from the church and that you'll probably be fired tomorrow."

"Well," I said, "that's certainly comforting to know."

"I wouldn't worry about it too much, though, brother," said Elizabeth.

"Why shouldn't I?"

"Because you're supposed to be the pastor at Lee Community Church. Everybody knows that, Brad. Deep down, everyone knows this is a misunderstanding, at least as far as you're concerned. They're just enjoying the process."

"What about the accusations?" I asked as the semitruck went flying by.

"Those don't matter," she said as her hair blew slightly in the wind. "You might have made a mistake or two, but in the end, everyone knows you are a good preacher."

"I'm not so sure," I replied.

"Well, it is true," she said. "I don't know much about God, and I haven't been to seminary like you, but one thing's for sure: the Lord wants you to be the pastor at Lee Community."

"How can you be sure?" I asked.

"It just makes sense, Brad. Everybody knows it. It's like it's been stamped on your forehead since birth. We've always known it."

"Thanks, Elizabeth," I said. "But what's happened here might interrupt God's will, at least as far as my position is concerned."

"We'll see," she said.

"Yep," I said.

"Yep," she repeated.

"So," she said, "do you think someone's stealing money from the church?"

"Maybe," I said. "I hate to say the words, but I think so."

"Well, you'll figure it out," she said.

"I hope so."

The awkwardness started to creep back in.

"So anyway," I said, "aren't we here to talk about you?"

"I guess so," said Elizabeth, sitting on the ground and leaning back against my car.

"So go ahead and tell me," I said.

She stared at me for a moment, took in a breath, and blew it out. A tear formed in her left eye, and I watched silently as she wiped it away.

"Well," she said, "I haven't told you or Mom or anyone about this, but about a month ago, I found out I was pregnant."

I swallowed hard. The thought of Elizabeth being anyone's mother seemed ludicrous. "Really?" I asked, feigning excitement. "You are going to have a baby? That's unbelievable."

"Brad, I—"

"You're going to need some help," I said, moving quickly into pastor mode. "Does the father know?"

"Uh, yes," she replied, "but I don't ..." She stopped midsentence and began to tear up once again. It wasn't like Elizabeth to not know what to say.

"Look," I said, "this might be the best thing for you. It would have been better if you were married, but I can perform a small, simple ceremony for you. There's nothing like being a parent to help someone—"

"Shut up, Brad!" she cried. "Just shut up!" Literally, she cried, in a way I had never seen her cry before.

I watched her face become hollow, and she leaned into the car behind her. I wasn't sure what to do, so I sat down across from her.

After a moment, between sobs, she managed to say, "Aren't you going to say anything?"

"You told me to shut up," I said.

She laughed through her tears. "It's okay, Brad," she said. "You can talk now."

"I know having a baby can be scary, but you will—"

"I'm not pregnant," she said.

"But you just said you were."

"No," she said. "I told you that I found out that I was pregnant. I'm not anymore."

"Oh no, Elizabeth," I said, reaching out to touch her on the shoulder. "I'm so sorry."

Elizabeth lowered her head once again and sobbed. And I just sat there. In that moment, I desperately wanted to offer some great words of wisdom, to offer her some form of comfort, but no words came. So I just sat there, on the pavement, watching my sister mourn the loss of her unborn child.

Then, unexpectedly, I thought of my own Gabe not having a cousin to play with, and tears instantly came to my eyes. This child I had just learned about was suddenly so dear to me, even considering the circumstances. I was reaching up to wipe my eyes when Elizabeth slapped at my arm.

"You know what?" she asked.

All at once, I felt like we were kids again, fresh off the pew after sitting next to my mother in church and arguing about something meaningless.

"What?" I asked.

"You," she cried with a pointed finger, "are the worst pastor in the world!"

"I am not," I replied like a five-year-old.

"You are too!" she answered in kind.

"Why do you say that?" I exclaimed. "You just said I was a good one."

"Well, I was wrong. You're supposed to offer me some kind of comfort. At least you could offer to pray for me."

"I'm sorry," I said. "I guess I took off my pastor hat for a moment and just tried to be your brother."

"Well, you're a lousy brother too."

"I am not."

"You are too," she said. "You didn't even try to hug me or anything."

"Well, come here then," I said, reaching for her.

She slapped me away once again.

"Why are you mad at me?" I asked.

"Because you didn't tell me to stay away from Tom."

"Who's Tom?"

"He's the father," she said.

"Oh, I just assumed it was Bill."

"Oh, gross! Never!" she cried.

"I'm sorry," I replied. "I didn't know."

"That's why you're a lousy brother."

Suddenly, time suspended as I looked into her hollow eyes, realizing what had happened. "Did he hit you?" I asked.

For once, Elizabeth had no words, and that told me enough.

"What did he do to you?" I asked.

Elizabeth suddenly stood and started wiping her clothes. I rose to my feet and pulled her to me.

"No!" she screamed, pushing away. "I don't want to hug you."

"Yes, you do," I yelled back. "I'm your brother who loves you. I'm not going to hurt you." Slowly, I pulled her to me once again, but more gently this time. As I wrapped my arms around her, she slowly reached out for me to hold her and then gripped my back tighter than anyone ever had before.

"Oh, Brad," she said quickly, "I loved him so much, but he was so bad for me. I knew he wasn't a good person and that I should stay away from him, but I just couldn't. It was like something inside me was pulling me to him. When I told him I was pregnant, I thought he was going to be ecstatic. Instead, he became furious and started throwing things around and cursing."

"Oh, Elizabeth," I said. "That alone must have hurt you so much."

"Yes," she said. "It killed me inside. I thought he wanted to be with me forever, you know, get married and start a family. Instead, he screamed, 'Why didn't you do something to keep this from happening?'"

"What did you say?" I asked.

"I told him I had taken precautions, but they're not always 100 percent effective. He called me a liar and pushed me down. From the floor, I cried and asked, 'Why are you so angry? Would it be such a terrible thing?'"

"How did he respond?" I asked.

"He pointed his finger at me and said, 'Get rid of it today and don't ever talk about it again.' I stood back up to plead with him, but he slapped me hard, then threw me across the room. I flew over the sofa, and I must have hit my head because I passed out."

"Is your head okay?" I asked, releasing her to look at her head.

"Yeah, I think so," she replied, stepping away from me.

"What happened then?"

"When I came to, he was gone. I was suddenly so ashamed and depressed, I went out and got drunk with a girlfriend. The next morning, I had terrible cramps and started bleeding. I went to the emergency room and discovered that I had lost the baby."

"You know alcohol is not good for—"

"Don't you think I know that, Brad? I'm not stupid."

"I know that, Elizabeth."

She wiped her eyes and said, "I don't know, Brad. Maybe I am stupid. I lost my child. It was my fault. I shouldn't have gotten involved with him like

I did. I shouldn't have told him like I did. I shouldn't have gotten drunk. I shouldn't have even looked at alcohol. I'm so ashamed."

I reached out to her again. This time, she moved to me immediately and hugged me hard. I pulled her closer to me and cried along with her.

"I'm so sorry, God!" she cried out. "I'm so sorry."

CHAPTER 25

It was 11:17 p.m. when I arrived home on Tuesday evening. The house was dark and quiet. I tiptoed through the living room, where Ashleigh was asleep on the sofa. As I walked down the hallway past Gabe's room, I envied the sleep he had already accomplished this evening. And then, finally, I came to the master bedroom door. Slowly, I turned the knob and pushed the door open, expecting Allison to be in bed sleeping. Instead, she was sitting in a kitchen chair in the corner of our bedroom.

"Well, Pastor Brad," she said, "it's so good of you to come home this evening."

Oh man, I thought. *We're going to have to talk about it.*

"I had all that car trouble," I said as I set my car keys on the dresser. "And then, of course, Elizabeth …"

"Yes, I heard," she replied. "You look awful."

"Thank you," I said. "It's because I got caught in the rain, fell in the ditch, and later had to change a tire by myself."

"Yeah, I heard about that too."

"I need to go take a shower."

"That's probably a good idea," she replied. "You kind of smell bad too."

I rummaged through my drawer of underwear and sleeping shorts and selected some clean clothes. "Well," I said, "here I go."

"Brad?"

"Yeah?"

"I'm glad you made it home, but I do have one question before you go into the shower."

Oh well. Here it comes. "Yeah?" I said.

"When all of this happened with the car, was that before or after you were caught kissing Sally Mae Watson at One Stop Shop?"

I had to think for a minute. She had me in one of those questions that I couldn't really answer. I couldn't just say it was after because that would mean accepting what she had said about Sally Mae and me. "No hablo inglés," I wanted to say. But she would have killed me, literally. Instead, I said, "Okay, let me tell you what happened."

She raised one eyebrow, leaned back in her chair, and crossed her arms.

I took in a deep breath and thought, *Well, here goes.* "Okay," I said. "Let me start at the beginning."

"I'm all ears," she replied without changing expression.

"First of all," I said, "the deacons' meeting was not good. At first, I thought everything was going to be okay, but then Earl and Jimmy stirred everyone up. So they've called a business meeting tomorrow night where they're asking everyone for a vote of confidence. If it goes badly, I may be fired."

"Yes," she said, "I've heard about all of that, from lots of different people on the phone tonight."

"People called here looking for me?"

"Yes, they did. They said your mobile number was going straight to voice mail. I didn't realize at the time that I should have just referred them to Sally Mae Watson's number."

I chuckled nervously but then saw Allison's face and realized the situation wasn't funny at all to her. Not one bit.

"What happened then?" she asked.

"Well, on the way home, I realized I needed some gas, so I pulled into the One Stop Shop to fill up. I inserted my card into the pump, but it wouldn't work."

"So that meant you had to go inside and kiss Sally Mae?" she asked.

"No," I replied, trying not to become angry. "I did have to go in and pay for my gas, though."

"That's understandable. What happened then?"

"Then Sally Mae told me that my church credit card had been canceled. Can you believe that? I can understand canceling it if I get fired tomorrow night, but doing it tonight is just another slap in my face."

"Yes, Brad, that's terrible, but why did you kiss Sally Mae?"

"I didn't kiss her. She kissed me."

"Why?"

"I don't know," I said. "I walked in, and she started flirting with me like she does sometimes, and—"

"You mean she's tried to kiss you before?"

"She's never tried anything like tonight, but she has made me uncomfortable with her conversation."

"Why haven't you ever said anything about it before now? Did you secretly like it?"

"No, I just … I don't know, honey. I guess I just didn't want you to worry."

"Should I be worried now, Brad?"

"There's nothing to worry about!" I cried. "She propositioned me, and I resisted her advances."

"It doesn't sound like you resisted! It sounds like you jumped right into her arms!"

"You're going to wake Gabe and your sister if you keep yelling," I said.

"So what happened?" she asked in a softer tone.

"Okay," I said. "Sally Mae's always had a crush on me since I was nice to her in high school. Tonight, she did corner me in the store and tried to kiss me. I didn't kiss her back, though, and I told her I was very much in love with you."

"Why did Earl and Archie tell everyone they walked in on the two of you kissing then?"

"They saw her last-ditch effort to win me over. I promise, I tried to push her away. What they saw was unfortunate."

"Unfortunate?"

"Well, yeah."

"To say the least," said Allison.

"If it helps matters," I said, "Sally Mae apologized to me about the whole thing."

"She did?"

"Yeah, but I told her the one she really needed to be worried about was you."

"At least you got one thing right."

"Listen, I know what it sounds like, especially coming from Earl, but it's not the way it looked. I was trying to be a perfect gentleman, committed to his wife, and she put me in an awkward situation. But I only want to love you. I only want to kiss and hug you. You're my wife. I'm committed to you, I promise."

"Really?" she asked.

"Yes, baby," I said, reaching out for her.

She stood and began walking toward me. "Do you promise that you will never cheat on me?"

"Absolutely," I said. "I love you and will be faithful to you for as long as we both shall live."

She smiled, and everything seemed better. "Well," she said, "you had better be faithful to me even after we're dead."

"Yes, ma'am," I said. "Forever and ever."

She hugged me tight, and I leaned down to kiss her. My lips were almost touching hers when suddenly she pulled away.

"Ah, no," she said.

"What?" I asked. "I can't kiss you?"

"Not yet," she said. "Your mouth has touched Sally Mae's mouth, and I'm not putting my mouth on it until you take a shower, shave, brush your teeth, and use Listerine."

"Yes, ma'am," I said, heading toward the bathroom and sighing a huge sigh of relief.

CHAPTER 26

"Honey," said Allison, "are you going to get that?"

I rolled over in bed at the sound of her voice and placed my arm over her waist.

"I didn't tell you to grab me," she said. "I asked if you were going to get that."

"Am I going to get what?" I asked.

"Someone's knocking on the front door."

That's when I heard the knocking for myself. It was a consistent light pounding with no pauses. I wiped the sleep from my eyes and glanced at the clock. It was five thirty on Wednesday morning. "Can't your sister get it?" I asked. "I mean, she is in the living room, and we're way back here."

"No, she can't," said Allison. "She's probably in there scared to death because someone's beating on the door at this ungodly hour."

"Yeah, I bet," I replied. "She's probably slept right through it. She does live in a dorm at college, you know."

The knocking continued.

"Brad?"

"Okay," I said, throwing the covers aside. "I'll go see who it is."

I stepped lightly as I made my way down the hall, checking on Gabe in his room and Ashleigh on the couch. Both were dead to the world, even though the knocking was much louder from this end. "Who could it be at this time of the morning?" I said to myself.

The knocking stopped when I unlocked the deadbolt. I opened the door and saw my dad smiling. "Hey, Daddy," I said. "What's up?"

"Morning," he said.

I looked around to confirm. "Yes, I guess it is morning. Is everything okay?"

"You planning on sleeping the day away?"

"No, I just had a late night."

"Yeah, I heard about that," he said.

"You did, huh?"

"Yep."

"Already?" I asked.

"Well, you know how news travels around here, especially bad news and gossip."

"That's just great," I moaned.

"Why don't you get changed so we can go have breakfast? I know a great place."

I yawned. For anyone else, I would have declined, but this was my dad, and he was concerned about me. "Okay, give me a minute," I said. "Do you want to come in?"

"No, I'll wait in the truck," he replied.

Ten minutes later, I was sitting in the passenger side of my dad's truck as he drove away from my house. I wondered for a moment if we would be back in time for me to get to work, but then I figured it didn't matter since I was about to be fired anyway.

"So," I said, "where are we headed for breakfast? Kentwood? McComb?"

"Nah," he said. "I have another place in mind."

"You know it's not best for me to go to the One Stop right now, right?"

"Yeah," he replied, raising his eyebrows. "I heard about that too, son."

"Oh my," I said, looking down. "I don't know what people are saying, but you know I didn't do anything with her, right?"

"Well," said my dad, "I heard that Earl and Archie caught you in a passionate lip-lock with Sally Mae behind the counter."

"Oh, Daddy …"

"However," he continued, "I also know that you can't always believe exactly what you hear around here, especially when Earl Bishop is involved."

"Do you want me to tell you what happened?"

"You can if you want, but I think I know my son well enough to know that he loves the Lord and loves his wife."

"Thank you."

"You're welcome, son. Sally Mae Watson is a terrible flirt, but your wife would have killed you by now if you had really done anything."

"Yeah," I laughed. "I guess so. So we're not picking up breakfast at the One Stop?"

"Nah, I only go there for gas really, but I take your mother there for milk, and I do hear good things about their pies."

"Then where are we headed?"

"Just hold your horses."

I've never really understood that term because I've never owned a horse, but I replied, "Okay," just the same, trying to be patient.

I looked out at the Aucoin countryside and suddenly felt like I was ten years old, riding with my dad to some surprise destination. One of the things I'd always loved about him was that he would wake me early on Saturday or Sunday mornings so he could show me some pretty landscape he had found sometime during the week. To him, exploring the world, or at least our Louisiana parish, was what it meant to be alive. As a child, I never liked rising early, but I loved spending time with my dad. Even though he could be tough as nails, I never doubted that he wanted the best for me and desired for me to enjoy my life and his company. He certainly seemed to enjoy mine.

After a few minutes, he turned onto a gravel road and drove for a couple of miles before turning onto an even smaller gravel road.

"This looks familiar to me, Dad," I said. "Have we been here before?"

"Yes, a few times," he answered, "but it's been a while."

For as long as I could remember, my dad had never liked to reveal the location of our surprise places before it was time. He liked to build up the tension with hints and then enjoy watching our faces when we arrived. Today was no different.

In the distance, the corner of an old wrought iron fence came into view. Suddenly, I knew exactly where we were going. "Really, Dad?" I asked. "A cemetery?"

"Well, this is not just any cemetery," he said. "It's the old Aucoin cemetery.

We've got a lot of family members buried here, plus it's just a lovely old spot." Dad slowed his truck and parked it underneath the limbs of a large cypress tree covered in Spanish moss.

"It has been a while since I've been here," I said. "What made you think of coming here today?"

My dad held up an index finger, and I smiled.

"First things first, son," he replied.

"Okay," I said, realizing he had a plan and I wasn't going to rush it.

He reached behind the seat and pulled a small lunch cooler into the front seat. "Enjoy your breakfast," he said as he stepped from the truck. "Then come over and join me."

"Yes, sir," I said, opening the cooler. Inside was a bacon and egg sandwich and a mason jar filled with milk.

I smiled when I saw the milk and called after Daddy, "Did Mama make this?"

He returned my smile and said, "Who else?"

I offered up a quick blessing and then watched him open the latch on the old iron cemetery gate. It swung open slowly, creaking with every inch. He stepped through with the respect and reverence of a Benedictine monk.

"This is hallowed ground to him," I said to myself as I watched him walk to several graves, wiping the dust from the headstones and taking time to read each one as if he'd never seen them before.

I quickly gulped down my sandwich, drank most of the milk, and finally stepped from the truck. The fallen leaves crunched beneath my feet as I joined him, where he was now squatting by the grave of his mother. We knelt there together in silence until I felt my legs could take it no longer.

Fortunately, Dad slowly rose to his feet and said, "Whew, son. Being in that position is hard on an old man."

I leaned on a tree for support and joked, "You're not old, Daddy."

He smiled and patted me on the back. "What makes you think I was talking about me?" he asked.

I returned his smile but didn't say anything.

"Brad," he said, "do you see all of these graves out here?"

I took a look like I had never seen them before and answered, "Yes, sir."

"Son, at least a quarter of these graves belong to people we're related to who have gone on before us to the hereafter."

I glanced around at them again, not knowing what to say.

He continued, "My parents are buried here. My grandparents, your great-grandparents, are buried right over there, next to all of their brothers and sisters."

Being a pastor, I thought it was up to me to say something meaningful at this point. "Well," I said, "I just hope I can live up to their example."

"What is that supposed to mean?" asked Dad.

"I, uh, meant that they were all godly people, and uh, I hope I can live up to their standard."

"Their standard?" asked my dad with a grin. "Son, you've got nothing to worry about there."

"What do you mean?" I asked. "All of these people were strong, outstanding Christians, right?"

"Sort of," he replied.

"From what I've heard, they were leaders in their churches. Wasn't your grandfather a pastor here in Aucoin?"

"Yeah, he was, but he was also a raging alcoholic."

"What?" I exclaimed. "I've never heard that before."

"Well," he said, "that's because nobody ever wants to speak ill of the dead, but he had a serious drinking problem he tried to kick for many years, but he just couldn't seem to shake it."

"How did you find out?"

"I was spending the weekend with my grandparents one time when my parents had to go out of town. On Saturday night, I was sleeping in the living room and woke up thirsty. I walked into the kitchen for a drink of water and found him passed out on the floor. I ran for my grandmother, who didn't seem surprised at all. She and I helped him to their bedroom and stretched him out on the bed."

"How did you know he wasn't just sick?"

"Well, there was an empty whiskey bottle next to his side of the bed, and he smelled like he'd been bathing in it. I pointed it out to my grandmother, but she told me he just needed to sleep it off and that I shouldn't worry."

"What happened?"

"I went back to sleep, and the next morning when I woke, he was already up at the church, getting ready for Sunday services. Later, as I sat on that hard wooden pew, listening to him preach, I looked at his face and listened to the words he was saying, but now I don't remember a single word he said. In fact, instead of seeing him standing behind the pulpit preaching, I envisioned him on that kitchen floor, passed out from intoxication."

"Surely that was a one-time thing?"

"No, I mentioned what had happened to my daddy a couple of weeks later, and that's when he told me about grandpa's drinking problem. He said it was a hard thing being a preacher, and sometimes they just need some type of relief from all the stress. I guess the alcohol was his escape."

"I guess so. Why didn't you ever mention this before?"

"I didn't think it was important then, but I do now." He smiled and put his hand on my shoulder.

"Why is that?" I asked.

Ignoring my question, he said, "My daddy is buried right over there. You probably remember his funeral when you were a boy."

"Yeah, I remember," I said.

"Do you remember much about him?"

"Not too much," I said. "I remember him taking me fishing one time."

"He was a deacon in the church."

"Lee Community?"

"Yeah."

"I never knew that. Was he a godly man?"

"He was very religious, but he cursed like a sailor."

"Really?"

"It's true, but he held his tongue in church, for the most part. His brother Jimmy taught Bible study at Lee Community, but he also frequented the horse tracks in New Orleans on his day off."

"Why are you telling me all of this?" I asked.

He looked me straight in the eyes and said, "Here recently, you've made a few mistakes, but you're in good company. Everyone makes mistakes. But you don't have to let those mistakes define you. You can admit your mistakes, confess your sins to the Lord, stand up to your accusers, and set an example for the rest of your family and for Lee Community Church."

"Do you think so, Dad?"

"I know so, Brad. I knew these people buried here. They were great people, and we wouldn't be here without them. But I know you even better. You're not just playing games here. You're a man of God. You've studied and prepared yourself. You've got what it takes to lead that church. And best of all, you know what you don't know, and you ask the Lord for His help. You're the real deal, Brad."

Tears welled up in my eyes. I quickly wiped them on my sleeve. "Thank you," I said. "That means a lot to me."

"Good," he replied. "I meant every word."

I smiled, not quite knowing what else to say.

"And son?" he asked.

"Yes, sir?"

"Don't you quit," he said, pointing straight at me. "Don't you dare quit."

"I don't intend to," I said, "but I am worried about our finances."

"Well, that makes sense."

"I haven't been stealing money from the church, Daddy. I did find a hundred dollars, but I didn't steal anything."

"I know it, son."

"But I do think someone has been stealing money from the church."

"Do you know who?"

"No, I don't, but I'm trying to find out. I think it's someone who has access to my office. I found paper clips all over my office. A few of them were even taped to the bottom of my desk and under the bottom lip of the trash can."

"Under the trash can?"

"Yeah, they were hanging down from the tape so someone could slip money into them easily."

"Do you think it might have been one of the deacons?"

"I don't know, Daddy. Maybe. Archie, Ernie, Burt, Earl, and Jimmy are the only other ones with a key to my office. I don't know why any of them would want to steal from the church, though."

"Earl's always had it in for you, though, hasn't he?"

"Yeah," I said, "but it just doesn't seem like something he would do. It doesn't seem like something any of them would do."

"Well, you're right there."

"Do you have any other words of advice?"

"Not about finding the thief," he replied with a smile. "But you had better finish that jar of milk because your mother's going to ask me if you did."

CHAPTER 27

I've heard it said that every man, whether he knows it or not, wants to hear his father tell him that he's got what it takes to succeed in life. My dad had just given that to me. I'm sure he'd conveyed it many times before in different ways, but not like this. This affirmation ignited my inner confidence and created a drive within me to press forward. It was awesome.

Needless to say, after my breakfast meeting, I was feeling pretty good. No matter what anyone said, I was a good pastor and a good preacher. I had made a couple of mistakes, but I was big enough to own up to them publicly and to work through them if people would allow me. If not, so be it.

Back at home, I showered quickly and changed into Sunday church clothes. I kissed Allison and Gabe, waved bye to a sleeping Ashleigh on our sofa, and headed out to the car. As I walked down the driveway, I pulled my phone from my pocket and noticed that I had three missed text messages, from Archie, Ernie, and Earl, in that order.

I clicked on the first text: "Good morning, Pastor Brad. This is just a reminder. Under the circumstances of tonight's business meeting, the deacons think it best that you not work from the church office today. If you have visits you need to complete in homes or the hospital, that's fine. See you tonight."

"Come on!" I shouted as I slapped my phone against my thigh. "I wanted to go look for more clues."

"Are you okay?" I heard from the end of my driveway.

I looked up and saw the boy who always rode his bike in front of my house at inopportune times. He was standing near the sidewalk with his bike to his side.

"Good morning," I said. "I'm sorry you had to hear that."

"It's okay," he said. "I understand."

"You know, I'm not normally the kind of guy who screams."

"Oh, I know that."

"How's that?"

"You're my neighbor. You're a nice man and a good preacher."

"Where did you hear that?"

"My mom and dad."

"Oh, well, I'm sure they're very nice as well."

"I like them."

"That's good," I replied, not sure what else I should say.

"Are you moving away?" asked the boy.

"What did you say?" I asked, wondering what the boy had heard. Quickly, I walked to the back end of my car to be closer to him.

"Are you moving away?" the boy repeated.

"What do you mean?" I asked, placing one hand on the trunk of my car. *This kid knows more about my future than I do.*

"I heard you might be moving away," he said.

"Where did you hear that?"

"My mom and dad."

So people want me out of town as well. It's worse than I thought.

"So are you moving?" he asked.

"I'm not planning on it," I answered. "Why would I?"

"I heard you were in trouble."

"You did?" I replied. "Who said that?"

"My mom and dad," he said.

"I see."

"I know. My mom and dad talk a lot."

"Well," I said, "your mom and dad are right about me. I am in trouble."

"Did you do something bad?"

"Ah, well, it's more like I made some bad decisions."

"What does that mean?"

"Well, I guess it means that if I had to do it over again, I would have done something different."

"That happens to me all the time," said the boy.

"I think it happens to everyone," I laughed. "What's your name?"

"Bobby," he said.

"Well, Bobby," I said, "the important thing is to work through the problems you created and to try to make better decisions next time."

"I guess so," said Bobby.

"You guess so?" I asked. "Don't you know it?"

"Yeah," he said with a shrug. "It's just hard to be good, especially when I don't want to."

I patted his shoulder. "I think that's everyone's problem, Bobby. I know it's mine."

"I've got to go," said Bobby. "I hope you don't have to move."

"Thank you, Bobby," I replied. "I hope so too."

I watched him ride away, stepped into my car, and started the ignition. I was just about to back away from my house when I realized I had no idea where I was going. I pulled my phone out and reread Archie's text two or three more times.

Awkwardly, I sent the only reply that came to mind: "Okay." After hitting send, I realized I should write a bit more, so I texted, "See you tonight."

I watched the dots bounce and waited for a reply. None came, but at least I knew he had received my replies. I decided to click on Ernie's text message next, hoping for some encouragement. I was slightly disappointed by what I read.

"Hi, Pastor Brad. Sorry about last night. That's not at all how I expected things to go. Earl and Jimmy are stirring up the members about tonight, but I still think you'll be okay in the end. Just remember that all is not lost."

I appreciated Ernie's words. He'd really had my back through all of this. But it was my experience that whenever someone said, "All is not lost," it meant "something has been lost."

I quickly replied, "Thanks, Ernie. I appreciate your encouragement."

I hated the dreadful anticipation of Earl's lingering text message. "Whatever!" I cried. "I'll just read it quickly. It will be like yanking off a Band-Aid all at once."

After a brief pause, I clicked on Earl's text message and began to read: "Just wanted to let you know that a few of us will be guarding the church office today in case you decide to come in and hide any evidence. Tonight's meeting has been a long time coming, seminary boy. And don't think I've forgotten about that nasty text message you sent me on Sunday. I'll be bringing that up at the meeting as well."

My eyes grew large, and my jaw dropped. "Oh no!" I said aloud as I remembered the biting text message I had written to Earl after this past Sunday's deacon altercation about the offering. I thought I had erased it. I must have sent it by mistake.

Quickly, I scanned my message history with Earl. There I found the culprit. I had sent it. I reread the text message I had sent. "Thank you, Earl, for challenging me today regarding the offering. Obviously, 60 years of tradition could never be wrong, especially in a church that is shrinking every year because they are afraid of trying anything new. And thank you for informing me that my preaching, the main emphasis of my lifelong ministry, is so bad that no one actually listens. You've given me such hope! By the way, you are a jerk!"

I closed my phone and dropped it into my lap. "Well, Lord," I prayed, "things just went further south than I thought they could go. I've been drowning here, and now someone's just handed me a baby. What am I going to do? Why am I so stupid? Why did I write that text message, even if I didn't plan to send it? That's why Earl's been extra angry this week."

Any confidence I had received from my dad was gone now. I had behaved badly, and things were catching up to me. It was one thing to make a mistake with finances or to have a lapse of judgment. It was something altogether different, especially in the eyes of the members of Lee Community, to speak (or text) in an ugly manner toward someone. I didn't know what else to do, so I decided to text Earl back. "Earl, I didn't realize I had actually sent that text. It was uncalled for, and I apologize."

I watched the dots bounce and imagined Earl reading the message and literally laughing out loud. In a moment, he replied. "It's too late for you to take it back, preacher boy! You've got a mouth on you and it's time for the whole church to know."

With everything that was in me, I wanted to respond harshly, even viciously, but I didn't. I had admitted my mistake and apologized to Earl and would do so again publicly if it came to that. "Help me to do the right thing, Lord," I prayed. "Help me stop reacting and start leading. Help me to act like You."

About that time, my phone started buzzing. I looked down and recognized Nettie Longwood's number. "Good morning, Nettie," I said into the receiver.

"Good morning, Pastor Brad," she said. "Do you think we'll need music at tonight's meeting?"

"You know, Nettie," I replied, "it couldn't hurt at all and might even be a good way to bring people together."

"Okay," she said. "Do you have anything special in mind?"

"Not really," I said. "I'll leave that to your discretion."

"Thank you, Pastor. I'll see you tonight."

"Thanks, Nettie," I said as I ended the call. "Lord," I prayed, "I've never seen a more faithful servant than Nettie Longwood. Even in this moment of crisis, she's remained steady in her duties. I'm tempted to walk back into my house and watch TV all day, but help me to endure in my calling until the very end."

I leaned back in my seat and thought about Nettie asking me if I wanted anything special for tonight. Then it came to me. I did want something special for tonight, but it wasn't something Nettie could give me. I wanted something entirely different.

Suddenly determined, I pulled my car into the street and headed toward the interstate. As I drove, I called Allison. "Honey," I said, "I won't be home for lunch."

"Is everything okay?" she asked.

"No, it isn't," I said. "I've been told that I'm not allowed into the office today."

"What?" she cried. "That's crazy!"

"You're right. It is. They did say that I could visit people in the hospital or in homes, but I don't think that's what I want to do today either."

"Are you okay?"

"Yes," I said, "but if I'm getting fired tonight, I really want today to count. I'll call you in a couple of hours."

"Okay," she replied. "I love you. Be careful."

"I will," I said. "And I love you too." I ended the call and quickly searched for another number. I found it quickly in the recent category, pressed it, and then placed my phone on speaker.

"Hello," said my sister.

"Hi, Elizabeth," I said. "Today, I need your help."

"What are you talking about?" she asked.

"I know you have your own set of difficulties right now, but how would you like to make a difference in someone's life today?"

"I guess so," she said. "What could I possibly do?"

"You'll see. Get dressed, and I'll pick you up in ten minutes."

"Where are we going, Brad?"

"Someplace you know much better than I."

CHAPTER 28

Ralph Waldo Emerson once wrote, "The purpose of life is not to be happy. It is to be useful, to be honorable, to be compassionate, to have it make some difference that you have lived and lived well." I could see that quote coming to life as Elizabeth rode with me to New Orleans. This was one of the first times in her life that she was heading there to do something other than sell paintings and party. It showed on her face. At least for one day, she had a mission to make a difference in the life of someone else.

Multiple times, I thought about bringing up her pregnancy, but I held back. I couldn't stand to end this semblance of happiness in her life, no matter whether it was temporary or not.

"I can't believe we're doing this," she said as we walked through the myriad vendors in the open-air French Market.

"I just hope we can find him," I replied. "There are a lot of places to hide in the French Quarter."

"What is his full name again?" asked Elizabeth.

"Paul Plaisance. He's Ernie and Connie's son."

"I know who he is," she replied. "I've actually seen him play in a few clubs down here. He visited my table after his set one time. Why don't you just call him?"

"I've tried, but his phone keeps going to voice mail."

"He may be practicing somewhere now, but if he's trying to survive in his business, he'll get his phone back up soon."

"What makes you say that?"

"I'm an artist. He's an artist. We're all about whatever the next gig is. We pretty much live and breathe through our phones."

"That makes sense," I said as we passed a table filled with alligator heads and teeth. "Where did you last see him play?"

"Snug Harbor."

"Oh yeah. I didn't know he played there."

"I can check it out, but it's in the Faubourg Marigny. It's a few blocks back."

"Did you bring your phone?"

"Like I said," she replied, holding her phone high, "we live and breathe through this."

"Excuse me," asked the crystal deodorant lady in a strange Beirut-meets-Beijing accent. "You want deodorant rock? It's made from crystal. You never need deodorant again."

"Ah, no, thank you," said Elizabeth as she motioned for me to move on. "You've got to keep moving here, Brad."

"You're right. Why don't you circle back and check out the area around Snug Harbor and then give me a call?"

"Where are you headed?"

"I'm going up by Café du Monde and Jackson Square. That's where I found him last time."

"Okay, Brad," she replied. "What if we don't find him?"

"I don't know," I said. "I guess we'll just go from there."

"Sounds like a plan."

"Call me if you get any kind of lead," I said before taking a step away from her.

"Hey, Brad," she called after me.

"Yeah?" I said, turning back to her.

"Thanks for asking me to come with you. It's kind of cool, getting to help someone."

"No problem," I replied. I then turned and walked toward Jackson Square.

A few minutes later, as I stood between the statue of Andrew Jackson and the St. Louis Cathedral, I desperately scanned my recent calls. Saxophone music from a nearby corner artist filled the air. I wanted to stop and listen but realized it wouldn't help me in my search, nor was it calming my nerves.

"Which one of these was his number?" I asked myself. "For the life of me, I can't remember."

Searching for hope, I glanced at the buildings around me. The cross on the top of the St. Louis Cathedral caught my eye. "Lord," I prayed in a whisper, "if this is the last thing I do as a pastor, please help me do it well."

"You look as if you are searching for something or someone," said a voice behind me.

Could this be Your answer, Lord? I wondered. I turned and saw a lady sitting at a tarot card table. She was smiling and reaching her hand out to me.

I smiled back and replied, "I'm sorry, but I don't think you can help me."

"Are you certain?" she asked. "I help many people find what they are looking for. With these cards, I can predict your future and possibly help you connect with another person."

"No, thanks," I said. "Unfortunately, I think I already know what's going to happen."

"Then please move away from my table," she said, waving me away with her hand.

"Sorry," I said as I stepped away and dialed another familiar number. The saxophone began playing louder, so I held the phone tightly to my ear.

After three rings, Ernie answered. "Hello, Pastor Brad," he said.

"Ernie," I replied, "this may sound strange, but would you please resend me Paul's number? I'd like to speak to him this afternoon, and I must have an old number."

"It's no use, Pastor," said Ernie. "Paul's phone went dead this morning in the middle of a conversation with his mother."

"He called Connie?"

"Well, she actually called him, but he spoke to her for five minutes."

"That doesn't sound like much."

"You're right about that," Ernie replied, "but it really is considering that Paul hasn't spoken to us, at least not for more than a few seconds, for a long time. It was a treat to speak to him. But then his phone went dead. At least that's what we think happened. We don't know for sure."

"Maybe I can find him," I said. "Do you know the names of any of the places where he plays music?"

"Are you going to New Orleans today?"

"Yes, I'm actually here in Jackson Square right now."

"Really? With everything going on at Lee Community, you went to New Orleans?"

"Well, there's not much I could be doing in Aucoin today anyway."

"What do you mean?"

"Archie banned me from the church office today. Earl has people guarding it so I can't enter."

"I'm sorry, Pastor."

"It's okay, Ernie. Thank you."

"What are you doing in the French Quarter?"

"I came here to find Paul."

"Oh, Pastor Brad," said Ernie. "Are you serious?"

"Yeah, I am. If today's my last day of ministry, at least with Lee Community, I'm not going to spend it moping. I want to help someone. I want to find Paul."

"I don't know what to say. What you're doing means so much to Connie and me."

"Do you remember any of the club names?"

"I'm sorry, I don't remember," he replied. "I do know that some of them are on Bourbon Street."

"It's okay," I said. "I'll find him, somehow."

"How?" he asked. "How are you going to find him? The French Quarter can be a big place when you're looking for one man."

"I understand," I said, "but I've got to try. Can you send his number to me once again? Who knows? Maybe he'll answer."

"Sure thing, pastor," he replied. "I'll text it to you."

"Thanks," I said and hung up. I looked up at the cross on top of the cathedral once again. "Well, here we go, Lord," I said as I lowered my head and took my first step toward Bourbon Street.

Even though Allison and I had spent our fair share of time in the French Quarter, we—like most seminary students—had steered clear of Bourbon Street, which was world-renowned for its bars, strip joints, and clubs. One of my professors used to say that the street itself smelled like sin. I never was sure what he meant by that. I always figured he just didn't want the sin to rub off on us.

Within a few minutes, I came to the famous den of debauchery and, after looking both ways, stepped onto Bourbon Street itself. Even though it was late morning, I could already feel the partying in the atmosphere. For a moment, I thought I caught a whiff of the sin my professor had warned me about, but it turned out to be the steam blowing from an oyster bar. I passed a painted mime setting up a ladder for a performance. The sight caused me to stop in my tracks for a moment and stare at the painted-faced performer.

Breaking a cardinal rule, the mime said, "Hey, pal. Unless you've got a tip for me, move it along. Next show is in ten minutes."

I realized how stupid I must have looked, so I replied, "Sorry, sir. I didn't mean to cause you to break character."

"I'm not breaking nothing!" he shouted. "Get away from me!"

"Okay, bye," I said with a wave.

He waved back but used only one finger.

I grimaced, turned, and continued down the street, hoping to find Paul walking down the street with his guitar. "What was I thinking?" I asked myself. "This is not like finding someone on the streets of Aucoin."

I checked the time on my phone and noticed Ernie's text message with Paul's number. I quickly saved it to my contacts and then called Paul, hoping he would answer. After four rings, Paul's voice mail picked up, stating that his mailbox had never been set up.

"How can he make it as a musician without setting up his voice mail?" I asked myself, thinking about what my sister had said.

I stepped into the doorway of a closed business and texted Paul: "Paul, this is Pastor Brad from Aucoin. I need to talk to you today. I'm in the French Quarter on Bourbon looking for you now. Please contact me. It's important." I sent the text and was depositing my phone in my pocket when the door of the business opened and bumped into me from behind.

"Sorry," I called out. "I didn't realize you were open."

There was no response as I turned around. I looked up at the sign of the establishment and noticed it was called the Funky Chicken Strip Club. As if on cue, heavy bass music started pulsating from inside the building, to such an extent that the door began shaking noisily.

In that moment, an older lady, obviously not one of the entertainers, stepped out onto the stoop with a broom. She noticed me staring and said, "You coming in, or are you just taking up space, baby?"

Startled, I replied, "Uh, no. Sorry. I was, uh, just looking for a friend."

"Well," she said, "we've got plenty of friends inside if you're looking, honey."

"Ah, no, thank you," I said awkwardly. "I'm looking for a musician, a guitarist."

"I've got a few girls who can play a G-string pretty well."

"Oh, uh, no," I stammered. "You don't understand. You see, I'm a pastor, and it's a man I'm looking for."

"Figures," she said, looking me over. "Two doors down."

"Ah, that's not exactly what I meant," I replied.

"Whatever," she replied as she opened the door wide, trying to entice me inside. "Are you sure you don't want to come in? You can take a load off, grab a bite to eat, and even catch one of the shows. Come on, today is Wednesday, which means no cover charge for pastors."

I shook my head but glanced inside. The stage was empty except for the flashing lights and the exotic-dancing poles. The seats were empty except for one close to the front, occupied by a long-haired middle-aged man. He wore an obviously fake wig and beard, mirror sunglasses, and a white leisure suit. He looked my way, and his smile suddenly disappeared.

"What's wrong with him?" I asked.

The lady laughed and let the door close on its own. "He's probably embarrassed to be seen by a normal person," she said, "especially in that terrible-looking wig."

"Was that a wig?" I joked.

"Guys like that come in here every day. They come to New Orleans for a wild time but are then embarrassed to be seen. So they buy some weird outfit and ugly wig and either drink themselves into not caring or leave because they feel stupid."

"How did he get seated so quickly? You just opened the door."

"He must be eager," she replied. "Besides, we have another door on the other side of the building."

"Okay, thanks," I said. "I'm going to keep looking for my friend."

"You sure I can't interest you in a show?"

"Yeah, I'm sure. I really am a pastor. I'm here trying to find my deacon's son. He's given up on life and his family, including his parents, and I want to remind him that God loves him."

The woman's eyes opened wide. Her demeanor changed as she broke into a smile. "Well, Pastor," she said, "that's something I don't hear very often here on Bourbon Street."

"I don't know why I told you all of that just now, but it just came out. I'm sorry if I bothered you."

"No problem," she replied. "You ain't bothering me. I hope you find him, and God bless." With that, she turned away.

"Man," I said aloud. "I just had a conversation with a lady who works at a strip joint on Bourbon Street. If only Earl could see me now."

I spent the next hour walking up and down Bourbon Street, hoping to somehow catch a glimpse of Paul, but he was nowhere to be seen. My only real accomplishment was angering the talking mime whenever I passed.

"What was I thinking?" I asked myself again as I leaned against a lamppost. "He could be anywhere. He might not even be in town."

"I wouldn't lean on that if I were you," someone said from behind me. I turned quickly to see Elizabeth walking toward me.

"What are you doing here?" I asked. "I thought you were going to call me."

"Oh yeah," she said. "Sorry about that. Are you enjoying your time on Bourbon, Pastor?"

"Not especially," I answered. "There's a mime who's about to kill me."

"What?"

"Never mind. Did you go to Snug Harbor?"

"Yeah, I did," she replied. "The bartender told me that Paul had been there earlier but had just left. He said he had a gig on Bourbon, so I got here as fast as I could."

"Okay," I said. "I was about to give up. I'm glad you came along."

"Me too," she said. "Are you going to answer that?"

"What?" I asked.

"It sounds like you're getting a call," she said, pointing to my pocket.

I reached for my phone and answered without looking at the caller ID. "Hello? Paul?"

"Sorry, man of God," replied the voice on the other end.

"Pastor Jeremy?" I asked.

"It sure is," he replied. "What's up with you today?"

"You wouldn't believe me if I told you," I said.

"Sure I would," he said.

"Okay then," I said. "I've spent the last hour on Bourbon Street searching for the son of one of our deacons."

"Really?"

"I knew you wouldn't believe it."

"Oh, I believe it all right," he replied. "And I know what that's like."

"You do?"

"Absolutely," said Jeremy. "I once searched the French Quarter for two days, looking for my own cousin who disappeared there one Mardi Gras."

"During Mardi Gras?"

"Yeah," he answered. "I saw some pretty raunchy stuff."

Elizabeth waved her hand in front of my face and asked, "Who are you talking to?"

"I imagine you did," I said, holding my index finger up to Elizabeth. "Did you ever find him?"

"No, I didn't," he said. "I was still searching when my uncle called me to say that some of my cousin's friends had dropped him off at home, thoroughly intoxicated, completely broke, and absolutely dead to the world."

"Yeah," I replied. "Unfortunately, I don't have two days. Today's my last chance to help this man."

"What do you mean?" asked Jeremy.

"You see," I answered, "there's a called business meeting tonight where the deacons are going to call for a vote of confidence. I may be relieved of my responsibilities by the end of the day."

"What does that have to do with you helping this man?"

"Didn't you hear me?" I asked. "There's a good chance I'm going to be fired tonight."

Elizabeth shook her head. "You're not going to be fired tonight, Brad," she said. "It can't happen."

"Is that your wife in the background?" asked Jeremy.

"No," I replied. "It's my sister Elizabeth. Did you hear me tell you that I'm about to be fired?"

"Yeah, I heard you," he said calmly. "Let me ask you a question."

"Okay."

"When you answered my call, how did I address you?"

"You called me 'man of God.'"

"That's right," he said. "Do you know why I used that terminology?"

"Well," I said, "I suppose it's because I'm a fellow pastor, at least for now."

"No," he replied. "Almost anyone can get the title of pastor nowadays. I'm not giving you an extra title because titles don't really mean anything. I called you 'man of God' because I sense that you are a real man of God, someone who will serve the Lord no matter what position you might hold. Am I right in my assumption?"

"Yes," I replied thoughtfully. "You are absolutely right."

"Just remember," said Jeremy. "Even if you're fired tonight, all is not lost. You will continue to serve the Lord, and He will protect you and provide for you."

"Thanks so much," I replied. "I appreciate it."

"You're welcome. What time is the meeting tonight?"

"It's at seven."

"I'll be praying for you," he replied.

"Thanks again," I said before ending the call. I dropped the phone in my pocket and stood a little straighter. "He's right," I whispered to myself. "I am a man of God."

No, you're not, I heard a voice within me say.

"Elizabeth?" I asked, hoping it was her. I looked around, hoping to see her standing there, but I didn't. She was nowhere to be seen. "So, man of God," I asked aloud, "what's going on?"

There's no way you are a man of God, I heard the voice say. *You're masquerading as a pastor, but you stole money from your church, and then you used it to gamble. If that wasn't bad enough, you then lied about it. You can never get over this, Brad Johnson. Never.*

"That's not true," I answered. "I made a few mistakes, but that doesn't mean I can't get through this."

You're about to be fired.

"No, I'm not!" I shouted, earning me another dirty look from the mime, now across the street from me.

You're about to lose your ministry and maybe your marriage and family. You let Sally Mae kiss you last night. You could have stopped her, but you didn't. You're a sex addict and completely worthless.

"She admitted it was her fault. She apologized, for crying out loud."

Absolutely worthless, repeated the voice.

"It's not true," I said. "I'm a man of God."

No, you're not.

"Yes, I am," I replied. "I'm a holy man of God!"

"Pastor Brad?" someone said behind me.

I turned and smiled. "Hello, Paul," I said. "How are you?"

Paul suddenly looked self-conscious and avoided direct eye contact. He appeared to still be wearing the same T-shirt and jeans from two days earlier. "I'm okay," he said. "How are you? Were you just talking to yourself?"

"Not really," I laughed. "It's hard to explain, but it was sort of the opposite of praying."

"Okay," said Paul. He shifted uneasily, and I could tell he wanted to bolt.

"Hey," said Elizabeth, suddenly walking out the door of a bar. "You found him?"

"Yeah," I replied. "Why did you go in there?"

"I had to use the bathroom, okay?"

"I'm sorry," said Paul. "You two were looking for me?"

"Yes," I said. "We've been walking around for quite a while trying to find you."

"Why?" he asked.

"Would you like to join us for some beignets?" I asked. "My treat."

He looked me in the eye. "You came all this way to eat beignets with me?"

"I'd like to talk with you, and I rarely get within walking distance of the original Café du Monde."

"Yep," said Elizabeth. "Beignets are good."

"Okay," he said. "We can get some beignets and talk, I guess."

"Great," I said.

"But I can't for a little over an hour," he replied. "I have a gig in about five minutes. I'm almost late."

"Oh," I said. "That's okay. No problem."

"We can wait," said Elizabeth.

"Would you like to come?" asked Paul. "It's just around the corner. You could get some lunch, and the beignets could be our dessert."

"Sure," I said. "Where is it?"

"It's a dive called the Angry Broad."

"Sounds like me," said Elizabeth.

I rolled my eyes at her comment.

"What?" asked Paul.

"Don't worry about it," I said. "We all have our own set of issues."

"Sorry, Pastor Brad," said Paul nervously. "But I really need to get there."

"Oh, okay," I said. "Let's go."

CHAPTER 29

The Angry Broad had an enormous bar on one end of the room and a miniscule stage on the other. Paul and the other band members were arranging their equipment onstage as Elizabeth and I sat at a table in the middle of the floor.

"I'm starving!" said Elizabeth, who frantically scanned her menu.

Food was the last thing on my mind, so I just nodded and continued to watch the musicians attend to their setup.

"What'll you have?" asked a waitress, suddenly beside us.

Elizabeth spoke up quickly. "I'll have the bourbon club sandwich with a side of red beans and rice."

"Anything to drink?" asked the waitress.

Elizabeth shot a hopeful look at me. I raised one eyebrow.

"I'll just have water with lemon," she said.

"What about you, baby?" the waitress asked in my general direction.

I looked up and smiled. "Oh, uh, nothing for me, thanks."

She rolled her eyes. "There's a ten-dollar cover unless you order something to eat or drink. You want to start with a beer?"

"Oh … uh, no, thank you," I replied, glancing up at the wall, at the menu written in chalk. "I guess I'll take a cheeseburger and a Coke."

"It'll be out soon, baby," she replied.

We watched as she turned from us, and then Elizabeth punched me in the arm.

"Ow. What was that for?" I asked.

"I'm going to tell Allison you've been flirting with a woman in the French Quarter."

"What? I wasn't flirting with her."

"After what happened with Sally Mae last night, this is scandalous!"

"I have no idea what you're talking about," I said, leaning back in my chair.

"She called you 'baby' twice. Next thing she'll be asking for your phone number."

"You're being ridiculous," I said. "I'm a happily married man."

"Whatever," she laughed. "Yep, this is the end of the line for you, Pastor Brad."

"Shut up," I said. "The band's about to start."

As if on cue, the drummer counted off the first song. For the next forty-five minutes, I slowly ate my cheeseburger and listened as the band played covers from the last several decades. Elizabeth wolfed down her food and then disappeared into the bathroom. The drummer was fun to watch because he constantly laughed and nodded his head. The bass player seemed content with his role and very amused by the antics of the drummer. The keys player was also the spokesman for the band. He smiled a lot but often brought his lips together tightly if he was especially pleased with the music. And then there was Paul, who was featured in almost every selection. He had improved musically over the years. However, unlike the rest of the band, he never smiled or seemed as if he was enjoying himself.

About halfway through the set, as I watched Paul, I suddenly felt strange, as if someone was watching me too. I looked around at the other tables, only half-filled because it was the early part of the day, but all the customers had their eyes either on the band or on each other.

The waitress suddenly appeared, bill in hand. "Here's your ticket, baby," she replied. "You want anything else?"

"Oh, no, thank you," I said. "Did you see if my sister left the building?"

"I think she's still in the bathroom," she replied. "I'm not surprised with the way she downed that whiskey earlier."

"I'm sorry, what?" I asked. "I don't understand. She only had water with lemon."

"She ordered it right in front of you, baby."

"What did she order?"

"The bourbon club. It comes with a shot of bourbon at the end of your meal. The only problem is, she had more than one shot."

"Good grief," I said. "Thanks for letting me know."

"You're welcome, baby," she replied. "I'll be back in a moment for your payment. Anything else?"

"There is one thing," I said. "Did you notice anyone strange in here watching me?"

"Honey, this is Bourbon Street. This place is called the Angry Broad. Strange is everywhere you look."

"I guess you're right," I said and glanced toward the door, just in time to see it close.

Fifteen minutes later, Paul and I sat awkwardly across the table from each other in the corner near the green and white awning of Café du Monde. His guitar case leaned against one side of the table. Elizabeth was once again in the bathroom, regretting her recent decision to sneak several shots of bourbon.

"Thanks for coming to see me," said Paul. "I'm curious as to what you want."

"Well," I started awkwardly, "I'm not sure I know how to say this, but I'm saying it anyway."

"I'm sorry," said Paul. "What?"

"Sorry," I said. "I know this must be confusing to you because it's even confusing to me."

"Okay," he replied.

"I'm a pastor, right?" I asked.

"Yes," he answered. "At least for now."

"Oh, you've heard about my predicament."

"Yes," he replied. "My aunt Shirley contacted me. She wants me to come to the church business meeting tonight to help get you fired."

"Are you going?"

"No, I'm not," he answered. "No offense, but I really don't care what happens at Lee Community Church in Aucoin."

"I can understand that. I wonder what I did to cause your aunt Shirley to dislike me so much. I just saw her on Monday, and she was really pleasant."

Paul shrugged his shoulders and replied, "Well, that's my aunt Shirley for you. She gets caught up in stuff like that. I wouldn't take it personally."

Suddenly, the waiter arrived, and we ordered beignets and café au lait. The diversion gave me a chance to gather my thoughts. I had been so consumed with finding Paul that I hadn't considered what I might say if I actually found him.

"What did you want to talk about?" asked Paul when the waiter stepped away.

"Sorry," I said, catching a glimpse of his eyes for the first time. They were the eyes of someone who was tired, hurt, and confused. The pain communicated by his glance almost brought tears to my own eyes.

"Paul," I said, "you look terrible, and I'm not talking about your clothes. You look tired and beaten down and worn by this life you've chosen."

"Really?" he asked, raising one eyebrow.

"Yes," I replied. "When I first saw you play music, you inspired me. You enjoyed playing so much that passion seemed to pour out of you. Now it just seems like you do it to survive."

"What are you trying to say, Pastor Brad?"

"I'm saying that I think you need to come home to Aucoin and refresh your body, mind, and spirit. Come renew your relationship with your parents, find joy in your music again, and spend some time talking with the Lord. It's painful to watch you now when I've seen the real you, enjoying your musicianship so very much."

"Wow," he replied softly, looking away to avoid eye contact. "It's that noticeable?"

"Yeah, it is."

Paul cocked his head to one side, took in a breath, and let it out slowly. He stared directly into my eyes for a few seconds, blinked, and then looked away. "Did my parents ask you to come talk to me?"

I chuckled and answered, "No, they didn't, but they do know I'm here."

"I spoke with my mom this morning."

"I heard it was pretty brief."

"Yeah, well, my phone died. It's hard for me to keep a good charge with my schedule."

"What do you say, Paul?" I asked. "Want me to drive you home this afternoon?"

"Why are you doing this?"

"What do you mean?"

"Why are you trying to help me?"

I smiled and scratched my head. "Well," I said, "I care about you and your parents."

"But aren't you getting fired tonight?"

I smiled again and said, "Maybe so, but that doesn't change anything."

"Sure it does," he said. "If you're going to lose a gig, why should you show up to play?"

"Well," I said, "I guess it's because what I'm doing is not a gig. It's a calling. Sure, I might lose my paid position at Lee Community tonight, but that doesn't mean I stop caring about people, restoring broken relationships, visiting the sick, and introducing people to the one who loves them so much."

"And you're here to bring me home?" he asked.

"Yes," I replied, "if you'll come."

"Wow," he said dispassionately.

"What do you say, Paul?"

Paul closed his eyes for a moment, started to say something, and then paused.

"What is it?" I asked.

"Okay, whatever," he said. "I'm caught in a trap, and I don't see how I can get out of it. I love being a musician. I love playing with musicians all over this city. But over time, I've made some bad decisions, and now I live in ways I never wanted to live. I'm not who I used to be. I have some addictions, and I have some debts. Those weigh heavily on me, even while I'm playing music."

Suddenly, the waiter approached our table with our order. He placed the beignets and coffee on the table and handed me the bill. "That will be $12.86," he said.

I turned to him and stood to remove my wallet. I pulled out a ten and a five, handed them to the man, and waited for my change. Quickly, he pulled out a small wad of cash from his pocket and made change.

"Thank you," I said, handing two dollars back to him.

"Thank you, sir," he replied.

I turned back to my seat and saw that both Paul and his guitar case were gone. I stopped the waiter and asked, "Did you see my friend leave?"

"Yes," he replied. "While you were paying, he stood up, grabbed his guitar case, and left."

"I can't believe it," I said, knowing there was no way I could find him again.

"Do you need anything else?" asked the waiter.

"You know," I said, "I'm going to need a bag for these beignets."

"One moment," he replied and stepped away.

Meanwhile, Elizabeth emerged from the bathroom holding her head. She collapsed into the seat next to me and placed her forehead flat on the iron table.

"Did you enjoy your bourbon club?" I asked.

"Not at all," she replied as she straightened into a normal sitting position. "It had too much bread."

"Yeah," I replied. "Too much bread always ruins a sandwich. Shots of bourbon whiskey never help matters either."

"I'm weak, Brad. Just tell me what I should do."

"Well, for starters, you should wipe all the powdered sugar from your forehead. I have a table full of beignets here."

"Oh, great," she replied as she reached for the napkins.

I couldn't help but smile at my sister.

"Where's Paul?" she asked.

My smile turned to a grimace. "He's gone," I answered. "He took off while I was paying the waiter."

"You let him get away again?"

"I didn't let him do anything. I stood to pay, and when I sat back down, he was gone."

"That sucks," she said before putting her head back on the sugar-sprinkled table.

"You're right, Elizabeth," I replied. "It does indeed." I took my first bite of the sugar-smothered beignets. It wouldn't be my last.

CHAPTER 30

It took me nearly thirty minutes to get Elizabeth back to the car, where she collapsed in the back seat. I practically fell into the driver's seat myself from exhaustion. I set the bag of beignets in the seat next to me, pulled one out for the road, and started the car. As I drove through the backstreets of New Orleans, headed toward the interstate, Elizabeth moaned.

"Are you okay?" I asked, looking back at her. She lay in the back seat with her arm draped over her face, covering her eyes.

"The sun is so bright today!" she cried.

I looked up at the sky. "Looks overcast to me," I said.

"Shut up, Brad!"

"No problem," I said, vowing not to say anything else until she demanded it.

"It's all my fault!" she suddenly cried. "I was finally going to be someone's mama. But I messed it all up, and my baby's gone."

I started to say something but quickly changed my mind. Instead, I said a quick prayer in my mind. *Lord, help my sister.*

During the drive back to Aucoin, I felt a sense of great loss for my sister and a sense of impending doom for myself. If I was going to be fired, I had really wanted my last day as pastor of Lee Community to be spent making a difference in someone's life. With Paul's disappearance, the whole day now seemed to be a waste. Paul certainly hadn't responded well to my visit. I might have even driven him further away from his parents.

I did call Ernie to explain what had happened. "I'm sorry," I told him. "But Paul just disappeared while I was paying the bill."

"It's okay, Pastor," said Ernie. "He's done the same thing to us, many times. I appreciate you trying to help. I pray for him every night, but I'm to the point where I've simply left him in the Lord's hands."

"I hope you've added me to your prayers today, Ernie. I'm afraid it doesn't look very good for me. Some of the people are determined to believe the worst about me."

"And your run-in with Sally Mae Watson last night isn't going to help your situation any either," said Ernie.

"You're right there," I said. "I don't know what I can do now except pray."

"Well, that is the most you can do, Pastor."

"Yeah," I said. "I guess so."

"But you still need to hold on to the truth, Pastor Brad, because in the end, it will set you free."

"Thanks, Ernie," I said. "I just hope it sets me free before I'm released from my job."

Ninety minutes later, when I crossed into the Aucoin city limits, Elizabeth was still asleep in the back seat, so I opted to drive home. When I pulled into my driveway, I realized I was covered with powdered sugar. The empty Café du Monde bag now lay on the floorboard. "I can't believe I ate them all," I lamented.

I stepped from the car and began to wipe the sugar from my clothes. Suddenly, a wave of nausea came over me, and I vomited all over the lawn. I reached for the beignet bag, blew the powdered sugar residue from the napkin inside, and then wiped my mouth with it. As I turned back to the car, Bobby pulled up on his bicycle.

"Man!" he said. "I haven't seen anyone throw up like that in a long time!"

"Yeah," I replied.

"You must be really nervous about getting fired tonight."

I closed my eyes and grimaced. "I'm okay, thanks."

"Who's that lady in the back seat of your car?"

"She's my sister," I said. "She's not feeling well."

"Looks like you're not feeling good either. What's all that white stuff on your clothes?"

"It's powdered sugar."

"Wow," he said. "That's a lot of sugar."

"Yeah, I guess it is."

"Okay," he said. "I'll see you tonight, Pastor Brad."

"You're coming to the business meeting?" I asked.

"Oh yeah," he said as he rode away. "Everyone in town is talking about it. That church is going to be packed."

"Wonderful," I said sarcastically as I walked to the side of the house and turned on the waterspout connected to the garden hose.

"So," said Allison from the front door, "are you nervous about tonight?"

I aimed the hose at the vomit and watched it dissolve into the lawn. "No," I answered.

"Then why did you throw up?"

"I'm pretty sure this is the remainder of a greasy cheeseburger from the Angry Broad and nine powdered sugar beignets."

"You ate nine beignets?"

"Yeah, maybe I am worried about tonight. I must have been stress-eating."

"Who's the angry broad?"

"Oh, it's not a who. It's a place."

"I see," she replied. "That's a relief, I guess. What were you doing there?"

"Listening to Paul Plaisance play."

"Did he come back with you?"

"No, he didn't. That's why I had nine beignets. I ordered us each three and confronted him about coming home, and he split while I paid the bill."

"I'm sorry, honey. I know you really wanted to help him."

"Elizabeth is asleep in the back seat of the car."

"Why?"

"She's sleeping it off."

"You two were drinking?"

"No," I said, "just her, behind my back. She'll be all right. I just heard from Bobby on his bike that the whole town is coming out tonight to watch me get canned."

"Do you think that's going to happen?" she asked.

"I don't know," I said. "I hope not."

Allison walked over to me and hugged me gently. "Oh!" she cried, pushing away quickly. "You're covered in powdered sugar."

"It's from the beignets," I said.

"Ah," she said. "You don't smell all that great either. You've got a couple hours before the business meeting. You'd better go get showered up."

"That sounds like a good idea," I replied, and I started up the stairs to our home.

"Oh, and honey?" said Allison.

"Yeah?"

"You better use some mouthwash too."

CHAPTER 31

It was six thirty when Allison and I arrived for the seven o'clock business meeting. I had wanted to arrive early and collect my thoughts as the people entered. However, the church parking lot was already full.

"Oh my!" said Allison as we pulled into the lot. "I've never seen so many cars here. Will you be able to find a spot?"

"I'm sure I can manage," I replied.

"It's like Easter Sunday," she said.

"Well," I said, "I guess tonight we're the best show in town."

Allison put her hand on my cheek and said, "It will be okay, honey, no matter what happens."

I smiled and said, "I wish I could be so confident."

As we both stepped from the car, I checked on Elizabeth, who was still asleep in the back seat.

"How is she?" asked Allison.

"Looks like she's out cold," I replied. "Let's not wake her. She'd probably make things worse anyway."

"Is that any way to speak about your sister?" asked Allison.

"Who are you trying to be?" I asked. "My mother?"

"I guess I do sound like her, but now is not the time to get all bent out of shape about your sister. You've got enough to worry about."

"You're right," I said. "She can sleep it off, and we'll take her home after my execution—I mean, the meeting."

As we turned toward the church building, I could hear commotion coming from inside the building. "Sounds like an angry mob," I said to Allison.

"Brad, why would people act like that? You grew up in this church, and now you're the pastor. These people love you. You get to pastor in your own hometown."

"Yeah, that's where Jesus said a prophet was without honor."

"Come on, honey," said Allison. "At least try to be upbeat and positive."

"Okay, I'll try."

"Pastor Brad!" cried Ernie, suddenly appearing from the door. "I'm glad you're here. Some of the people said you weren't going to show up."

"Why wouldn't I be here?" I replied.

"Well," he said, "the word on the street is that you've lost your mind. Someone said that your affair with Sally Mae has been going on since high school and that you've been paying her to keep it quiet with church money."

"What?" I asked.

"Yeah," he said. "The same person said you were going to leave Allison and Gabe and were planning to run off with Sally Mae on a cruise."

"These rumors are really getting out of hand," I replied.

"And now it's been reported that you were driving around with a drunk lady in the back seat of your car, claiming she was your sister."

"That one's true," I said. "Elizabeth, my sister, did go with me to New Orleans, and she did sneak a few drinks, and yes, she's asleep in the back seat of my car, even now."

"Is that it?" Allison asked Ernie.

"No," he said. "I don't know how to say this, Pastor Brad, but you're also being accused of something far worse."

"Something worse?" I exclaimed. "What do you mean?"

"Apparently, a neighbor kid saw you covered in a white powdery substance, vomiting all over your front lawn."

"I did throw up in my front yard today, but it was from the food I ate in New Orleans. I was covered in powdered sugar."

"There's the white powdery substance," said Ernie.

"Yeah," I replied. "It was all over me from the beignets."

"Well," said Ernie, "you're going to have to explain that to everyone. Like I said, everyone thinks you've lost your mind."

"I don't know if I've lost my mind or not, but I'm not having an affair with Sally Mae, or anyone else for that matter, and I haven't booked a cruise with anyone. I wanted to take Allison on a cruise for our anniversary, but it's going to be hard to do that if I don't have a job."

"You wanted to take me on a cruise?" asked Allison. "When were you planning to tell me about it?"

"Well," I said, "I didn't want to say anything if I couldn't make it happen."

"That's sweet, honey," she said.

"I should probably warn you, Pastor Brad," said Ernie.

"Warn me about what?"

"Well," he said, "as you can tell, the place is packed. Earl has turned all of Aucoin against you. He called people last night, talking to folks until late into the night."

"Really?" I asked. "Everyone in town is against me?"

"Some of them are really angry," said Ernie. "But you should keep calm as you enter. Church people tend to get mean in situations like this, and they'll analyze every move you make and every word you say to help their argument."

I swallowed hard. "Okay. Thanks, I guess."

He smiled. "I know everything looks grim at the moment."

"Yes, it does," said Allison.

"However," said Ernie, "even though things look really bad, I still think everything will be okay in the end."

"I hope so," I said. "I mean, how bad could it really be?"

I opened the door for Allison, and we stepped inside. Instantly, all conversation ceased, and every head turned to face us.

"Hi," I said with a slight wave. No one responded.

After an awkward moment of silence, Archie stood and said, "Pastor Brad and Allison, won't you please come in and have a seat up front? We have two reserved spots just for you. Is your son with you?"

"Ah, no, he isn't," said Allison. "He's at home with my sister."

"I see," said Archie. "Just this way."

I smiled at people as we walked down the center aisle, accompanied by Ernie. Every deacon was present, along with his wife and children. Sally Mae sat in the back row, looking down. Shirley Plaisance, Ernie's sister, was seated with the members of the Dorcas class, who were no doubt wishing they had their seat cushions. In the front row, next to Nettie Longwood, sat my neighbor Bobby and his parents. Bobby's parents, Bill and Jennifer, eyed me suspiciously, but Bobby smiled and waved, seemingly unaware that his reports about the white powder had complicated my situation. I smiled back at him and then glanced again at the filled sanctuary. No one else was smiling except for Nettie Longwood and Freddy Lambano.

I turned to Ernie. "Do you still think everything is going to be okay?"

"Yes, Pastor," he replied. "It's going to be fine. Remember, the truth will set you free."

"Yeah," I said. "Thanks."

Ernie winked and gave me a thumbs-up before walking to the back of the room.

I rolled my eyes and whispered to Allison, "I think Ernie may be the one who has lost his mind."

"He's just trying to be nice, I'm sure. Where's Earl?" she asked.

"That's a good question," I replied. "Who knows what he's up to?"

Slowly, the conversations in the pews resumed, and I relaxed a bit. After a couple of minutes, Nettie Longwood went to the piano and began playing in a minor key. Archie stood and slowly made his way to the pulpit, trying to time his approach with the ending of Nettie's musical piece.

I whispered to Allison, "I feel like I'm being led to my own execution."

"Oh, Brad," she replied.

"It's been nice being married to you, honey," I said. "Take care of our son and know that I love you."

"Good evening," said Archie, interrupting any comfort I had been about to receive from my wife. "It's good to see everyone here this evening. I'm sorry it has to be under such dire circumstances."

A few grunts were heard from the congregation, but nothing intelligible.

"I, Archie Arceneaux, chairman of the board of deacons for Lee Community Church, do hereby call this business meeting to order. Since this is a special called business meeting, we will dispense with the reading of the minutes from our last meeting. Tonight, we have only one order of business, that being the recent accusations and semi-confession of Pastor Brad Johnson."

"What's a semi-confession?" whispered Allison.

"I'm not sure," I replied.

Archie continued, "Pastor Brad has been accused of stealing church funds, lying to church officials, carousing with both local women and New Orleans floozies, and finally, as of this afternoon, engaging in substance abuse." Archie paused for dramatic effect as the congregation gasped in unison and momentarily sucked all of the oxygen from the room.

"Goodness gracious," said Mrs. W. P. Gurdon, the teacher of the Dorcas class.

I glanced at Allison, who tightened her lips and blinked her eyes.

Archie continued with the accusations against me. "We even have official reports that he was seen today in the French Quarter of New Orleans visiting an establishment called the Angry Broad."

"Oh my!" repeated Mrs. Gurdon, who started fanning herself with both hands.

Jimmy Rice stood and shouted, "What was the name of the unhappy broad he propositioned?"

Gasps could be heard across the congregation.

"I say we call for a vote right now!" yelled Jimmy. "He's guilty. Everyone here knows about him and Sally Mae Watson! And his neighbor kid saw him with suspicious powder all over his clothes."

The congregation seemed to roar in agreement as they suddenly broke out into applause.

"I didn't know they knew how to clap," I said to Allison. "I guess it takes me getting fired to build excitement around here."

"Quiet, please!" boomed Archie over the crowd. "I can appreciate your enthusiasm, Jimmy, but we have to conduct ourselves in an orderly, efficient manner, or this meeting will give way to sheer anarchy."

Finally, the crowd grew silent again.

"Now, folks," said Archie, "you have to listen to what I say. I said that Pastor Brad visited an *establishment* called the Angry Broad. Please don't jump to conclusions, or pandemonium will break loose."

"Can I talk now?" asked Jimmy.

I glanced at Allison. She reached over and placed her hand on my own.

"Now, Jimmy," said Archie, "you can't make suggestions or comments until I open the floor for discussion. We have to follow procedure."

"I'm sorry," said Jimmy. "Why don't you open the floor for discussion then?"

"Now just hold on," said Archie. "I'm getting to it."

"Please do," said Jimmy.

Archie stood tall behind the pulpit and said, "I now open the floor for discussion on the matter."

Jimmy raised his hand. "May I speak now, Your Honor?"

"Very funny, Jimmy. What is it that you have to say?"

"I say we call for a vote right now," repeated Jimmy.

The crowd once again cheered and clapped.

"This is going to be a long night," whispered Allison.

"Yep," I replied, wrapping her hand in my own.

Archie raised his hands and said, "Now hold on, everyone. We've only heard the accusations so far. We need to at least give Pastor Brad a chance to respond and then give folks a chance to ask questions and comment."

A few louder grunts erupted from the congregation.

"Pastor Brad," said Archie, "would you please come to the podium?"

"Certainly," I replied, standing and taking in a huge breath. The walk to the podium seemed to take an eternity. I felt every eye watching my every step, as if waiting for me to commit all seven deadly sins.

When I finally stood beside Archie, he said, "Now, Pastor Brad, would you please take a few minutes and address the accusations that have been made against you?"

"Certainly," I replied. "Any particular order you want me to follow?"

"No," he said. "Just tell us what happened from your perspective."

"Okay," I replied.

"And Pastor Brad?" added Archie.

"Yes, sir?"

"We're expecting you to be completely honest as you share today. Do you understand?"

"Absolutely," I said.

Archie stepped away from the podium and sat in a chair on the platform. I stepped into his position and smiled awkwardly at the people. "Well," I said, "I guess there's no better place to start than at the beginning."

I was about to begin when the back door opening caught everyone's attention. "Sorry I'm late," said Earl as he stepped inside.

"It's okay," said Archie. "Come in please, all of you."

Earl shuffled in, revealing a handful of others behind him, including Paul Plaisance, my sister Elizabeth, and Pastor Jeremy Sullivan.

"Oh my," I said, inadvertently speaking into the microphone and catching the attention of the congregation.

"Please continue, Pastor Brad," said Archie.

I nodded politely and smiled. I surveyed the congregation once again and noticed Mama and Daddy sitting in the third row. Daddy smiled and nodded his head as if to say, "You've got this." Earl shuffled in and found a seat between the deacons and the Dorcas class members. Paul and Jeremy managed to find seats beside Ernie in the back row.

"Sorry," I said as the attention of the congregation shifted back to me. "As I said, let me start at the beginning. This past Sunday morning was difficult for me. After a harsh altercation with the deacons during the Sunday school hour, my confidence was shot. I feel as if I did a poor job of preaching, and for that I am sorry."

I noticed a few nods across the crowd, but the angry stares persisted.

"Following the service, I turned off the lights and went to retrieve my bag from my office."

"You mean the church office, don't you?" asked Archie, half-standing.

I grimaced briefly and then replied, "Yes, excuse me. I went to retrieve my bag from the church office, where I have a desk. It was then and there that I noticed a hundred-dollar bill on the floor. I figured it had been mistakenly dropped by one of the ushers, so I picked it up. Now, I don't have the combination to the safe in the office, so I texted Ernie Plaisance, our church treasurer, and then placed the bill in my Bible for safekeeping."

"See?" said Jimmy Rice loudly to his neighbor. "I told you he stole that money."

I swallowed hard and continued. "My intention was to keep the hundred-dollar bill in my Bible until I met up with Ernie on Monday to count the offering, but unfortunately, that is not what happened. I stopped by the One Stop on my way home to pick up some milk and—"

"That's not all he picked up from what I've heard," said Shirley Plaisance.

The room filled with laughter.

"May God spare us all!" cried Mrs. Gurdon, who resumed fanning herself.

Allison rolled her eyes. Ernie shook his head. Sally Mae looked down at her feet and grimaced.

"Can we please have order?" asked Archie.

When it was almost quiet, I said, "While at the store, I learned that their card machine wasn't working, so in desperation to get milk to please my wife and my mother, who was visiting, I used the money I had found."

"And there you have it!" cried Jimmy, standing and pointing at me.

This time, however, the congregation remained quiet.

"Please, Jimmy," said Archie, "let Pastor Brad finish."

I caught Jimmy's eye for a moment, but he looked away. I glanced at Earl, who had surprisingly said nothing. He stared back at me without expression. Mama, who sat a few rows behind Earl, smiled gently and shook her head.

"My plan," I continued, "was to replenish the money and give it to Ernie on Monday when we counted the offering. I was going to tell him about it when he responded to my message, but then he and Connie were in a car accident in McComb."

As I spoke, Earl shifted uncomfortably in his seat but still said nothing.

"Then," I said, "when Ernie and I met Monday to count the offering, I was finally able to return one hundred dollars to him. He received it and placed it in the offering. Earl was there and witnessed the whole thing." I stepped back from the pulpit and glanced at Archie.

"Is that all you have to say?" he asked.

"What else would you like for me to say?" I asked.

"Well," said Archie, "I suppose that would be up to the congregation to decide. I now reopen the floor for discussion. Does anyone have any questions for Pastor Brad?"

"I have a question!" shouted Jimmy Rice, standing up.

"Okay, Jimmy," said Archie with slight hesitation in his voice. "What is it?"

"I heard the rest of his confession last night at the deacons' meeting. But that was before you and Earl found him in the arms of Sally Mae Watson at the One Stop Shop last night. I'd like to hear from you and Earl about what you saw. Then I'd like to know how long this affair has been going on."

"Okay," said Archie. "This is somewhat out of order, but I'll allow it. Since

I'm moderating this meeting, I think it best that we hear Earl's testimony about last night."

Earl's head shot up, and he rose from his seat.

Oh my, I thought. *Now I'm done for. Earl has been ready to drive the nails into my coffin for years.*

"Earl," said Archie, "would you please come up here to speak about what we saw last night?"

Earl slid past the other deacons in his row and made his way down the aisle to the front. He wasn't wearing his usual evil smile. In fact, he looked nervous. As he approached, I moved from the pulpit and sat next to Archie. Earl swallowed hard and faced the congregation but said nothing.

"It's worse than we thought," said Jimmy. "It's left Earl speechless!"

"The details must be horrific!" said Mrs. W. P. Gurdon.

"Come on, Earl," said Jimmy. "We're all waiting."

"Go ahead, Earl," said Archie. "Tell them what we saw last night."

Earl gripped the podium and started to speak but then hesitated. "Wouldn't that be better coming from you, Archie, since you're the chairman of the deacons and all?"

I glanced at Allison, who raised her eyebrows. It wasn't like Earl to back down from the opportunity to put someone in his place, especially me.

"No," said Archie. "Since I'm the moderator, we need the testimony of someone else. You were the only other witness to what we saw."

"Okay," said Earl, turning back to the people. Gripping the pulpit, he said, "Well, last night, after the deacons' meeting, Archie and I stopped in at the One Stop Shop and found Sally Mae Watson and Pastor Brad behind the counter in each other's arms."

Somewhere in the building, a woman gasped, and the whispers began. I closed my eyes and swallowed hard. When I opened them, in the midst of the chaos, all I could see was Allison smiling. I loved that smile.

Archie shouted, "Now settle down, everyone! Let Earl finish."

"What were they doing behind the counter?" asked Jimmy.

"Well," said Earl, "they appeared to be kissing."

Again, the woman gasped, and the whispers turned to full-blown conversations. Earl stepped away from the podium, looked at me, looked down at the floor, and then walked back toward his seat.

"Earl?" said Archie. "Do you have anything else to say, Earl?"

"You want to hear more?" asked Earl.

"Come on, Earl," said Jimmy. "Go on back up there and let him have it!"

"I believe I've said enough," said Earl.

When have you ever said enough, Earl? I thought. *Why are you being so timid?*

Archie stood behind the pulpit and gripped it with both hands. He grimaced and looked out at the crowd, which slowly grew quiet.

"Well, folks," he said. "I don't see any need to move forward with talking about the money. It looks like we have a pastoral moral failure on our hands. That in itself is enough to call for a vote of confidence."

"It sure is," cried Jimmy.

"What's your pleasure?" asked Archie.

Jimmy stood and pointed at me. "Since we have a preacher who can't keep his hands off of women, I make a motion that we terminate Brad Johnson at once!"

The crowd burst into angry applause.

I looked helplessly at Allison. She mouthed, "I love you," and smiled once again.

"Do I hear a second?" asked Archie.

"Wait a minute!" screamed a voice from the back. "Don't you want to hear the whole truth?"

CHAPTER 32

Archie's eyes opened wide as he gripped the podium with both hands, leaned in, and cried out, "Sally Mae Watson? Is that you?"

Sally Mae looked up with wide eyes, rose to her feet, and responded, "Yes, sir, Mr. Chairman."

"She wouldn't dare come in here!" cried Mrs. W. P. Gurdon.

"Can you believe such a thing?" asked Shirley Plaisance.

"Ha!" cried Jimmy. "This oughta be good."

Sally Mae ignored the comments and said, "Wouldn't you like to hear the whole story about what happened between Pastor Brad and myself?"

"I think so," said Archie, "but I believe we need a motion to—"

"For crying out loud, Archie!" said Ernie. "I make a motion that we hear what Sally Mae Watson has to say about the night in question."

"Do I hear a second?" asked Archie.

Suddenly, the sanctuary was filled with silence. In a way I was grateful because no one wanted Sally Mae or me to be embarrassed. However, I was also upset because sometimes people would rather believe a lie than uncover the truth.

"Anyone?" asked Archie.

After another brief moment of silence, Allison stood and said, "I'll second the motion."

"What?" asked Archie. "I'm not sure that's fitting now, Allison."

"Why not?" asked Allison, turning toward Sally Mae. "I'm a full-fledged member of this church. Besides, I'm very interested to hear the full story of what went on between Sally Mae Watson and Pastor Brad Johnson."

Even from a distance, I saw Sally Mae flinch.

"Okay there, Allison," said Archie. "All in favor?"

Every hand rose high, with the exception of mine and Archie's.

"The ayes have it," said Archie. "Sally Mae, would you be willing to share with everyone here about what happened that night at the One Stop Shop?"

"Yes, Archie," said Sally Mae. "I do believe I would."

"Then come on up."

Sally Mae practically ran to the stage.

"Thank you," said Archie. "I know this must be difficult for you."

"Not really," said Sally Mae. "Well, maybe a little. Do I need to be sworn in?"

"No," said Archie. "This is not a court of law."

"Oh, okay," replied Sally Mae. "It sure seems like one."

This brought a slight chuckle from the crowd. Sally Mae nodded her head.

"Can you just tell us what really happened?" asked Archie.

"Absolutely," she replied, looking out over the crowd. "Well," she began, "I'm not sure how to say this, especially with Allison sitting right here in front of me, so I'm just going to spit it out and ask for forgiveness later."

Every eye across the room, including Allison's, was glued to Sally Mae, partnered with every ear listening in fascination.

"Most of y'all know me from the One Stop Shop. But I've known some of you longer than others. I've known Brad—er, Pastor Brad Johnson—for quite a while now. You may not know this, but he and I once went out on a date."

"What?" asked Archie.

"I guess I should clarify," said Sally Mae. "We went on a date when we were in high school together. You see, I moved to Aucoin from Kentwood during my junior year, and even though that's just down the road from here, I really didn't know anyone. Even back then, I dressed in overalls and high-tops, and some of the girls were making fun of me by the lockers. Brad didn't like seeing this happen, so he walked right up to me in front of them and asked me out on a date."

"What does this have to do with anything?" asked Jimmy.

"It has everything to do with everything," said Sally Mae. "I'm explaining to you about the type of man Brad Johnson is. He cares about people. Him asking me out back then meant the world to me. It not only resulted in a date to the movies and dinner with him, but it also introduced me to Aucoin and to Lee Community Church."

"Can you tell us about the night in question?" asked Archie.

"Yes," said Sally Mae. "You see, I've always been unlucky with love. In high school I had hoped Brad would ask me out again, but he just wanted to be friends. I went along with it, but I kept a secret from him from then until now."

"What was it?" asked Shirley Plaisance.

"Shirley!" cried Archie. "You have to let me ask the questions unless I give you the floor!"

"Sorry about that, Archie," said Shirley.

"Thank you," said Archie. "Sally Mae, would you please tell us your secret?"

"Certainly," she replied. "What Pastor Brad doesn't know is that for all these years I've secretly been in love with him."

"I knew it!" cried Jimmy. "What do you think of that, Earl?"

Earl uncharacteristically shrugged his shoulders.

"Okay," said Archie. "Can you please just tell us what happened last night?"

"I was getting to that," said Sally Mae. "Pastor Brad came into the store. It had been pretty quiet all night. I saw my chance to make a move on him, so I did."

Allison raised one eyebrow and crossed her arms but kept herself under control.

"And can you tell us how Pastor Brad responded to your advances?" asked Archie.

"He rejected me and tried to push me away," she answered.

"But when we walked in, we saw you kissing each other!" snapped Archie.

"I know it looked that way," said Sally Mae. "Pastor Brad was actually trying to push me away, but I fought back and kept coming at him."

"Come on, Sally Mae!" cried Archie. "Do you expect the good people of this church to believe that you managed to trap Brad Johnson into the awkward situation he was in when Earl and I walked into the store?"

"Yes, I do," snapped Sally Mae. "It's amazing what you can accomplish if you put your mind to it."

A few chuckles could be heard from the crowd. Allison showed no emotion but gripped her purse tightly.

Archie pressed on. "Do you have anything else to say, Sally Mae?"

"Just one thing," she replied. "I want to apologize to Pastor Brad and everyone here for what I've done, especially you, Allison."

Allison, who had been staring down at her purse during much of Sally Mae's testimony, looked up and raised her eyebrows again.

"I'm so sorry, Allison!" said Sally Mae. "Can you please forgive me?"

Allison tightened her lips and looked up at Sally Mae. The crowd grew quiet as Allison stood.

"My gracious!" cried Mrs. W. P. Gurdon.

"Shhh!" said Shirley Plaisance. "I can't hear what she's saying."

Allison stepped up to Sally Mae and stared at her.

"Please forgive me?" repeated Sally Mae.

Allison suddenly let out a breath, smiled, and nodded yes.

Sally Mae took a step forward and asked, "Really?"

"Yes," said Allison. "I can't believe I'm saying this, but yes, I forgive you."

"Oh, thank you!" cried Sally Mae as she suddenly grabbed Allison and pulled her close.

The two ladies hugged each other tightly for a moment until Allison pulled away. I wanted to applaud, but instead I just smiled.

"I hope we can be friends," said Sally Mae.

"I think we can," said Allison. "I'm certainly going to be seeing more of you."

"Why is that?" asked Sally Mae.

"Because I'll be the one buying gas and milk for our family in the future."

Both women laughed, as did most of the ladies present. Sally Mae and Allison hugged once again, resulting in applause from the congregation.

Archie raised both hands for the congregation's attention once again. "Excuse me, everyone!" he said. "We still need to continue in an orderly manner. Do I hear a motion that we accept Sally Mae's testimony and therefore excuse the compromising position in which Pastor Brad was found last night at the One Stop Shop?"

"So moved," said Earl.

"Earl!" cried Jimmy. "What are you doing?"

"Leave me alone," said Earl. "Go ahead, Archie. I made the motion, so let's proceed with the meeting."

"This night is certainly filled with surprises," said Archie. "Do I hear a second?"

"I second the motion," said Ernie.

"Is there any discussion that needs to take place?" asked Archie.

"I should say so," cried Jimmy. "These ladies hugging is all very touching, but I think we need to hear a full description from Earl about what he saw last night at the One Stop."

Earl grimaced and stood. "I don't think that's necessary," he said. "We've heard from Sally Mae, and that should be the end of it."

"What's wrong with you, Earl?" cried Jimmy. "You brought us all here to see justice prevail, and now you're backing down."

"I am not," said Earl. "I just believe Sally Mae's story, and that's all there is to it."

"Now just a cotton-pickin' minute, Earl! I think—"

A loud whistle suddenly cut through the commotion. Every person present turned to see Sally Mae with two fingers in her mouth.

"Archie, I did forget one part of my testimony," she said. "Can I share it?"

"Uh, okay," said Archie.

"Well," she said, "I just wonder if it would help matters if I shared about some of the men from this congregation who come into the One Stop Shop and flirt with me. Would that help move the discussion along?"

Jimmy sat down without another word.

"Even though that's a very good point," said Archie, "I don't think this is the best time for that discussion."

"Can we vote then?" asked Ernie.

"Is there any other discussion from the floor?" asked Archie.

The room remained silent.

"All in favor?" asked Archie.

I watched as almost every hand was raised.

"Opposed with a like sign?" said Archie.

Only Jimmy, Shirley, and Mrs. W. P. Gurdon raised their hands. Almost nothing was ever unanimous at Lee Community.

"Motion carries," said Archie.

I sighed a huge sigh of relief.

"I'm sure we're all happy to know that our pastor was the victim and not the conspirator of the unfortunate happenings last night at the One Stop Shop," said Archie. "However, we now must return to the issue of his mishandling, and possible theft, of church funds."

Oh yeah, I thought. *I almost forgot.*

"I now open the floor for discussion," said Archie.

All eyes went to Earl, who closed his eyes to avoid eye contact.

"Anyone?" prodded Archie.

"I'll speak," said Ernie from the back.

"Very well," said Archie. "It is only fitting that we hear from our church treasurer. You have the floor. Any objections?"

Ernie? I thought. *Oh, of course. He's my character witness. He's got my back, right? He knows I gave back a hundred dollars, which is exactly what I found.*

Ernie walked deliberately down the center aisle and up the steps, gave me a wink, and then turned and faced the people. "Good evening," said Ernie. "Before talking about the financial issue, I feel I must share a few things. First, I want to thank Pastor Brad and Allison for the love and concern they have shown my wife and me this week. I don't know how we would have made it without him. He was the first—in fact, the only—church leader to visit us while Connie was in the hospital. He and Allison prayed with Connie at home and then drove to New Orleans to deliver a package to my son Paul. Then, after a rough deacons' meeting and unfortunate incident at the One Stop Shop, Pastor Brad drove once again today to New Orleans and searched all over Bourbon Street for my son Paul. That's why he was seen in the Angry Broad earlier today. He was waiting for my son, who was there playing a gig. Because of his efforts, my son Paul has come home and is here tonight."

The congregation turned to look at Paul, who smiled but looked down and away from the congregants.

Ernie smiled. "No matter what happens here tonight, I want each person here to know that I will always be grateful to Pastor Brad for his ministry here and especially for how he's helped me and my family over the past week."

As several people across the congregation nodded in agreement, I breathed a sigh of relief.

"However," said Ernie, "we're not here to speak about those things, as good as they are. We're here to explore the facts in order to discover whether Pastor Brad did indeed steal funds from the church."

Silence filled the room as Ernie paused. From the look on his face, I could tell he was about to tell the whole truth and nothing but the truth. Even though that should be a good thing, I was afraid that it could very well get me fired.

"I've served as church treasurer of Lee Community for many years, since long before Pastor Brad was pastor. Most of you know that I've kept meticulous records tracking our church finances. My records indicate that over the last quarter our deposits have been down considerably, by close to one thousand dollars a week."

"A thousand dollars!" said Bobby to his parents. "That's a lot of money!"

Members of the congregation chuckled but quickly returned their attention to Ernie.

"If I'm correct," said Ernie, "our financial condition is considerably bleak for a church of our size. Before figuring in this past weekend's offerings, we're about $15,000 in the red for this year."

A sullen hush fell over the congregation.

"But I've recently updated the giving records of our people, and I see that the giving of our people actually has not decreased over the past year. In fact, it's up by 1 percent."

"What are you saying, Ernie?" asked Archie.

"Well," said Ernie, "as much as it pains me to say this, there's a discrepancy between what's been collected and what has actually been deposited into our account. It's obvious that either someone has stolen funds from our collections, or our records are wrong."

"Heavens sakes!" cried Mrs. W.P. Gurdon.

"I must note at this point," said Ernie, "that I'm certain our records are not wrong."

I raised one eyebrow. Ernie was setting the scene for someone to take the blame, and it looked like it was me.

"Pastor Brad," said Ernie, "claims to have found a one-hundred-dollar bill on the floor of the church office this past Sunday afternoon. He says he put it in his Bible for safekeeping and texted me. When I called him back, I was too caught up with Connie to discuss the church finances, so I asked him if it could wait. I came in late Monday to count the offering, and once we were back in the office, he presented me with a hundred-dollar bill. Money found, the same amount returned."

"But it wasn't the same hundred-dollar bill," said Jimmy Rice. "That rascal had spent some of the money. If he took that one hundred dollars, then he's probably stolen the entire fifteen thousand!"

"Excuse me, may I say one more thing?" asked Sally Mae.

"I'm sorry," said Archie, "but you've already had your turn to speak, Sally Mae."

"I know," she replied. "But what Pastor Brad has not told anyone is that he first broke the one-hundred-dollar bill because Billy Ray and Melissa Broussard were on their way to have a baby and desperately needed gas. Our card machine was down, and I'm not allowed to extend anyone credit under any circumstances, so Pastor Brad paid for their gas from the hundred-dollar bill."

"Likely story," said Shirley Plaisance with a smirk.

"Thank you, Sally Mae," said Archie. "That does put a different spin on our understanding of why Pastor Brad didn't give us back the exact same bill."

"I thought it might," said Sally Mae.

"Thank you," said Archie. "Ernie, would you please continue?"

"Well," said Ernie, "you're right that it wasn't the same hundred-dollar bill. Isn't that what you said earlier, Pastor Brad?"

I stood from my chair and replied, "That is correct. I knew I could replace it later, but my using that original money caused this whole series of events."

"Now, Pastor Brad," said Ernie, "that is where I would disagree with you."

What is he saying? I thought. *Is he turning against me?*

"I'm sorry?" I asked. "Why is that?"

"Well, this whole series of events was set in motion a few months ago, long before you found that money."

"Can you please explain?" asked Archie.

"Yes," replied Ernie. "As I said earlier, the church is about $15,000 in the red with this year's budget. It's easy to see that our offering totals have been lower than they should have been, even though our average church attendance hasn't really changed much in the past year."

"What are you saying, Ernie?" asked Archie.

"Well, it's pretty obvious that if our attendance has not changed, and if the people have not been reducing their giving, then someone has been stealing money from the church."

"That's right!" screamed Jimmy, standing suddenly. "Besides this whole hundred-dollar nonsense, Earl said he and Ernie found hidden money all over the church office. Isn't that true, Earl?"

Earl shifted uneasily but replied, "Yes, it's true that we found money hidden in the office, but we don't know how it got there."

"Ernie," shouted Jimmy, "didn't you and Earl both see Pastor Brad carrying about a thousand bucks in cash in his wallet?"

"Well," said Ernie, "yes, I did say that, but—"

Jimmy pointed a finger directly at me. "Doesn't it seem likely that if we're missing money, and Pastor Brad has a wallet full of it, that he might be stealing funds?"

"It might seem that way," said Ernie, "but—"

"Ernie?" I said. "Can I address that question?"

"Are you sure?" he asked.

"Yes," I said as I stepped once again to the platform. I glanced down at Allison, who smiled back at me. I then looked out at the congregation. "On the day in question, Earl and Ernie did see nine hundred dollars in cash in my wallet, I'll admit that. I had already given Ernie one hundred."

Suddenly, whispers and louder conversations broke out across the congregation. Bobby, my supportive neighbor, looked up at me and shook his head in disapproval.

"Can I finish please?" I asked loudly, causing the sound to diminish.

"Where did you get that money?" asked Jimmy. "Earl told me that you said you had earned it. Is that true?"

"In a manner of speaking," I replied.

"What is that supposed to mean?" he asked.

"I guess it's more correct terminology to say that I won it."

"What?" asked Archie. "How did you win it?"

"Well," I stammered, "I'm ashamed to say it, but I won it from a Mississippi scratch-off lottery ticket."

A hush settled over the crowd for a moment, as if they were all mulling over the meaning of the words I had just spoken.

"Wait a minute," said Archie. "You're telling us that in between the time you found the money in the office and the time you returned it, you not only spent some of the money to purchase milk and gas, but you also drove to Mississippi, purchased a lottery ticket, and won?"

"Yes," I replied. "That's what I'm saying."

"Our pastor is a gambler?" cried Mrs. W. P. Gurdon.

"And you expect us to believe that's how you had so much money in your wallet?"

"Yes," I replied, "that's exactly what I'm trying to say."

Heads turned, and whispering began.

I rubbed my eyes gently and continued. "In fact, Allison and I would like to give what's left of it to Lee Community. It should be a little over eight hundred dollars." I pulled my wallet from my pocket, pulled out the rest of the cash, and handed it to Ernie, who placed it in an offering plate and set it on the front pew.

"Earl," said Ernie, "would you please come sit by this offering plate, so this cash can be guarded?"

"Okay," said Earl as he made his way to the front.

"Now," said Archie, "we're thankful that you gave this money to the church, Pastor Brad, but it sounds like you're being accused of stealing close to $15,000. That eight hundred is just a drop in the bucket."

I froze, not knowing what to say. I felt the congregants' stares on my very soul and felt ashamed, as if I were naked before them, even though I hadn't stolen the money.

"May I continue?" said Ernie.

"Oh," said Archie, "of course. I had forgotten you even had the floor. Please do."

Ernie nodded solemnly at Archie and then looked back at the crowd. "I have to say that I believe Pastor Brad about him winning the lottery."

"You do?" I asked aloud.

"Yes," he replied. "I believe he is a man of integrity who made a slight error of judgment in buying that lottery ticket. He was planning on paying the church back the entire hundred dollars, so it really doesn't matter. He probably never imagined that he might actually win."

I nodded but said nothing.

Ernie continued, "I'd venture to say that most of the people here have purchased lottery tickets at one point or another. We've all done many things we're not proud of, right? I sure know I have."

A few heads nodded while a few eyes turned away.

"Pastor Brad is a good man and a good pastor. I for one stand beside him."

"What are you saying?" asked Earl, sounding more like his old self. "You just said you think he's been stealing the church's money."

"That's not entirely correct," said Ernie. "What I actually said was that when you look at the books, it's obvious that *someone* has been stealing money."

"Okay then," said Earl. "If it wasn't Pastor Brad stealing the money, then who was it?"

Ernie looked back at me and then, one by one, at Archie, Earl, and Jimmy.

"Well?" asked Jimmy. "Who's responsible?"

"I'm responsible," said Ernie, "so much so that I feel I must resign as church treasurer."

"Come on, Ernie," said Archie. "Isn't that a little drastic? Just because you were the church treasurer when the theft happened doesn't mean you are to blame for it happening."

"Yes, it does," replied Ernie.

"Why?" asked Earl.

"Because I stole the money," said Ernie.

CHAPTER 33

A "gasp" is defined by *Merriam-Webster* as when someone "breathe[s] in suddenly and loudly with [his or her] mouth open because of surprise, shock, or pain." All three of those latter feelings were evident in the gasps around the room following Ernie's confession. The members of the deacon board rose and stared at each other in appalled disgust. Mavis Jeansonne, a member of the Dorcas Sunday school class, fainted. And me? Well, my heart ached from the news.

Mrs. W. P. Gurdon said nothing, but instead began fanning Mavis and herself at the same time with both hands.

I looked into Allison's eyes, seeking a smile filled with hope, but instead I watched the tears form and stream down her cheeks. I sat still, a part of but somehow separate from the scene before me, numb from what I had just heard.

Archie let the chaos reign for a moment, with his hand over his mouth. He was probably trying to figure out what to say next. Finally, he raised his hands and cried, "Everyone! I know this is a huge shock to us all. It certainly is to me. However, we must continue."

Ernie looked back at me and caught my eye for a moment. I smiled gently and realized tears were in my eyes too.

"Ernie?" said Archie, pulling him away from our silent conversation. "We're all shocked at your confession. Just to make sure, you weren't speaking metaphorically or anything like that, were you?"

Come on, Ernie, I thought. *Just tell them you were making it up to save me.*

Instead, he smiled gently and replied, "I am being completely serious and sane. Pastor Brad simply found a hundred dollars and got caught up before he could return it. I took money from the church over a period of weeks."

Archie pursed his lips together, as if stalling while he searched for wisdom. Then, after what seemed an eternity, he asked, "Could you please explain your actions to everyone?"

"Yes," said Ernie. "I can." He paused, took in a deep breath, and said, "This is sort of hard to confess with my son here in the crowd, but I'm going to try anyway."

"Please do," snarled Jimmy.

"Connie and I have been worried about Paul for a long time. He's an excellent musician, but he's made some bad decisions in his life. We learned he was in trouble financially, through his friends at first, and we wanted to help him so badly. Over a year ago, we wiped out our savings in a bad investment, so we've been barely making it financially."

"Why didn't you tell anyone, Ernie?" I asked. "We could have helped you."

"I don't know," he replied. "I almost mentioned it several times, but I was embarrassed. I also thought it would be bad for business at my store if the word got out."

"That must have been hard," I said.

"Yeah," he said, "but I was determined to help my son, even it meant doing something extreme. I knew what I was doing was wrong, but I did it anyway. I kept telling myself I could pay it back. Now I'm afraid we've simply gone too far."

I glanced at Paul. His face looked drained of all life, his eyes empty, as he took in every word his father was speaking.

Ernie continued. "It started when Connie and I got a call from a bookie in New Orleans, saying that Paul owed him $15,000. He said that if we didn't pay him the money, Paul was never going to be able to play music again."

Paul looked down at the floor, gripping his guitar case so tight that his knuckles had turned white.

"Well," said Ernie, "I couldn't stand the thought of someone hurting my son. I tried to sell off some equipment at the store, but nothing went through. I didn't know what to do. Then one day, somehow, it just happened while I was counting the offering." Ernie paused and swallowed hard, desperately trying to not become emotional.

"What happened?" cried Bobby, unable to take the suspense any longer.

"Now, son," said Archie, "please be quiet. We've got to follow procedure."

"Sorry," said Bobby, slinking into his seat.

Archie then turned to Ernie and asked, "What happened, Ernie?"

"That's what I just asked," whispered Bobby to his mother, who in turn held her finger to her lips.

"Well," said Ernie, "I found myself slipping $250 cash into my pocket. I knew it was wrong, and I felt terrible about it, but I just couldn't stop. The next week, I did the same thing, only it was five hundred that time. Soon, I found an easy way to start hiding cash between the safe and the wall, and I created my own system for slowly stealing money."

"So," I said, "when you found the two hundred dollars between the safe and the wall when I was with you, that discovery wasn't real?"

"That's right, Pastor," said Ernie. "I'm sorry. I was afraid you were about to catch me in the act, so I acted as if I had found it."

"So did you also hide money in other places in the office?" I asked.

"No," said Ernie. "I only hid cash between the safe and the wall."

"Huh," I replied. "Are you sure you never hid money under the trash can or beneath my desk?"

"I'm positive," said Ernie. "I would have been afraid you would discover it there."

"Why do you ask, Pastor Brad?" asked Archie.

"Well," I said, "this may sound strange, but I found some suspicious-looking paper clips in those places."

A slight chuckle spread throughout the congregation.

"I'm serious," I replied. "I thought someone might be using them to quickly hide cash before coming back for it later."

"Well," said Archie, "I'm sure we all appreciate your amateur sleuth attempts, Pastor Brad, but let's just stick to where actual money has been found."

"Okay," I said.

An awkward silence settled over the congregation as Archie slowly turned his attention back to Ernie. His countenance dropped as he looked into the eyes of our church treasurer turned thief. "Oh, Ernie," he said. "How could you?"

"I don't know," cried Ernie. "I wanted to stop, but I had gone too far, and I just wanted it to be over so I could start paying everything back. This past Sunday, I had finally amassed the $15,000 for Paul. I called the bookie after church, and he told me he needed the money by Tuesday, or he was going to break Paul's fingers. That's why I drove to McComb on Sunday."

"I thought you were going out to eat," I said.

"I'm sorry I lied to you, Pastor Brad," said Ernie. "Connie made sandwiches, and we ate them on the way. We didn't have the money to eat out. Please forgive me."

"I do," I said.

"What happened then?" asked Archie.

"Well," said Ernie, "I wanted to wire the money instead of delivering it to the bookie in person. I didn't want to look at the man who wanted to hurt my son. Then, as you all know, as we were driving in McComb, our car was struck, and Connie was put in the hospital, all because of my stupid pride."

Paul Plaisance suddenly stood and shouted, "Dad, you don't need to—"

"I have to, son," said Ernie. "I stole that money. The hundred-dollar bill that Pastor Brad found had fallen from where I had hidden it beneath the table. The package Connie asked Pastor Brad and Allison to deliver to Paul was actually a package of money for him."

"The package Allison and I took to New Orleans contained $15,000?" I asked.

"Yes, Pastor," replied Ernie.

"Heavenly Days!" cried Mrs. W. P. Gurdon.

"I don't believe what I'm hearing!" said Shirley Plaisance.

"Ernie!" I cried. "Allison and I could both be charged as accomplices to your theft!"

Ernie tightened his lips. "I didn't think of that. Oh my. Connie knew you and Allison had too much integrity to open the package on the way to New Orleans, and apparently, she was right."

I took in a deep breath, not knowing what to say.

"I'm sorry we did that to you, Pastor," said Ernie. "I'm sorry about this whole thing. This entire meeting is my fault. Someone needs to call the police. I'm guilty of a heinous crime, and I deserve to be punished."

"Don't do that!" shouted Paul, running forward with his guitar case.

"Please don't. My dad was only trying to help me. He's an honest man, and he loves the Lord. For him to steal for me ... I mean, he must have been really worried because that's just not how he operates. I drove him to it, I tell you. I drove him to it."

The room was quiet as Paul ran up the steps to the platform and embraced Ernie, who in turn wrapped his arms around his son. "I love you, son," said Ernie. "I'm sorry I'm putting you through this."

"It's my fault, Dad!" cried Paul. "I drove you to it. I'm so sorry!"

"Archie?" asked Earl from the front row. "What about the church's mon—"

"Hold on a second, Earl," replied Archie, standing and patting Ernie on the back as Ernie continued holding his son tight.

After a moment, Archie stepped back and asked, "Are you okay if we proceed, Ernie?"

Ernie slowly pulled away from his son, wiped his eyes, and said, "Absolutely. You're right, we do need to continue."

"Dad?" said Paul. "I need to—"

"It's okay, son," interrupted Ernie. "Even though I had good reasons, what I did was still wrong and—"

"What if we gave the money back?" asked Paul.

"What do you mean?" asked Ernie. "Didn't you give the money to your bookie?"

"No, I didn't," said Paul. "I paid the man back all right, but not from the money in the package. I paid him off fair and square, legally, from money I made from gigs. That's why I was staying with friends and working some terrible gigs in some of the worst places in New Orleans. Sometimes I played all night, only to leave for another gig in the morning."

"But that man called and said you still owed him money."

"I did at the time. I told him I was going to pay him soon, but he wouldn't believe me. He was probably just trying to get the money out of you sooner."

"So everything's okay?" asked Ernie.

"Yes," he replied. "I'm safe. Thank you."

"What did you do with the money?" I asked, unable to help myself.

"I'm glad you asked," replied Paul with a smile. He opened up his guitar case, pulled out the large manila envelope we had delivered to him in New Orleans, and handed it to Ernie.

Ernie smiled at his son and then passed the envelope to Archie, who in turn passed it on to Earl.

"Wow," said Archie, looking out over the congregation. "This is unbelievable. We've heard two confessions tonight dealing with church funds, and everything has been returned. As soon as it is deposited, our budget-to-actual should show us eight hundred dollars in the black."

Applause suddenly broke out in Lee Community Church.

"However," proclaimed Archie, "we still have to proceed because wrong has been done. Crimes have been committed, and we have a full confession."

"Archie's right!" said Jimmy Rice. "Just because the money's been given back doesn't change any of the facts about the wrong that's been done."

The clapping stopped, and a sobering chill fell over the congregation. Suddenly, it seemed as if all eyes were looking to me, not as a perpetrator or as a victim but as their leader.

I glanced at Ernie, who gave me a nod of reassurance, and then said, "I'm glad all the money has been returned, and I'm glad to know that the good people of Lee Community never ceased giving over these past three months. But Archie is right. I've confessed to doing wrong, and so has Ernie. You must deal with our actions. Archie, please continue."

Archie sighed heavily and said, "Okay then. Everyone here has heard the confessions and discussion. What's your pleasure?"

Nettie Longwood stood from her seat in the front row and faced the congregation. "May I say something?" she asked.

"Certainly, Nettie," said Archie.

"I've been paid to play the organ and piano here for twenty years. I've enjoyed every service, and I love all of you here."

"We love you too, Nettie," said Archie. "Is that all you wanted to say?"

"Absolutely not," she replied. "What I wanted to say is that I've been paid a stipend every month for playing the piano. Part of that money is my salary, part of it is to purchase music, and part of it is for instrument maintenance."

"What does this have to do with anything?" asked Earl.

"Well," said Nettie, "I've secretly believed all of these years that I'm underpaid, so in my own form of rebellion, I have only had the piano tuned every other year."

"Well," said Archie, "that's not that big of a deal. I'm sure everyone here forgives you for that."

"No," replied Nettie. "Just like these men, I've done wrong. You've just heard my confession."

"Nettie," I said, "don't you think—"

"Hush up!" she shouted as she picked up her purse. "Nobody say another word!"

Everyone obliged Nettie and watched as she pulled out her checkbook, quickly wrote out a check, and handed it to Earl.

"Now," said Nettie, "as I see it, I received payment from the church for the tuning of the piano for twenty years. On average, it costs us around a hundred dollars a year for the piano tuning, so as I see it, I owe the church a thousand dollars for ten years of non-tuning. Please accept this check and consider us even."

"But Nettie," said Earl, "you made the check out for eleven hundred. That's a hundred more than—"

"Hush up, Earl!" snapped Nettie. "I've given what I've given. I figure if everyone is coming clean, I might as well too and pay some interest along with it."

"Yes, ma'am," said Earl with an actual smile.

Nettie turned once again to the congregation. "I'm sorry, everyone. Please accept my apology."

"Okay, thank you, Nettie," said Archie. "Now, let's continue with the business at hand."

"Hold on a minute," said Nettie. "I've got one more thing to say."

"Okay there, Nettie," said Archie. "What is it?"

"I just wanted to say that if you bring charges against Pastor Brad and against Ernie, then I'd like you to do the same to me."

"What?" asked Archie. "You want us to bring charges against you? I'm sure everyone here forgives you."

"No!" said Nettie. "I knew what I was doing was wrong, but I did it anyway. I deserve to be punished. So when you choose to prosecute these two men, prosecute me as well, for I am also guilty."

"Thank you, Nettie," said Archie.

"You're welcome," said Nettie as she returned to her seat.

"Okay, everyone," said Archie. "You've heard the confessions of Pastor Brad, Ernie, and uh, Nettie. What's your pleasure?"

"Archie?" said Burt Luketich. "After hearing Nettie's confession, I might as well make my own. Last year, I was going through a low business season when Pastor Brad called me to work on the plumbing here at the church. As I look back on it now, I overcharged the church by close to $250. I'd like to refund that money to the church tonight and give another $250 to make it right."

"Okay, Burt," said Archie. "Thank you for making it right and for your donation."

"Oh yeah," said Burt. "I just did some work this week in the nursery. You can just throw away that invoice, Pastor Brad, because I'm not going to charge the church anymore for my services."

Again, applause broke out at Lee Community. I was sure this was some kind of record in our church.

"Oh, and one more thing," said Burt. "If we vote to press charges against Mrs. Nettie here, then you might as well do the same to me."

"Okay there, Burt," said Archie. "Uh, thank you."

As Burt walked to the front and pulled out his checkbook, Archie rubbed his head. He, like many others, was baffled by the situation. After a moment, he stepped up to the podium and asked, "Are there any more confessions?"

"I have a confession," shouted a voice from the back.

"Who said that?" asked Archie.

"I did," said my sister Elizabeth as she stepped into the aisle. "I have a full confession as well."

"Good grief, Elizabeth," I said. "This isn't the time and place for it."

Elizabeth stopped halfway up the aisle and put her hands on her hips. "Archie?" she asked.

"Yes, ma'am?" he replied.

"Am I still a member of Lee Community Church?"

Archie looked at me and then at her and replied, "Yes, as far as I know."

"Then can my brother, Pastor Brad, keep me from speaking at this meeting?"

"Well, uh, no, I guess he can't," said Archie.

"Good," she remarked as she resumed walking toward the podium. "Then I'd like to say something."

I shook my head slightly, trying to figure out how my sister, who had been drunk the last time I saw her awake, who had until recently been sleeping it off in the back seat of my car, could stand in front of this crowd and speak to the rest of this congregation. "Good grief," I repeated as I dropped my head into my hands.

CHAPTER 34

Elizabeth stood before the people of Lee Community and grinned. "Well," she smirked, "I never thought I'd be standing here in front of this crowd."

Archie looked at his watch and asked, "What was it you wanted to share, Elizabeth?"

"Oh yeah," said Elizabeth. "Sorry, I'm slightly under the influence."

"So what else is new?" asked Mrs. W. P. Gurdon.

"That's right," said Elizabeth. "It's a problem I have that I'm dealing with. My brother is helping me work through it. You see, the rumors of Pastor Brad carrying around an intoxicated woman today in his back seat are true. It was me."

"Elizabeth," I said, "you don't have to—"

"Yes, I do, Brad," she replied, before turning back to the people in the pews. "I've had some personal issues as of late, and earlier today, I tried to drown them in several shots of bourbon. My brother found out and took care of me, just like he always does."

Elizabeth paused, and the congregation leaned in, hoping to hear more.

"You see," she continued, "to me, Brad has always been a pastor. Even when we fought as kids, he always ministered to me. When my dad ran my boyfriend away when I was a teenager because he caught us kissing behind the church building, Brad was there for me. When I wanted to become a freelance artist and everyone told me I didn't have what it takes, Brad believed in me. And when …" Elizabeth paused. She looked like she was holding back tears and debating with herself as to whether she should continue speaking. A tear formed in her left eye, and she wiped it away quickly. "When the world I had created for myself turned against me, causing me to do the unthinkable, he was there for me. Even when he didn't want to be, he was there. Even when I pushed him away for giving me the help I sought him out for, he continued to be there for me."

Every eye in the building was locked on Elizabeth. She smiled gently as she looked across the crowd. "I guess what I'm trying to say," said Elizabeth, "is that Brad helps me be a better person. Even when it frustrates him, he is accepting of me while still pushing me to be the best me I can be."

What I did next was completely out of order, but I practically ran to Elizabeth. As I hugged her tightly, the tears streamed freely from her eyes.

"Thank you, Elizabeth," I said as I released her.

"You're welcome," she replied before sniffling slightly and then facing the congregation once again. "I guess that's all I have to say," said Elizabeth. "Well, except that I realized tonight that I haven't given to Lee Community Church in over two years." She reached in her back pocket and pulled out a folded check.

"Elizabeth," I said, "you don't have to do this."

"Oh yes, I do, Bradley," she replied. "Didn't Mama and Daddy teach us to always tithe to the Lord?"

"Yes," I said, "they did, but can you afford it?"

"Dear brother," she replied as she handed the check to Earl, "shut up."

I laughed, and a few others chuckled.

Earl opened the check and couldn't help but exclaim, "Ten thousand dollars!"

I opened my mouth to speak, but Elizabeth held up an index finger. "Not one word, Brad," she said. "Not one word. It may be hard to believe I have that kind of money, but I'm not a starving artist. I'm good at what I do, so let's just leave it at that."

I smiled and nodded.

"Well," said Archie, "I guess that settles that. Any questions?"

For once the room was silent. Elizabeth tightened her lips, nodded politely to everyone, and returned to her seat, winking at me on the way.

Before Elizabeth could be seated, Bobby walked the steps to the platform, much to the surprise of his parents, and tapped on Archie's shoulder.

"Well, hello there, young fella," said Archie. "How can I help you?"

Bobby turned and faced the congregation. "Can I say something?"

"What's your name?" asked Archie.

"Bobby."

"Thank you, Bobby, but this is a business meeting for Lee Community Church. Are you a church member?"

"No," said Bobby, "I don't go to this church. I'm Pastor Brad's neighbor."

"If that's the case, then I'm afraid you're going to have to—"

"Let the kid talk!" cried Nettie Longwood.

The congregation turned and looked at Nettie in shock. Never before had she been so assertive, even indignantly forceful, as she was tonight.

"Well, okay," said Archie. "Go ahead Bobby."

Bobby smiled then said, "I'm Pastor Brad's neighbor from down the street. I like to ride my bike near his house because there's a long sidewalk. Every time he sees me coming, he acts funny and makes me laugh. I've never been to church before, but if people in church are like Pastor Brad, I think I want to start." Bobby turned and smiled at me.

I smiled back, not knowing what to say.

"Thank you, Bobby," said Archie, interrupting the moment. "But we've got to move on now."

"Wait," said Bobby, holding out one hand while reaching into his pants pocket with the other. "Here's a dollar I've been saving. I'd like to give it to Pastor Brad's church."

A collective hush filled the room. After a moment, Archie took the money from Bobby, and everyone watched as Bobby rejoined his parents. His dad tousled his hair, and his mother pulled him close to her. Both of them were beaming with pride.

"Thank you, Bobby," I said, interrupting the flow of the business proceedings slightly.

Archie nodded at me and then faced the congregation. "Okay," he said. "What's your pleasure?"

"Just a minute!" cried Jimmy from his seat. "Isn't that the kid who saw white stuff all over the pastor's clothes?"

"Yes, I believe so," said Archie.

"Get him back on the stand," ordered Jimmy. "We want to hear about that."

Archie turned to Bobby and asked, "Son, would you mind telling us about the powder you saw on Pastor Brad?"

"Yeah!" cried Jimmy. "What was it?"

"What was what?" asked Bobby.

Archie looked back at Bobby and said, "He's talking about the white powder you saw all over Pastor Brad earlier today."

"Okay," said Bobby. "Yeah, he was covered with it. I think it came from that donut bag he pulled out of his car."

"Donut bag?" asked Archie, turning to me.

"Beignets," I replied.

"Pastor Brad," asked Archie, "were you covered in powdered sugar from eating beignets while driving?"

Suddenly embarrassed, I replied, "Yes, Archie. That's right."

Archie smiled at me and then at the congregation. "Everyone satisfied?" he asked.

No one spoke.

"Good," said Archie. "Let's continue. Pastor Brad ..."

"May I say something?" asked Earl, rising to his feet.

"Come on, Earl!" snapped Archie. "We've just about destroyed order in this meeting as it is. We've got to do things by the book."

Earl suddenly became animated and blurted out, "Just give it a rest for a moment, Archie, okay?"

"What are you saying, Earl? You're normally such a stickler for rules here."

"I know," said Earl, "but since we've concluded that the powdery substance was actually powdered sugar, there's one more accusation I'd like to make against Pastor Brad, something only he and I know about."

My heart sank. I was finished at Lee Community. Earl was about to read them my text message. I just knew it.

"Folks, we came to this building tonight with the intention of calling for a vote of confidence. Even with all we've heard, I feel like that still needs to happen. I'll admit, everything up to this point has been very touching, especially with this young man here giving his savings to our church. But I feel that we can't leave this place tonight without everyone hearing what I'm about to say. I don't know if it will change your feelings or sway your vote, but it certainly has determined mine in both instances." Earl glanced in my direction for a moment and then reached into his pocket and pulled out his phone.

Here it comes, I thought.

"It will come as no surprise to you that Pastor Brad and I do not always agree."

"That's putting it mildly," said Sally Mae, causing a slight uneasiness across the sanctuary.

"In fact," declared Earl with his index finger pointing up, "most of you are probably here tonight because I contacted you. I've shared with everyone I can think of in this town that Pastor Brad is a thieving, manipulative, uncaring, underdressed, woman-chasing coward. And most recently, in front of the entire deacon board, I also made the statement that Pastor Brad is a bad preacher."

"Amen!" cried Jimmy Rice, who started clapping but suddenly stopped when no one joined him.

Earl looked around the room, catching the eyes of almost everyone. He waited for the awkwardness to fade and then said, "But I was wrong."

My eyebrows raised, Archie's mouth dropped open, and Nettie's hand covered her mouth.

"Could you repeat that?" asked Archie.

"Certainly," said Earl. "I was wrong to say those things about Pastor Brad. They're not true. I have argued with him quite a bit over these past few years, but none of that has anything to do with his abilities or his character. It has to do with me. I've been jealous of Pastor Brad."

"You've been jealous of me?" I blurted out. "Whatever for?"

"Well," said Earl, "I've always felt like I should be in your position, preaching and leading the people of Lee Community Church."

I stepped from my position and stood next to Earl. "You've wanted to be the pastor?"

"Yes," confessed Earl. "When I was in college, I felt like I was supposed to be in ministry, but I was afraid. I even visited the seminary in New Orleans a couple of times, but I never could bring myself to fill out the application."

"I thought you hated the seminary," I said.

"I suppose," said Earl. "I guess deep down I was just upset I never went there myself." Then Earl turned to face me completely and said, "Pastor Brad,

I've fought you every step of your ministry here at Lee Community because I secretly wished I was in your position. I found a little bit of power as the assistant chairman of the deacons and let it go to my head. I'm sorry."

Archie suddenly raised his hand and interrupted. "I'm confused, Earl."

Earl's eyes softened, and he looked at his feet. "I'm sorry I never told you, Archie. I'm sure this is confusing to you."

"That's not what I'm talking about," said Archie. "You said you had one further accusation to make regarding Pastor Brad."

"Oh yes," answered Earl. "When I learned that Pastor Brad was going to New Orleans to find Paul, I convinced myself that he was going there to have a wild fling on the church's dime, so I followed him there."

"What?" I exclaimed.

"Yes," he replied. "I parked behind you, followed you around, and took pictures of your every move."

"You did?" I asked.

"Yes," said Earl. "I even disguised myself on Bourbon Street with some wild clothes and a wig so you wouldn't recognize me, but even with that, you still saw me."

"Wait a minute," I said. "Was that you at the table in that, uh, restaurant?"

"Yeah," said Earl, hanging his head. "I heard you talking to the lady at the door. Then I watched as you and Paul met and you waited for him while he played a gig. In all of those situations, you had every chance to compromise your integrity, but you didn't stumble as you reached out to Paul or to the woman at that, uh, establishment."

I smiled and looked down, slightly embarrassed.

Earl continued, "You were a godly example to all of what a pastor should be, a light in the darkness. I couldn't even keep my thoughts while I was trying to catch you in the wrong. You're a better man than I."

"So what's your accusation, Earl?" asked Archie.

Earl laughed—maybe the first time I had ever witnessed him laugh—and said, "I'd like to accuse Pastor Brad, in front of this entire assembly, of being a good preacher and, even more than that, of being a good pastor."

"Here, here!" yelled Nettie Longwood, once again surprising everyone.

Allison stood and began clapping, followed by Nettie, Bobby, Ernie, Paul, and then the entire congregation, with the exception of Jimmy, who finally rose but opted not to clap.

"Now!" exclaimed Archie. "If there's no further discussion, can we finally call for a vote of confidence?"

"Sounds good to me," says Earl.

"Thank you," said Archie. "Is there a motion that we keep Pastor Brad as the pastor of Lee Community Church?"

"So moved," said Earl, reaching for my hand. "Forgive me, Pastor."

"You are forgiven, Earl," I replied.

"Do I hear a second?" asked Archie.

"I second the motion," said Ernie.

"Very good," said Archie. "All in favor, raise your right hand."

Across the sanctuary, every right hand went up but one, and all eyes were on the owner of that hand.

"Come on, Jimmy," said Earl. "What do you say? I was wrong. Let's do the right thing together."

"But I thought we were all going to be mad at the pastor," said Jimmy. "We wanted him gone."

"We were wrong, Jimmy," said Earl. "Let's stop being so angry and try to work with him. What do you say?"

Jimmy looked as if he was going to explode but then suddenly said, "I suppose, as much as I hate to admit it. It's too tiresome to be angry all of the time anyway." He quickly raised his hand.

Archie laughed and said, "Let the record show that Pastor Brad is still our pastor by a unanimous vote. Do I hear a motion that we adjourn?"

"Excuse me," called a voice from the back. "May I say something?"

What now? I thought.

"Excuse me," repeated the voice. "May I say something before we adjourn?"

Archie replied, "It's not necessarily in order, but nothing really has been tonight. Would you mind standing and identifying yourself?"

"Certainly," said the man as he stood up. "My name is Jeremy Sullivan."

I smiled when I saw Jeremy, but Archie did not seem as pleased.

"Thank you, Mr. Sullivan," said Archie. "Tell me, are you a member of Lee Community Church?"

"Well, no," answered Jeremy. "I'm actually the pastor of Grace Church in Baton Rouge, but I've been here this evening for the meeting, and I'm a new friend of Pastor Brad."

"Isn't Grace Church that big church in Baton Rouge with the fountains and the café'?" asked Archie.

"Yes, sir," said Jeremy.

"Why would you want to come to a Wednesday business meeting at Lee Community?"

"Well," said Jeremy, "I've actually come tonight more as a delivery boy than as anything else."

"What do you mean?" I asked.

"You see," said Jeremy, "Pastor Brad came to a meeting for pastors yesterday at Grace Church. He filled out a card for a door prize, and he won. I'm here to deliver it to him."

"What?" I asked. "I told you I didn't think I should accept."

"I know you did," said Jeremy. "But fortunately for you, I didn't listen, so you have to take it."

"This is highly irregular for a business meeting," said Archie.

"Come on, Archie," said Earl. "You've got to lighten up."

After a brief moment of awkwardness, Archie said, "I guess you're right, Earl. We should allow this to take place."

"Enough of this!" cried Sally Mae. "What did he win?"

"Pastor Brad, thanks to some generous laypeople I know who love the Lord and those who share His Word, I'm pleased to give you these two reservations for a Caribbean cruise leaving from New Orleans. A two-night stay in the Riverfront Hotel is included with the cruise."

The congregation broke into cheers, another first for Lee Community. I glanced at Allison. Her beautiful smile beamed back at me.

I took the tickets from Jeremy and glanced at them. "Wait a minute," I said. "These tickets are for this Saturday. I couldn't possibly arrange to be off by then. I'm not even sure I still have enough vacation time."

Nettie Longwood jumped to her feet and cried, "I make a motion that we give Pastor Brad ten days of paid leave starting this Friday as punishment for playing the lottery with church funds."

"What?" said Archie. "I didn't call for discussion yet."

"I second the motion," cried Ernie.

"Me too," said Earl.

"This is highly irregular," said Archie.

"I know," said Earl. "Isn't it great?"

"Oh, whatever," said Archie. "All in favor, raise your right hand."

I glanced around the room. Every right hand was held high.

"The motion passes!" cried Archie. "Congratulations, Pastor Brad and Allison! You're going to the Caribbean!"

Once again, cheers and applause filled the room.

When the noise finally died down, I said, "Thank you all! This means so very much to Allison and me. We're so thankful for this surprise vacation and for the time off."

"That time off is your punishment!" cried Nettie with a smile. "You go on that cruise and think about what you've done."

"Thank you, Nettie. Thank you, everyone," I said. "I feel so very blessed. I'm blessed to be your pastor. I can promise you this: I promise to be the best pastor I can possibly be. I have so many dreams of what Lee Community can become. I want to share them all with you and—"

Allison interrupted, "And he promises to share them all after we return from our cruise!"

Laughter filled the sanctuary.

I hugged Allison tightly and said, "You know, I could get used to this."

Allison smiled and said, "Me too."

"Now!" cried Archie. "Do I hear a motion that we adjourn?"

"So moved!" cried Earl.

"Seconded!" cried Ernie.

"All in favor?" cried Archie.

"Aye!" cried everyone in unison.

"Finally!" exclaimed Archie. "Meeting adjourned!"

"Oh my," I said to Allison, "I'm going to have to find someone to preach this weekend."

"Maybe your friend Jeremy has an associate who could fill in," she replied.

"Maybe," I said, "but I have another idea."

"What?" she asked.

I walked across the room to where Earl was speaking with Jimmy.

"Pastor Brad," said Jimmy. "No hard feelings?"

I reached for his hand and shook it. "Absolutely," I said. "Absolutely."

"I'm sorry, Pastor," said Earl. "I've not treated you fairly."

"It's all over," I said to Earl, shaking his hand too. "Will you forgive me as well, for being too sensitive and not responding properly?"

Earl looked up suddenly and stared me right in the eye. "Yes, I will, Pastor."

"Thank you," I said, pumping his arm vigorously. "Just think about what we can accomplish if we work together."

"I'm willing to give it a try," said Earl.

"That's good, Earl," I replied, "because I'd like for you to preach this Sunday."

Earl's jaw dropped. "What?" he asked.

"Would you be willing to preach?" I asked. "You know, I'll be on the cruise this Sunday, and you would really be helping me out."

Earl swallowed hard. "Yes, Pastor. I'd be happy to preach for you. Thank you."

"No," I said. "Thank you, Earl."

CHAPTER 35

The ocean wind blew in my face as I reclined in my chair with my bare feet on the railing of our private balcony. I watched Roatan Island growing smaller as our cruise ship sailed away toward our next tropical destination. I sipped from my soda and picked up a mystery paperback from my favorite author.

Well, Lord, I prayed without closing my eyes, *I can't believe I'm here. Less than a week ago, I was pretty sure I was going to be out of a job. Now here I am on a free vacation with the blessing of the Lee Community congregation. The church was in dire straits financially, and now we're ahead of the game. Earl and I are even being pleasant toward one another. I feel like I'm dreaming again. Thank you.*

Allison peeked out from our stateroom and smiled a big smile.

"Well, hello there, Mrs. Johnson," I said.

Allison returned my smile and took a seat in the chair beside me. Then she leaned over and kissed me gently on the cheek. "This is a wonderful vacation, honey," she whispered in my ear.

"It really is," I replied. "This ship is amazing."

"Yeah," she said. "I do have a question for you, though."

"What's that?"

"Well, it's about you buying the lottery ticket."

"What about it?"

"You knew how the people of Lee Community would feel about it, right?"

"Yeah, I did."

"Then why did you do it?"

"I'm not really sure, baby. I've asked myself the same question. It was like something came over me, and I felt like it would change my whole situation."

"But it's not something you would normally even think of, is it?"

"No, it's not," I replied. "I don't know why I did it, Allison. I just did, even though I knew I shouldn't."

"Huh," she said.

"I guess it's like Burt overcharging the church when he needed money, like Nettie withholding the piano tuning because she felt slighted, or even like Elizabeth drinking when she's supposed to be helping me reach out to Paul. People just get caught up in life and end up doing things they'd never dream they would do. The apostle Paul struggled with it as well, saying he didn't understand why he did sinful things he hated."

"What did he say was the solution?"

"He said Christ was the only one able to conquer sin. I think we often sin when we don't depend on Christ and instead try to live and work and even minister apart from Him."

"Is that what happened with Ernie?"

"Yeah, I'm sure of it. I'm glad everyone's forgiven him."

"I am too," said Allison. "Will it be strange for him not to be church treasurer?"

"Probably a little," I replied. "But he's going to be busy helping Paul establish himself as a musician outside of Bourbon Street."

"Paul's moved home?"

"Yes. He's even going to try helping out with the music ministry."

"Really?" she asked. "That's going to change things up a bit."

I laughed and said, "I can envision the rehearsals with Paul, Nettie, and Freddie. It will be interesting to say the least."

"Yeah, it will," she replied, tightening her lips for a moment.

"What is it?" I asked.

"What do you mean?" she replied.

"You look like you're worried all of a sudden."

"Oh, I'm sorry," she replied. "I was just wondering how Gabe was doing."

"I'm sure he's fine. Ashleigh was so nice to agree to stay with him every night."

"I was glad your parents could watch him during the day."

"Yep," I said. "One thing's for sure: his bones are going to get plenty of calcium while we're away."

Allison chuckled and replied, "Well, the way he's growing, he's going to need it. He runs around so quickly, he knocks things over without even knowing it."

"What do you mean?" I asked.

"Last Sunday, we didn't have any other kids his age in the nursery, so I took him to your office. He was running around so fast and knocking things over. I told him to sit on his bottom while I cleaned up the mess, and before I knew it, he had grabbed all of the paper clips from your office and had taped them all over the room."

"You're joking," I said.

"No," she answered. "I pulled him out from under your desk, set the trash can back in place, and removed the taped paper clips I could find."

"Really?"

"Yes," she replied. "Why?"

I blew out a long breath that ended with a chuckle. "Oh, no reason at all," I said. "At least none that matters."

We both turned back to the ocean and watched silently for a few minutes as the island disappeared in the distance. I reached for Allison's hand and pulled it to my lips. "I love you," I said, kissing her hand twice before interlocking my fingers with hers.

"I love you too," said Allison. "I'm so thankful for this vacation."

"It has been nice," I replied. "Now I'm just curious about one thing."

Allison's eyes caught the reflection of the Caribbean water. "And just what might that be?"

"Well," I said with a smile, "would you like to celebrate in a special way?"

"What do you mean?" she asked. "In one of the fancy restaurants?"

"No," I replied. "Right here in our room. We may have to order room service tonight."

Allison smiled, leaned in close, and kissed me again, on my lips this time.

"I'll take that as a yes," I said.

Allison nodded as she reached for my hand. I took it in my own, rose to my feet, and pulled her close to me.

"My, my, my, Pastor Brad," she teased. "You are a bad preacher."